SERPENT

A NOVEL BY MICHAEL COLE

SEVERED PRESS
HOBART TASMANIA

SERPENT

Copyright © 2021 By Michael Cole

WWW.SEVEREDPRESS.COM

ISBN: 978-1-922551-82-5

CHAPTER 1

"...and then, the damn smoke alarm goes off. My wife and I woke up and rushed into the kitchen. First thing I notice is the damn LEGO I step on."

Brian Uhler chuckled at Captain Ross Margo's retelling of his midnight misfortune. He kept his eye on the horizon, watching the grey clouds passing by the cockpit of Lockheed L-100-30 Hercules they piloted.

"So, what happened after that?"

The Captain shook his head and rolled his eyes at the memory.

"So, after I shoot off about twenty F-bombs, I go into the kitchen. Of course, my wife feels she needs to ask me if I'm okay like twenty freaking times. 'Yes, I'm fine. What the hell's burning?!' Then we see Brandon standing there."

"Oh no," Brian laughed. Anything involving the Captain's four-year old grandson always ended in some form of disaster. "Oh, boy. What'd he do?"

"Well, the poor kid's got this shit-eating smile on his face. He already heard Grandpa cussing over his spilled toys, so he thinks I'm mad to begin with. He tends to grin like that when he's caught doing something he shouldn't. So, my wife asks him what he's doing up so late, while I can already tell the smell's coming from the oven."

"Uh-oh. He decided to cook himself a midnight snack?"

"Well—yes and no. I guess you can say yes if you consider a plastic LEGO a midnight snack," Captain Margo replied. Brian laughed, while simultaneously wincing from imagining the smell of the fumes that filled the Captain's house. "God, I think it took two hours to air out the place," he continued. "But I have to give the kid credit."

"Credit? Did he season the LEGOs with parsley?"

"No, but he did place them on a cooking sheet, and he actually remembered to spray it down with pam. That, and I think he preheated the oven, because it was set to four-hundred."

"The same temperature you set for his chicken nuggets?" Brian asked.

"Mmhmm." The Captain nodded. Brian had to be careful not to laugh too loudly. His high-pitched voice and the confined space of the cockpit didn't go together very well. "Gotta hand it to the kid: he's not dumb. He always watches his grandma work the magic, and is just fascinated at seeing the little frozen nuggets go in, then come out crispy and hot."

"He just wanted to see what happened if he did the same thing with LEGOs," Brian said.

Ross sighed. "Yes." Finally, Brian couldn't help himself. He laughed loudly at the Captain's misery.

"Well, thanks to the pam, it was surprisingly easy to scrape those little—" The plane jolted from within, causing both men to look to the back door. "Jesus, what the hell was that?"

"It definitely wasn't a cargo shift," Ross said. They had only one container, and that thing was strapped tight. The crew that loaded it had specific instructions to make sure the container was doubly secured in their cargo hold. He adjusted his mic to his lips. "Tillman? Gibson? Want to tell me what's going on back there?"

Tillman had awoken with a jump. The banging noise had echoed through the hold, ending his nap short. Gibson was already on his feet. He had tossed his novel to the side and started to inspect the large container. It was different than anything he had shipped in the past. It was fifty-feet long, resembling a giant fuel cannister. A steel hose was fastened to ports on the front and back end, circulating something that sounded like water through the thing.

All four men were no strangers to shipping cargo. They had made this specific trip over a dozen times in service of the medical corporation Timestone. It was a simple trip: Five-hundred miles from a private airstrip twenty-miles east of Jacksonville, North Carolina, to Isle Mendoza, a privately owned island a hundred miles north of the Bahamas. It was an easy four-hour round trip that always promised good money, as the CEOs of Timestone entrusted them with shipping extremely important technology and machinery, some of which were experimental prototypes. The company had made its fortune with medical breakthroughs, and it seemed par for the course that this weird thing was just another piece of technology. Neither of them had any idea how an oversized water pump would be a medical breakthrough, but hey, as long as the check cleared, they couldn't care less.

Unless it threatened to bring the plane down, that is.

"Hang on, Captain. I'm taking a look," Gibson said. He shone his flashlight over the container. Immediately, his eyes noticed the dozen warning signs posted all over it. The straps were tight, the bolts secure. There didn't appear to be anything wrong with the pump mechanism. "I'm not noticing anything off. I think it's just—"

He heard a thud from inside. A second, louder, crash made him jump back. He could hear water swirling within. Something was inside, moving on its own free will.

"Is it just me, or is there something alive in there?" Tillman said. Gibson panned his light to his crewmate. The scrawny thirty-year old Tillman already had sweat glistening on his brow. His skin was turning pale, his lips tight, unintentionally holding his breath.

"Get ahold of yourself," Gibson said. Tillman finally took a breath. Several seconds passed without any sort of noise.

"Maybe it was nothing," he said. Gibson continued inspecting it, then shook his head. He adjusted his headset mic to speak to the Captain.

"Captain, the container's secured. Straps are tight. Pumps are working. No breaches to be seen."

"Then what was that noise?"

"I—I'm not sure. Whatever it was, I think it stopped. I—" He smelled something. Fumes of some kind. Tillman flashed on the overheads. Immediately, they saw smoke billowing from the underside, near the front of the container.

"Holy shit!" Tillman said.

"Captain, something's burning back here."

Immediately, the toxic smell filled the hold.

Captain Ross Margo recognized the burning smell of corroding metal. Something was burning from inside the cargo hull. He was a hundred miles away from the coastline, and three-hundred miles from his destination. Whatever was happening back there, it was dangerous. Ross was not dedicated enough to the company to risk his neck flying over the Atlantic with potentially lethal cargo.

"Alright, we're turning west. Let's get over dry land and set down at the first airport we can find," he said.

"I'll get a message out to Dr. Hugh," Brian said. "It's his toy. He'll know what's wrong with it."

"Holy Christ! Captain?" Gibson's voice filled his headset. Another crash shook the aircraft. The Captain looked back.

"What's going on back there?"

The entire cargo hold was rapidly filling with twisting fumes. Both crewmen placed gas masks over their faces and gloves on their hands before proceeding to check the container.

"There," Tillman said. He pointed at a series of hot droplets coming from the bottom of the container. The metal was extremely hot, darkening at a spot where the droplets seeped through.

"Oh God. Captain, this container is...MELTING!"

"Melting?"

Gibson pointed his flashlight at the floor. The droplets were forming a cavity. Whatever was eating through this container was now eating through the deck.

"Captain, whatever this shit is, it's gonna eat through the hull!"

The softened metal broke away from the container. At that moment, they realized that the container had been weakened in multiple sections. It cracked open like an egg, unleashing a wave of boiling hot saltwater onto the two crew.

Gibson and Tillman screamed, their faces and arms blistering. The water swashed in the cargo hold like the contents of a half-empty water bottle, repeatedly assaulting the two men.

The plastic mask was now starting to melt, threatening to weld itself to Gibson's eyes. With no other choice, he ripped the straps off. Hot water felt like it was melting his feet through to the bone. Steam and fumes mixed together. He couldn't see his hand in front of his face, much less whatever was thrashing violently in the hold with him.

Whatever was in that container was now writhing like a worm, bashing the bulkheads on both sides. He heard Tillman let out a high-pitched scream. His voice broke apart into violent sounds of struggle. Despite the chaos, Gibson was able to notice one particular detail; his crewmate sounded as though he was being whipped back and forth. Warm fluid splattered his face. Tillman's struggle ended with a violent gargling sound, then something else that sounded like crunching gravel...or bone.

He wiped his severely burnt hand over his face and held it an inch in front of him. It was blood, and not his own. He shined his light over his chest and brushed the clouds away. Before they swirled back, he saw that he was coated in Tillman's blood.

Something sizzled in front of him. More steam spiraled up from the floor. Whatever corroded the container was now eating through the hull. In addition, he heard scraping. A shape took form in the grey steam cloud. It was angular, split into two segments. Then he noticed the teeth, and realized he was looking at an upper and lower jaw, coming right at him. The body behind it was snake-like, slithering its way right at him.

Gibson screamed and turned to run into the cockpit. But the snap of those jaws snatched him off the floor. Ten-inch teeth skewered his body, crunching his ribs and spine, while scissoring the soft tissue with each munching motion. Gibson felt his body break apart and suction into the throat behind those teeth, his dying wails echoing loud in the pilots' headsets.

"I'm gonna go back there," Brian said.

"Wait!" Ross shouted. Brian quickly sank back into his seat. The Captain rarely raised his voice, and when he did, it meant the situation was serious. And it was.

An alarm blared overhead. *Hull breach imminent.*

"Descending to eight-thousand feet," Ross said. Brian re-secured his straps and braced for the inevitable plunge. The plane dipped radically and dove for the ocean. They heard the thing in the back, unsecured, being thrown against the back ramp. Its impact was enough to jolt the whole plane. Whatever it was, it weighed thousands of pounds. And it was moving.

When the plane hit eight-thousand feet, they leveled it out.

"Alright, let's get a Mayday signal out," Ross said. Another alarm blared. *Hull breach.* They could feel the wind current suctioning out the inside of the plane.

In addition, the thing back there was still thrashing about. It was getting closer, snarling like a pissed off dragon from ancient legend. Its sound confirmed what the two pilots were worried about. It was alive.

The situation was going from bad to worse—*much* worse. The breach widened, cracking the plane across its center. The sheer velocity of its travel did the rest of the work. There was no choice. They had to ditch, or else break apart in midair.

"Come on!" Ross muttered as he initiated the descent.

Something struck the backdoor, folding it out into the cockpit. Both men looked back, just in time to witness a second hit.

"What is that?!" Brian shouted.

"It doesn't matter at the moment! Let's just get this plane—" A third hit flung the door into the console, its corner bashing Ross's right temple. He shook from the impact, then faceplanted against the console. Brian froze, his eyes briefly locked on the sight of his Captain with his skull split open. A high-pitched screech filled the cabin, shattering the windows, as well as his eardrums. Now deaf, he couldn't even hear his own screams as the giant mass filled the cockpit and seized him in its jaws. Razor teeth mashed his body, spraying his blood all over the console.

The plane continued its plunge, then pierced the ocean's surface. The wings broke apart, the engines erupting in brief orange flashes. The fuselage cracked wide open and departed from the cockpit. Both sections continued their plunge, before finally crashing down into a reef fifteen-hundred feet below the surface. The fragments settled into their final resting place.

CHAPTER 2

"We're here," Captain Ronald Tyler said. He walked to the middeck of the vessel *William Travis,* where his client Dr. Hugh Meyer waited. He was a tall, skinny man, his face beginning to show the lines of age. At fifty years old, his thin hair was showing the first shades of grey.

Hugh Meyer closed his eyes and took in the cool ocean breeze. Its refreshing scent was the only good thing he had going for him today. When he opened his eyes, he was gazing at the vast, seemingly infinite stretch of Atlantic Ocean. The sky was cloudless, the morning sun bright and welcoming.

Behind him was a seven-thousand-pound Triton submersible. The doctor turned around and gave the Triton submersible a third look-over. It was a remarkable piece of machinery, capable of descending to two-thousand feet. It was ten-feet long and eight-feet wide, with a hull designed to withstand ten atmospheres of pressure. Its main battery was designed for twelve kilowatt hours, more than enough for its pilot to complete his inspection. The morning sun beamed through the cloudless sky, reflecting its light off the spherical cockpit. Behind that glass was a single seat.

Hugh sighed. As it was a one-man submersible, he would not be able to go down to investigate the crash site. Unfortunately, he had spent more of his career in the lab, rather than on the field, and had never undergone the appropriate training to handle such equipment.

That job belonged to Howard Liss, a four-year Navy veteran with ten additional years of submarine diving for private and state run institutions. At thirty-five years old, he was in better shape than most men in their twenties. His thermal suit hugged his muscular frame. He was sweating right now in the summer heat, despite the breeze coming off the ocean. In ten minutes though, he was going to be surrounded by dark ocean. Even on a clear day like today, visible light only penetrates to a hundred meters. Below that, the only natural light left would be the dim blue-green light of the aphotic region. He would certainly have to rely on his searchlights when inspecting the seabed.

"Alright, doc, the check has cleared. I'm ready to do your bidding," Howard said. Hugh didn't smile. To him, this wasn't a fun scenario. Four men had certainly died, his specimen likely lost. Though they hadn't recovered the black box yet, he couldn't shake the feeling that the organism was responsible for the crash.

Hugh checked his watch. It had been twelve hours since the crash.

"The point of interest is the cargo hold," Hugh stated. "Start your search there and see if you can aim the camera through any breach in the fuselage."

"Do we have any idea how intact this cargo plane should be?"

"No idea, unfortunately," Hugh said. "We were in contact with the Captain and suddenly the signal went dead."

"I'm certain it won't be a pretty sight," Captain Tyler said. "I don't know how squeamish you are, Howard, but just be prepared when you come across the cockpit."

"I'm prepared," Howard said, slightly annoyed. The Captain should've known this wasn't his first rodeo. Howard had conducted rescue dives as well as participating in investigations for sunken ships, oil rigs, crashed aircraft, as well as individual boating accidents. He had seen bodies eaten by fish, sawed into sections by debris, bloated to the point of looking more like squid than human beings. That was what he expected to find down there, assuming the current hadn't suctioned them out of the cockpit entirely.

Howard climbed aboard the Triton and opened its circular hatch. Before lowering himself inside, he gave Hugh a glance.

"So, all you want to know, is whether that container inside is breached?"

"That's correct," Hugh said. "It's imperative that I know."

"That *you* know," Howard said. "Is this being funded by you, or Timestone?"

Hugh didn't answer. He lifted his two-way radio to his lips.

"Ryan, how's the video feed?"

"Nice and clear, Doctor. I'm looking at your pretty face right now. Straighten your collar, for godsake. You look like hell."

Hugh felt like hell. He wanted to laugh at his assistant's attempt at humor; he could use the levity. Unfortunately, he felt too much weight on his shoulders. Much of that fell from guilt. He hoped the black box would indicate engine failure, or something mechanical as the cause of the crash. At least then it wouldn't be his fault. But first, he needed to know if the specimen was still down there. It was unlikely it had survived the crash. Unlikely. But he needed to be sure.

He shut his eyes. A tsunami of memories flooded his mind. He saw the creature, then only ten-feet in length, leaping from its pool and assaulting the feeder. He remembered the sensation of warm blood spraying his hands as he pulled the worker away, and the horrible gut-wrenching sensation when he saw the man's leg detach. If it could be eaten, the specimen would go for it. Whether the prey was alive or dead, it didn't matter.

When it reached twenty-feet in length, there was no choice but to isolate it. It would actually attempt to breach the glass, and slither across a dry metal floor, in order to get to other specimens across the exhibit. Its metabolism also generated various problems. For one, it was constantly hungry. No matter how much the caretakers fed it, it was constantly ready for more. It was considered cute when the specimen was only two-feet long…until it took off the index and middle finger of its handler. Additionally, sedation had limited effect. The second time it escaped, they had to shoot it with a milliliter of Xylazine, which wore off in the five minutes it took for them to get the creature into a secondary tank.

Hugh was sure that by the time they got the specimen to Timestone's private island facility everything would be fine. The medical breakthroughs they had already acquired from its DNA were immeasurable, and there was too much at stake, as long as they could keep it isolated.

"I'll be up there in two minutes," Hugh said. He looked back at Howard. "Be careful down there. If you see anything unusual, ascend."

"Doc, it would take a ton of TNT in order to break through this hull. I think I'll be fine. Trust me, it's not my first time down there. I've seen every weird looking creature you can imagine," Howard said.

"I hope not," Hugh said. He turned around and walked to the bridge. Howard sealed the hatch and fastened himself to his seat, while the crane operator prepped to hoist.

Hugh entered the superstructure and ascended a flight of stairs. He found his assistant, Dr. Ryan Burg seated at a table to the left of the helm. Ryan was ten years younger than Hugh, and had a perfect suntan that most college students would dream of, due to his many years diving with sharks and working aboard research vessels.

The bridge overlooked the main deck. Hugh walked past Ryan and watched through the window. The crane was slowly lifting the submersible over the side. He could see the Captain and other crewmen guiding it over, while communicating with the crane operator through radio.

"Jesus, Doc," Ryan said, spinning in his chair to face him. "If you get any more nervous, you'll give yourself a stroke. God knows you haven't invented a cure for that, yet."

"I was on my way," Hugh said. He didn't mean to say it; his thoughts just escaped verbally. His voice was solemn. His eyes went from the activity below to his dim reflection in the glass. He hated the man looking back at him. "So many breakthroughs. I convinced myself I was saving lives. Instead, I've cost the lives of seven people now."

Ryan stood up. "Oh, for crying out loud, Hugh. That's a crock of shit and you know it. You didn't accelerate the growth rate. And hell, you had no idea how vicious that thing would be. Nobody did. You can't blame yourself for the people it killed in the lab, or for the crew. You had good intentions. You were developing new research that could change the lives of millions."

Hugh resisted repeating the famous line; *"the road to hell is paved with good intentions."* He sucked in a deep breath and watched the sub touch the water.

"Well, if it was turbulence or engine failure, and if that container is intact, then the specimen is dead. No way the pump would still be functioning. The damn thing should've suffocated within thirty minutes after crashing."

"You sound hopeful," Ryan said.

"Wouldn't you be?"

"I'm not sure," Ryan said. "I was there studying it with you, Hugh. The specimen is a living medical breakthrough. I've studied thousands of species, memorized their biology and immune systems, and I can tell you, we've never had anything like that creature. We might finally learn the cure to cancer, you know."

"I know," Hugh said. "And we can try again. You know Timestone will just have me engineer another one. But first, I need to know *that* one is dead. If it isn't, we can't let it roam free." He looked at Ryan. "You know it isn't compatible with the ecosystem. And if it were to make its way to a populated area—"

Ryan nodded. There was reluctance in his eyes, but he couldn't deny that Hugh was correct. He was there the first time it injured someone, and nearly lost a hand on a couple of different occasions. Then there was the day he arrived to work and found a frenzy of activity in the lab, as several workers had to sedate the thing after it had pulled a feeder into its pool. The creature was hyper-aggressive, and had a taste for human flesh. If it was still alive, it would likely migrate to the coast. "Timestone might not do anything about it."

"Likely not. If it can't be captured, they'd rather just engineer another specimen," Hugh said. "Hence, we must hope that container is sealed." *Please, God, let it be sealed.*

He took a seat next to Ryan and watched the computer monitor. He saw the bright blue ocean, just a few feet below the surface as Howard began his descent.

"Radio check. You hear me, Doctor Meyer?"

"Loud and clear, Howard," Hugh replied.

"Alright. Beginning descent. Hope you enjoy the virtual tour."

The camera feed angled down toward the deep, dark abyss.

Howard applied thrust, watching the light as he ascended two-hundred feet. He was already a third of the way through the photic zone, where the light was sufficient enough to support photosynthesis, if there were any reefs at this depth. At six-hundred-and-fifty feet, the particles had scattered, leaving him in a blue-green abyss.

"Approximately nine-hundred feet to go," he said.

"Your lights aren't on," Hugh replied.

"Turning them on right now, Doc. Don't worry, I know how to run this machine. You just sit back and enjoy the tour." Howard shook his head. *Backseat driver.* He watched the barometer. 371 PSI at a depth of eight-hundred feet.

Had he not made hundreds of dives in the past, Howard would've described his surroundings as the atmosphere of an alien planet. Now, he just saw it as what it was: water simply too far from the sun's reach. With every hundred feet of descent, it grew another shade of dark. He activated the forward beams. Small fish darted from view, their eyes stung from the sudden flash. He could see whitetip reef sharks gliding across the seafloor, accompanied by several species of deep dwelling fish. The light brought out the dull brown color of the ocean bottom below them.

Dark biogenous material, made up of hard parts of sea animals, drifted across the seabed like dust bunnies. Crabs clustered around them, picking for pieces of protein.

Howard banked gently to starboard, searching for the reflection of a steel hull. He spotted cuttlefish gliding across his sphere. A few yards past him were several specks that turned out to be a school of shrimp.

"This might take a bit," he radioed.

"The signal came from here," Hugh replied.

"I believe you, Doc. But it's still a big ocean, and I'm only one guy. Just bear with me, and I'll find it."

Hugh sighed, nervously tapping his fingers against the desk. He was anxious to see the container. He needed to know it was still sealed.

Had it been any other circumstance, he would've allowed himself to be in awe of the ocean bottom. This was the closest he had ever been to it. Being a biological engineer, he had spent the majority of his career between the lab and the office, rather than out in the field. It was moments like these that he wished he pursued something like marine-biology. He watched the fish zipping through the lights, moving about like futuristic shuttles traveling through space. For Ryan, it was nothing new. Still, it was a sight to behold.

As Howard panned to starboard, his light streamed across an area that resembled a miniature mountain range. There was no flat area of seabed. It was a valley of canyons, cracks, ravines, and large rolling peaks. He ascended a few meters to get over a hill covered in residue and crabs.

Scattered along the seabed was inorganic material. Aluminum. At first, Hugh thought it to be parts of the plane.

"What's that?" he said. "Lower left. Something shiny…"

"Not wreckage, Doc. Just an old soda can somebody tossed over." The camera panned down and zoomed in on the object. Hugh sighed. It was a beer can, its label peeled into ribbons, the top covered in the residue. *"Whoa! What do we have here?"*

Hugh leaned toward the screen. He half-expected Howard to start poking fun at him. At the same time, the hairs on the back of his neck rose. As the camera panned, he braced himself for the sight of the plane. Instead, he saw the severed head of a whitetip reef shark. Little threads of flesh danced from the edges of its wound. Its jaw was clenched shut, its eyes open and pale. There was no sign of its body.

Ryan sucked in a breath.

"Something had lunch today." He and Hugh looked at each other.

"Could anything else have done that?" Hugh asked.

"Yes. A bigger shark, or a good-sized squid, which we'd be lucky to see," Ryan said. "Then again, I don't think a squid would leave a head intact like that. And any shark big enough to do that doesn't normally travel this deep."

"Should we call him up?" Hugh asked.

"No," Howard's voice blasted through the receiver. Hugh realized he'd left the transmitter pressed.

"Howard, you might be in danger…"

"Doc, as you can see with all the sea life down here, there's no danger. If there was something that terrifying, the sharks and fish would scatter." Hugh looked at Ryan for confirmation on that fact, and got the nod he was looking for.

"Alright. Proceed."

The bio-engineer took a rag from his pocket and swiped the sweat from his brow. He watched the canyons pass below the submersible, as though it was aerial footage.

"And look at what we've got here," Howard said. The two scientists watched the monitor as the sub turned to port. Lying flat against the sediment was a rounded section of steel. Wires dangled from the edges, waving in the current as though the debris was an anemone. Several feet behind it were several solid objects scattered in the sediment. The light hit them, causing a blinding reflection.

"Glass," Hugh said. Howard proceeded, traveling over a dip in the terrain. He passed over a large ravine, panned slightly with his flashlight to make sure nothing was there. The bottom was ten or fifteen feet below the edges, with no sign of wreckage lodged inside. Sharks and bony fish swam over it, zipping back and forth to chase after squid or shrimp that lingered too close to examine the sub.

One shark bumped against the sphere, sparking laughter from Howard. But Hugh wasn't laughing. He watched the landscape, his eyes not daring to blink. His handkerchief was now scrunched in his fist, which was pressed against the table.

"It's fine," Ryan said. "That sub's meant to absorb pressure. It'll take more than a few bumps to rupture that cockpit."

"It's not the pressure I'm worried about," Hugh said.

"The specimen is tough, but he won't be able to damage it," Ryan assured him. The shark swam out of view, unveiling another community of fish and crustaceans. They were gathering over a large grey hill. Then Hugh realized it wasn't a hill.

"There it is: the fuselage."

Howard ascended another few feet to give the scientists a wider view. The cockpit and fuselage had broken apart entirely and had landed within several meters of each other. A hundred feet behind them was the starboard wing, which had broken in half. The engine looked like the pop can, only a thousand times bigger. Its shaft was bent outward, the outer casing chipped away.

"Damn," Howard whispered to himself, his voice carrying through on the radio. He steered to port to get a look inside the cockpit. The hull was crumpled inward, looking as flexible as tarp as he neared it.

"Careful," Hugh warned him.

"Careful is my middle name," Howard replied. He doubled his speed and descended, then did a one-eighty turn to get a look inside the cockpit.

Hugh winced, unsure if he was prepared to see the pilots' corpses. They'd be malformed by now, bloated by seawater and pressure. The camera focused through the windshield. There was nothing but splintered control instruments inside. No bodies, no sign that life was ever there other than the technology it created.

"The hell?" Hugh muttered. It was possible they could have fallen out through the back while it sank, though both men should've been strapped to their chairs. Before he could look closely enough to see if the belt buckles were attached, Howard had already panned slightly upward. He steered the sub over the hunk of metal that was the cockpit, and lined himself up with the wingless body of the fuselage.

Pieces of metal and glass were scattered all around it. Deep dwellers were already in the process of making it their home. Crabs were bunched up at the edges, fish were swimming through the windows and cracks, while cuttlefish attacked some of the weaker crabs that had found themselves in the path of falling debris.

"You see everything you need to see, Doctors?" Howard asked. Hugh tried to look, but the sub was not at the correct angle. He was positioned over the wreckage, and the cracks and

windows were not wide enough for an adequate view inside. It had to be fine though. The fish and other wildlife were undisturbed, except for that dead shark, but down here? Hell, that could've been caused by anything. Still, he needed to be sure.

"I need you to go down and point your light straight down the neck of it. I need a clear view inside," he said. He watched the sea bottom seemingly 'reel' back as though on a conveyor belt while Howard put the Triton in reverse. After clearing the neck of the plane, he descended, nearly touching the ballast to the seabed.

Hugh and Ryan watched as the light filled the plane's insides, escaping through the cracks in the hull. Casings of the container were scattered against the bulkhead, with pieces of pump lying about, fulfilling a new destiny of providing shelter to small fish and crustaceans. The container had not only been breached, it had been decimated.

"Jesus. It's out. It escaped!" Hugh said. Ryan got on the phone and started making a call.

"It might've been killed in the crash," he said. Hugh knew by the way he was dialing numbers that he didn't believe that idea. "Shit," he slammed the phone down, "no signal."

"It must've left the area. It could be anywhere," Hugh said.

"We know from our studies that it prefers shallower water. It will likely be heading inland," Ryan said. Hugh pressed the radio transmitter.

"Alright Howard, it's time to ascend," he said

"No need to panic, Doc. Whatever was inside that thing is clearly not large enough to bust open this sub."

"Howard, your task is done. Now, COME UP!"

The Triton pilot shook his head. *Jeez, was the doctor off his rocker? Did he need some stress medication, or what?*

"As you wish," he said. He backed out from the fuselage and initiated ascent. He rose a hundred feet, then noticed that the ocean floor was alive with activity. Sharks, fish, squid, EVERYTHING was scattering. Some moved further to the south, some north, passing under his sub, but most darted to his left, disappearing east into the thick darkness.

Never had Howard witnessed such a vast exodus.

He saw sediment billowing like smoke from a volcano. Bits of rock was rolling off the crested edges of the ravine he passed over a few minutes prior. He turned the Triton for a better look.

Something was shaking the rock which formed the ravine. A few other fish darted for their lives, while crustaceans scurried across the bottom.

Like the tongue from the hideous mouth of the ravine, something rose. Its skin was a dark brown and scaly. Its face was reptilian, its neck lined with three long gill slits on each side. Behind them were a pair of jagged pectoral fins, with four antennae-like feelers protruding from their rigid points. The creature continued to rise from its hiding place.

Howard's heart pounded the inside of his chest. For a second, he questioned what he was looking at. It was no whale, and it was way too big to be a shark. It was at least forty-feet long. Forty-five maybe. He could only describe its snout as the cross between a crocodile and a moray eel. Its eyes opened, reflecting the light from his sub. Catlike pupils focused on him.

"Howard! Get out of there!" Hugh screamed through his receiver.

The pilot failed to hear the words over the terrible rush of water. Like a snake striking a rodent, it lashed its upper body at him. Its mouth hyperextended, impaling the sphere with eighteen-inch long teeth.

Water invaded the cockpit in thick streams, hitting Howard's face with an intensity that scraped away the upper layers of skin. He threw his hands wildly, lost in complete panic. The sub shook side-to-side then shook violently as the creature slammed it against a rock. The control instruments flashed like firecrackers, their internal systems ravaged by the seawater.

The thing's feelers scraped the glass above him. Its teeth sank further in. Its jaws had encompassed the sphere entirely, sucking it toward the throat. Even through the rush of water, Howard could hear the groaning of metal and cracking of glass.

Red lights flashed. *Pressure alert! Pressure alert!*

The sphere imploded. The jaws clamped shut through the now-empty space, impaling Howard between the rows of spike-shaped teeth. It yanked him back, snapping the harness like a rubber band. It chomped once more before swallowing, then inspected the wreckage. It tasted the inorganic material comprising the sub, learning that it was not viable as sustenance. The creature backed away, unused to the increased weight gained from its recent growth. It slowly ascended toward the distant sunlight above. It relied on its eyesight as much as it did its other senses, thus, it needed to hunt in shallower waters.

"Goddamn!" Hugh shouted. He stood up and hit his fist against the table. "It's bigger! It's *much* bigger! It wasn't that large when we loaded it into the container."

"Ms. Brown must've had the staff hit it with another round of the growth hormone," Ryan said. Now, he was sweating too. Neither of them expected to see the creature so large. It was almost twice the size of when they last saw it, and now, it was twice as deadly. He tried making another phone call to headquarters.

"Forget it," Hugh said. "They're not gonna do anything about it. This thing is responsible for four deaths already. As far as they're concerned, they can write this thing off as engine failure or some bullshit. When the creature inevitably kills someone, they will act as though they know nothing about it. Let the public think it's a new species, or just a series of shark attacks. But they won't make any effort to catch it. Right now, Ms. Brown is gonna make every effort possible to distance the company from this thing's existence."

"So, what can we do?" Ryan asked. Howard looked down at the monitor. It was fuzzy now, the camera crushed against the bedrock. Before the sub crashed into its final resting place, they could see the specimen swimming to the surface.

"It's my fault he's dead," Hugh said.

"No. Hell no." Ryan pointed a finger. "I approved the choice of submarine myself. The creature wouldn't have been able to breach the sphere had it not grown. You didn't know."

"Maybe not. But I'm not going to stand by and let that damn thing kill anyone else. I'm going after it."

"It's gonna head for shallower water. And knowing that thing, it's gonna seek out an area teeming with activity," Ryan said. He sighed, dreading the inevitable carnage. "Where's the nearest beach?"

CHAPTER 3

"Welcome back, all you sunbathers, speedboaters, and parasailers of Spiral Bay. And if you're still at work instead of vacationing, then all I can say is: Sucks to be you! Hope you are all enjoying this Thursday morning, and thank you for joining us on Z-108, Spiral Bay's home of classic rock. We have the weather for you. Clear skies and a high of ninety-two, winds no higher than twenty-miles per hour. Best part is, that forecast is projected to last all through the weekend! So, everyone not stuck in an office, get your butts on out there! It's almost like nature is trying to get as many people in the water as possible! Or maybe I am, because I'm looking at it through my window, and let me tell you, it's calling my name. Or could it be the senoritas."

"Definitely not them," Samantha Russell said, chuckling to herself. She had personally seen the radio host and it totally brought to mind that phrase 'a face for radio.' He wasn't wrong, though: the weather was absolutely gorgeous. And the residents and vacationers of Spiral Bay were out taking advantage of it.

Sammy carefully steered her silver and green Police Interceptor through town, carefully monitoring the thousands of people moving between the cafes, hotels, and shops. Several people were loading up their trailers and trucks with surfboards, skis, and sailboats, while those without those things were either content with staying on the beach, or would make arrangements with local charters to try parasailing, waterskiing, or—what Sammy loved most—marlin fishing.

Sammy took the main road out of the town area, passing through a thousand feet of lime-green grass and recreational parks before reaching the beach. Spiral Bay was a small recreational bay, home to three-thousand residents, and housed three times that number in the summer months. The public beach area stretched for four-point-three miles, completely comprised of golden-white sand. On the south end, a series of docks separated the public area from the harbor. Beyond that was nothing but private beach houses all the way to Beggars Cove, where local residents could enjoy their privacy without a stampede of tourists zooming around them.

It was nine-o'clock, and the beach was alive with vacationers enjoying the cool morning breeze. The water was a perfect crystal blue color. The waves rolled gently onto the shore. Almost equally as blue was the sky. As the radio host had said, there wasn't a cloud to be seen. Just golden sun embracing the hundreds of people who headed out for their morning swim.

For first responder convenience, the beach was divided into numbered sections, usually marked with signs on the thirty-foot lifeguard towers and tents stationed at each 'border'. Each section was five-hundred feet in length, allowing for precise coordination should an emergency occur. Aside from the signs, all sections of the beaches were exactly the same: just golden sand, mashed under the feet of crowds eager to let the ocean embrace their bodies.

Sammy took a left turn and headed north, remembering her father said he would be near Section Seventeen. She kept her eyes on the beaches, which were covered in sunbathers and people enjoying morning breakfast while watching the horizon. Kids chased each other along the shore, their feet splashing waves of sand. She waved at a couple of her officers who were out on foot patrol and they waved back. As long as the crowds didn't get too riled up, and they usually didn't, the officers were essentially getting paid to hang out in the sun and socialize, which Sammy encouraged.

Out in the water, jet skis and motorboats were speeding in their full glory. The horizon was marked with multicolored sails as vacationers took to the ocean. Even from the road, she could feel the sense of freedom that each sailor was experiencing. During their stay, they were liberated from the mundane aspects of paying bills, house chores, and coasting along in work zones that most of them didn't want to be at. Sammy recognized a couple of fishing charters. Every day, the local fishermen took out ambitious tourists, hoping to hook the big one. And some of them did, though most turned up empty handed.

Speaking of which—

As Sammy approached Section Seventeen, she noticed several camera vehicles and cautioned off areas. From the road, it looked like a crime scene. In truth, it was a sports series production, featuring the eccentric outdoorsman Derrick Crevello. His trailer was right at the edge of the beach, his staff occupying the top three floors of the Zoller Holiday Inn. Crew and cameramen were gathering on the beach, setting up shots, while gorgeous women in bikini tops applied makeup to the star. He had a Rockstar physique, his skin a butterscotch tan color from a lifetime in the sun. Sammy smirked, amused by the glimpses of interaction she caught whenever they weren't blocked by the crew. Either those women really enjoyed working with him, or they were extremely good at faking it. She suspected the former. She couldn't deny that Derrick rocked that blond bro flow hairstyle.

Sammy had never heard of Derrick Crevello until her father stated his production company had rented out a section of beach for two-days of shooting. For her father, the mayor, to actually rent out this public space, must've meant they brought in loads of money and business to the town. After looking him up on *YouTube* she learnt of his high-energy charisma. The guy loved to fish, and the internet was full of images and videos of the guy hooking seabass, salmon, tuna, marlin, swordfish, and even some sharks. Between all of those adventures were specials featuring him interacting with and rescuing dolphins. Whether that was his genuine personality or simply scripted to further improve his public image, she had no idea.

When the news first hit her, she was worried it would put a strain on the local businesses. Of course, it went to show how little she knew about the entertainment business, as it did the opposite. Business was booming, and as a result, there were many more last minute bookings in the local hotels for people wanting to catch a glimpse of the production. The local residents were quick to voice their approval. As usual, her father made a good call.

And there he was, dressed in grey slacks, a white dress shirt, and blue tie. He was smiling, in conversation with someone similarly dressed, at least ten years younger. Likely a producer or executive producer. Sammy parked her vehicle along the side of the road and stepped out.

Mayor Richard Russell turned around and saw his daughter approaching. She held two iced coffees. He checked the time, then smiled at her.

"You're five minutes late, Chief."

"Oh darn. I dropped the ball again," she quipped. Richard asked the producer to excuse him, then walked over to greet his daughter. He took the iced coffee, and resisted the urge to give her a kiss on the forehead. It was, technically, a formal meeting, after all.

"First time on a TV set?" she asked him.

"Eh, first one that's actually *intended* for entertainment," he replied. "Beaches looking good?"

"Nothing really to report," Sammy said. She sipped her coffee and watched the camera crews position their cameras, while writers spoke with the talent. "If this guy's a fishing guru, what's he doing here on the beach?"

"Just some intro stuff for the episode. He's gonna say stuff like 'Okay, folks, here I am at Spiral Bay, home to the world's largest recorded marlin.' He'll probably talk about the lighthouse on Lebbon Rock, and other stuff to set up everything the episode will cover," Richard said. "Most of the shooting's gonna be out on the water."

"I'm surprised you're not making a cameo!"

"I don't look so good in a bikini," Richard quipped. "These guys are asking for a police escort, however. Basically, he'd like a couple of officers on standby while they're out just to keep any fangirls from getting too close during the shoot."

"Nothing I can't handle," Sammy said. "Any idea when they plan on heading out?"

"Eleven o'clock. I hate to spring this on you. I know your staff is stretched thin as it is."

"Dad, I'm always looking for an excuse to get out on the water," she said. "I'll handle it myself. The beaches are fine. Sergeant Shier has a good handle on things on the beaches. I'll head out with Jesse. I warn you though, I can't ensure I'll be able to deter any fangirling from her."

"Somehow, I think you can handle it, sweetheart!"

The crowd opened up, making way for Derrick Crevello as he marched over to the Chief. A smile came over his face. He knew the Chief would stop in on set, but he anticipated someone in his late forties, early fifties. Not a twenty-eight year old woman with almond hair that hung to her neck.

"I must be in heaven," he said. Definitely the words of a TV star whose fame has gotten to his head. He was exactly what Sammy expected, down to the southern drawl and the sudden brushing back of hair, which was nothing more than an excuse for his biceps to flex. He reached out and shook her hand. "Derrick Crevello. Pleased to meet you, Chief."

"Pleasure's all mine," Sammy replied.

"Oh, I don't think so," he said.

"Careful, Derrick. I've got fifty bucks that she'll floor your ass and cuff you for sexual misconduct!" a tall man in an American flag t-shirt said. Sammy recognized the two sidekicks from the *YouTube* clips she'd seen. The one in the flag shirt was Melvin. From what she gathered, his persona was that of someone in constant competition with Derrick but always falling short. The other man was Josh. She learned that he was never intended to be a co-star, but a drone camera operator. Somehow, probably through ass-kissing, he ended up working his way in front of the camera. His personality was the opposite of Melvin's. Rather than being an antagonistic presence, he was a yes-man who always agreed with every idea that came from Derrick's mouth. Yet, even on film, he still served as the drone operator.

"You would like that, wouldn't you?" Derrick said to Melvin.

"I would, actually!" Melvin said. "Then I would become the show's new lead."

"Yeah, enjoy the ratings plummet. Bastard," Derrick said.

"Yeah," Josh said. Melvin bumped his shoulder against his other co-star.

"Don't you have a drone to fly?"

Josh held the control device to Melvin's face. "Yeah. I'm gonna use it to film you lose. As usual."

Sammy began to wonder if the TV personas were just that— personas.

Derrick looked back at her, smiling and pointing his thumb at his sidekicks.

"Don't mind them. They're like puppies. They follow me wherever I go. Haven't gotten Melvin neutered yet, which is why he's so cranky." He turned to Richard. It was the first time they'd met, as all the prior meetings had been conducted by agents and producers. "Mr. Mayor! Pleased to meet you as well. Thanks for hosting our show!" Richard shook his hand, noticing the star's eyes glance back to his daughter.

Could be worse. Successful TV career. Not much older than her. Both love the ocean. Might not make a bad match. He then noticed the models behind Derrick, some of them wearing outfits so small that they barely covered the goods. *On second thought—*

"Just say the word, Chief, and I'll get the writers to sneak in a cameo," he told her. Sammy smiled.

"I appreciate it, Mr. Crevello, but I've had more than enough TV exposure."

"Not like this. We can arrange something great!" Derrick turned toward the ocean, waving his hands as though painting a picture. "We can do something fun, like feature Derrick Crevello, assisting law enforcement in pursuing illegal poachers! We could even do a speedboat chase!" He cleared his throat and spoke like a narrator, "Derrick Crevello thought it would just be another average day in the hot sun, smoking cigars, and bringing home the trophy. Until he witnessed the wanted criminal, Rico Matteni, attempting to net a dolphin. Unwilling to sit back and do nothing, he and Spiral Bay Police Chief—" he leaned to look at her nametag— "Samantha Russell pursue the crook into the open ocean!"

Sammy allowed a chuckle to slip through. There was something contagious about his outgoing personality. In her mind, most people couldn't get away with speaking about themselves in the third-person without sounding stupid, but it definitely suited Derrick.

"Might work," Josh said. Just like in the show, agreeing with everything Derrick said.

"We could make it so *I* almost catch him first," Melvin said.

"But fail miserably, of course! Until Lady Chief and I save the day!" Derrick retorted. "Hell, we can fly Jake Smith's stunt crew over from Miami. I hear the *Robbie Justice* show just got cancelled, so they might be looking for work."

"Yeah, I'm not sure that'll work, Derrick," the producer said. "This is a fishing program, not an action series."

"I guarantee it'll bring us our highest ratings," Derrick replied. "Plus, we'd make a star out of this gorgeous cop!"

"Thanks, but I'm good," Sammy said.

"You sure, Chief? We could do something less intense, like shoot a special where Derrick Crevello mentors Spiral Bay's Police Chief in catching a fifty-pound dorado! I guarantee fans would love it. You'd be a star overnight."

Sammy could feel herself starting to blush. *God, I hope they're not filming this.*

"I'm extremely flattered, but I think I'll stick to shooing all the ladies away while you film," she said.

Derrick shrugged, though his smile never left his face. It wasn't often a woman turned down any chance to be on screen with him. At least he wasn't taking this as a personal challenge to pursue too hard, though Sammy anticipated a few hints during the shoot.

"Well, if you change your mind, hit me up. The writers here will figure something out. Right, guys?!"

"Uh-huh, yep," somebody in the crowd behind him retorted. Another man, dressed in a Hawaiian shirt, sandals, and shorts burst from the crowd.

"Alright, Derrick! We're ready to go. Come on, let's get started."

Derrick rolled his eyes. "That's Marty, our director. Gotta get to work. Ratings don't raise themselves. Nice to meet you, Chief. I'll see you on the water at eleven!"

"I'm looking forward to it, Mr. Crevello," Sammy said, shaking his hand again. Derrick winked before returning to the set, with Josh and Melvin tagging behind him.

"You're lucky she didn't kick your ass," Melvin pestered him.

"I'd let her cuff me," Derrick retorted.

"Now *there's* your ratings boost!"

It took everything to keep herself from falling apart in a fit of laughter. She wasn't sure if she was flattered, or embarrassed, or both. Luckily, she didn't act star struck, probably why Derrick was taking such an interest in her. Or maybe she was overthinking these things.

"Good lord, I feel like I woke up in Hollywood," she said.

"You think you can handle him out there?" her father asked. She could tell he was amused by the encounter.

"Yes, Dad," Sammy said. "Not sure if Jesse will, though."

"Oh, God, she'll melt like butter," Richard said.

Sammy closed her eyes and thought about it for a minute. "You know, that'll be fun to watch in itself!" She got on her radio. "Unit One to Unit Four."

"This is Four. Go ahead."

"Hey, meet me at the dock at quarter to eleven. We'll be heading out on harbor patrol."

"Ten-four, Chief. I'll see you then."

Sammy felt evil.

"Don't let her make too much of a fool of herself on camera," Richard said. "I don't want everyone thinking our police department is made up of goofballs and fangirls."

"*Every* police department is made up of goofballs," Sammy said. Richard chuckled then sipped his coffee.

"Well, I wouldn't have appointed you to your position if I wasn't confident you could handle such things."

"Oh, please, Hollywood won't be a problem. This town hasn't thrown anything at me yet that I can't handle."

CHAPTER 4

The great white glided twenty feet below the surface, heading east to avoid the distortion caused by human activity. It had been three days since its last feeding, and now its body was demanding sustenance to support its three-thousand pound mass.

The fish typically hunted in a shallow, rocky region, where seals and fish were constantly in abundance. At eighteen-feet in length, it was the most fearsome predator lurking in these waters. Bony fish and eels scattered the instant it appeared. Capable of bursts up to thirty-five miles per hour, the great white could easily outpace most of the puny creatures that attempted to flee. However, hot pursuit was not its preferred method of hunting. Like most of its four-hundred fellow species, the great white preferred to go after wounded prey, or unsuspecting seals floating along the surface.

The shark repeatedly circled the landmass in the center of the shallow region, finding nothing but small, insufficient fish darting about. The few seals in the area had gathered up on the shore of the tiny island. They watched its dorsal fin slice through the water during its futile efforts to seek them out. Some of them barked, as though heckling the big fish. Being king of the ocean meant nothing when your meal was on dry land.

After five long passes, it was clear that the seals were not coming off that island. Giving up, the shark branched further out, relying on its lateral line to pick up the distressed motions of fish. Meanwhile, it used its network of jelly-filled pores concentrated in its head called the ampullae of Lorenzini to detect minute electrical signals from the muscle contractions from prey. There were small eels hiding in the rocks, and a few small fish darting out of its way. But so far, there was nothing hiding nearby worth seeking out.

The smell of blood filled its nose, drawing the fish slightly north. It didn't detect any distressed movements from struggling prey, but there was a lot of blood in the water. The shark increased speed, following the trail as though magnetized to its source. Water passed through its gills, carrying thin strands of blood and tissue.

At one hundred yards, the great white could see the whale floating along the surface. Long pectoral flippers waved lifelessly with the swells. The whale was dead, its flesh pale from the loss of blood. Still, the great white circled with caution. The whale was nearly three times its size, and it needed to be sure there was no risk of being thrashed by its mighty fluke.

After circling twice, the shark closed in on the enormous gash in the whale's midsection. The wound was large enough for the fish to fit its entire head through. The shark did not detect any movement nearby, thus wasn't concerned with the presence of rival predators.

It lined up for a strike and darted for the wound, plunging its entire head between the soft, fleshy edges. It sank its teeth into a mouthful of meat and thrashed its head to tear it loose. The shark circled back, mashing the torn flesh in its jaws, then swallowed. It wasn't done. Opportunities like this were few and far between. The great white could feed at its leisure and not waste energy on chasing down and killing the meal. A few more mouthfuls of this whale, and it wouldn't have to eat again for a week. It circled back and lined up with the wound. It was wider now, thanks to its own contribution. The shark bit at the edges, snapping a piece of rib while peeling a ten-pound slice of blubber from its underside. It attacked the dead flesh as though it were a mortal enemy. Serrated teeth sliced effortlessly, mincing the food until it was safe enough to be digested.

The shark took a few minutes to pass water through its gills. Though the agonizing need to feed had lifted, the shark was not ready to quit yet. It circled back for another go. Its attacks had stirred a fresh cloud of blood, draining what little remained from the carcass. The scent spurred the shark further. It closed in and closed its jaws on a mouthful of meat. It whipped its head, shaking the entire fifty-foot whale, while its teeth acted like sawblades.

Electrical impulses filled its pores. Water disruption hit its lateral line like sonar pings. The shark was no longer alone. Something was closing in, and from the heavy distortions, it was big and not injured.

The great white released the whale and dove under it, clearing the path of the huge creature rising from the seabed.

The Serpent had watched the unsuspecting fish while it rested in the rocks. During this time, it had remained perfectly still, as to not deter its potential meal from approaching. It allowed it to feed on its previous victim. It was no loss—it would get that sustenance back.

However, the Serpent underestimated the shark's burst of speed, and its jaws snapped shut on nothing but seawater. The shark fled to the east at its maximum speed of thirty-five miles per hour. Swinging its enormous snake-like tail, the Serpent darted after it, weaving under the carcass. Its large eyes were fixed on the target, watching its every move. The shark would not travel in a straight line for long, especially since its pursuer was faster and more agile. And unlike the white, it was fully rested, and did not tire easily.

It gradually closed in.

The fish could sense the much larger creature nearing its caudal fin. After a few seconds, it would be within reach. The shark turned to the left and dove deep. The Serpent's massive eyes immediately spotted the first twitch of motion leading to the evasive maneuver. It completed the turn before the shark, and shot in a straight line into the anticipated trajectory.

The shark completed its wide arch, only to find the creature suddenly on a collision course on its left side, as though it materialized out of nowhere. There was no escape this time. The elongated jaws snapped shut, driving huge dagger-like teeth into the white's hide directly behind the pectoral fin. The fish struggled to free itself, its nerves alerting its brain of the massive injury, which was widening by the second. Much like it had done to the whale carcass, the shark found itself thrashed back and forth, helpless in the jaws of this unknown predator. It writhed like a worm, twisting its body, unable to free itself.

Its own blood clouded the water, blinding any spectators to the white's slaughter. The Serpent ripped and tore mercilessly, loosening its grip only to create a new, stronger one. Each disruption in the attack lasted only a split-second, the shark not fast enough to act on it. Not that it would make any difference.

The Serpent yanked its head backward, carrying with it a lump of flesh and a series of pink intestines. A huge plume of blood expanded from the shark's wound like smoke from a gas explosion.

The shark sank, its stomach and inner abdomen fully exposed to the elements. It was still alive. There was no conscious recognition to the severity of its injuries. It didn't grasp the scientific reality of infection, exposure, and the basic loss of blood and tissue. For the shark, the math was simple: it was alive, and it needed to do whatever it could to prolong that.

It fluttered its caudal fin, propelling itself to the open ocean. Intestines and loose tissue trailed behind it like ribbons from a battered flag waving in the wind. The fish retreated thirty feet, when suddenly, it felt intense pressure crushing its tail.

The Serpent slammed its jaws shut like a clamp. Teeth punched through the tissue and cartilage. The Serpent twisted back and forth, slicing away at the joint. The shark wiggled, literally being wagged by the tail, until finally, the caudal fin tore free.

Without its caudal fin to push it forward, the shark's mass was nothing more than a three-thousand pound paperweight. It spiraled down into the seabed, twisting and attempting to swim.

After swallowing the cartilaginous material, the Serpent angled its head down to the trail of blood. Like a bolt of lightning, it shot down the three hundred feet of distance to continue its assault. It bit and ripped away, splitting open the white's U-shaped stomach and retrieving the whale flesh it had consumed. Loose sediment billowed up and mixed with the blood cloud, creating a strange, greenish-red mixture that resembled the atmosphere of a foreign planet.

It only took a couple more bites to split the shark in half. Its head rolled like a bowling ball along the seabed, the Serpent preferring to feed on the tail and stomach regions. Fatty tissue ascended to the surface, where it would eventually drift past the whale carcass and be plucked up by the sea lions.

Momentarily satisfied, the Serpent slithered along the seabed toward the island. It found a large rock and studied it with its feelers before gliding over it. Behind it was an entire valley of rocks and chasms, perfectly suited for providing a natural habitat, even for a creature of its size. The creature weaved in-between them, effortlessly sliding out without its fins or tail getting snagged. In addition, it could feel distant vibrations coming from the distance. The area was rife with prey, enough to sustain it for a lifetime if necessary.

The judgement was made. This would be the Serpent's new habitat. It decided to circle the island before resting, its anal fin cutting the surface.

The seals proceeded to bark at it, warning the creature that it was incapable of reaching it. Though it was different in appearance, they believed its hunting patterns were the same as the great white that had hunted before it.

Drawn by the noise, the Serpent lifted its head above the surface. The barking swiftly stopped, and in a few moments, the seals started backing up to the side of the island. The thing approached the rocky shore. There, it waited for a few minutes, before slithering up the slope like a horrifying snake. It was just as fast on land as it was in the water.

The seals scattered, the largest also being the slowest. Eyes bulged as those massive jaws closed over its body, splintering its bones and grounding its flesh. Its brethren dove into the water and swam for their lives, their splashes dwarfed by the enormous one caused by their pursuer.

One by one, it picked them off. Scattering didn't make a difference, nor did staying together. The creature was faster than them, and was spurred by an appetite unmatched by anything sharing the ocean with it.

The attack was over within minutes, leaving an aftermath of tissue strands that would be nibbled by small fish and birds.

CHAPTER 5

"Alright, ladies and gentlemen. Thank you for joining me out here on the North Carolina coast. As you can see, I'm out on the aft deck of my beautiful Long Lydia Yacht, *Liddy*. I'm out here with Josh and Melvin, and our lovely assistants." Derrick paused to allow the cameras to focus on the bikini girls. They smiled and waved, a couple of them holding up lures, while one prepped the star's fishing rod. "They'll help us weigh the catch when we bring them in. Plus, cheer us on to keep up the good morale."

"Not to mention pass out the beers," Melvin said.

"Amen to that," Derrick said, wrapping his arms around the waists of two of the models. They smiled ear to ear, hugging the star close as he continued playing to the camera.

"Now, for those of you that are new, here's some basic info about the blue marlin: They are found all over the Atlantic Ocean, with the exception of the extreme northern and southern ends. When fishing for them, you're most likely to find them on the mid-Atlantic coast, the Gulf of Mexico, the coasts of the Bahamas, and the Caribbean Sea. They tend to prefer warm tropical waters, but are found through almost all of the Atlantic. These fish are known for their smooth, tubular body— essentially, they are the swimsuit models of the sea. Of course, they are most well-known for their bill, which extends as far as three feet. It acts like a skewer, plowing through other fish as though this were the Middle Ages. Some marlin fishermen have even suffered injury as a result of marlin jumping onto the boat headfirst. So, whenever you're out on the water and you have a marlin on the end of your line, always be cautious when the battle nears its end."

"You'll want to have gloves for this," Melvin said. "When the fish comes near the boat, a partner will have to grab the fish by its bill. It'll fight, and if it's too big, you might need a winch to bring it on board."

"That's right. Hence, as always, we have our lovely assistants at the ready," Derrick continued. "A marlin's diet consists of mackerel, bonito, ballyhoo, and mullet—not the Patrick Swayze kind, ha-ha-ha. Now, for you at home watching this, it'll only be a ten or fifteen minute wait to see whether we find something, or come up empty handed. As you can see here—I'm *never* empty handed. In fishing or in life. However, fishing for the blue marlin is a game of patience. You could be out here for hours. Hence, the need for beer and other entertainment—if you *Catch my Drift*." He hugged the girls tighter.

"Oh, Derrick," one of them giggled.

Behind the camera, the director, Marty, shook his head and mouthed, "Remember, this is a family show."

Had the cameras not been rolling, Derrick would've rolled his eyes. *Uh-huh, sure. Because these ladies were clearly hired to bring in young viewers. Most of this is gonna be used as a voiceover anyway.*

"But take my word for it: when you hook into a blue marlin, it becomes a battle of willpower and stamina. And believe me, it's the experience of a lifetime when you see these bad boys in the flesh, leaping ten feet out of the water."

"Right," Josh said.

"To do this, you need the right equipment. For smaller marlin under two-hundred pounds, you can use a stand-up belt. But anything larger, I would suggest you sit in the fighting chair. The trick of the fight is to pump and reel in quick bursts. Raise your rod to sixty-degrees—" as he spoke, one of the girls sat in the angler chair, demonstrating the necessary actions with the rod "—then reel down to put the line back into the reel. You'll want to do roughly five-feet of line at a time."

"I can do eight," Melvin said.

"Yeah. Hence all the lines you've busted," Derrick retorted. He turned back toward the camera. "If it jumps, let it do its thing. *Don't* reel while it runs—you'll just tire yourself out. Slow and steady wins the race."

"Speaking of slow, when the hell are you gonna stop talking?" Melvin said.

"Why? Eager to watch me haul in a thousand pounds of protein?" Derrick replied.

"The only protein you'll see is the bucket of chicken you'll eat while you mope about coming up empty handed, while I reel in the big one!"

"Alright then, prove me wrong, tough guy! It's a competition between Melvin and myself. I've got a nine-hundred pound swivel, with a five-hundred pound mono leader fixed with a trolling lure. I'll be using tuna as bait, while Melvin there thinks he'll be content with an artificial lure. Reminds me of our time as kids fishing in Grandma Jean's pond, and how afraid he was to touch the worm!"

"Right," Josh repeated.

"Let's get to it!" Melvin said.

"Just remember, the best catch usually goes to the guy with the bigger rod—if you *Catch my Drift,*" Derrick winked at the camera. "But first, a word from our sponsor..."

"Alright. Cut!" Marty said. The talent and crew broke their formation and moved about to set up for the next shot. Marty looked over his notes. "Nice work there, everybody. Derrick, you're quite the natural at this. One take and we got it all."

"A hundred-and-fourteen episodes," Derrick bragged.

"Okay. Give me a few minutes to communicate with the other boats, and we'll get ready for the next shot. Who knows, we might get everything filmed today with a little luck."

"That's to imply he'll actually catch something," Melvin joked.

"I say the odds are in my favor," Derrick replied, holding his reel.

Marty shook his head. *Are these guys aware that the cameras are off?* Melvin prepped his rod and lure and awaited direction for the next take. Five feet back from the transom were two fishing chairs, spaced six feet apart. Both were equipped with harnesses, footrests, and equally as important, cup holders. Between them was a red cooler, packed with soda, beer, water, and ice.

"Alright," Marty said, his eyes going from the script to the ocean, "So, you're going to cast out that direction?"

"Correct," Derrick said.

"Alright. Let me coordinate with the camera boats. We'll need someone filming about eight-hundred feet to our eleven o'clock, pointing east. That'll give us a good view of anything that happens, and... oh, damn it. Where's the police radio? The Chief will be in the shot and we'll need her to move."

"Is she now?" Derrick said. He gazed to the right at the blue and white police vessel rocking gently in the current. The bow was faced north, the two beautiful occupants standing out on the main deck. "I'll take care of that." He grabbed the police radio and leaned on the port railing, making sure to be seen. "Hey, Chiefy. Captain Derrick here. Did you happen to reconsider taping that law-enforcement special?"

Officer Jesse Roper let out a high-pitched laugh, immeasurably amused by the star of *Catch my Drift*. They leaned on the railing together, watching the shoot from a couple hundred yards out. Jesse's tan face was almost red from blushing from the celebrity attention she never thought she'd ever get.

Sammy shook her head, knowing what her subordinate and best friend was about to suggest.

"No. We're not doing it," she said.

"Come on!" Jesse replied. "It would be totally good for our image! Who knows, we could be getting calls from producers if it all goes well!"

"Oh, lord help me," Sammy muttered. What was she thinking, bringing Jesse out here? The girl had a list of celebrity crushes, though Derrick Crevello was never listed. Probably because she didn't watch a lot of sports shows, though that was likely to change now.

"Officers?" Derrick's voice was nagging. It was as though he could sense the inner conflict. Sammy picked up the radio.

"We appreciate the offer, Mr. Crevello," she said.

"Gosh, you make him sound like an old man when you say that," Jesse said.

"Shut up," Sammy retorted.

"Can't blame me for trying," Derrick said. *"However, my director has a request. We're lining up the next shot, and it looks like you'll be in it. He's hoping you'll throttle south a hundred meters or so. Personally, I think it'll add to the magic having you there, but unfortunately, I can't make every call."*

"Aww," Jesse moaned, making a pouty face.

"Will do," Sammy said. She turned to Jesse, who leaned against the railing, arms folded while watching the *Liddy* with envy. The girl was clearly questioning her choice to give up modeling in California in favor of following the family line of police service. With her sunflower blonde hair and cheerleader physique that she maintained since high school, and blossoming personality, she probably would've made it.

"What's that look for?" she said.

"You know he's just looking at you as an object," Sammy said. "The women over there—they're just props."

"I can think of worse ways to make a living," Jesse replied. "You think those girls hate their jobs? HELL NO!"

"I just know a bunch of them go crazy when they hit their forties," Sammy said.

"Beats going crazy in your twenties," Jesse joked.

"I don't understand what you mean," Sammy lied. She knew what her friend was getting at. Jesse knew the Chief better than anyone; maybe even her father. There was a specific reason she didn't want to get on that boat with Derrick.

"If you were completely over him, you wouldn't hesitate to climb up on that deck and toss a line out," Jesse said. She was smiling, confident in her analysis. That confidence elevated when she heard the predictable lie.

"I don't know what you're talking about," Sammy said. The predictable lie was followed by a predictable action of walking to the cockpit. Jesse wasn't going to let her off that easy.

"Don't play dumb," she said.

"I'm not playing dumb. I'm just moving the boat, like your crush asked," Sammy replied.

"You know, officers, we did a show on Lake Michigan, and we got the Mason County Fire Department to do a show with us. Big hit. Just saying—"

"He doesn't quit, does he?" Sammy said.

"Could be a sign," Jesse joked.

"Oh, for crying out loud. I'm a police chief, not a bikini model," Sammy said, pretending to be annoyed. Had it been anyone else on the boat with her, she probably would've been genuinely irritated. But there was something about Jesse that, no matter how hard she tried, she just could not be mad at her.

"You could be," Jesse retorted, shrugging her shoulders.

"Nice try. We're not getting on that boat."

Jesse mocked a disappointed sigh. "You just don't believe in fun."

Those words were chosen intentionally, as Sammy had repeated them to Jesse six months ago in a three-hour venting spree after her breakup. They were the very words, among others, her ex had said on their last night together, though in a less comical tone than Jesse's. Ever since, Jesse had tried to talk her into getting back together with him. "Soul mates," she had always put it. "Oh, you guys were made for each other!" Apparently not, as apparently Sammy didn't know how to balance life and work.

She attempted to put it from her mind, which only caused her to fixate on it more. Nearly ten times she looked at Ben Stacie's name on her contacts list, and considered whether or not to tap that screen. That number dwarfed the number of incomplete texts that she started to type, only to delete midway through. As always, she resorted to painting Ben in a broad brush to make her believe the breakup was best. The bastard never tried calling *her*, so he was clearly over her. Right?

She started the engine, immediately hearing a rattling sound from the engine.

"Damn it. We're gonna have to get this thing serviced again," she said.

"Hate to tell you how to do your job, girl, but you're gonna have to get with your dad for better funding for our equipment," Jesse said.

"Yeah, yeah, I know. I'll get it fixed."

"Not just fixed. We need new boats," Jesse said.

They listened to the crews setting up for the next shots. From where they drifted, they could only see the fishing seat on the right. To Jesse's delight, that was the one Derrick chose to sit. He peered over the railing at them and blew a kiss their way. Sammy noticed Jesse starting to blush.

"Oh, my god. Hon, you're hopeless."

"Remember what I said about fun? I *like* it."

"Enough to make a fool out of yourself," Sammy replied. The radio crackled again. This time, it was the director's voice.

"We'll be shooting in five."

Sammy got the message. She throttled the boat a few hundred feet back. The rattling worsened. Sammy's stomach sank. Before, it didn't sound like anything serious. But now, it seemed as though the engine was about to explode.

"Ohhhhh, shit, shit, shit! That doesn't sound good," she muttered. She switched off the engine and opened the hatch into the engine room. Immediately, she could smell something smoking. She didn't need to be an expert on engines to know it was dead. "Great. Just great."

"Fabulous," Jesse said. "Any idea what's wrong?"

"I'm no mechanic," Sammy said. She backed out onto the deck and looked over at the yacht. It didn't seem the cast and crew were aware of their predicament. That was the way she wanted to keep it, as she didn't want this embarrassment caught on national TV. Oh, how her father would kill her.

She peered at the surrounding ocean. Luckily, there weren't any boats close by. Most of the yachts, sailboats, and other fishing vessels kept a fair distance. Hopefully, that would continue, as she wouldn't be able to go after anyone with the engine in its current condition.

"Why today? Why *now* of all freaking times?!"

"We're gonna have to get someone out here," Jesse said. Sammy pulled out her phone and tried to call Dispatch. She didn't want this predicament broadcasted over the department's frequency. The resulting series of jokes from the other officers would be ruthless. She held the phone to her ear. There was no ringtone.

"Come on," she muttered. The phone continued loading, failing to get a signal out. There was no choice but to communicate by radio. "Son of a bitch." She braced herself for the inevitable onslaught, then pressed the transmitter. "Unit One to Dispatch."

"Go ahead."

"Hey, uh," Sammy tensed as she spoke, "Could you get in touch with Henry's mechanical service. We need a tugboat out here. We're having engine difficulties."

A short pause followed. Sammy immediately envisioned the laughter taking place in the office.

"Ten-four, Chief."

As expected, a storm of transmissions came through the radio.

"Lost at sea, are ya, Chief?" She recognized the voice of Sergeant Robert Shier. The guy had a commanding voice that made him sound like a USMC Fireteam leader—probably because he was.

"Maybe she'll find a desert island!" another said.

"Farewell and adieu to you fair Spanish ladies…"

Jesse and Sammy smiled as the transmissions continued to roll in.

"I'm starting to think about unpaid overtime for you all," the Chief replied.

"You'd have to make it to the office to do that!" another officer joked.

"Don't know about you guys, but I'm off to the office for pizza!"

"Ooo! I know where she keeps the department's credit card!"

"Alright, you knuckleheads, that's enough," Sammy said. "Oh, and don't you even think about it, Officer Barber. Go anywhere near that card and you'll be scrubbing toilets for the jail cells."

There was a pause. Finally, Barber's voice cracked through the transmitter.

"So, who likes bacon on your pizza?"

Sammy threw her head back and sighed. "Oh, those bastards." She went to the transom and set the anchor. Last thing she needed was to drift further out.

"Dispatch to Unit One."

Finally! Sammy unclipped her speaker mic. "Go ahead."

"Henry's not in today. Turns out he had a big job somewhere up the coast. Had to take the tugboat with him." Sammy felt an overwhelming urge to kick something. It really did seem like this boat waited for the literal worst possible moment to crap out on her.

"Any good news?"

"The Bulldogs are up by three points," Sergeant Shier chimed in.

"Oh, shut up," Sammy retorted.

"I'm on hold with Beggars Cove Boat Repair. I believe he has a tugboat. From what I hear, he's pretty good."

Sammy's stomach sank. *She did NOT say Beggar's Cove Boat Repair!* This couldn't be happening. Not him!

If Jesse's smile had gotten any wider, it'd have split her face.

"Don't you even say what I think you're gonna say," Sammy said, pointing a finger.

"I'm saying it!" Jesse laughed. "This is FATE! I knew you two were gonna have to run into each other eventually!"

"Jesse, I don't want to see him."

"Bullshit. You're dying to see him."

"I am not!"

"Well, we'll just have to see," Jesse said. She grabbed the radio and turned to face the yacht. Sammy felt herself getting even more nervous.

"What are you doing?"

"Helping you out," Jesse said. She cleared her throat and spoke into the radio. "Spiral Bay Police to Mr. Derrick Crevello?"

The celebrity fisherman was instantaneous in his response, which was highly enthusiastic.

"What's going on, badass babes?!"

Jesse struggled to keep from giggling into the transmitter. "I hope it's not too late to request a transfer over to your boat. Probably with the jet ski you have in the back." She turned to watch Sammy's expression grow increasingly sour as she spoke. "You see, the Chief has changed her mind and is allowing me to make an appearance on your deck. She'll have to stay behind and take care of some managerial duties on the radio, but *I* have free rein to show you guys how it's done."

"Hell yeah! I'll be there to pick you up myself!"

They could hear Derrick telling Marty to hold off for a few more minutes. Jesse put the radio down and smiled at Sammy, who looked as though she was about to throw her best friend overboard.

"What the hell are you doing?"

"I'm helping you," Jesse said.

"*Helping* me?"

"Uh, yeah!"

"How is this helping me?"

"You really think those guys aren't gonna get you on camera at some point? When they do, they're gonna find you, drifting aimlessly with a dead engine. I don't think that'll do well for the department's image. *Unless*, I keep their attention on me. Also, Derrick's a goofball, but I don't think he'll bother you if he thinks you're busy with actual work."

Sammy's expression softened. Jesse had a point: she absolutely did not want to be filmed in this current predicament. Of course, there was nothing she could do when the tugboat got there, but with a little luck, they'd be done before the repairman would arrive.

"Please don't make TOO MUCH of a fool of yourself," she begged.

"Remember to tell yourself the same thing when Ben gets here," Jesse said. Sammy grimaced. Jesse could read her mind: *I hate you.* "Love you too."

The Chief leaned on the guardrail and stared out to the west. Somewhere over there, Ben Stacie was receiving a call that his ex, the town's young police chief, needed his help.

CHAPTER 6

Ben Stacie wiped his handkerchief across his face. It was his third one for the day, and already, it had turned brown from the oil stains. He always referred to it as 'mechanic's sweat', and it was a sign of a good day's work. He had been hard at work on Professor Jeb Bordain's fishing boat all morning. It had been brought in the previous night, with the Professor complaining of a rattling sound. As Ben predicted, it was the piston pin bushing, which needed to be replaced.

He heard the bell ring as the front door opened. Ben lifted himself out of the engine compartment and climbed up on deck. After climbing off the boat, he crossed the dock into his shop. Standing at the check-in counter was Professor Bordain.

"Hey, Ben," the Professor said. "I got your call. How's she looking?"

"Nothing too serious," Ben replied. "I was able to replace the bushing, as well as give her an oil change. Just remember to treat your boat engine as if it was your car. It needs to be regularly maintained. I see a lot of cracked cylinders that could easily be prevented."

"I appreciate that, Ben," Bordain said. Ben had known the Professor since high school, when the administration forced him into taking a chemistry class that he absolutely detested. Specifically, he detested the equations; the mixing of chemicals was actually pretty neat. Now, Bordain was teaching chemistry at the community college a couple of miles inland. "What do I owe you?"

"I had the parts on hand. Just make it seventy bucks and we'll call it even," Ben said.

"Don't let yourself get shortchanged," Bordain said, reaching into his wallet.

"Well, it's the least I can do for you giving me a C," Ben joked.

"I can't argue that," the Professor chuckled. He handed the money over and Ben started ringing him up.

"So, how are things at the school? Any summer classes?"

"Why? You interested in a course?"

"Hell no!"

Bordain smiled. "Yeah, things aren't too bad for the most part. Some of these kids are..." he paused, trying to think of a delicate way of putting it, "Eh, screw it. They're dumb as a box of rocks. I don't know if they're frying their brains looking at computer screens all day, or just don't have an appreciation for learning, but they're not smart. We had an acid spill the other day. The dummy didn't use the correct protective gloves, despite the fact that I specifically told him which ones to use. Apparently, they didn't 'look' like they would protect against acid. "Too thin," he had told me later. He didn't realize it's the material itself that matters, not the density."

"Surprised you let him play with such acid," Ben said.

"That was my error. I shouldn't have," Bordain said. "Luckily, the kid admitted he didn't follow instructions, so that's the only reason I'm not getting my ass investigated. But the damn stress was enough for me to finally go out on my boat, and, well, you know where that led."

"Luckily, it wasn't too bad. I just need to make some finishing touches, and it'll be done. You can have someone come and pick it up at any time. If it gives you any more trouble, just bring it on in and I'll give it a look."

"Ben, you're a saint. I'm glad you've found something you enjoy doing. Keep putting your mind to it, and you'll be successful."

"Thanks, Professor." Ben cleaned off his oily hand, then shook Bordain's. The Professor turned around and left, the bell chiming as the door opened. As the tune settled, the phone rang. Ben recognized the number. *The Police Department? Interesting.* "Beggar's Cove Engine Service. This is Ben speaking."

"Hi, Ben. I'm calling from Spiral Bay Police Department. We're hoping you have a tugboat available for a towing service. One of our patrol boats is having engine trouble three miles north of Lebbon Rock."

"Uh-oh! Yep. I can start heading on out there in about twenty minutes or so. I'm just finishing up touches on another job, and I can get started afterward, unless it's a dire emergency."

"No, nothing like that. I'll let her know you're coming."

Her... Ben's mind started to wander. There was only a handful of 'hers' on the police force, and if he remembered correctly, only a couple of them worked during the day.

"I'm just curious, which officer is it on the boat? I'm familiar with a lot of the staff, that's why I'm asking."

"It's the Chief," Dispatch replied. Ben smiled. *Oh, I knew this was gonna be a good day!*

"Alright. Three miles north of the lighthouse. Thanks, Dispatch, I'll be out there as soon as I can." He hung up the phone and hurried out to the dock to finish up work on the Professor's boat. He replaced a couple of valves and finished adding the oil. After wiping his hands, he proceeded to test the engine. It ran as smooth as though it was fresh off the assembly line; a stanch difference than when it came in. He knew the Professor had his spare key, and had instructed him where to leave the main key when finished.

Ben finished locking up, then hurried to the restroom to wash his hands and face, and to change his shirt. It had been a while since he'd been this excited for a job.

CHAPTER 7

"Fish on!" Derrick shouted. The cameras recorded the crew roaring in celebration as the marlin snared itself on the hook. It made a bounding leap out of the water, its body twisting, thrashing its bill like a rapier.

Nobody was happier than Jesse Roper. Of course, as a play to the camera, Derrick had relinquished his seat to her, narrating the event as they drifted. It had only taken twenty minutes for the fish to strike the bait, leaving her competition, Melvin, flabbergasted.

"Look at this! LOOK! AT! THIS!" Derrick cheered, looking back and forth between the camera and the action. "This is amazing! The Spiral Bay Police Department doesn't only produce the hottest officers I've ever seen, but they can also rival me as the world's greatest fisherman!"

Jesse pulled the rod high, then reeled in the slack. The fish jumped again and crashed. The line went taut as it tried to run.

"Let it tire itself out," Derrick said. He glanced up briefly at the drone, then back at Josh, who spun his laptop monitor for the star to see the perfect aerial shot. He saw the fish from a hundred feet up. It jerked its head back and forth, then tried to dive. He spun back toward Jesse and spun his fist, like an athletic coach mentoring a student during a competition. "You've got it on the ropes! It's committed a heinous crime, and it's trying to get away from the police!"

Several hundred feet back, Sammy watched the event from the foredeck. She couldn't believe it. Jesse had actually caught something.

At least someone's having a good day. She was actually happy, though admittedly for the wrong reasons. She just hoped they managed to shoot enough footage and head to shore before Ben arrived.

Oh God, I can't believe he's coming out here. They hadn't seen each other in six months. Each passing minute added nervous tension. A million possibilities rolled through her mind. Would he be pissed off to see her? What would she say to him? What would he say to *her*? Would there be an argument? He wasn't really a confrontational guy, but then again, she was the one who broke off their engagement. For plenty of people, that'd be more than enough to cause resentment. Worst of all, would this all be captured on camera? Just the thought of it was making Sammy turn red.

Unfortunately, there was nothing she could do but watch and wait, and hope the yacht didn't drift too close to her. She could hear Jesse whooping from the *Liddy's* deck, and listening to her joy was enough to brighten anyone's day.

The marlin twisted in a miraculous display and crashed, sparking thunderous applause from the crew. Even Marty was clapping his hands. His concern of including the local PD as a stunt had immediately faded. This officer seemed to handle the fish pretty well. And Derrick was having the time of his life, which was all being captured on camera.

The marlin was two hundred yards out. Jesse held tight to the rod, the straps pressing against her midsection. This marlin was undoubtedly much heavier than two-hundred pounds.

Jesse tugged it back, then brought in some of the slack.

"You won't see any of those Miami or L.A. cops doing this!" she cheered.

"Not at all!" Derrick replied. He faced the camera. "Just look at that, folks! We've got a natural here showing Melvin how it's done! Look at him there, holding his pole in his hand. Line looks a little limp there, bud."

Melvin held up a middle finger, first to Derrick, then up at the sky where Josh's drone was hovering.

"Here's two for ya!" He held up his other middle finger.

Marty put a hand over his face and shook his head. *Another clip for the editing department.*

Jesse was starting to sweat through her uniform now, but she didn't care. She was having the time of her life. She was about to be on TV! Not only that, but she was reeling in a thousand-pound marlin. Hell, they ought to do a spinoff show about *her*!

She pulled back and reeled in another few feet of line.

Then, suddenly, another round of applause exploded. Melvin's line went taut. A moment later, they saw another spray of water in the distance. A second marlin broke the water.

"Here we go, ladies!" the fisherman exclaimed.

"No way!" Derrick shouted. It was unbelievable. TWO marlins within twenty minutes of each other. The *YouTube* clips of this episode were sure to get millions of views. Hell, there'd be articles written about this spectacle.

Derrick faced the cameras again, his face and hands animated as he went off-script to explain the events.

"We've got two marlins, folks. TWO! Now, our fisherman and fisher-lady are in stiff competition to bring in the best catch! Who'll bring in the larger fish? Will it be Officer Roper of the Spiral Bay Police Department? Or will it be Melvin, who once snapped a line reeling in a bluegill in Ohio?"

"It got snagged under a branch!" Melvin corrected him, struggling to pull the rod back. He reeled in the slack, then jolted as the fish tried to run. It leapt again, twisting wildly. At the same time, Jesse's fish jumped, both showing their vibrant blue and silver colors.

Josh steered his drone for a closeup view of Melvin's fish.

"Oh, man, I hate to admit it, Derrick, but I think Melvin has the bigger fish!" he said.

Derrick watched the screen. He couldn't deny it; Melvin's fish was trophy size at the very least. Even from this distance, he could tell it was well over the average length of eleven feet. His guess was that it was at least thirteen or fourteen, probably weighing near thirteen-hundred pounds. He was tempted not to acknowledge it on camera due to his bias in Jesse's favor—of course, he wanted the pretty lady to win. But the facts were the facts, and no matter the result, it was still a great moment for the show.

"Oh yeah!" Melvin shouted. "Sorry, Officer! But your fish's bill looks a little small!"

"You seem to know a lot about small appendages," Jesse retorted. The crew erupted with laughter and applause, which increased as both fish leapt from the water again.

Melvin smiled. He was a good sport—he'd be in the wrong business otherwise. He started to whoop, which transformed into a sharp grunt as the fish tried to run again. He felt as though it would pull him right through his harness. He straightened his cap and gripped the rod. The damn marlin was not surrendering easy. It was going deep now.

He felt a warm mist as Jesse's fish struck down again. The dumb thing had actually leapt *toward* the boat, making her job easier. She only had about thirty or forty feet to go, while his was maybe a hundred-fifty feet out. No problem. The competition was not about who could get their fish in first; it was who brought in the best catch. And his fish was undoubtedly the heavier of the two.

The Serpent lifted its head, alert. Its sensory receptors had lit up across its long body. There was something struggling for dear life in the water. The Serpent had chosen to rest in the rocks after consuming the shark and seals, but already, its metabolism was burning the recent fuel. There was no question of why it was always so hungry—the beast wasn't capable of such critical thought. It only knew that it *was* hungry, and that food was in its vicinity.

It fluttered its long tail and traveled north toward the vibrations. The increased intensity of their patterns informed the beast that it was getting nearer. There was a slight hint of blood in the water, but it wasn't clear whether it was related to the struggling prey. But the prey was there.

After crossing nearly three miles of water, the creature's gift of eyesight served their purpose. There were two large floating objects in the water, holding several creatures that could easily be consumed as prey. But first, it wanted the vulnerable target swimming below the surface.

There were two of them! One was near the floating objects, the other much further out, and deep. Its movements were that of something attempting escape.

The marlin could detect the approaching mass. Its brain was a hurricane of warning. First, it was trying to escape the strange, unseen force that dragged it toward the floating mass. Now, there was something approaching from its right. It turned left but only managed to go a few feet. It had already exhausted itself and was making no progress. It pointed its bill skyward and shot for the surface.

It attempted a leap, but only its head escaped the water. Jaws snapped around its body, cracking bone and splitting its flesh as though it was soft as bread. It pulled down and twisted its jaws, snapping the spine. With one final tear, it tore the body free from the trapped, useless head.

"Holy—" Melvin had leaned forward with the pole, as though his fish had quadrupled in weight in a single instant. After a few sharp tugs, he suddenly felt a sharp release, and he was flung backward in his chair.

"Jesus!" Josh said. Everyone on deck muttered in awe and confusion. There was a huge splash where the fish was, and there was no mistaking the huge red cloud back there.

"What the hell happened?" Derrick said.

"I don't know," Melvin said, straightening himself out. He cranked the reel a few times. There was definitely no thirteen-hundred pound fish on the end of it. However, there was still some weight, and it was more than the lure and bait. "I've got *something*."

Jesse continued to focus on her fish. It was twelve-feet from the deck now. It had worn itself out drastically, though it continued to thrash violently. Two wiremen stood on the portside, ready to grab the fish by the bill.

Derrick, remembering the cameras were still rolling, focused on the event taking place. He didn't want Jesse's thunder being overshadowed by the bizarre event that just happened.

"Alright, guys! Officer Roper's victory is almost complete! Just a few more cranks...there you go...just a little more...there!"

The men grabbed the bill and held tight. The marlin wiggled, its tail slapping the hull of the boat. After letting it wear itself out further, they pulled up with all their might. Others rushed in to help. Finally, the deck was filled with cheers as it was held by six men standing in a line.

Jesse threw a fist in the air and screamed triumphantly, then proceeded to high-five everyone on the deck.

The carnivore thrashed the headless fish, mashing its body into portions that could easily be swallowed. The vibrations from the other marlin had disappeared completely, as though it had simply vanished. Still, there was the prey on top of the boats. It remembered the taste of their soft flesh, how easily the bones splintered between its teeth. They were no match for it, and once the marlin was fully consumed, they would be next.

Suddenly, other distortions filled the sea. The Serpent sensed incoming movement. Nothing threatening, but still large enough to get its attention.

Blue sharks, five feet in length, dove into the cloud of blood, stealing bits of flesh from the dead marlin. There were several of them swarming the water like bees. The Serpent extended its jaws, and snapped them shut over a shark that dared to come in for a bite of the ravaged carcass. With a shake of its head, the Serpent split the shark in half, its head and caudal fin twirling to the seabed trailing blood streams. The other sharks turned back, realizing the large lifeform sharing the water was a violent predator. They raced out into the open sea, but the Serpent was not intending to let them escape so easily.

It grabbed a fleeing shark by the caudal fin, its teeth grazing each other as they plowed through its midsection. With a quick snap of its jaws, it impaled a second row of injuries, rupturing the fish's insides. After tearing it in two, it chased the others further out to the east, favoring them over the land-based prey, who remained oblivious to its presence.

As the crew continued to praise Jesse for her catch, the cameras focused on Melvin as he reeled in his lure. A few times, they noticed the three-foot bill of his 'catch' poke through the waves.

"What the hell?" he muttered.

More people gathered. He unclipped the harness and reeled in the remainder of his slack. Out of the water came the severed head of his marlin. Thin strands of flesh dangled, the spinal bone splintered like a toothpick.

"Well, would you look at that!" Derrick said. "Poor Melvin! Just when he finally catches something worth keeping, Mother Nature says "Nuh-uh, boy! Not having it!"" The crowd laughed, while Melvin grimaced. He looked over at his other co-star.

"Josh. Did you catch that?"

"No. My camera was on the officer's fish. I didn't swing back in time," Josh said.

"Looks like our lovely officer wins this round," Derrick said. He took Jesse's hand and raised it to the sky as though she was the winner of a UFC fight. "Give it up for our champion, ladies and gentlemen!"

Melvin let the head drop to the deck. Being a good sport, he shook Jesse's hand.

"Well done, Officer," he said. "Now we know we no longer need Derrick on the show. We can have *you* for a host!"

"Nice try," Derrick retorted.

Melvin glanced back at the head. "So, nobody's gonna mention this oddity?" The others circled it, the show host kneeling to inspect the severed area.

"Whatever did this was big," he said. He shrugged. "Must've been a shark, I guess." He wasn't fully convinced. It would have to have been a big shark to bite through this marlin with such ease. Then again, he couldn't think of anything else that could have done this.

"What about an orca?" Josh asked.

"I think we would've seen it," Jesse added. "Killer whales often surface for breath after taking down prey." She looked out to the water. There was nothing to obscure the view. Had a whale breached, they would've had no problem spotting it, even by mistake.

"Hmm, who knows," Derrick said, directing one of the cameramen to line up with him. "Maybe we have a monster somewhere out in these waters. Perhaps our new fishing competition won't come from the land, but from the sea itself!"

"Alright, cut," Marty said.

"Hey, what are you doing?" Derrick complained.

"Everything's good, Derrick. We've got TONS of fishing footage, more than enough to fill the episode. But we're still gonna need to script and shoot some connecting shots."

"Hell, I can do that now," Derrick said.

"You know the process," Marty groaned. "We have to review what we have and write around that. Plus, we'll need the officer to sign release forms before we can even begin the process."

"What about this, though?" Derrick pointed at the fish head. "We could have our next episode right here! 'The Hunt for the Spiral Bay Monster!' Think of it; we've never had a to-be-continued episode before. And these won't air until September, anyway. We could push it back and have this be like a Halloween special, or something."

The director thought about it, then nodded. Derrick Crevello was more than a little eccentric, but he did often bring good points to the show.

"I'll have to speak with the studio heads," he said. Derrick rolled his eyes. Knowing the producers, they wouldn't send an answer back until morning at least. Oh well. At least he got Marty on board with his idea. More than likely, they'd be back out to shoot some more tomorrow.

Jesse turned toward him and shot him a smile. "Don't I get a picture with the star of the show?" Derrick felt a glow that only a stroked ego could bring.

"Damn right you do!" He put an arm around her waist then stood next to the marlin. Cameramen took several snapshots. Once they were done, Jesse leaned over the side to look at Sammy.

"Chief, you should've come aboard!" she said on the radio.

Sammy waved back at her. "I saw it. Well done. You've done the department proud." She wanted to ask whether they were about to head back, but didn't want to sound eager. *Please*

SERPENT

head back. She thought of a better way to inquire. "So, did they get a ton of footage of you? Worthy of an Emmy?"

"Worthy of two Emmys," Jesse replied. *"I have to sign some stuff with them. Can't wait to show off to all the guys!"*

"They'll be impressed," Sammy said. "You gonna try again?" She winced when asking that, fearing the answer to be 'yes'.

"No. They're wrapping it up for the day."

"Okay, ten-four," Sammy said, then immediately lowered the radio to exclaim, "Oh, thank God." She had dodged a bullet. They'd be gone, and she wouldn't have to worry about being caught on video with a busted engine...

She noticed orange lights in her peripheral vision.

Sammy turned, then sank into a chair. The sight of that approaching tugboat brought with it a strong desire for Sammy to hurl herself overboard. So much for that dodged bullet.

CHAPTER 8

Ben couldn't withhold his glimmering smile as he steered his tugboat close toward the broken down police vessel. The woman on deck was as beautiful as ever. It was the first time he'd seen her since she ended their engagement. Even from a few hundred yards out, that glare on her face was unmistakable. He had been on the business end of that a hundred times. Only this time, it was because *she* was in trouble.

"Hey, what's going on here?" Derrick said. He had heard a large boat pulling close ahead of the *Liddy*'s bow. Everyone instantly recognized it as a tugboat, and there was no mistaking the fact that it was lining up for service on the police vessel.

"Is your Chief having boat issues?" Melvin asked Jesse. She smiled.

"Yeah, she blew the engine," Jesse said, giggling.

"Turn the boat around," Derrick said. The helmsman carefully maneuvered the yacht to position the aft deck into view.

Sammy bit her lip. The very thing she was afraid of had happened. So much for Jesse keeping the crew's attention off of her. She tensed for a moment, then eased up—she didn't want to be caught on camera looking unprofessional. And Ben was here to help, though she could tell by that shit-eating grin that he was enjoying the hell out of this.

There he was, in his typical blue jeans and black t-shirt. His brown hair was shorter than usual, roughly finger-length. And…it was hard to tell from here, but had he lost a little weight? He was never really hefty to begin with, but when she last saw him, the double-cheeseburgers were starting to leave their mark on his midsection.

That last encounter—oh, how she wanted it erased from her mind.

Ben stepped out from the cabin, leaned over the gunwale, and smiled at her.

"You know? Last time I saw a police chief on a broken down boat, a big great white was leaping out of the water to get him."

Full of jokes. There's one aspect of him that didn't change.
Suddenly, it hit her: Did Ben know about the film crew? Would he seize the opportunity to make her look like a complete idiot—more so than she already looked?

Relax. Respond.

"Only marlins out here," she replied.

"I saw it splashing on the way in," Ben remarked. Finally, he struck her with that gaze. She could sense the many phrases and questions competing in his mind. *"How have you been?" "I miss you." "Never thought I'd see you again." "You seeing anyone?"* Going by the way those eyes were looking at her, it had to be something like that.

Ben grabbed the tow cable.

"Told ya you'd need me back in your life in some way!" he quipped. Sammy closed her eyes.

Don't reply. Don't...

She was suddenly extremely aware of the crowd watching her. Standing right in the middle was Jesse Roper, still looking bright from her big catch. Even with that considered, she seemed too happy to be witnessing this encounter.

"Looks like they know each other," Derrick commented. To his right, one of the cameramen shot B-roll footage.

"Oh, they know each other very well," Jesse said. Derrick felt some excitement building within him.

"Please elaborate," he said.

"They're in love," Jesse told him. Sammy started to whip toward her, eyes briefly wide.

Stay cool. Don't look deranged—I can't believe she's telling them!

Jesse waved to the maintenance man. "Hi, Ben! How you doing?!"

He waved back. "Doing great, Jesse! How's life been treating ya?"

"This has been the best day of my life!" Jesse said, winking toward Sammy. It took effort for the Chief to not crawl into the cockpit. That bitch! She planned this! *"Oh, you two are meant to be together!"* Well, damn if she wasn't going to make that happen herself. And here she was, using Derrick and his film crew to work her magic.

"Oh, this is too good!" Derrick said. "Former lovers?"

"Yes," Jesse said. She leaned in to whisper in his ear, "They broke up, but they're still in love."

"Okay, well it's time for Saint Derrick to work his magic. In addition to being an expert fisherman and charming TV personality, I'm also a love doctor."

"I don't think jerking off qualifies you," Melvin said.

"Hey! Who set you up with Susie McKinley?" Derrick said.

"You! And we know how that turned out. She dumped me!"

"Yeah? You told me you wanted to date someone smart," Derrick said. More laughter consumed the deck. Derrick leaned over the rail and cupped his hands to call to Ben. "Welcome to the set of *Catch my Drift!*"

Ben looked at all the cameras on the yacht. He had heard of the show coming to town, but didn't realize right away that *this* was their crew.

"Oh, this is good," he said to himself.

"We can add this to the special," Derrick loudly told the director, who immediately rubbed his forehead. *Another change. Another addition. Oh, God.* Derrick pointed to the former lovers. "She's in love with the mechanic! Perhaps Derrick can help rekindle their romance!"

Marty shook his head. "I don't know if the studio will—"

Derrick whipped around and called out to Ben, "How long were you two together?"

"Three years," Ben replied.

Sammy's fists clenched. *Stop talking.*

"Was she a nice girlfriend?" Derrick continued. Hot breath burst from Sammy's nostrils. What would Ben say? And Jesse—she was dead. So dead!

Ben thought about it. "In the beginning. We kind of drifted afterwards."

"Aww," Derrick moaned. "Why? Just looking at you, I can tell you'd make a pretty couple! And judging by the way she's looking at you, I think she misses you!"

Sammy's eyes widened. *My 'I'm gonna murder you' look comes off as ROMANTIC?!*

Ben thought about his next answer. Sammy felt the nervous shakes finally taking hold of her. This was his way to get back at her: make a fool of her on camera. It probably wouldn't air, as she never signed any release forms. But hell, how would she know none of this would make it on *YouTube* or something? She braced for the emotional impact of Ben telling them how she chose her career over him, and how she thought he had no ambition and drive. Of course, that would be followed-up by the founding of his company less than a month later, probably to show her up.

And now, she was at the mercy of his services. That damned engine!

"Hmm. Well, first of all, Sammy is a nice considerate person, and that carried through our relationship. I guess things went downhill after I focused on my career. It's just one of those things where I started at the bottom and began working my way up the ladder. Next thing I know, I'm the boss, and it gets to my head. It wasn't long before I start throwing myself into the field for long hours, taking calls at home, and constantly attending meetings, even ones that don't particularly require my presence."

"Well, damn, Mr. Ben," Derrick said. "You should've known better!"

Sammy cringed.

"I know. But I've paid the price. And I've moved on just fine. I'm just happy to be here in Spiral Bay. Gotta say: there's hardly any criminal activity here, and you can thank the Chief for that."

"Well, we have a celebration tonight on the beachfront. Officer Roper here brought home the prize and we're gonna celebrate her victory at Section Seventeen. Eight o'clock! And you, sir, are formally invited. Food and drinks provided! The only requirement I have for you is to bring a date! If you need help with that, though, I can help set you up."

Sammy noticed a couple of the models smiling and waving at Ben. The bastard didn't hesitate to wave back!

Wait...he's single. YOU broke up with HIM! She chastised herself in the realm of her mind.

"Really?" Ben said, looking excited. "You know what? I think I'll be there."

"Excellent!" Derrick smiled, then glanced over at the Chief. "I think he'll choose well." Finally, he turned and headed into the cabin. "Alright, let's head in. Officer Roper, I presume you could use a lift since the Chief is preoccupied."

Jesse smiled one last time at Sammy, then replied, "Please. I'd greatly appreciate it." She disappeared into the boat, which proceeded to throttle east toward shore.

Finally, their audience had disappeared.

Ben prepped the tow cable, then slowly brought his vessel a little closer to hers.

"I guess this is one of those very interesting days," he said. "Got myself a party to attend tonight!"

"You're a dick," Sammy said.

"Wha—?" He wasn't sure if she was playing along, or genuinely pissed off; an issue that persisted as she advanced through the department. *Two can play at this game.* "Well fine. I think I'll head on back. Have fun floating out here."

"Oh, Ben," she said, shaking her head.

He chuckled. "How've you been?"

"I've had better days," she said, tilting her head down at the boat. "But overall, good. Working a lot."

"Me too," he replied. He secured the towline onto the cleats on her transom. "Wanna ride with me?" Sammy nodded, then climbed over. "What kind of rattling sound is it making?"

"Sounds like something has, or is about to, break loose."

"Well, let's get it into my shop and I'll get a look at it," he said. He double-checked the towline then climbed back onto his boat. As he went over the cockpit, he couldn't help but notice Sammy's eyes on his mid-section. "Oh! Yeah, I'm the same guy, just cut out the chili dogs and burgers. I came to realize how much I enjoy freshly baked fish with some salad. Silly it took me this long, considering I live on the coast."

Sammy made a nervous laugh, feeling stupid for getting caught blatantly checking him out. Her ex, of all people.

"You—" she paused. She wanted to say 'you look good.' It seemed like a reasonable response, but would it somehow come off as…admitting she missed him? "You've done good. I'm impressed." *God, that sounded stupid too!*

Ben walked to the helm and started the engine back up. He took it slow, accounting for the mass of the smaller police vessel behind him. Gradually, he increased speed.

"Alright. We'll be there in twenty, thirty minutes," he said. He tapped on the wheel as though to a beat. He was in a good mood. "Wow. Big party tonight for a big fishing show! And *I'm* invited. Did not expect this! I just gotta figure out who I'm gonna bring."

"I'm gonna kill Jesse," Sammy said aloud.

"Why? Did she steal your thunder by catching that big marlin? Like I said, I caught a little bit of the action on my way in."

"She's a little drunk on fame right now," Sammy said. "And she actually managed to trick me into letting her go on that yacht, all so she could get us alone together. Of course, I never considered the fact that she planned on using Derrick and his show, let alone actually be successful."

"You say that like it's a bad thing," Ben said.

"Well, I, uh…" Sammy was aware of her stuttering, which made it worse.

"She's a master planner," Ben said.

"Yes. She is," Sammy said, relieved to have a way out of the stuttering rabbit hole she was in.

"Still! Doesn't change the fact that I have a party to look forward to tonight. Did he not invite you?"

"Of course he did…not…" Sammy's voice trailed off. She thought for a moment. She remembered Derrick inviting Jesse, and of course Ben. But not her. "Come to think of it, he didn't."

"Shame."

Sammy knew the game he was playing, and unfortunately it was working. She couldn't tell if he was bantering or rubbing in the possibility that he was gonna dance with some gorgeous models on the beach tonight. The worst part was that the thought of it made her jealous, and she didn't want to feel that way. She left him for a reason! His lack of progress in his career. His gaining of weight. The fact that he was wasting his time trying to set up a business that was doomed to fail—except that it didn't.

The self-awareness crept in. Who was she to judge? Especially when she put all of her energy into her career instead of supporting him. Wow. He had really improved on all fronts since their breakup. Hell, even his haircut was better!

It seemed the best thing she contributed to his life was…leaving him.

Damn. If I thought this day couldn't make me feel lower…

CHAPTER 9

Hugh kept his forehead to the window. For two hours, he watched the ocean pass underneath him as the helicopter he chartered took him up along the Georgia coast. The pilot, a former contractor for CBS News, was slightly hesitant to take up these two mysterious men. Their instructions were simple, fly up and down the coast in search of anything unusual. Usually, his clients had a specific destination in mind. When asked what they were looking for, they remained vague. But the zeros on the check were enough to put his reservations to rest.

"Perhaps we should go further out?" Ryan suggested.

"You said yourself it prefers shallower waters," Hugh reminded him.

"True, but it could be anywhere," Ryan said.

The pilot glanced back at them. "Uh, I know people that can search for whatever it is you're looking for by boat."

"That'll take too long," Hugh said. He didn't disagree with the pilot per se, but he needed to cover as wide an area as possible, as quickly as possible. So far, there were no obvious signs of the creature. In a way that was good, as some of those signs would include boat wreckage and death—something he was trying hard to prevent.

"How much longer can we stay up?" Ryan asked the pilot.

"With current speed and weight, we've got another three hours tops. But keep in mind, in about thirty minutes, we'll have to head back, or else we'll be forced to land on some other airstrip, and I'm not paying for their fuel."

"Alright. Keep pushing south then," Hugh said.

"You get what you pay for, doctors." The pilot took a swig of whatever was in his flask and pressed forward. Ryan and Hugh glanced at each other nervously. Suddenly, there was little mystery of why this pilot had been terminated from his high-paying job at CBS. Unfortunately, he was also someone who wouldn't ask too many questions, especially when presented with money. And if he did see something and attempted to make it public, who'd really believe him?

Hugh's phone buzzed. *Linda Ayres*. Finally, the Timestone CEO was returning his dozen calls.

"Dr. Meyer here."

"Doctor. I thought I instructed you to let it go." Her voice was cold and lifeless, like it was when his lab assistants had been slaughtered back in the main facility.

"No deal," Hugh said. "I'm not letting it go loose. Any action taken from here on out is our responsibility. We created it, and now there's a possible danger posed to the environment and the population."

"There's nothing to connect the creature to Timestone," Ms. Ayres replied. *"I'm not wasting resources to capture something that we've proven we can just recreate. Capturing it will be more trouble than it's worth, because THAT would bring attention to our involvement, especially if it does kill someone else. We've already harvested DNA from its spinal column and extracted bone marrow. We have everything we need to grow a new specimen, and we can do it in our new facility. It's money that has already been spent. If the creature is seen, it'll be chalked up as an anomaly."*

"I understand you're only concerned with your company, Linda, but—"

"It's MISS Ayres, Doctor. Don't mistake me for your friend."

"No mistake there," he mouthed, aiming the device away, only to reposition it. *"Miss* Ayres, Dr. Burg and I are certain we've narrowed down the approximate location to the specimen's whereabouts. We just need the resources to exterminate it. We need boats, manpower, possibly some—"

"Negative, Doctor. You're on your own. If you and Dr. Burg want to hunt that thing, fine. But do it quietly. Go to the press, and believe me, it won't go in your favor."

Hugh hesitated, holding back a hail of 'fuck-you' and 'eat shit', among other derogatory remarks. None of which would benefit his purpose beyond feeling good in the moment. He took a breath, cooling off enough to reply.

"Fine." It was the best he could do. "I'll do it myself. But I'll need funds."

"I'll provide you a hundred grand to take care of the problem, as long as you do it quietly."

"Done." Hugh was surprised to even get that much, though a hundred grand was pocket change to Timestone. Hell, he'd seen her spend twice that on a corporate dinner once.

"Make it quick." The dial tone bopped in Hugh's ear. He stuffed the phone in his pocket then returned his eyes to the water.

"Pleasant conversation?" Ryan asked.

"You know Linda. Oh, excuse me, *Miss Ayres*."

"Bitch must think she's the God of War," Craig said. Hugh scoffed. The pilot must've dealt with plenty of egos as large as Linda's.

"So, she's actually providing funding for our little excursion?" Ryan asked, his expression a surprised one.

"She's not concerned about the specimen being loose. That said, I think the way she sees it is if we catch it, then the tiny risk of exposure is eliminated. Plus, I think she wants to appear like she gives a damn so I won't send in my resignation."

"So, what is this specimen?" Craig asked. He was getting braver in his prying after overhearing the phone conversation. Hugh scowled. He would've spoke in private if possible, hence his many attempts to call before the flight, but Linda wouldn't pick up. And he couldn't ignore his one certain chance to speak with her.

"Something big and mean," Hugh said. He hoped the vague answer would suffice. It must have, because for the next several minutes, Craig didn't broach the subject again.

He flew in silence, the microphone brushing against his black beard. He mumbled a few lyrics from some song the doctors didn't recognize, then glanced at the fuel gauge.

"We'll have to turn around soon," he said.

"Understood," Hugh replied. For another few minutes, they continued straight south. So far, there was nothing but water underneath them. Maybe the occasional boat. Nothing to suggest the thing was nearby.

Suddenly, Craig straightened in his seat. "Uh-oh."

Both doctors leaned forward.

"What? You see something?" Ryan asked. Craig descended a few meters, then pointed straight ahead. There was something floating in the water. It wasn't a boat or any kind of inflatable they recognized, though its texture did appear to be rubbery. As they got closer, they saw a long, white flipper rippling with the swells.

"It's a whale," Ryan asked.

"A very dead whale," Craig added. Hugh looked at the marine biologist.

"You think it could be—?"

"Only one way to know for sure," Ryan replied. "Craig, how close can you get me to that thing?"

"Hell, I can touch the water if I felt like it," Craig replied.

"Good. Bring me over that carcass. I need to get a closer look."

"Alright. Just be aware of that draft when you open the door," Craig warned. He steered the chopper over the whale and slowly descended. Ryan watched through the window, until they were almost directly over the dead mammal. He slid the door open and was immediately hit with a gust of wind current driven by the rotors. The water swished, the carcass rocking slightly.

Its skin was pale, almost bloodless. He checked the sides, then saw the meaty edges where something had ripped a chunk of it free. There were technically many explanations for why it would have such wounds. Adrift at sea, anything could've taken a bite out of this creature. However, the tooth marks along the humpback's head were unmistakable. It was as though a series of stakes had been hammered into its head, clearly reminiscent of smooth, pointed teeth. Not only that, but their placement indicated a creature with an elongated snout.

Ryan pulled himself back into the chopper.

"It's here."

"You sure it didn't just pass by?" Hugh asked.

"Pilot? What's our location?"

"Spiral Bay is a few miles that way," Craig said, pointing west.

"Busy area?" Ryan asked.

"Very."

"How shallow it is around here?" Hugh asked.

"It gets shallow around Lebbon Rock, a small island where the lighthouse is. A lot of rocks. Gotta be careful when boating around there."

"It's there! It's the prime environment where it would want to lurk. Lots of prey, places to hide" Ryan said to Hugh. The genetic engineer nodded.

"We need to start now. We need to get supplies and a boat ASAP."

"You guys need a boat?" Craig looked back at them and smiled. It was clear he was offering his services. The guy needed money, preferably under the table, and the scientists proved they were willing to pay high rates for standard services.

"We're not talking about a little motor yacht for a getaway cruise," Ryan said.

"I already determined that," Craig said. "I fish. I have a small trawler that'll get you here by nightfall."

"How big of a boat?"

"Fifty-feet."

The scientist considered the proposal. "What about weapons?"

"Ha!" Craig laughed. "My brother was a police instructor before he died. Left me with all his guns! Shotguns! Rifles. Pistols. My favorite is the .44 Magnum."

Hugh glanced at the marine biologist sitting beside him. By the look on his face, Ryan was wrestling the dilemma over. On the one hand, he didn't want to involve anyone else in this hunt. On the other hand, they didn't have the luxury of time. And shopping for boats and weapons would take much of that.

"How much are you willing to let it go for?"

"Oh, I'm not willing to let it go," Craig said. "I still plan on using it for fishing. But I'll be more than happy to bring you on out. Guns and ammo included. Fifty-grand."

Damn it! Hugh was stuck between a rock and a hard place. He had an opportunity right in front of him, yet, this idiot was wanting to tag along. Linda *had* to call while he was here in this helicopter.

"Well, I'm not waiting all day. Offer stands for two minutes, then it's off the table," Craig said. He ascended and started speeding north, watching Hugh's indecisive expression. His tactic was working. Hugh suspected the time limit was a bluff, but could he really risk turning him down? Not when they needed to move fast.

"Fine," Ryan answered for him. "Fifty-grand. Half when we land, the rest after the job is done. Deal?"

"Deal!" Craig said, before taking another chug from his flask. He burped, filling the chopper with the aroma of whiskey, and whatever he ate before getting in the cockpit.

Hugh looked back at the whale one last time before the chopper carried him from view. He had initially suspected the specimen would not go after organisms and objects larger than itself. That whale was at least fifty-feet long, if not sixty. And it wasn't even entirely devoured, which only meant one thing: The Serpent was killing everything that moved.

Hopefully a twelve-gauge to the head will be enough to stop it.

"So!" Craig's voice echoed through the fuselage, "What is it that we're hunting?"

"Long story."

"Good thing we have time."

Hugh sighed. There was no point in holding back now. "It's a forty-foot, prehistoric, carnivorous eel."

CHAPTER 10

"Alright. Let me take a look here," Ben said. He had finished tying the boat to his dock. Sammy stood on the deck, arms crossed, waiting to take in the mental blow of what this would cost the department—while trying to ignore the fact that her ex-fiancé was the one doing the repairs. Ben climbed down into the patrol boat's engine compartment, immediately taking in the smell of burnt oil. "Gosh! Don't you ever get these things in a shop?"

"We have a contract with Howard to get our boats in every three months," she answered. Ben popped his head back up.

"You kidding me? Three months?!"

"Yes," Sammy replied.

"Chief, you need to service these engines every hundred hours, especially this time of year when they're being used twelve hours a day."

Sammy gulped. Her lack of mechanical knowledge wasn't more evident than in this moment.

"How bad is it?"

"You've got a cracked cylinder. Crankshaft looks bent. And your pistons are fried. And I've only just got started. You might be looking at a brand new engine."

"Oh, Jesus," Sammy said. "The mayor's gonna kill me."

"You can call him your dad," Ben said. "Don't know if you know this, but I think I dated you for three years. I met him somewhere in that time. Plus, the last names kind of give it away." He ducked back down. "How's he doing, by the way?"

"Not bad," Sammy replied.

"Did anything ever come back from that scan?"

Sammy was silent for a moment, having forgotten that their engagement ended not very long after her father's doctors discovered a lump on his thyroid. Thus, Ben never got to hear the results of the biopsy.

"Benign, luckily," she said.

"Oh, thank God," Ben said. "That's very good news."

"Yes, it is," Sammy said. She couldn't restrain the smile. Her dad always liked Ben, and acted more heartbroken than her when she announced their engagement had ended. Her father was a business owner, and with Ben being an aspiring one, they always bonded with discussing the topic. Of course, Sammy didn't have the knack for it, so she never understood what they were talking about.

"Think there's something wrong with the oil pump too," Ben said. Sammy's smile vanished.

"Gosh, might as well toss a stick of dynamite in there, see if we can make it even worse," she remarked.

"That'd be the one way to do it," Ben said. "Does your dad know of the contract?"

"No. He just leaves it to me to take care of it. He has other things to do, and doesn't feel like micromanaging me."

"Good strategy. Unfortunately, it bit him in the ass in this case."

"Thanks," she replied.

"Just saying," Ben said. He stepped out, his arms and shirt covered in grease stains.

"You're loving this, aren't you?" Sammy said.

"Loving what?"

"Don't play dumb," she said.

Ben chuckled. "Okay, maybe a little."

Sammy let a smile slip through. "I never asked how you've been."

"Living the dream," Ben said, his voice triumphant. He climbed off the boat, his boots thudding hard against the wooden dock. "Working long hours doing something I enjoy. Making good money. Hell, now I might even get a contract with the police department if the Chief is smart."

"I'll point it out to the Chief Financial Officer," Sammy replied. She was trying to keep her spirits high, and failing miserably. It wasn't that she didn't like seeing Ben so happy—it was *why* he was happy. It brought to mind the phrase 'ball and chain', at least, that's how she was now seeing herself when thinking of their relationship. Once she cut him loose, he flourished.

"So, how much will a new engine cost?"

"I'd have to look, but for a boat like this, probably somewhere around thirty-five grand. Shouldn't be too hard on the budget, right?"

"No, but you know Dad. Hates unnecessary costs. So fiscally responsible. Why does my dad have to be the ONE fiscally responsible politician?!"

Ben laughed. "Well, it doesn't HAVE to be replaced. It can be repaired. It'll just take a bit of work. And patience."

"I'm assuming that's cheaper?"

"Very much so."

"How much?"

"Oh…considering everything that needs to be replaced, probably four-grand. Roughly. And a few days to get it done."

Sammy breathed a sigh of relief. It was just an estimate, but even the actual cost was higher, it would still be a hell of a lot better than thirty-five thousand. Still, she'd have to get the bill to the Chief Financial Officer, and explain that their boats have not been properly handled.

"So…are you saying you'll do it?" she asked, her voice shaky. Ben leaned against the back of his shop and gazed at her, while wiping his hands off with a handkerchief.

"I might. I have the parts."

Oh, great. He's up to something. Sammy felt nervous, yet excited at the same time. Yet, she had to play it straight.

"You want payment up front?"

"Considering what I'm about to ask for payment, I'd say so." Sammy cocked her head, her eyebrows raised. Ben winced, then snickered. "Okay, that came out a bit creepier than I intended. What I meant was; instead of money, you could pay by…being my date to Derrick's party."

That was the answer she was hoping for, even if she didn't want to admit it to herself.

"You're still going to that, huh?" she said, trying to sound reluctant.

"Hell yeah!" Ben said. "And I gotta bring a date. That's the condition, remember? But if you don't wanna go, I understand. Derrick Crevello did say he'd hook me up if I couldn't—"

"What should I wear?" she said, cutting him off. Ben paused, caught slightly off guard by her response. He figured it'd be a staunch 'no'.

"Well, uh, it's a beach party, so you won't wanna wear anything you don't want to get dirty. Now that I'm thinking of it, even though it's for a TV series, I don't see Derrick as the kind of guy expecting to see tuxes and dresses."

Sammy brushed her hair back, a gimmick of hers when nervous.

"I'll figure something out."

They heard a vehicle pull up in the front parking lot, on the other side of the building. A moment later, the front door chimed. Ben pushed the back door open. There stood Jesse, her face and uniform still moist from being repeatedly splashed by seawater.

She leaned on the counter and smiled.

"Hey." It was long, drawn out, the tone that of somebody who knew her master plan had worked.

"Hey," Ben replied. Jesse leaned to her right to look at Sammy through one of the back windows. Ben stepped aside to let her in.

"You!" Sammy said. Jesse covered her mouth to keep from laughing. She knew the Chief wasn't genuinely pissed.

"So!" Ben interrupted. "Shall I pick you up, say, a quarter to eight?"

Jesse let out a squeaky giggle, while Sammy closed her eyes. *Yeah, yeah, you have your moment, girl. I'm still gonna bust your ass to midnights.*

"Yes. That'll be fine," she replied.

"See you then," Ben said, twirling a small wrench in his hand. Sammy waved goodbye, then followed a jovial Jesse to her Police Interceptor. The Chief fastened herself into the passenger seat and scowled at her friend.

"I'm gonna kill you," she said, sarcastically.

"Oh, I'm so afraid," Jesse retorted. She pumped her wrist against her chest, like a throbbing heart.

"It's just one date," Sammy said.

"Uh-huh," Jesse said. "Must explain those rosy cheeks of yours."

"Oh, shut up!" Sammy laughed. Jesse honked the horn as she pulled out of the driveway, leaving a blissful Ben Stacie to ponder what he would wear to the event.

CHAPTER 11

"You want to leave? Then go ahead. Leave!"

Brianne Vase thought she had prepared herself for the verbal storm. As it turns out, there was no way one could brace themselves to witness the heartbreak they caused. There was no way around it. Her staying out late and sneaking into motels was fun at first. Exciting, intoxicating...addicting. How else would Jared respond to the admission of her three-year affair, let alone the news she was leaving him for the guy she'd been sneaking around with?

Brianne shuddered from a thunderous crack of a picture frame crashing against the bookcase. Jared seethed, his tie strung around his buttoned shirt. There were pads of sweat. His heart was racing. He was a slightly heavier man in his mid-forties, and Brianne was just now thinking of his family history of heart conditions. Perhaps she should've left out the affair and simply stated she was leaving him. Then again, what lie would she tell this time?

Luckily, she had taken the day off, and packed a few things while Jared was at the docks. At least, it prevented her from having to scrounge up a few items in a hurry.

"Jared, I'm sorry. You know it hasn't been working out for us."

"Well, no shit. How could it work out when you're banging every dude you see?" he snapped.

"I wasn't—" She stopped. The small inaccuracy didn't matter. He was just having an emotional breakdown. It was best to get it over with quickly. "There's nothing I can do to make this better. I do ask that you get with your friends and use them to help you get through this. Please." Her words were genuine. Despite her actions, she did care about him. She would not go gunning for alimony or his retirement. She just wanted out, regardless of whether it was the right thing to do.

"Yeah? A friend like yours?" he asked.

"No, just—*maybe* that's what you need," she said. "Seriously. Go out and meet someone new! Do what you need to do to heal."

"Yeah, you'd like for me to go out and find a new pair of legs! Probably be watching to see if I bring her home, so you can tell your lawyer. Be a nice way to shift the blame of this divorce on me."

Oh, shit. She shouldn't have taken the bait. She should've just told him to get with his friend Leon, or Aaron, and left it at that. But, in her desperate attempt to make him feel better, she went with the 'get laid' route. It made her realize how emotionally detached she was from the marriage, that she had forgotten he was still in love.

"That's not what I want," she said. "And I'm sorry. I'm so, SO sorry. But this is happening. All I can promise is that I'll make the process as quick as possible. I don't want anything. The house and truck are yours. They're both paid off. I won't fight for them."

Jared scoffed as he sat on the sofa.

"This guy must *really* be good in the sack, or he's got money."

Brianne didn't answer. *Both* answers were right, but saying that would just pile onto the list of stupid she'd accomplished already.

"I'm sorry, Jared. I know that doesn't mean much. For once, I'll be honest with you. I've given up. *I* did. Not you. You've stuck it out."

"Damn right I did," he said. "Thirteen years down the drain. Should've listened to my parents back in the day."

Brianne nodded. His folks hated her from day one. A small, dark part of her was happy they weren't around right now, just because she knew there'd be a barrage of phone calls aimed her way. Then again, she deserved it.

There was nothing else she could do now. The message had been delivered, the damage done. The next time she would see him would be to sign papers. Hopefully, he would cool off by then and let the process go relatively quick. They didn't have kids, and she was already willing to relinquish most of their assets, which usually caused the battles that dragged out divorce proceedings. With a little luck, they'd be one of those rare couples that simply met with a lawyer, then a judge, sign some papers, then be done with it. The judge would probably make Jared pay a lump sum, or agree to an alimony amount, but she already planned to tell him to simply not pay it.

All she could do right now was go out the door. Anything she would say from here on would not register in his mind.

Right now, she was just the evil bitch who'd been cheating on him for three years.

She wrapped her hand around the doorknob, then gave him one last glance.

"All I'll say is: please do what you can to heal."

"I see you're healing just fine. Have a lot of screwing to make up for the thirteen years of boredom, or sexual inadequacy, or whatever the hell I was doing wrong all this time," Jared retorted.

"No! It's not you, Jared. It's just—"

"Get the hell out. Go bang that fucker for all I care! Hell, play it on a tape so you can watch your own mess! Get out! Go! And while you're at it, go skinny dip with Mr. Rich-cock in shark infested waters. Do the world a favor!"

He stood to his feet and kicked the coffee table, flipping it over and launching its contents across the living room.

"Okay, I'm leaving," Brianne said. She hurried out the door. Her eyes welled up as she went to her car. She should've left sooner. The boiling point was near, and she knew it, and desperately wanted to avoid it. She heard something else smash as she got in her car. Going back and checking on him would make the situation worse.

Brianne started the car and started backing out of the driveway. As she made the turn, her phone lit up. It was Sean. She hastily answered.

"Hey."

"Hey, babe. You alright?"

"I'll be fine." Her words came through a series of sniffles.

"He'll cool off," Sean said.

"I hope."

"Why don't you come with me out on my boat? It'd be nice to get away from the crowds and just enjoy the ocean."

Brianne inhaled deeply. Her stomach was still in a knot, and she wasn't in the mood for anything. However, she did leave Jared for Sean, so she may as well enjoy the fruits of her pain. Perhaps some time together would help calm her nerves. Also, it was past seven in the evening. Most of the boaters had come in for the day, and the few that were out were likely romantic getaways that wanted to keep their distance.

"I'm heading over there right now."

She took a left turn at the next intersection, then left again at the one after that, taking her east toward Sean's private beach house.

****

Sean Douglas waited in the pilothouse of his seventy-foot motor yacht *Tropic Fire*, eagerly awaiting the arrival of his date. He could already imagine the smell of her butterscotch cream lotion, which never failed to get him worked up. He didn't care she was seven years older than him; she had a body that rivaled girls in their twenties, and the fire of someone who'd been unfulfilled her entire life.

Speaking of that fire…

He stuck the champagne into a bowl of ice and placed two glasses beside it. He considered keeping his shirt unbuttoned, but realized it would probably take a little longer than usual to get her in the mood this time. Coming on too strongly would not seal the deal.

He watched the sun as it dipped in the west horizon. Its rays burned right into his eyes.

"Damn," he muttered. He lowered the shades, only peeking every so often to see if he could see her pulling in. The main cabin was already set up for the night, the furniture cleaned and vacuumed, the rug freshened, and, most importantly, the bed. All he needed right now was her.

And there, she was. Finally.

Sean grinned, watching the Chevy Blazer park on the righthand side. The door opened, and out stepped Brianne. His eyes went straight for her legs. She wore regular office slacks today. Nothing particularly sexy, but he had memorized the muscular tone hidden underneath, and that was enough for him. Her white blouse had a couple of buttons undone—definitely more than what the mortgage company would allow. She definitely had plans in mind.

He stepped out onto the dock to greet her. "Hey. I'm glad you're here."

"Hi," she replied. Her face was moist from tears. Sean wiped his fingers near her eyes, clearing up her face. "Sorry. I seriously thought it'd be easier." He hugged her.

"It's fine," Sean said. After burying her face in his chest, she leaned up and gave him a long kiss. Already, his hand was creeping its way under her blouse. *Not yet, as much as I want to.* "Why don't we head on out. The water's great. There's hardly anyone out right now. We'll go by the lighthouse like we always do."

"Yeah," she replied, nodding. "That sounds great." Except, it only increased her guilt. She was doing the very thing that put her husband in dismay. Hell, what was he doing right now? Still destroying the house? Would he go out and get drunk? *Oh God...* she failed to consider the firearms he owned. What if he went out and hurt someone? Or turned a muzzle on himself? It'd be her fault, even if nobody else knew of her affair.

Her stomach stiffened. She moved Sean's hand away from her waist.

"Sorry. Just...not yet. Need to clear my mind."

"Whatever you need," he said. She forced herself to kiss him again, hoping it'd help loosen her up. Besides, no amount of dismay would take away from the fact that he was a smoking hot vice president of a new speedboat manufacturer: *Douglas Mako*. And he was only twenty-nine years old!

There's a reason I'm leaving Jared, she reminded herself. Right now, the only other thing to do was to put in her two-weeks at the mortgage company. *That* would leave no regrets! In fact, the thought was so good, it actually kind of helped to alleviate that knot in her stomach.

She tapped Sean on the rear and started for the ladder. "Come on. You said you'd take me out!"

Sean enthusiastically hustled after her.

"Your wish is my command!" He climbed up onto the deck then led her into the pilothouse. Brianne took a deep breath when she saw the champagne and glasses.

"I'm gonna need one of those right away," she said. He went right to pouring her a glass. As she sipped it, he started the engine, then throttled out to sea.

****

It wasn't long until Lebbon Rock appeared in the distance. Already, Brianne was on her third glass of champagne. And knowing how nervous she had been all day, it was fairly likely that she was drinking it on an empty stomach.

"Gosh, I know what you're going through, but don't go too hard on that stuff," he said.

"Believe me, I'm doing *you* a favor," she said, slightly wavering back and forth in the cough. Sean kept his eyes on the horizon, keeping her from seeing his facial reaction.

Don't really see cleaning up your vomit as a favor.

Brianne finished the glass, then leaned back against the arm of the couch. She had kicked her heels off, and was considering undoing the rest of the buttons on her blouse. She needed to feel good. That's why she came here. It was one of many things that drew her to Sean. She never thought she'd score a younger man, let alone one as accomplished as him.

Still, that stupid feeling of guilt haunted her. She stared at her champagne glass, studying the lines in its design. Her eyes moved down to her wristband. It had slipped a little, revealing a couple of marks from her tattoo. She would get it removed soon. She and Jared had gotten tattoos of each other's names eleven years ago. It was marriage; she figured it was safe to get her spouse's name on her body. Turns out, whenever she'd hear somebody say NEVER to get somebody's name tattooed on your body, spouse or otherwise, they were right.

"I need a little fresh air," she said.

"That sounds like a good idea," Sean said. He steered the vessel slightly to starboard and engaged the autopilot. He then followed Brianne out onto the fly deck. They leaned against the railing together. It only took a few moments for his fingers to find their way under the back of her shirt, exposing the small of her back.

"I see that grin," Brianne said.

"Can you blame me?"

"No," she chuckled, shivering at the touch of his fingertips. He wasn't sure whether it was the alcohol or his touch that was so intoxicating. Hell, as long as the end result was the same...

He leaned over to kiss her neck. It was obvious she was still a little tense from the encounter with her soon-to-be ex.

"So? You gonna come to Maine?"

"It's so chilly up there," she replied.

"I know of a way you can keep warm," he said. She smiled. The fact that this was real was so scary, but exciting at the same time. Sean had mentioned taking her to Maine and starting a life together up there, instead of meeting up a few times every year. Then it became a promise, but up until an hour ago, it seemed like a fantasy. Telling Jared she was leaving made it suddenly seem real. The more she thought of it, it seemed like the better choice. Her family, and Jared's, lived close to this area. It wouldn't take long for the news to spread, and once it did, she'd be their most hated person on the planet. Yeah, better to move several states away.

She could hear her mother in her head right now. "How do you know that guy's not gonna ditch you when he's done with you?" Brianne definitely wanted to avoid that conversation, specifically those words. It was a concern she had herself, but refused to consider.

No, Sean and I have a unique bond, and nobody can tell me otherwise. Though she didn't hate Jared by any means, there was a reason she wanted to leave that mundane life. No romance. No chemistry. No real relationship. They had fallen into the trap of practically being roommates. What she felt with Sean was so real. Intoxicating. Exciting.

His hand was now completely up the back of her shirt. She slung her head back, eyes closed, her smile pointed at the sky. Her internal justifications, as well as the champagne, had eliminated the guilt. Whether it'd return in a couple of hours, she didn't care. It was time she lived for the moment.

In the blink of an eye, she came alive with a passionate energy, practically throwing herself into Sean's arms. She pressed her mouth to his, tongues intertwining. Her hands went for his waist and dug underneath, while his worked on undoing the remaining buttons on her shirt.

Brianne was breathing passionately as his lips worked their way along her neck to her cleavage. The shirt peeled back, revealing her shoulders. His hands went around her back to unclip her bra. Meanwhile, she got to work unbuttoning his pants, while nipping at everything beneath his completely unbuttoned shirt.

Suddenly, she pulled back, right as Sean had located the clasp. He stood, puzzled and disappointed.

"What the…?" He noticed she was squinting hard at the water. At first, he was afraid she was feeling nauseas, but then realized she was looking at something specific. "What's wrong?"

"I don't know. I saw something in the water," she said.

"Probably just a fish. Or a seal. They gather around here a lot," Sean said.

"No, it wasn't what I saw. It was something else."

Sean exhaled slowly, and quietly, preventing a frustrated sigh from potentially ruining the mood. Maybe if he indulged this nonsense, they'd get back to business sooner rather than later.

He stood beside her and studied the water. The first thing he noticed was the boat's shadow stretching far to the east. The water surrounding that shadow was glistening from the sun's final stretch of rays as it descended into the western horizon.

"Want me to take us somewhere else?" he asked. Brianne didn't answer. She kept her eyes to where she saw the thing.

"Back there," she said.

Sean looked again, gradually losing patience. Something sparkled in the water. He squinted and leaned forward. Was there actually something there? If there was, it was a few hundred feet off the starboard bow.

"Hmm. Let's take a quick look." He reentered the pilothouse and started the engines back up. Brianne kept watch while he steered the boat closer. She was right; there was something floating. Something long and flat. A door? Sean stepped back out to look. "What the hell?" He shook his head, confused. He'd seen garbage thrown out before. Hell, he'd seen coolers, even electronic consoles tossed away. But a door? He climbed to the aft deck for a better view. Upon leaning over the railing, he saw that the door itself was heavily cracked. The lower corners were chipped, as was the entire side containing the hinges. There were still splinters of wood attached to the hinges, as if the interior walls had burst apart.

"What the hell? Did somebody take a sledgehammer to their cabin?" he said, half-jokingly. He looked back up at Brianne, only to notice that she was looking further east. He followed her gaze, then saw the additional floating fragments. Drifting in the sea was a gathering of floating mixture of wood, light metal, soda cans, paper plates, as well as a dozen other commodities. No way all this stuff was tossed overboard. "Oh, shit," he said. "Brianne, you know how to operate a boat?"

"Uh, yeah," she said, nervously.

"Just steer the wheel a tad to the right and throttle slowly. I wanna get a better look at this. We're probably gonna have to report this." Brianne entered the pilothouse and steered the boat to the center of the debris field, then cut the engines. The water was shallow here. Sean could see the rocks below the surface. They were deep enough to safely pass over, but they still needed to be careful. Looking at them, he thought he was looking at a miniature mountain range under the water.

He moved to the other side of the deck and looked down. A sharp chill ran down his spine. The hairs on the back of his neck stood up.

"Oh...shit," he said. Below the water was a sunken motorboat. Its bow was propped up against one of the rocks.

The hull was caved in on the starboard side, as though a torpedo had plowed into the vessel. Judging by the scattering of debris, the cloud of soot and residue that had accumulated, this happened recently.

Very recently. As in, they literally just missed it.

"Jesus Christ."

"Let's get out of here," Brianne said.

"Oh, we will. But I need to call this in," Sean said. The sound of splashing water caused both of them to spin back. Rippling water caused the debris to scatter further. "What the hell was that?"

"Sean, let's go," Brianne pleaded. He took a minute to gaze over the railing. There was a cloud of soot under the water. A BIG cloud, and growing. Something was moving down there. Whatever it was, it was big, and Sean was not about to question what it could be. He was never a believer in sea monsters, but something about this wasn't sitting right. He turned and went for the ladder.

"Alright. We're going—"

Like an angry god, the ocean came alive with explosive force. A huge wave of water spilled onto the deck, knocking Sean against the ladder. He lost his grip and fell, spiraling like a top as the water swished. An ear-piercing scream from Brianne forced him to open his eyes.

The beast slithered over the railing like an enormous snake. Feelers, like the antenna of an insect, extended from its snout. Two enormous eyes gazed down on him. Its mouth opened, baring enormous teeth, and a dreadful stench of decomposing flesh. It cocked its head back slightly, then tensed, ready to strike.

Sean tried scurrying back, but found himself trapped against the structure.

The next scream was his own.

The Serpent lashed like a cobra. Overwhelming force pulverized Sean's body. Its jaw mashed like a crocodile's, reducing its prey to mush. The boat rocked as the creature rolled, its huge tail swishing the water beside it.

Brianne staggered, holding onto the rail for balance. She looked back to the pilothouse. She needed to get to the helm.

The beast thrashed again, splintering the aft deck. The stern dipped under its weight, letting in a huge surge of water over the transom. That water turned red with Sean's blood, the last remnant of his existence, other than a few snippets of clothing. The beast gazed up at her, its toothy grin lined with red.

Brianne screamed and sprinted for the pilothouse. She slammed the door behind her and locked it. The boat rocked backward again, then continuously shook. She could hear creaking all around the structure, as though it was straining to hold together. Pieces of deck imploded from overwhelming weight. The cracks could be heard from the bow as well as the stern. The beast was actually climbing on board entirely.

She grasped the helm and tried to throttle. The engine roared, but the boat didn't go anywhere. She kept trying. Maybe she was doing something wrong! Her mind raced through a hundred possibilities, deliberately avoiding the reality that the propellers were gone.

Brianne froze, then stared ahead through the forward windshield. Like an alpha predator from the Mesozoic era, the beast raised its enormous head until it was staring straight into the eyes of its prey.

She froze, terrified and helpless. She was at the point of questioning whether this was reality. Was she really about to be eaten by a real-life sea serpent? Somehow, despite all the horror, adrenaline, and intoxication, she was suddenly very aware of her open shirt and slipped wristband. Was this punishment for her betrayal? Had God sent His wrath in the form of this horrid monster?

The beast burst through the glass, sending huge shards rocketing through the pilothouse. Brianne's last scream was no more than a squeak before she was scooped into those powerful jaws. Teeth punctured her body throughout, rupturing her flesh and organs and fragmenting her skeleton. Blood drizzled from the beast's gums as it withdrew its prize from the enclosed room, leaving behind a trail of blood and severed limbs.

CHAPTER 12

Sammy checked the clock again. It was the tenth time in only two minutes. Seven-thirty-eight. Her heart was racing. For the first time in years, she was obsessing over how she looked. She had waxed her legs, applied her lotions, did her makeup a trillion times, and tied her hair every which way imaginable before simply settling on leaving it straight.

"Oh, Sammy Russell. You've been in front of news cameras a hundred times in the past six months. You're always dealing with people. You *never* care how you look," she said to herself. "Hell, it's not like you've never dated him before—"

Except she had. More than that; she was engaged to him. And in the months since, she had failed to convince herself that it wasn't a monumental mistake. Now, she was given the opportunity of a lifetime—she could make things right. Not only that, but if Ben really took her back, she'd get to do better.

Sammy went back to the mirror again. She had opted for the neon colored dress. It was one of those sights that, while not bad, just didn't leave the impact she wanted. The more she looked at it, the less satisfied she became. The clock was running out. She had to make a choice. But what other options were there?

She went through her closet, then found her crop top and lace top. She always felt she looked better with a more modest look. She had to make a choice.

"Oh, I hope I'm not overthinking this," she muttered. She threw the dress off her body, then put on the lace top with a pair of jean shorts, then modeled in front of the mirror again. She liked that better. Then again, she wasn't the one she was trying to impress.

Oh no! Is this too modest? Am I looking like a cheapskate? Here I go overthinking this.

She heard the knock on the door. Her heart fluttered. She took a deep breath and approached. Ben hadn't knocked on her door in years. Hell, they'd always had keys to each other's places. All of this was so familiar, yet so new at the same time.

She opened the door. There he was, dressed in khaki shorts with a blue shirt tucked in. Casual too. She made a good call with the denim shorts.

In his hand was a bouquet of lilies.

"Hey," he said. Sammy smiled and accepted the gift.

"Hi," she said. She took the flowers. "Thank you. I'm uh," she chuckled nervously, "I just got finished getting ready." Ben glanced into the living room and saw the several discarded dresses.

"I can see it was quite the challenge," he said. "Too bad. I really like the sunflower dress."

Sammy's stomach knotted again, and she whipped around to look at the dress she had changed out of a minute earlier.

"Oh! I can, uh—" she stammered.

Ben laughed. "I'm just giving you a hard time." Sammy smiled and jabbed him lightly in the gut. He made a dramatic 'ow!' then straightened his posture. "Really, though. You look great."

"You too," she replied. "Ready for your moment of fame on the set of *Catch my Drift*?"

"You know, I watched a few episodes of that while I was getting ready, and I gotta say, it's kind of addictive. You know he caught a barracuda once?"

"Are you really surprised?"

"I know who will be surprised," he said. "All those chicks Derrick has with him! Once they're shown up by my date!"

"Oh, stop," she said. "Let's get out of here."

Ben pulled the door shut behind him then offered his arm out to her. Sammy smiled; she could tell he was enjoying the hell out of this. So was she, and the evening had barely started.

She took his arm and walked out to the driveway.

CHAPTER 13

As the clock struck eight, the coastal waters at Spiral Bay became increasingly vacant. The sun blasted its blinding gaze into the world as it slowly sank into the horizon. A few paddleboaters enjoyed the peace and quiet, but stayed close to the shallows to not risk getting turned around in the night. The beaches, save for one section, were quieting down, as vacationers settled in for the night.

Further out, the ocean was quiet. Fishing trawlers had come in for the night to bring in their daily load, while the three-week voyagers remained hundreds of miles out. At eight-fifteen, the lighthouse on Lebbon Rock flashed its stream of light out to sea.

It was eight-twenty when Dr. Hugh Meyer started watching the southern horizon intently. Had night fully settled in, it would be easy to see the lighthouse from a distance. Unfortunately, it was too bright, which forced him to rely on Craig's supposed knowledge of the sea. For a few minutes, the geneticist watched for the landmark, but the strain of shielding his eyes from the horizontal rays was giving him a migraine.

Hugh sank into a chair that Craig had set up. Sitting across from him was Ryan, with his back to the sun. Each minute seemed to drag longer than the last. The *Red Autumn* was a fifty-foot vessel, its main deck taking up almost half that length. It had the wear and tear of a thirty-year old ship, though the boat was constructed in 2010. Craig had zero entertainment on the boat, leaving Hugh and Ryan to converse about past endeavors to pass the time. Adding to the misery was their subjection to Craig's horrendous singing voice during this whole time.

The chopper pilot, now boat captain, kept the back door of his wheelhouse propped open to maintain constant communication with his clients. Hugh decided it was best for him to remain seated on the main deck, as the fly deck smelled of tobacco, something he could never get used to. At least he'd been around enough marine animals to be used to the stench of fish on the deck.

The sun was setting now. Ryan had the lanterns set out and ready to go. He'd probably light the first one in another twenty minutes or so. Up above, Craig stepped out on the fly deck and glanced down at the scientists.

"You boys look like you're getting nervous? If you need, you can take a leak over the side there." He chuckled.

"Of course we're nervous," Hugh said. "Why aren't you?"

"Because I'm not the one who'll end up in a mental institution," Craig said, then cackled again.

Hugh turned to gaze far into the water. Back in the chopper, when they explained what they were hunting, he had burst out in laughter. He didn't buy into their stories of a giant, extinct species of eel that could possibly hold countless secrets for the healthcare industry. He probably couldn't even comprehend the medical aspects, as his mockery focused entirely on the creature itself. However, the money was successfully transferred to his account, and that was all he cared about in the end. Whether or not it was a waste of time was no concern—he'd go on TEN wild goose chases a day for this kind of money!

Hugh glanced at the large bucket of chum at Ryan's feet.

"You sure it'll be drawn to that? We've learned it prefers live prey," he asked.

"Don't have much of a choice," Ryan replied. "Unless you wanna throw the Captain overboard." Hugh shrugged suggestively, then grinned.

"I knew a guy who thought he saw a sea serpent once," Craig retorted. He pulled a pack of cigarettes and his flask out of his torn breast pocket. "Guy went on for weeks about how he chased after it. I tried to convince him that it was probably just a shark. He said, 'No, Craig! It was real! I saw it with my own eyes! It had a tail like a dragon, the eyes of a cat, and the spirit of a demon!' Gotta say, he was adamant about it."

"Yeah? What happened to him?" Ryan asked.

"Died of a stroke after a month," Craig said. "Dumb fool. Should've watched his diet a little better." He proceeded to drain his flask, then light a cigarette.

"I don't know about mythical sea serpents, but what we're chasing was built in a lab," Ryan said.

"I'll believe it when I see it."

Hugh closed his eyes. "I'm afraid you might." Just the thought was getting his heart racing. The image of his horrible creation staring into the monitor was frozen into his mind. He had seen it bloodthirsty before. He'd seen it attack and kill before. But there was something increasingly menacing about it now—it was free! And twice as large as when he last saw it.

"I—" Craig belched, "Eh-hem! Excuse me. I remember. Should I be worried about it constricting my boat?" He chuckled as he took another draw.

"Not big enough for that," Hugh said. "Besides, I doubt it'd bother doing something like that. It'll just slither on board and rip you apart in its teeth."

"Well, good thing I have *this*!" Craig drew his deceased brother's .357 Ruger from its holster. Hugh and Ryan stood, alarmed by the idiot's poor trigger discipline. The muzzle was pointed right at the deck. He waved it around, finger on the trigger, not even paying attention to what he was doing as he blathered on about some story of his brother doing something at a shooting range. Only when he holstered it did they catch anything he was saying. "—So, I took the gun and told him, 'Jesus, kid, you couldn't hit the broad side of a barn if you were leaning on it.' So, I aimed at the paper target and put a round right through the nose of that dumb face drawn on it."

"Congratulations," Hugh said, disinterested. He sat back down.

"Thanks," he said. "You guys sure you know how to use them shotguns and rifles I brought for you?"

Both scientists glanced over at the gun cases secured along the portside. Most of them contained Remington twelve-gauges, while two of them stored AR-15s with ten-round magazines.

"Yes. I can handle them," Hugh said. Ryan didn't provide an answer. He hadn't shot a weapon since he was sixteen. Hugh was not aware of this until they were already on the boat. Had he known, he probably would've tried talking Ryan into staying behind. Then again, the marine biologist would still be useful. They needed someone to operate the spotlights and maintain the chum trail.

All Hugh could do was hope he could land a shot right between its eyes. Craig had allowed him to fire a few practice shots before they began their voyage, which he appreciated. After shredding a few paper targets, it had all come back to him. Now, he just needed to replace that paper target with a forty-foot serpentine creature.

Several minutes passed by, and the remaining daylight was reduced to an orange glow lining the western horizon. Ryan stood up and switched on the interior lights. Craig stepped back into the wheelhouse to flash the forward beams. His voice echoed across the boat.

"Look at that!" he said. The scientists both glanced past the structure. Way off in the distance was a dim light, appearing like a star over the horizon. "Ladies, may I present to you, Lebbon Rock!"

"Finally," Hugh muttered. The structure itself wasn't visible yet. Hell, the light was so dim, it had to be a couple of miles away at least. But that distance would be shortened in a few short minutes. He released a nervous breath, then knelt to open one of the shotgun cases, then looked at Ryan. "You ready?"

"Let's get this over with," the marine biologist replied. He peeled open the bucket of chum, then launched a scoopful of the oily tuna mixture into the water. Craig chuckled, then lit another cigarette as he watched the two scientists go to work.

"Alright. Let's catch ourselves a cat-eyed dragon fish!" He returned to the helm. Before adjusting their trajectory, he made sure to refill his flask.

CHAPTER 14

"Look at that," Ben said as they arrived at the beach. Fireworks popped high in the sky, their sparkles flashing a series of vibrant colors. Country music blasted from speakers. To the right, a team of crewmembers were finishing up the last touches of a small karaoke stage. Dancing in the sand were roughly a hundred crew members and guests. In the center of the large gathering was an enormous bonfire. Its flames danced ten feet above the artificial pit in the ground. Its orange glow stretched beyond the shoreline, where several of the bikini girls were taking photos. Several meters beyond them, a few wild crew members zipped about in the water on jet skis.

Catering vans drove in and out, delivering all kinds of gourmet food. Sammy rolled down the window, and immediately took in the scent of pasta, burgers, seafood, fresh cuts, and so much more.

"Wow, Ben. You really went all out with our first date," she joked.

"I have a rich friend," he retorted. He pulled the truck to the side behind one of the crew vehicles and parked. He got out, then quickly stepped around to open the door for Sammy. She enjoyed the gentlemanly efforts—so much so that she was probably blushing. "May I?" He offered his arm, which she happily wrapped hers around. Together, they walked to the edge of the party.

Two security guards immediately approached. Sammy quickly pulled her badge from her back pocket, then revealed her Chief of Police ID. The two large men glanced at it, then at her, surprised to see such a young face holding a high position. For a moment, Ben suspected they would question it, which wouldn't please his date.

"Guys! They're good!" somebody shouted from the crowd. The guards each put on a smile and stepped aside.

The entire beach section was alive with people dancing, eating, with several couples walking off together to make out. Tables were lined with all kinds of mouthwatering food and alcohol. Immediately, Ben and Sammy saw a very energetic

Derrick Crevello dancing with…Jesse! She was laughing hysterically, sporting a bikini top and jean shorts.

"Oh, Jesse," Sammy muttered. The girl was a free spirit, and was eager to show off as much skin without coming off as a skank. Either she was hoping to hook up with Derrick for the night, or just wanted to show off her body for the cameras. *Well, those abs deserve it. I can't deny that.*

To her surprise, there were only a couple of cameras, each on body mounts to be carried by a single operator wherever he lingered. B-roll footage, likely. That, or Derrick was hoping to catch something on film.

"There she is!" the star announced, pointing his finger to the approaching couple. Right away, the cameras turned. Sammy smiled and waved. *Yep. They wanna catch US on camera.*

Derrick and Jesse quickly approached to meet them.

"I *knew* it! I knew you'd manage to get her to come with you! Well done, my friend." He raised his hand to slap Ben's, who reciprocated the gesture. Their hands met with a thunderous clap, then they pulled each other close for a manly hug, as though they were lifelong buddies. Derrick turned and met Sammy with a big white smile. "Chief! I'm so happy you came along!" He extended his arms wide for an embrace.

"Thanks for the invite, Mr. Crevello," she said, accepting his hug.

"The pleasure's all mine," he replied.

"Told ya you couldn't stay apart!" Jesse called out, bragging.

"Just repaying him for his help with the boat. Plus, I wouldn't dare skimp out on celebrating your victory," Sammy said. Nobody was convinced.

"Your connection is far more important than any film reel," Derrick said. He took her hand and Ben's, then brought them together. "A leaping marlin on a fishing line will create a spectacular moment, but *this* is forever."

A series of cheers and whoops came from the left side of the bonfire. Sammy listened to them for a moment, then realized she recognized the voices. She looked over and saw Sergeant Robert Shier, in full uniform, holding a plate full of food. Standing alongside him were Officers Murphy and Barber, both raising a hand high, celebrating the Chief's arrival with her date.

"Oh my gosh. What are you guys doing here?"

"They wanted police presence!" Shier said, crumbs shooting between his teeth. "I didn't want to miss out, so I put in for the overtime!"

"Well done, man!" Officer Murphy said to Ben. Sammy glanced down at their plates, which were overloaded with all kinds of food. "They insisted! You've always said it's good to interact with the people. It maintains good will. Would've been irresponsible for us to turn down their offer!"

"Very true," Sergeant Shier said, struggling to hold back a laugh. She noticed a second plate on a table behind him. The jock had no reservations about helping himself. Sammy shouldn't have been surprised. He was a big guy; a whole head taller than the other two, and compared to their average builds, he was practically *Mr. Olympia*. With those hours at the gym came a ferocious appetite.

"Oh, screw it. You guys enjoy yourselves. Just no alcohol!"

"Like you have anything to worry about," Murphy joked.

"Uh-huh," Sammy muttered.

Like an explosion, the speakers blasted Garth Brooks' *Calling Baton Rouge*. Right then, several of the crew started dancing around the fire.

"Come on! Make this a party!" Derrick shouted, heading out to the 'dance floor' with Jesse. "Hey! Where's the Chief?!"

Sammy felt Ben take her by the arm.

"Be my guest?" he asked. With a warm smile, she pranced off with him toward the flickering glow of the bonfire. The three officers started whooping in unison.

"You go, Chief!" Shier called out.

Sammy looked back, faking anger through her laugh. "You're all fired!"

"Alright! That means free reign on the booze!" Barber called out.

The beach was alive with people dancing energetically with their partners, while others blasted fireworks high into the sky.

Jesse and Derrick clutched their hands with the other's, thrusting their arms high with the beats, their feet kicking up waves of sand. Derrick, a southern boy himself, sang along with the classic lyrics with the enthusiasm of a rock star. Dancing ten feet away from them was Ben and Sammy, their eyes locked together while mirroring each other's movements.

More fast songs followed, along with endless dancing. Derrick and Jesse led the way, occasionally calling out for Ben and Sammy to keep up with them. Their dance turned into a four-way routine, with the duo switching partners. The new teams locked arms with each other, then danced in tight circles before reuniting with their original partners.

After five songs, Sammy was ready for a break.

"Damn. I was gonna hold back, but screw it. I need a drink!"

"Bar's open!" Derrick said, pointing to a large portable bar counter positioned over by the karaoke stage. There was even a bartender present, with a host of different beverages. There were the typical beers, mojitos, margaritas, vodka mixes, and other expensive drinks, along with foreign beverages that neither of them had ever heard of.

"What can I get for you?" the bartender asked.

"Mai Tai, please," Sammy said.

"Make that two," Ben said. The bartender proceeded to shake the ingredients in a mixer with ice, then strained it into a glass. He floated the dark rum on top, then added a lime slice and pineapple spear.

"Compliments of Mr. Crevello," he said, passing the drinks to them.

"I might be in the wrong business," Ben joked. He walked with Sammy to the shoreline, watching the fireworks popping high in the sky. Anyone else who wasn't eating was dancing away to the music. Center stage was Derrick and Jesse, much to the amusement of the Chief and her date.

"Gosh, I think she's in love," Sammy said.

"Hey, that girl's gonna have to get in line," Ben said, taking in some of his drink.

"Heck, it could've been me," she said. "He tried getting me on that boat."

"Yeah? Why didn't you?"

Sammy sipped on her drink. "Because I'm the Chief of Police. I don't want to be filmed looking like an idiot, especially on duty."

"And now Jesse's his date for the night," Ben said. "Jealous?"

Sammy laughed. "Maybe a little." It wasn't true, but she wanted to gauge his reaction. It still seemed unreal that he would take her back so easily. If she was dumped in favor of a career, she'd be bitter for years. *Maybe that mindset should be evaluated.*

Ben saw right through the lie. As the drink started doing its magic, he couldn't resist looking at her legs. They were like those described in the bro-country sub-genre, and he missed them.

"There you are!"

They heard someone approaching from behind. It was Marty, the episode director.

"Hi! Sorry to interrupt. I was told you arrived," he said.

"No problem," Sammy said. She noticed a few sheets of paper in his hand.

"Even though we did all of that filming, we still need to get some forms signed before we can legally have you on the air. Of course, you can decline, but as much as it pains me to say it, Derrick was right. The footage we got was spectacular, and the heads of the studio think it'll be a ratings high."

"I guess you really are star material," Ben said, nudging Sammy's shoulder.

"If you'd be willing to sign, the show will pay each of you twenty-thousand dollars," Marty said. Ben's eyes lit up.

"Where do I sign the paper?!"

"Right here," the director said. They walked over to a dining table for Ben to write. He skimmed over the formalities, which stated that he couldn't sue provided he agreed with all the listings of everything that was aired. He had watched the show, and the guests it had were never shown in a negative light.

"I want to add an extra condition," Sammy said. Both men looked at her, each slightly puzzled. Was twenty-grand not enough?

"Well, that's the standard deal," Marty said. "I'm not sure the producers will agree to much more."

"Don't worry, it won't cost them anything extra. I just want the check for me to be written in Benjamin Stacie's name." Now, both men were very puzzled, especially Ben.

"Huh?"

"You want all forty to go to him?" Marty said, thinking he had heard her wrong.

"That's right."

"Okay. That shouldn't be a problem. Let me just get another piece of paper printed out stating that deal. I'll be back in five minutes or so." Marty hurried off, leaving Ben alone, staring at his ex-fiancé with wide eyes.

"I...what the...just..." he stammered, struggling to get a cohesive sentence out. Finally, it all escaped in one word. "Why?!"

"Because," Sammy replied.

"That's not an answer," he said. "That's twenty thousand. You've still got a mortgage, unless that Chief's salary is way better than what you originally told me."

"Not *that* good, unfortunately," she chuckled. "In seriousness, though, I want you to have it."

"I gathered that from the 'sign it over to Ben' part," he replied. The extreme excitement from getting such a lump sum of money had dwindled to a crushing guilt.

"The reason is, you've been there for me, always helping me with my career. You always made it to my house in time to have breakfast and dinner ready when I got home, no matter what the shift. Had to listen to my sob stories about bad calls I had to handle. Helped me study to work my way up the rankings, even bought me extra studying gear, which really came in handy by the way. You did all of that, and so much more. And all you got in return was me telling you not to bother pursuing your ambition of opening a shop."

"Not true," he said. "You also called me a deadbeat in the same sentence."

Sammy cringed, remembering that. It was an argument, and people say stupid things. However, she should've been smarter and less harmful with her words.

"Yeah, I did say that, and I'm sorry," she said.

"Oh, don't worry about it," he said. "I've gotten over it a long time ago. Is six months considered a long time ago?"

"It feels like a lot longer," Sammy said.

"Maybe. But the point is I'm fine! You don't need to give me twenty-thousand bucks to make it up to me."

"It's not just making it up to you, it's me doing my part to support you," Sammy said. "I know you're doing well, but I can't imagine you don't have expenses you're still paying off. The tools; the tugboat; the shop itself; probably a bunch of other things I wouldn't know about."

Ben scratched his nose, unsure of what to say next. She wasn't wrong. The tugboat alone cost sixty grand, though he had it paid down to thirty. The shop started out at eighty, a relatively cheap deal after it was foreclosed in its previous ownership.

"I, uh—you don't owe me anything. What about your bills? This could put a real dent in your mortgage. Imagine how much you'll save if you can…"

Sammy hurried past him and took a seat at the table. Marty had returned with the papers.

"Here we go," he said. Sammy quickly signed her name and dated it before Ben could protest further. "Alright. And it looks like Mr. Stacie has signed his, so we're all set. I'll send notifications to the emails you listed to inform you when the episode will air."

"Sounds great," Sammy said. The director shook hands with each of them, then ventured off.

Sammy laughed at Ben's dumbfounded expression. There was nothing he could do about it now. The deed had been done.

"I don't know what to say."

"Well, you bought me lilies, and I *love* lilies, so I'd say we're even," she quipped.

"They weren't forty-thousand dollar lilies!" he replied.

"It's not about dollar value," Sammy said. She walked up to him and took his hands. "I'm sorry I wasn't there for you when you needed me most."

"Oh, Sammy. It's okay," he replied, shrugging his shoulders. "I mean, you weren't really wrong to think of me as anything but a perfect angel. I brought baggage home from Afghanistan, and I can admit now that I took a little while to get my life in order."

"Stop making excuses for me. We were going to be married, remember? I just wish I could turn back the clock and make things right."

Ben shrugged his shoulders again. "You don't have to turn back the clock." Her hands tightened around his fingers.

"I don't know if I deserve it. I'm sure there're women out there better suited than me to spend their life with you."

"Yeah, but they don't have your legs," Ben quipped. "Some came close, but not quite enough. Deal breaker for me."

They both smiled, then wrapped their arms around each other. As they kissed, a barrage of fireworks pummeled the sky like anti-aircraft artillery. Suddenly, the whole beachside lit up in applause. The couple looked to the bonfire, seeing Derrick and Jesse whooping in the middle of the crowd, all of which were looking at them. In that crowd were the two cameramen, catching the money shot that Derrick predicted would occur.

"That's what I'm talking about!" he shouted. "Now, Ben, my new friend, don't be like Melvin over here and let your catch go! She's a keeper! Don't let her go!"

"To be fair, something took my catch," Melvin said.

"Yeah, your fishing life is the same as your dating life," Derrick retorted, sparking laughter from the crowd. He snapped his fingers at the DJ, who proceeded to play more music. Jesse blew a kiss to the reanointed couple, then proceeded to dance with Derrick.

After sharing a loving hug, Sammy and Ben joined in on the fun. They danced through another series of fast-beat tunes, before finally a slow-dance song embraced the crowd. All at once, everyone found a partner and rocked gently side to side.

Sammy let Ben hold her close, his hands wrapped around her waist, while she rested her head on his chest.

Damn it, Jesse. How the hell did you pull this off?

Sammy didn't care. This was the happiest she'd been in a long time.

CHAPTER 15

The swarm of seagulls flocked to the patch of rock four miles off the coast, where they often hunted for the small crabs that came ashore during the night. The big bright light illuminating from the tall structure flickered as they passed by it, then settled down on the rocky shore. There, they found their usual abundance of crabs. Some snapped their claws, trying to slice at the orange beaks that pecked at them. But size and hunger made all the difference, and the seagulls had both on their side. They flipped the little crabs like pancakes, then impaled the softer shell on their undersides. Legs coiled as the overturned crabs were helpless to defend themselves as their insides were viciously torn out.

The birds that struggled to successfully locate crustaceans searched for snails and clams, with varying luck. However, a new option presented itself. An aroma pierced their nostrils, drawing their attention to a speck of light circling the island. The object was a quarter mile off, but judging by the motoring sounds, it was one of those large objects that carried clothed biped creatures across the water. There was a strong smell of fish innards coming in that direction. For the birds unable to locate crabs or snails, it was worth investigating.

Hugh would hear the wings flapping in the night sky. He aimed the large spotlight out into the water, following the rope that dragged the large tuna that dragged in the center of the chum current. Right away, several birds flocked down to it and dug their beaks into its hide.

"Damn birds stealing the bait," he said.

"Oh, let 'em have a few mouthfuls," Craig belched. The captain was wavering back and forth on the fly deck. He had been chugging whiskey this whole time. Hugh refused to look at him. He should've told him not to come along, especially after seeing the whiskey flask in the helicopter.

Desperate times call for desperate measures, he had thought. Stupid good faith seemed to be his downfall: Good faith that Timestone would handle their specimens properly; good faith that the CEO wouldn't add steroids or hormones to the specimen behind his back; and good faith that Craig would limit his drinking to a buzz. Now he was worried the idiot would hurl at any given moment.

"Shoo!" Ryan said. The bait was trailing thirty feet off the stern. He tossed a large scoopful of chum out there, hoping to scare them off. Unfortunately, it splashed ten feet short. The tuna was completely covered in white now. The birds looked like bees gathering on a hive. It was almost one white shape now.

"I'll take care of it," Craig said. He yanked out that .357 revolver and extended it toward the flock. Ryan and Hugh glanced back and saw the drunkard's wavering aim, then dove to the deck. Several large cracks filled the air. Feathers exploded from the tuna as several bodies took to the skies in terror. "Yeah-hah!" he shouted, giving the word two syllables.

"Christ! You mind putting that gun away?" Ryan snapped. Craig continued laughing, the revolver now pointed to the sky while he took another drink.

"Why? That was the most entertainment we've had all night!"

"We're not paying you for entertainment," Ryan said. "We're trying to catch a dangerous organism."

"Oh, right! Your sea serpent," Craig said. He glanced at his revolver. "Did I fire five shots, or only five? Err, five shots, or only six? Wait…whatever it is, I'm asking genuinely. I didn't count."

Neither scientist entertained his question. They glanced back at the chum trail, their ears ringing somewhat from the sudden gunfire. At least when target practicing, they had ear protection on. Right now, the best course of action was to ignore Craig and focus on the task at hand.

They had been chumming for ninety minutes now, with no sign of the beast. Frustration was setting in, especially with Craig's behavior added to the mix. Both men were considering calling it a night and hiring a different charter, or getting their own boat entirely.

"You think we should?" Ryan whispered to Hugh, reading his mind.

"No way we're paying him the extra twenty-five grand," Hugh replied, glancing back to make sure they weren't being overheard. Craig had stepped back into the wheelhouse. The clanging of a whiskey bottle could be heard, along with some fumbling movements. He stepped back out then walked around to the front.

"Don't mind me. I just gotta take a leak," he said. He waddled around the structure until he was on the forward side.

Hugh groaned. "What a waste of time. I was sure we'd find it here. You think it might've moved on?"

"Research indicates they're territorial," Ryan said. "This is an ideal habitat for it, along with rich hunting grounds. It's got to be here."

"Then why haven't we found it?"

"First of all, we haven't put in enough time. And who knows what effect dipshit's gunshots did. Might've even scared it off."

"That thing survived a plane crash. I don't think a loud 'bang' is gonna intimidate it much," Hugh said.

"Fair point," Ryan replied. They heard the drizzle of Craig's urine stream hitting the water. Tobacco smoke wafted into the air, its smell permeating the aft of the boat.

"OW! SON OF A BITCH!"

Hugh and Ryan sprinted to the cabin, the former initiating the climb up the ladder.

"Craig?! You all right?"

"Just spilled some ash on my dick!"

Hugh immediately slid back down. He wasn't going anywhere near that conversation. For all he knew, he'd be opening the floodgates for Craig to rant about sexual experiences.

"Case and point," he said to Ryan. "Let's head in."

"You don't think we should wait longer? It's a large area," Ryan said. "And, any minute that thing stays out here is another chance for it to kill somebody."

"Damn, you *had* to remind me of that," Hugh chuckled. Oh, how he sometimes hated having a conscience. Ryan tossed another scoopful of chum in the water. Despite everything he had just explained, it was odd that the creature, considering its hunger and aggression, had not appeared. Perhaps it wasn't in the area after all. Then again, there was a sliver of evidence to the contrary.

Ryan panned the spotlight out onto the chum trail, then shone it out as far as the light would reach.

"Hard to tell in the dark, but it doesn't look like anything's going for this chum trail," he said. "No sharks. Maybe a few small fish, and of course, those damn seagulls. But as for anything of significant size? I haven't seen any sharks or tuna. Have you noticed anything?"

"No," Hugh said.

"These waters should be teeming with them," Ryan said. "Blue shark especially. It's almost as if they've been chased out. Or wiped out."

Hugh pondered in silence. Could the creature have done that already? Then again, it had doubled in size since he had last seen it. And if it had fed substantially, it would make sense why it wasn't attacking. Even with its metabolism, it would need to take small periods of rest.

"Hey! What do we have here?!" Craig's gravelly voice broke Hugh's train of thought.

What did the idiot do now? Considering the topic of their last exchange, he was afraid to broach the subject.

Instead, it was Ryan who did the honors. "What now?"

"Looks like a love yacht is adrift out here!" Craig laughed. "Oh! And the lights are out. Must be a different kind of 'fishing' going on."

Craig stumbled into the wheelhouse and cut the boat to starboard, taking them away from the island. Hugh leaned on the railing, barely able to see the shape in the dim moonlight.

Right away, Craig panned one of the forward spotlights onto the deck.

"Jesus! Don't do that, you idiot," Hugh said. "You don't know who they are. Leave them alone!"

"You're half-right," Craig called out, retracting the light. "Don't want to give them a chance to get their clothes back on."

"Oh, for Chrissake," Ryan muttered.

As Craig steered them closer, the boat came into definite view. It was slightly larger than the *Red Autumn*. There were no engine sounds, not even autopilot. The boat was simply adrift. In the open sea, that wouldn't be out of the ordinary. But this close to the island? Not to mention all the rocks surrounding it.

Craig steered the boat alongside it, then finally, blasted the light through the windows.

"POLICE! COME OUT IMMEDIATELY!" He hunched over and laughed at his own humor.

Hugh pressed a palm to his forehead, and turned around. His heart raced, his hands shaky from inevitable confrontation. Hopefully, the owner of this yacht wasn't armed.

"Jesus! Hugh?" Ryan muttered. His tone was urgent.

Hugh whipped back around and gazed at the gaping hole in the front of the structure. The whole front side of the pilothouse was in shambles, with pieces of the deck cracked and folded down onto the forward deck. The windshield was completely gone, the frames folded both inward and upward, as though an enormous hand squeezed its way in to grab something.

Craig slowed the fishing vessel to a stop, then stepped out to pan the starboard spotlight along the yacht. The golden stream entered the pilothouse, allowing the crew to catch glimpses of the blood splattering on the wall.

"What the hell did you guys create?!" Craig shouted. In the blink of an eye, he went from sceptic to horrified believer. "I thought you were joking when you said it would slither up on the boat!"

"Calm down," Hugh said.

"No calming down! There's *blood* in there!" Craig said. He yanked his revolver out and opened the cylinder. Empty cartridges hit the deck as he struggled to reload, dropping half of his full ones in the process.

Hugh gritted his teeth. Seeing the boat had confirmed his worst fears: the creature had now taken civilian lives, and only within a day of escape.

"It's here," he said.

"No shit it's here," Craig said. "It tore right through that boat!"

"Craig, I swear, if you don't shut up…" Ryan said. He panned the spotlight back and forth, now cautious of every ripple in the sea. He no longer felt safe on deck. Meanwhile, Hugh opened another case and pulled an AR-15. He loaded it and pulled back on the cocking lever, then propped it against his shoulder, with the Remington still slung over his left.

"Who knows how long this thing's been adrift," he said.

"That blood still looks fresh," Ryan replied. He took the spotlight while Hugh scanned the water with the muzzle of his rifle. "This didn't happen long ago."

"Still, Doctor, it's a big area. It could be anywhere. For all we know, it could be right behind us."

As though propelled by military explosives, the ocean erupted behind the transom, sending chum-filled water spraying over the deck. All three men whipped around in time to see the huge, narrow jaws seize the tuna, then immediately dive beneath the surface. Its whole body rolled with the motion, briefly coming into view a few meters at a time. The display ended with the tip of its tail whipping upward like a scorpion's, before following the rest of its mass underwater. The rope went taut, and suddenly, the stern dipped several inches.

"Holy fucking shit!" Craig shouted, falling back against the guardrail. He rolled against it, nearly flipping himself overboard as the stern dipped another few inches. The vessel was being pulled backwards. With an ear-piercing *crack*, the rope snapped.

The vessel rocked back and forth, its Captain frantically stumbling to the helm. Drunk and disoriented, he walked right into the edge of the doorframe. His forehead met the corner, snapping his head back and causing him to fall to his knees.

"Damn it," Ryan muttered. The bait was lost, the opportunity to shoot it gone. There was no way Craig was going to maneuver the boat in this condition. He rushed for the ladder and climbed to the pilothouse. Suddenly, as spry as someone half his age and sober, Craig sprung to his feet.

"Out of my cabin, fish-doc!"

"You're losing it, Craig. Let me take over!" Ryan said. The drunken boat captain shoved him back against the port railing. Ryan's shoulders hit the metal bars with a ringing *thud*. He grimaced in pain, then glared at the panicked, intoxicated man in front of him. "Damn it, Craig. If you keep this up, we'll all be—"

A spray of water struck the side of the boat. Ryan noticed Craig's eyes widening and pointing up behind him. His heart fluttered. He could hear the beast raising its ugly head. His mind replayed the hundreds of memories, in which he witnessed the creature in captivity, coiling like a snake to strike its prey.

He reached for the rail bar to fling himself down onto the main deck…only to be snatched up before his hand even touched the metal. His dying gurgle sent droplets of blood spitting at Craig's boots. The Serpent thrashed its prey above the water, then mashed its jaws. It was killing its prey right in front of the others!

Horror and fascination struck Hugh Meyer at once. It was *deliberately* flaunting its kill. Not only that, it had set them up! It remembered how people rushed to the aid of the people it attacked in the lab. It deliberately waited by the yacht, knowing someone else would soon come by.

The rifle shook in his grasp as he aimed for its neck. The recoil shook his body, throwing his aim. Despite this, he kept shooting. The target was huge and impossible to miss at this range, even for a novice shooter.

Bullets struck its neck, the sting causing it to jolt. As it swung its head to the side, it inadvertently flung the lower half of Ryan Burg's body into the sea, entrails flailing like tentacles. Its tail struck the hull, rocking the boat to the side.

"Jesus! Mary!" Craig shouted. He stumbled into the wheelhouse and started the engine back up. It sputtered the first few attempts, then finally came to life with a roar. The boat had spun in place, its bow now pointing toward the island. *Shore! We have to get on shore!*

He put the vessel in full throttle, the sudden jolt shifting Hugh against the transom. He watched the front of the vessel to see where Craig was taking them. For once, the guy had a good idea. Though the coast would be safer, it was four miles, and he was confident the thing would not abandon the chase.

"Come on, baby. I know you can get us there," Craig said, patting the helm. In the course of the next few seconds, his voice abandoned the gentle tone, and soon, he was almost screaming at the boat. "Come on! Come on!"

Hugh swallowed. The island was getting uncomfortably close…a little too fast! Did the idiot not know there was a boat dock on the south side? Even Hugh saw it, and he wasn't even familiar with the island.

"Craig! Slow it down! You're gonna put us on the rocks!" His words fell on deaf ears. He felt something strike the underside of the boat and slide down to the stern. He had already grazed a rock. The idiot was getting in the way of his own survival. Hugh rushed to the ladder and climbed to the wheelhouse. "Goddamnit, you dumb son of a bitch!" He stepped up onto the fly deck.

As though hitting a brick wall, the boat stopped in place with a thundering crash. Both men were thrown forward. Craig fell face-first against the helm, while Hugh caught the edge of the doorframe.

The Captain tried throttling back. The vessel reversed a few feet, then jolted forward. The bow plunged, as if being plucked from below. Craig spun the helm both ways, trying to wiggle the boat free. Had he been sober, he would've realized he wasn't stuck between two rocks.

Bile rose into the back of his throat as the spotlights embraced the dark brown scales of a snake-like monstrosity. It cocked its head back, pointing its head forward. Its lower body coiled around the tip of the boat, crushing the rails. It could see its victim through the glass.

Craig yanked his revolver, only for it to remain stuck in its holster. He tugged repeatedly with a tight grip. One of his fingers found its way into the trigger guard. A loud crack blew his eardrums. He didn't even feel the bullet burst his foot into a red splotch.

Before the sudden lack of support could teeter him to the floor, the beast plowed its face through the windshield. Craig convulsed as a dozen spiky teeth plunged his body. Blood sprayed the console as it pulled him out like a potato chip from its bag.

Hugh was on his knees now. He had attempted to grab Craig and pull him out of the wheelhouse, but was too late. Now, all he could do was watch as the Serpent continued mashing his body between its razor teeth. Arms and legs thrashed for a split-second before the life mercifully faded from the booze-soaked body.

The doctor only had a few seconds before it would come for him. He shouldered his rifle and fired off the three remaining rounds in the mag. They struck the Serpent's neck. He watched it twitch from the stings, proceeding to swallow its new meal.

"What?" There was no sign of any injury. The only blood was that which trickled from its victim.

Hugh dropped the rifle and unslung his shotgun. He winced in pain as the shots rattled his ears. Still, he kept firing, ejecting spent shells onto the deck. The beast jolted as though surprised by a needle prick. Hugh knew now that he was wasting his efforts. The beast's increased size meant it had thicker scales—which could now deflect bullets. It was like trying to impale knight armor with a stick. His plan was never going to work! This was all a fool's errand, which served no purpose but to get Ryan and Craig killed.

Now, Hugh was next.

Blood trickled from its jaws. It was already prepping for its next strike. Hugh had moments left.

He gauged the distance between himself and the island. The shore was five hundred feet away at most. The only thing between it and him was the beast and a few dozen rocks.

The time to act was now. Hugh turned and leapt out of the wheelhouse. The Serpent's head burst into the structure behind him. He felt the shockwave from its tremendous jaws slamming shut inches behind him. He turned to the right, paused just long enough to see that the creature had lodged its head inside the boat. Its body squirmed over the bow, crushing the deck like a soda can. Its feelers protruded out the back of the cabin. He estimated it would free itself inside of thirty seconds.

After a brief prayer, he launched himself over the side and braced for a possible impact against the top of a rock. To his relief, his body touched nothing but water. He surfaced, sucked in a breath, then paddled for the island.

The Serpent slashed its lower body. The walls cracked like eggshells, the ceiling gradually lifting off the boat like a lid. Hugh gasped frantically. Three hundred feet to go. He knew not to look back. It would only waste precious seconds. Unfortunately, his rational mind was overpowered by the instinctive need to gauge the threat level. He glanced back.

The boat was sinking now, its stern gradually yawning high as water seeped through large cracks in the bow. The beast had freed itself now, its body resting on the bow deck. Its head was arched over the pulverized wheelhouse, searching for Hugh on the main deck.

Just knowing that it had freed itself sparked a fresh adrenaline rush. Hugh stroked the water with the grace of an Olympic swimmer, quickly passing another hundred feet. He only had to cross a dozen more before he collided with a rock. Luckily, he had felt it with his hands and was able to turn his body in time to absorb the blow with his shoulder. He moved around it and found another.

The water was getting shallow now. He could touch the bottom. Up ahead, he could see the rocky shore. It was lined with seagulls. There wasn't the slightest hint of sand. It was rock all the way to a small grassy hill, which led to the lighthouse. Its light lit the entire east side of the island, the reflections against the ocean shining back at it, bringing to view its white color. At the base was a door.

He had found a place to hide!

The water came down to his midsection. He ran the last hundred feet. The increased motion, however, resulted in additional noise. The seagulls took to the skies as the intruder invaded their shores. Hugh threw his arms over his face as several white bodies grazed past him.

Behind the sound of fluttering wings was that of thrashing water. The beast turned its head and the cloud of birds. Behind it, the tasty human stood on the shore. It slithered on the surface at frightening speed, quickly putting itself on the rocks.

Hugh yelped and raced up the hill. He planted each step carefully; should he slip, it would certainly mean death. There was no margin for error.

Halfway up the hill, he could hear the crashing sound of his creation making landfall. This time, he didn't look back. Not due to strategic thought, but from pure terror!

Almost there.

Its body grinded against rock and soot, then dirt as it reached the base of the hill. He could feel it gaining on him.

The door was right there! It was now or never!

Hugh screamed for dear life and threw both hands out for the handle. To his great relief, it was unlocked. He leapt inside, turning only to pull the door shut. As he did, he caught a glimpse of the beast, initiating its strike. Its jaw struck the door, knocking it right into the scientist. Hugh fell back against the wall, and slid down to the floor. He was encased in darkness. The lighthouse was automated, thus the interior lights were not activated. The switch had to be somewhere nearby.

The tower shook again, the wall folding in slightly. The creature was determined to get in. It struck a third time, cracking the steel. Hugh pulled himself to his feet. It felt as though in the middle of an earthquake. Bits of ceiling tile rained down around him.

He proceeded up a winding staircase, which led to a large open lobby.

Another impact shook the structure. Glass shattered from somewhere above. Suddenly, it was darker. The spotlight had gone out. Hugh held his arms out and stumbled blindly. After a few unbalanced steps, he found a wall and pressed against it. Better to stay in one place than send himself tumbling down the staircase.

He inhaled deeply through his nose in an effort to calm himself. The walls here were sturdier than the *Red Autumn's* wheelhouse. This lighthouse was meant to withstand hurricanes. Surely it would endure the battering from an angry beast.

Hugh simultaneously heard the crack of impact and felt the blow of the wall denting in, shoving him off the stairwell. The doctor tumbled into the pit of darkness, hitting every stair on the way down. By the time he reached the bottom, he was in a different abyss. As his mind inhabited the dreamless sleep, he was oblivious to the next hour of assault. The creature continued to strike the lighthouse. It curled its body all the way to the top, and hammered its solid forehead into the structure. Huge cracks lined the walls. Support beams buckled. Yet, it would not succumb to its wrath.

After a seemingly endless assault, the beast had lost interest. The prey was not worth the effort to retrieve it. Sooner or later, it would venture out. But for now, the Serpent had easier prey in the water.

It slithered down to the shore and into the water, leaving behind a battered lighthouse and a wrecked fishing boat propped against the rocks.

CHAPTER 16

The morning sun rose around five-thirty a.m. at Spiral Bay. Sammy Russell usually loved the early sunrise, as it made getting ready for work much easier. But today, she wished it would stay down for a little longer, or that a severe rainfall would obscure it. She wanted to stay in bed, with her man's arm wrapped around her midsection.

The only thing she didn't miss about sleeping with Ben was his occasional snoring, which made a brief appearance during the night. A quick elbow to his side remedied that problem. Otherwise, it was perfect.

Her secondary alarm rang. She groaned and pounded her hand against it to cease its annoying chime. She wanted to call in sick, but it was her first year as Chief, and she didn't want to make a bad impression.

Ben awoke too and stretched, his naked body still pressed to hers. Immediately, his hand caressed the goods he hadn't felt in so many months. Sammy smiled, letting him enjoy his morning fondling for a few minutes before standing up.

"You know...we could take a few extra minutes and..." He winked.

"If it was Saturday, then you betchya," Sammy replied. She stretched, her skin looking like gold in the morning sunlight. "But I've already lingered in bed for too long. And I've still got to get a quick shower in."

"You're the boss. Tell them you're not going in," he quipped.

"I wish," she replied. She turned and leaned over to kiss him. His lips met hers, then continued down to her neck. She pulled away, much to his disappointment. "We'll pick this up tonight." She looked at the clock. She had lingered far too long. It was a few minutes past six, and she was usually on the road at six-thirty.

Ben sat up and scoured the room for his clothes.

"Nice thing about being self-employed; I can afford to run a few minutes late," he joked. "Speaking of work, I will get started on your engine today."

"Jumpstarted it just fine last night," Sammy said from the bathroom. That brought a smile to Ben's face. She entered the bathroom, relieved herself, then started the shower. It took a minute for the water to reach the desirable temperature. She stepped in and soaked herself, cleaning away the sweat and stickiness from the night's festivities.

She heard the bathroom door open, then saw Ben's silhouette appear on the other side of the frosted glass door. It was obvious what he was up to, and she wasn't about to stop him.

He let himself in.

"I gotta get clean too. I guess we can kill two birds with one stone." He shut the door, keeping the steam from escaping, then embraced her. Sammy laughed as he kissed her neck and pressed her to the wall.

"You know all I have is lavender body wash and shampoo," she said, feigning resistance...while keeping her chin cocked high to allow access to her neck and everything below.

"Perfect! I've always wanted to smell like flowers."

She smiled, then moaned her pleasure, caressing his flesh, and enjoying the sensations of his hands and mouth on hers. Only a few words managed to escape her breath.

"Babe. You're gonna make me late."

"Oh no," he said, his mouth now down to her breasts. "I guess crime's going to skyrocket. And it's all my fault."

"Yes. Yes it is," she moaned. She pulled him back up to her and dug her tongue into his mouth. So much for putting it off for later.

Eh, who cares if I run a little late? I'm the boss, damn it.

CHAPTER 17

Jesse Roper had a similar morning. She had gotten her wish with the big television star. She woke up in his hotel room at five o'clock, and surprised him with a round of morning lovemaking to start their day. After their vigorous activity which ended in simultaneous climax for both of them, they laid in his bed wrapped in each other's arms.

She thought she'd regret this, that she was acting like a skank. Maybe if it had been anyone else, she would've thought that very thing. But life was short, and she had the time of her life yesterday fishing on board his yacht, then the party, and of course, what came after. The only concern she did have was the hopes that she'd get to do this again tonight. Jesse didn't expect Derrick to hang around Spiral Bay for the rest of his life. He would move on, and both would be left with this memory. There'd be more women for him to entice with his charisma and good looks. Jesse knew that. She just hoped her continued desire wasn't a sign that she'd feel jealous later on when he eventually left. She had heard many stories of obsessed fans who thought they'd fallen in love with their favorite celebrities, usually music stars.

"You seem to have a knack for all kinds of talents," said a very happy Derrick.

"You probably say that to all the girls," Jesse replied. She smiled and nipped his chin playfully.

"Just you, Officer Sexy," he said. They made out for a few more minutes before finally rising out of bed. Jesse had to hurry home and change. Her bikini top and jean shorts would not make for a suitable police outfit.

Derrick took one last glance at her breasts before the bikini covered them up. He started the shower and poked his head out of the bathroom.

"I don't suppose you plan on joining me?"

"I wish, but I've got to get going," she replied. *Oh, how I really wish.* She wanted to ask so badly if he would see her again tonight. The words were bunched in her throat, ready to escape. *No! I knew this would be a one-time fling. Just take the memory and go out on a high note.* Apparently, her subconscious replied, *"To hell with the high note,"* and the words came out. "Do you, uh, want to see me again? Tonight?" *Damn it. I'm one of those crazy, obsessed fans, aren't I? He's gonna think I've gone off the rocker, probably get a restraining order, and—"*

"I was hoping you'd ask," he replied. Jesse struggled to contain her excitement. Outwardly, she smiled and did a brief victory pose, as though she scored a winning shot in a volleyball game. Inside, it escalated into a series of childish jumps and whoops that probably would've turned anyone, even with Derrick's persona, off.

"You guys planning another beach party?"

"Nah, not tonight," he answered. "Studio can't be blowing all their funds on good times. Nope, tonight will just be you and me, and whatever restaurant you choose. If that sounds stupid, then we can think of something else. In the meantime, we'll be out filming connecting shots on the water today. We'll probably need another police escort. I don't know if such tasks get assigned or if you can volunteer, but if you wanna take a police boat out with us…"

"I'm there," Jesse said. She approached, grabbed him by the chin, then pulled his lips to hers. "Seven tonight?"

"Seven's good."

"I'll come here," she said. "Who knows? Maybe I'll take a sick day on Friday, so I don't have to leave in a hurry."

"I like that. I think I'll have Friday off too. We're scheduled through the weekend, but thanks to you and the Chief, we got more than enough footage yesterday. After these connecting footage shots and some narration, we're pretty much set."

"The studio won't make you leave early?"

"Hotels and stuff are already paid for. Basically, we'd be paid to be on vacation. Great gig. You should try it."

"Maybe I should," she said. She kissed him again. "I'll see you later, okay."

"Damn straight," he said. It was a struggle for her to leave. She wanted to stay so badly, but duty calls, and time was quickly running out. She graced him with one last smile before exiting the room. This early in the morning, the halls were mostly empty, as most residents' view of vacation didn't include waking up at the crack of dawn. There were a few early birds getting breakfast in the lobby, including two familiar faces.

Melvin and Josh were seated on a couch, sipping coffee and eating toast. Josh saw her coming down the stairs first. His eyes widened. Then Melvin's did the same.

"Good morning," she said, her voice somewhat shy.

"Hi!" Melvin said. Judging by his expression, he was surprised to see her. It was obvious what room she came from. Highly unlikely she spent the night in the director's room.

"Early birds, huh?"

"Josh is. Me, not so much," Melvin said, holding up his coffee. "Sun's blasting right through my window, and those curtains are thinner than paper."

"Must be a pain." Jesse wasn't sure what else to say. There was still the unspoken question hanging in the air. 'What were you doing up there?' Not really any of their business, but unfortunately, she was self-conscious enough to address it.

"I guess you're probably used to seeing girls coming out of Derrick's room," she said, owning up to the night's post-party festivities.

"Actually, no," Melvin said. "Despite his personality, he's more of a—" he searched for a way to say it, "I guess you can call him a steady guy."

"He likes you," Josh said bluntly. He smiled and sipped on his coffee.

"Really?" she asked. It should've been obvious; he never left her side during the party, LOVED having her on his yacht, they slept together, but most telling of all, he agreed to see her again. Still, she suspected it was a love-em-and-leave-em type of deal. Sometimes, a man would use the same woman for a few nights. She never suspected that Derrick would have interest in her that would go beyond a few days.

Great. Now, I'm REALLY gonna go insane.

"I guess I thought I was just a fling, to be honest," she admitted. She immediately regretted telling them that. "Oh, God, please don't tell him I said that."

Both guys laughed.

"You've got nothing to worry about," Melvin said. "The way he acts around the bikini models, it's really all for the camera, but he's not really that kind of guy. Part of it is genuine, the other part is the year we live in. Seems like controversy is just waiting to happen nowadays. But, no, enjoy this. I could tell he enjoyed himself more than usual last night, and I've NEVER seen him only dance with one chick. How he plans to make it work after we leave, I have no idea. But you want my advice? Enjoy it while it lasts."

"Thank you," Jesse said. Her self-consciousness faded, and now she couldn't be happier that she asked to see Derrick again. Perhaps there was more to him than met the eye. Today was Thursday, and they were scheduled to leave Monday morning, leaving her with four days to figure it out.

"What time are you guys getting on the water?" she asked.

"Early, this time. Seven-thirty, eight o'clock, maybe," Josh said. "Did he ask you to join us?"

"Yes, actually."

"Yeah, he likes you," Melvin said. He raised his coffee cup. "Congratulations."

"Thanks," Jesse said. She nearly got so lost in the world of endorphins that she nearly lost complete track of time. "Shit, I gotta go! See you on the water, gentlemen."

"Bring a boat that doesn't explode," Melvin joked.

"Good thinking," she replied. Jesse had to keep from skipping as she made her way to the lot. She found her car and twirled herself into the driver's seat. She had less than an hour to mask the warm and fuzzy emotions that were plastered over her face. *Eh, screw it. Let everyone see.*

She started her car and raced for home. Already, she was counting down the minutes until she could be out on the water.

CHAPTER 18

Dr. Hugh Meyer awoke to a throbbing headache and the taste of his own blood. His back and joints felt as though someone had attempted to put an axe through them. Sunlight crept inside cracks in the roof and window frames, letting him see the bottom of the staircase where he had fallen. He was on his hands and knees now, glancing at his surroundings. As he moved, he became particularly aware of a pain in his left shoulder. The crease in his shirt was still there, right where it hurt. He glanced back and saw the edges of the steps. He must've hit a dozen of them on the way down.

Images of that horrible beast flooded his mind. Ryan Burg was dead, as was Craig the captain and helicopter pilot. He barely knew Craig, didn't even remember his last name, and didn't think much of him. Still, the guy didn't deserve what he got. And Ryan, he never had a chance. Hugh had worked with him for years and gotten to know him. He was single—at least that spared Hugh the pain of notifying a spouse, and he hardly mentioned family. Probably didn't have much, like Hugh himself.

Perhaps Ms. Brown looks for those kinds of things when hiring.

Hugh didn't care at the moment. He was trapped on this island without a boat. At least, a functioning boat.

He pushed the door open and immediately saw the *Red Autumn* half-sunken a couple hundred feet off the shore. The stern was propped up at a perfect forty-five-degree angle. The cabin, rather, the several fragments it had collapsed into, had washed up on the rocks.

The hill was marred from the creature's scaly body. He could see how it had spiraled around the lighthouse and slithered its way up like a snake. The water was calm right now, though that could change any moment. He questioned whether he should even be standing outside, considering how fast the beast moved. It certainly had no qualms about coming out of the water. If it discovered the beaches, it would be a catastrophe.

He would have to warn people somehow.

Hugh hurried back into the lighthouse and searched the lobby for a computer or a phone. Frustratingly, there was a computer, but it got pancaked by falling wreckage. Hugh knew better than to waste his time trying to make it function. The case was cracked, the screen was destroyed, and internal parts broken and detached. He was no computer expert, but he knew the guts weren't supposed to look like that. There was no phone that he could see.

He was alone on this damn island with no phone, no boat, no internet. No way to warn the authorities.

"Damn it!" he said. He went back outside and started looking around. There wasn't much to see. Most of the island shore was rocky, except for the dock. It was the one space where boats could come in safely, as the seafloor leading up to it had been spaced out carefully. He hoped maybe the maintenance crew in charge of this island would've left a jet ski or motorboat of some kind, but no luck.

Hugh found a rock and sat on it, then gazed at the deceptively calm water. His watch stopped working from being submerged, so he couldn't be sure of the exact time. Early morning still, judging by the position of the sun. It was blinding at this angle. Luckily, it was at his back.

He inspected his injuries as he sat. The cuts had already stopped bleeding and the throbbing pain in his joints was already settling down. He contemplated swimming, only to immediately realize how dumb that idea was. It went to show how desperate he was to get off this island.

Then again, maybe he wasn't as desperate as he thought…

A tiny shape formed on the western horizon. At first, it almost appeared like a bug paddling along the water. It was a little further to the north, less than a mile out. It wasn't a speedboat, judging by its slow speed. It took many minutes until it was close enough for Hugh to realize it was a kayaker.

"No…oh God, no!" The beast would shred that boat in a single bite. He sprang off the rock and ran to the shoreline, screaming at the top of his lungs, "GO BACK! TURN AROUND!" He waved his arms frantically. "GET BACK NOW!"

Jonathon Berndt smacked the paddles into the Atlantic, driving himself forward. His bare arms and chest glistened, not from seawater, but from sweat. His father had taught him to embrace the water at a very young age. He was an athletic trainer for aquatic athletes and Olympic kayaking. He had trained over a dozen silver and bronze medalists, and three gold.

The love for the sport passed down to Jon, who spent every summer morning paddling out to Lebbon Rock and back.

In addition to the love of kayaking, he enjoyed the whistles from the pretty babes watching from their sailboats or yachts as he passed by. One or two of those encounters led to 'additional workouts' later that day. Unfortunately, he was an early bird, and most people didn't venture this far out this early. Still, he didn't mind. He preferred having the open ocean mostly to himself.

He was arriving at the halfway mark of his journey. It was four miles from his home on the beach to Lebbon Rock, then four miles back, a distance that would overwhelm most people. The paddles sliced the surface, kicking up small swells. Drips of water splashed his face, mixing with the sweat droplets.

Just a little further. He just needed to pass the island, circle it, then he'd be on his way back.

However, something seemed off. He swore he could hear something. Shouting. He stopped paddling and tried to focus. Someone was yelling, but from where? He glanced around. There didn't seem to be any other boats. That meant it had to be coming from the island.

Indeed, it was. Someone was there, standing near the small dock. He was waving his arms frantically. Either a crazy person, or someone desperately in need of help. Whatever the case, Jon couldn't quite make out what he was saying.

He pointed the front of his boat at the dock and struck the water. He paddled as though his father was coaching him in an Olympic race.

There was no boat on the dock. Perhaps the guy was stranded. Maybe he hit a rock...

Jon saw the fishing boat's bow sticking out of the water on the northside.

"Holy shit!" He must've had an accident. Maybe the lighthouse wasn't working last night? It too, looked messed up. *Really* messed up. As he got closer, he spotted the finer details on the island. EVERYTHING looked messed up. It was like a giant garden rake had slid up the side of the hill and back, overturning the upper layers of rock and soil.

As he got closer, his ears picked up definite words.

"YOU'RE IN DANGER! TURN AROUND! GO BACK!"
What?

Jon slowed down a little, but continued forward. Now, there was only about eight-hundred feet to go.

"What happened, man? You run aground?"

"I said TURN AROUND!" The man waved his arms to the east. "THERE'S SOMETHING IN THE WATER!" *Yeah, okay, now I'm settled on crazy.* The guy was stranded, however. Jon figured he'd go back to shore and make a report. Hell, the guy would probably be picked up by then anyhow.

"I'll let someone know to pick you up," he shouted, then directed his kayak to the left.

"TURN AROUND!"

Jon rolled his eyes, carefully watching the rocks beneath him.

"Yeah-yeah-yeah, I'm doing it—"

He never noticed the large 'rock' beneath him unfold. The beast launched itself toward the surface, jaws extended. Jon and his kayak were launched several feet high with the wave. He felt the small boat crack and split apart. Before the jaws closed down, he had already fallen out of the seat and hit the water. Pieces of kayak rained down around him.

Jon emerged along the surface, gasping for breath, confused and terrified. He saw the tail breaching the water a few yards ahead of him. His eyes traced the body to the left, all the way to its head…which was coming right at him.

The Serpent turned its head and closed its jaws around his midsection. It raised its screaming victim high, legs and arms thrashing about. Blood erupted from every orifice and wound. It maximized the pressure, crunching its victim's stomach to mush. His tongue hyperextended with his dying gag, before his body broke in two. The Serpent snapped up both halves and swallowed.

Hugh backed up the hill, horrified at what he witnessed. The creature swam in tight circles, searching the red water for other traces of meat. For the moment, it didn't seem to have an interest in him. Still, Hugh wasn't about to bet his life on it. He carefully worked his way back to the lighthouse and shut the door.

He was trapped.

The beast concluded it had scooped up all the remains. The small meal only intensified its hunger. With its head resting on the surface like a crocodilian, it contemplated another go at the lighthouse. After brief consideration, it decided to go for easier prey. It ducked beneath the surface and swam east.

CHAPTER 19

Everything was going wrong for Gordon Bell this morning. Though he loved the water, his idea of a sailing trip wasn't to get up at six in the morning and sail five miles out. The wind kept pushing him to the north, forcing him to use his motor a little more than he intended. Of course, Martha took no issues with that.

"Let's head north!" she had said. So, they went north. Gordon tried to stick to the happy wife, happy life motto. It served him well so far, especially during this vacation. She was an early bird and he was a bit more of a night owl. Hard to work on your artistry during the day when the phone's ringing off the hook and a new appointment has to be made. But it had been a good year so far. He had sold five paintings in the last two months, each for five grand. Many had said he'd never make it and should put the dream aside in favor of a 'real' job. But now, he was getting the last laugh.

And it was all thanks to Connie. She encouraged him to fulfill his passion and not to listen to the naysayers. So, she deserved to have her husband get up in the morning hours with her and hit the water on their dinghies.

The hydrofoils were giving him trouble. The increased drag was causing him to fall a little behind. Connie, however, had no problems at all. A small wind hit their backs, propelling her a little faster than him.

"Hey, hang on a sec," Gordon shouted.

"Having trouble, dear?" she called back.

"Yeah, as always," he said. She slowed her sailboat and hooked back around. "You think you can troubleshoot it?"

"Maybe. I'd rather get it on land before I get a look at it. And we're almost five miles out."

"The lighthouse is over that way. We can let the wind carry us over there," she said. She pointed to the north. From here, the island looked like a small speck in the ocean. But at least it was within sight.

"Yeah, that's a better idea," Gordon answered.

Connie giggled. "And here I was thinking you were finally turning into a good sailor."

"I haven't had my coffee yet," he retorted.

"Oh, right," she said, poking fun at him. She knew not to press it too far. Sailing was her hobby, not his. Despite a modest interest, Gordon still had a competitive attitude. It was part of what fueled his artistry. Because of this, he wanted to get good enough to show her up in sailing. It was just the patience he lacked.

He tried to get a look at it, but his motions were causing the boat to waver and turn. And he wasn't able to get a look at it anyway. Connie was right, they needed to be on land.

Gordon gave a quick look toward the island. He'd have some drag, but the wind should be able to get him there.

"Alright. Let's make for land!" he said, his voice like a pirate's.

The wind took hold of their sails and pushed them to their destination. Of course, Connie was gaining speed. Her bow hit a swell, causing her to bump a few feet over the surface. She whooped as the boat touched back down with a mighty splash.

Gordon smiled, watching his wife performing tricks on the water like she was in some biker gang. He was impressed she managed such a leap, as the swells were minimal in size. Like yesterday, the weather was perfect. There was just enough wind to move them along, but it wasn't fierce by any means. In another hour or so, they'd be seeing more sailing boats, speedboats, parasailers, and jet skis taking to the water.

His wife was pulling further ahead. Normally, he'd ask her to slow down, but then again, what was the point? They were heading to the same destination anyway.

She hit another swell, which seemed to appear out of nowhere. Still, it gave her boat another bump, which led to another cheer. She waved back at him. He waved back, though surprised at the swell. She was five-hundred feet ahead of him right now, so it was hard to tell where the waves were coming from. Perhaps the tide was rolling back, and the waves were ricocheting off the island? He wasn't sure how tides and ocean physics worked. All he knew was that there weren't swells anywhere near him larger than six-inches.

He took his eyes off her to check his sail.

Then he heard another splash, and a scream. His eyes returned to his wife.

It all happened in a flash. The serpentine creature appeared, its mouth like something out of prehistoric times. By the time Gordon turned his head, the creature had vaulted, its body making a U-shape as it came down on his wife. Jaws crashed down on her sailboat, cracking it in half.

Her scream came to an abrupt end, only to be replaced by those of her husband.

Gordon tried to scream her name, but his shouts came out as crazed gibberish. His mind was contemplating the mythical creature he just witnessed, as well as the sudden death of his spouse, all at once.

Bits of wreckage floated about over a cloud of red water, pushed along by large swells—stirred by the creature's movements. After a minute, Gordon had stopped screaming. He tried to force himself to awaken. It had to be a dream. His wife couldn't be dead, and such a monster couldn't possibly exist! It was impossible!

His boat was starting to spin. The sail was lagging on the portside. He needed to correct it in order to get to the island. But his mind was lost in despair and confusion. He was not waking up, like he hoped he would. Whatever was going on, it was real.

He watched the water in hopes that Connie would miraculously pop up. Instead, all he saw was wreckage—and more swells. Large swells, rolling up around his boat.

Then he noticed the elongated shape moving in loops beneath him. When he first set sail, he couldn't get over his fascination of the water's clarity, which allowed him to see all the fine details below. Now, that clarity was granting him a glimpse of the evil thing that had taken his wife. He watched it tilt its head up at him. The sun reflected on its two enormous catlike eyes and white teeth. Fins flapped behind its head, allowing it to float. Whiskers, long and rigid, waved from its snout, grazing the underside of Gordon's sailboat. It was like the damn thing was taunting him!

Then it struck like a cobra. Gordon's boat rolled over and split, sending him tumbling to the side. He hit the water and rolled before submerging completely. He opened his eyes, saw the wreckage sinking, and the huge creature swimming between it all. It turned right for him and lashed again. Its front teeth came down on his head and shoulders, severing the spinal column and imploding the skull. It thrashed his limp body side to side, then swallowed it whole.

Food was plentiful in these waters, and the Serpent was not yet satisfied. It needed more, and it was favoring the taste of humans. They were small, but relatively easy to catch as long as they were on their floating devices. The only one who proved difficult so far was the one on the land. It would come back shortly. For now, it proceeded to hunt further out.

CHAPTER 20

Jesse went through briefing with a smile on her face, which brought good-natured jokes from her fellow policemen. Sergeant Shier was the first to ask questions about her and Derrick, to which she replied, "You guys know I don't kiss and tell."

"I think you just did," the Sergeant had replied. That invited jokes about how she was going to be a television star's trophy wife, which sparked new thoughts about where this could be going. This was all so new! She had accepted the fact that she was the fling for this particular trip of his. Not a typical thing she'd do, but it was fun and exciting. The fact that Derrick might have genuine interest in her was so unexpected, but magical.

Gosh, I've only known him for a day! Yeah, his personality was magnetic. His looks great. And they seemed to bond pretty well yesterday. But she wasn't in junior high! It wasn't the first time she had dated, either. She shouldn't be thinking so long term this early on. But, for some reason, she was. *Has to be because he's a celebrity.* Things did move fast in the Hollywood lifestyle. Maybe that's what it was.

"Just enjoy it," she muttered to herself.

Regardless, she couldn't wait to get out on the water and see him again. And her excitement now paled to that which came from knowing she would have an actual date with him later on.

She wasn't the only subject of jokes. Everyone noticed that the Chief wasn't in yet, and the news of her going to the party had already spread throughout the department. Sergeant Shier was obnoxious, but at least respectful enough to not talk about Sammy's private life. All he admitted was that she was running a little late today, meaning she must've called.

Jesse couldn't recall a time she was this happy. She had a fun and exciting thing going, and on top of that, her best friend had reunited with her fiancé! And she was partly responsible for them getting back together!

She had cleared it with the Sergeant about her going on harbor patrol. She knew the crew would be out by eight, so she would simply spend the first hour of the shift patrolling the town and the beaches.

It was a simple morning with little trouble. At seven-fifteen, she had a traffic violation. Twenty minutes later, she and a couple of officers responded to a quarrel taking place in front of a grocery store, where two young bucks thought they were entitled to the last beach blanket. Turned out, each of them had a girlfriend that requested one, so naturally, they had to impress. Luckily, the officers' mere presence was enough to deter the situation, which hadn't yet escalated into a physical brawl. It was just a matter of separating them and sending them on their way. No report necessary, as no further action was taken. Just a log for the dispatchers.

Other than that, there wasn't any trouble so far. Considering the vast quantity of people moving about in the town, it was pretty chill. Almost all of them wanted the same thing: to enjoy their vacation stress free.

At seven-forty-five, Jesse started for the harbor. She drove her patrol car along the main road which took her along the beaches. Already, people were hitting the waves. Surfers were riding the tide, most of them failing miserably. A few parasailers were already gliding in the distance, looking like mosquitos in the distance. A few people were swimming, while many others were enjoying breakfast on the beach.

The activity decreased drastically as she entered the southern side of town where the docks were located. There were still some tourists in this section of town, mostly chartering boats for the day. Beyond that, there weren't too many attractions.

A few docks down the bay, she saw Derrick's yacht, *Liddy*. Several crew members were arriving, ready to set out. She slowed her vehicle and rolled her window down all the way. There he was, sitting on the aft deck. He saw her, stood up, and blew a kiss her way. Josh and Melvin were beside him. Though she couldn't hear what they were saying, it was obvious they were throwing jokes his way.

Jesse continued a little ways down until she arrived at the police harbor. She parked the interceptor in the police lot, then checked with the officer on station to sign out some keys. She made sure to take Boat Two, which she knew had an oil change recently. Despite the amusement that Sammy's fiasco gave her yesterday, Jesse didn't want to live out that misery again.

Two minutes later, she was on the water, traveling a few hundred feet ahead of the *Liddy*. She could imagine Derrick getting into character for the cameras. Maybe he would make an adlib about 'having the best catch of my life, if you *Catch my Drift*."

God, that's corny, she thought. *Good thing I'm not a writer.*

After twenty minutes or so, they spotted Lebbon Rock in the distance. She watched the yacht to see where'd it'd go. As she suspected, they were turning to port to go a little further north. Probably looking for the same exact location as yesterday for consistency purposes.

All of a sudden, her radio crackled.

"Hey, Jesse. How's it going?" It was Derrick.

"Another day in paradise," she replied. Usually, she'd say that sarcastically. Not this time.

"Whatcha thinking of wearing tonight?"

She blushed, and was thankful nobody was around to see it.

"I don't know. You like dresses or casual? Or something in-between?"

"Hmm. I like green. Most people don't realize it, but I just LOVE green. Like forest green."

"I have a Berydress that's green. I bought it two years ago in a sale, but hardly ever wore it. Might be fate," she said.

"Took the words right out of my mouth!" he exclaimed. *"That has my vote."*

"You've got a deal," she replied. She could hear other chatter in the background.

"Come on Derrick. I know you're seeing stars and feeling like a cloud, but we need to fish!"

Sounded like Melvin. Probably was, because the next voice was definitely Josh's.

"Leave him alone, man! He's in love!"

Something about that word made her knees shake. Jesse took a seat, letting the boat guide itself as her mind pondered. Could he be? After one day? Sure, it was magical, but most first dates were. What was so special about *her?* It was possible that Josh was just poking fun. In fact, knowing those guys, he probably was. Still, she couldn't shake that morning's conversation from her mind. It came as a total shock that Derrick was not quite the womanizer she initially thought; that he wanted something steady. Even *they* were surprised to see her coming down the steps.

It all gave her so much excitement, which in itself brought concern. She was losing herself in the bliss of what could only be described as a fantasy. Famous, good looking, rich celebrity falls in love with local woman and they live out the rest of their lives together. It felt so real, but sounded so fictional. Yet, she wanted it to happen. At this point, she was unsure how'd she handle it if it turned out to be fiction. Unfortunately, all logical signs were pointing that way. He wasn't from here. He'd move on eventually to go with the shoot. Hell, she wasn't even sure where he lived! It all just seemed too good to be true. Yet, it didn't change the fact that she wanted it to be. It didn't make sense when described. It was just a feeling. She liked him more than anyone she ever met. Maybe it was because he was famous and it was more exciting. So what? It was still true.

As Jesse watched the water, she began noticing a few shapes beneath the surface. Rocks!

"Oh shit!" she said, realizing she had coasted too far north. The yacht had already angled a bit to the left, though it had slowed to almost a drift. Jesse cut the wheel, and waited for the inevitable radio calls from everyone joking that she almost ran aground.

The next transmission couldn't have been more different.

"Holy Christ! Jesse! You see that boat?!"

Jesse scanned the island perimeter. The sun was still low enough to be a nuisance, despite her sunglasses. She cupped a hand over her eyes, then looked to the north of the island. There it was, a battered fishing vessel smashed up on the rocks.

"What the hell happened here?" she said to herself. She throttled, carefully watching for the rocks below. As she came within three hundred feet of the shore, she realized there was no pilothouse…it was completely ripped away. There was clearly nobody on board. Wreckage had washed ashore and clumped against the rocks, as well as the shallow seabed beneath the boat. She looked into the clear water, fearful that she would see a body. To her surprise, and relief, there was none.

Did they not see the lighthouse? How the hell did they pull this off?

Jesse looked at the island. The blinding sunlight glanced off the thick walls of the tower, revealing its many cracks. The structure looked as though a giant hand had squeezed around it. The top looked even worse. It was almost completely caved in.

"Any idea what happened?" Derrick asked.

"No. I'm gonna have to get ahold of the Chief," Jesse replied.

"Maybe THEY know what happened."

"Who's *they*?" Jesse asked.

"Big yacht. Seventy-footer, I'd say, drifting twelve degrees off our port bow. Doesn't look to be operated. It's just...drifting."

Jesse found her binoculars and looked to her left. The *Liddy* was about a hundred-fifty yards off her portside, facing north. She panned left. There it was, about twelve hundred feet out. It was facing west at the moment, but slowly turning, but only due to the drift. Derrick was right; there didn't appear to be anyone at the helm.

Something looked off about the structure, but she was too far to tell. The only thing she could determine was that something was off. The lighthouse could wait. She cut the wheel to port and throttled toward the yacht.

As she passed Derrick's vessel and neared the destination, the oddities in the pilothouse became clear. There was a gaping hole in it! In addition, much of the decking had been smashed, and the hull showed signs of indentation in multiple locations.

She maxed her speed, then slowed drastically when she closed the distance. The name on the port bow read *Tropic Fire*. Behind her, Derrick's crew was moving in as well. She glanced back and saw him on the foredeck. The helmsman pulled them close enough to speak without radios.

"I think we've found one for *Sherlock Holmes*," he said.

"No shit," Jesse said. It scared her there was no movement on this vessel. She turned on her flashers. Red and blue strobes bounced off the cracked hull. "Hello! Spiral Bay Police Department! Is anyone there?"

That gut-wrenching feeling doubled after hearing no answer.

She could see a ladder near the stern. She slowly steered her boat around to the side.

"Hang on," Derrick said, seeing what she was trying to do. He motioned for the helmsman to steer him to the other side of the boat. With the *Liddy* being a larger vessel, it was easier for him to cross over onto the battered deck. "Holy Jesus." Walking the deck on the abandoned yacht was like hiking through the mountains in Tennessee—there was hardly any level flooring. There were several cavities in the vessel, as if it had been hit with a meteor shower.

He crossed the aft deck until he was on the port side, then leaned out over the crunched guardrail to look at Jesse. She tossed a line to him, which he caught and secured to the yacht. They pulled her boat up against the *Tropic Fire*, which enabled her to climb up.

"I'm no detective," Derrick said, helping to pull her up, "but I don't think it's common to see a sunken fishing boat, a roughed-up lighthouse, and a vacant love-yacht on the same day."

Jesse pulled out a flashlight and found the steps to the pilothouse.

"I need to make sure it's vacant first," she said. They entered the structure and checked the lower levels. All the lights were out. The kitchen and dining area looked untouched, aside from all the contents that spilled. There was no blood, or signs of struggle. It almost resembled the aftermath of a boat caught in a severe storm. The cabins were empty. Derrick kept his hands close to his chest. No way was he going to get his prints on anything, though, somehow, he didn't suspect human involvement in this case.

Nobody was on this ship. Engine room was vacant. Water had leaked in through the various breaches and flooded the lower levels, though not enough to sink the yacht. The only place left to check was the pilothouse.

Jesse knew that was the first place she should've looked, as that contained the most obvious and significant damage. However, she was afraid to go up there. She just knew she wouldn't like what she saw.

And she didn't.

The luxurious pilothouse may as well have been a cabin, with all the lush furniture and the bed. Unfortunately, in addition to the vast damage on the forward side, the walls and floor were covered in blood. Both Jesse and Derrick froze, astonished and frightened.

Jesse instinctively placed her hand on her Glock. Slowly, she stepped further into the large pilothouse. The blood had dried, though some spots were slightly moist, probably due to mist that drifted in from the sea. But almost all of it was discolored. It had turned a shade of brown.

It was everywhere, as though a person had burst like a balloon.

Jesse trembled. There was no need for the flashlight here, as the gaping hole in the wall provided enough light. There was something around the corner. Something white, and moving. She sucked in a breath, then braved the next few steps.

Seagulls! At least four of them, picking at something on the floor. They scattered and flocked out to the sky as the human approached, unveiling the severed arm that they had nipped at.

Jesse cupped her mouth and staggered back, ending up in Derrick's arms. He said nothing; only staring with unblinking eyes. The Officer sucked in a breath, gained control over the gag reflex which had threatened to go into overdrive, then grabbed her radio.

"Boat Two to Dispatch. There's an emergency here at Lebbon Rock…"

CHAPTER 21

"God, it's like I have no self-control," Sammy muttered, panting heavily from the strenuous activity between her and Ben. It was eight-thirty, and only now were they finally getting dressed. So much for that shower, it had only resulted in her feeling sweatier. The passion and longing had fueled the lovers into a lovemaking spree that had lasted for a couple of hours. Now, Sammy was considering calling in sick, considering how late she was already.

Maybe I can blame it on the food from the party. Right away, she knew everyone would see through the bullshit.

"You're being too hard on yourself," Ben said, throwing on his shirt. "You were just deprived all these months. It's like not having your favorite food, then suddenly you get presented with a buffet!"

Sammy clipped her belt and straightened her hair.

"I guess that's one way to put it," she said.

"Well, normally I'd try to convince you to call in sick and spend the day with me, but I do have a patrol boat engine to fix, as well as a couple of other appointments."

"What would I do without you?" Sammy said, leaning over for a peck on the lips.

"Go crazy," he answered.

"See you after work?" she asked.

"Is that even a question?" he replied. They kissed again, both surprised at the stirring they each felt. They literally could go at it again, if circumstances allowed.

Sammy pulled away from the kiss, but only to hear the faint transmissions coming in from her police radio. She had clicked it on as she got dressed, only hearing the usual chatter. But this was different. She turned the volume up.

"...at Lebbon Rock. We've got one deceased person confirmed. Two vessels vacant, heavily damaged. We've got damage at the lighthouse. We're gonna need a complete investigative team."

Sammy and Ben looked at each other. *What in God's name?*

"This is the Chief," she transmitted. "Jesse, is that you?"

"Affirmative."

"Can you identify missing parties?"

"There's a purse here. I'll phone the names to Dispatch in a minute. I've already collected some of the belongings. But Chief, it's bad. Whatever happened here, it...there's only a severed arm remaining. No other human remains. No bodies."

"Okay. Remain where you are. I'm on my way." Sammy took a breath, as did Ben.

"Well, this day didn't take long to go from zero to a hundred on the weirdness-scale," he said.

"No kidding," Sammy replied. "Ben, I know you have work to do, but I really could use your help. She mentioned two boats. We're gonna need to tow them to shore. Is there any way you could possibly...?"

"Babe, I'm all yours," Ben said. "Or, since we're on official business, I should say 'whatever you need, Chief!'"

Sammy smiled. "Only in front of the others." Unfortunately, it only took a moment for that smile to fade. Her head started to throb. She'd never had a murder case in this town before. Fatalities, sure, usually from car or boat accidents. An occasional drowning. But as far as crimes go, Spiral Bay was a pretty tranquil location.

"Let's go straight to your place, then," she said. "I'll drive. I'll pack a cherry to put aboard your boat."

"Let's get to it," Ben said. They finished gathering their belongings, then rushed out the door.

CHAPTER 22

Hugh hid in the lobby, crouched as far under the computer desk as he could fit himself. He made a strict point to keep out of sight in case the creature decided to slither up the tower and look in from above. It was probably unaware how easily it could get him at this point, as all it needed to do was pry apart a few sections of the service room above. Still, hiding in here was better than standing out in the open.

Despite the damage, the thick walls blotted out most sounds. The only thing he could hear were the seagulls that fluttered into the tower. Their incessant flapping of wings was maddening, and they went on for at least an hour. As the doctor remained motionless, they got more courageous, and flew closer to inspect him. They weren't even sure if he was alive. If not, then he would be some more fresh meat for them to pick at.

A few braved the chance and flew in close. That was finally enough to draw Hugh from his hiding place. He swatted his arms at the annoying birds, causing a huge frenzy within the lighthouse.

He thought he would lose his mind. Surely, these birds might attract the attention of the Serpent. It was as though he was in an exhibit with a hundred wild caught species put on display.

There was no way of keeping track of time. His phone no longer worked because of the water. Same with his watch. And the clock on the wall had fallen off during the attack. Was the beast still out there? Probably. The waters seemed peaceful enough when he saw the kayaker. Yet, the thing appeared. It had become a master of stealth, just as it demonstrated when it attacked the submersible. It didn't take much imagination for Hugh to suspect his creation was waiting and watching for him to step out that door.

After a period of time that he could not gauge, some of the seagulls settled, while the others descended to hunt for food elsewhere. He could finally hear the ocean breaking against the rocks. And there was something else; mechanical sounds. Boat engines!

Oh no!

Hugh sprang to his feet as though awakening from a horrible nightmare. He ran to the door and yanked it open, then gazed out into the water. There was a seventy-foot yacht and a police vessel inspecting the drifting yacht that he and his crew had found. He immediately remembered how it attacked when their attention was on it. It was probably gonna attempt the same trick with them.

He saw another boat approaching from the mainland. It was a little smaller than the yacht, though its motor was louder. It was a tugboat, clearly intended to bring in the vacant vessels. There was one person on deck that he could see, with another at the helm. And god knows how many people were on that yacht!

All of them had no idea they were lining up to be the special of the day.

Hugh threw his hands high and ran for the dock.

"Hey!"

Sammy Russell closed her eyes as the cool ocean breeze came over her face. She could see Jesse's boat and the *Liddy*. She then stared at the broken boat near the shore.

"What in God's name happened here?"

Ben didn't reply. He stared off into the horizon, confused. He put a hand to his ear and listened for a moment.

"Do I hear something?" He stuck his head out of the cockpit and glanced around. "Is somebody shouting?"

"No, I don't…wait…" Sammy stopped and listened again. Her eyes went to the lighthouse. "There!"

The man ran to the dock as though he had seen a ghost in that lighthouse.

"Looks like he's stranded. Probably was on that sunken boat," Ben said.

"I'm gonna radio Jesse. You think you can get us over there without ending up like that fishing boat?"

"Sure can." Ben cut the wheel to starboard and lined the bow up with the dock. By now, the man was on the dock. When they closed within a few hundred feet, his words became clearer, and more frantic.

"Get out of the water!"

"What the hell?" Sammy muttered. She clicked her radio, "Jesse?"

"Yeah?"

"Come meet us over by the island. We have a person that you might have to take to shore immediately. Might need medical attention first. We'll need your first aid kit."

Derrick walked with Jesse back to her boat.

"I'm on my way, Chief," she said. Derrick held her hand until she was over the side. She definitely lacked the spring in her step that he was fond of seeing. Then again, what was there to be cheery about in the moment. He definitely wasn't tooting one-liners, that was for damn sure.

"You sure you'll be alright?" he asked.

"Yeah," she said. With a bag of collected items strung over her shoulder, she climbed down to the deck. "Haven't seen anything like that since my rookie year."

"If you want to cancel for tonight…"

"Hell-fucking-no," she exclaimed. Derrick almost jumped. That spring returned with a little bit of spice.

"I suppose I have my answer," he said. He smiled and untied the ropes, then tossed them back to her. "Anything you need from me and my people?"

"We'll probably need to get more police out here, so you'll probably have to complete your filming without us."

"Alright. We'll vacate. Want me to call you?"

"Please," she said. "I'm off at three."

Derrick winked, then hustled over to the *Liddy*. It would be good to be back on his own, rather than this friggin' ghost ship. They began to depart for the north as Jesse throttled for the island.

She could see Ben's tugboat closing in on the dock.

"Hurry! These waters aren't safe!" the man shouted.

Ben was just a few meters from the dock. The man was on the tip, ready to leap out onto his boat. He glanced down at Sammy.

"Something's not right with this guy," he warned.

"I can handle him," she replied. As she spoke, the man actually did leap. He folded over the edge, blew the air out of his lungs, but didn't stop to pull himself in. He hurried to his feet. His hair was a mess. His face and arms were covered in bruises and cuts. His clothes were wrinkled and stained with dirt and slime. And his eyes were like those of someone who was personally on the run from Satan.

"Sir, we've got you. I'm the Chief of Police," Sammy said in an assuring voice. "You're safe now. Can you tell me your name?"

Hugh took a breath and took a split-second to think. He realized how he looked and how he was coming off. Even in a place as nice as Spiral Bay, it was safe to assume that the police had more than their fair share of mentally ill visitors. Unfortunately, what he was about to tell them wasn't going to improve that image.

"Chief. My name is Dr. Hugh Meyer," he said, his voice shaky, but with calm. "What I'm about to tell you might be hard to believe. But, then again, the evidence is right there." He pointed at Craig's fishing boat, then at the yacht, then the lighthouse.

"What happened?"

"We need to leave NOW!" he said. "There's something in the water. A predator! It's already killed a number of persons, and we're next if we don't vacate immediately!"

"A predator?" Sammy said. She looked at the lighthouse again. It looked as though a small breeze would push it over at this point. Her first instinct would be to write this man off as insane, but *something* did all of this damage. She looked up at Ben. "Let's go!"

As Ben put the vessel in reverse, she snatched her radio. "Jesse?"

Sensory receptors in its whiskers alerted the Serpent to the many vibrations originating near its new habitat. It had chosen its home well. Prey was abundant, both in fish, and in the tasty humans that foolishly lingered too close.

The Serpent returned to the rocks with haste. Its eyes caught sight of the floating shapes traveling along the surface. There were three of them, each the kind that carried the humans. The largest one was pulling away. Another was right next to the island, while the third was in the middle. It was the smallest one, and in its experience, the smallest prey was usually the fastest.

It had learned the previous night that the loud weapons used by the humans could not hurt it. Those tiny projectiles could sting, but ultimately, no harm was done beyond that. There was nothing stopping them from its wrath.

It coiled beneath the water, then in one lashing motion, it sprang for the surface.

Jesse had just lifted her radio to answer the Chief's call when suddenly she was knocked off her feet by an explosive force. The entire bow of her vessel had been lifted toward the sky, rolling her backwards over her shoulder like a pebble down a hill. She hit the transom, then felt the splashing of water against her body. She pushed up to her hands and knees, only to fall flat on her face again as the boat crashed back down. It rocked heavily as though caught in a hurricane.

The thrashing of water all around her made her realize that this was no rock. There was something *in* the water doing this. And whatever it was, it hit the boat again, causing it to fishtail.

Jesse pulled herself to her feet, then glanced out at the ocean. It was as though she was trapped in a whirlpool. Beneath those frothing waves, something was pushing the patrol boat.

She found her radio and pressed the wet transmitter.

"Chief! Help! There's something in the water!"

Another splash hit her. The thing had stopped assaulting the draft, and had now lifted its head above the bow like a python. Jesse gasped at the sight of the elongated jaws, razor-sharp teeth, and enormous eyes.

In that split-second, her brain debated on whether this was some horrible nightmare, or to draw her Glock and shoot the damn thing. She went with the latter.

The beast had opened its mouth to snatch her up, only to reel backwards from the unexpected sting in its mouth. Jesse let out a rapid hail of gunshots, the first of which had struck the soft tissue along the roof of the creature's mouth. It retreated and dove into the water, its tail swinging high and wide. It smacked the cockpit, resulting in an explosion of glass and metal. The boat teetered to stern, and once again, Jesse was thrown against the transom.

"Son of a bitch!" Ben said. "Sammy! You see that?!"

"Jesse! We're coming!" Sammy radioed. There was no response. They had watched the beast rise out of the water, its head like that of a dragon. The patrol boat was still spinning, with the portside facing them. The whole front was crumpled inward. Water was seeping in rapidly.

Ben gunned the throttle, then watched for the rocks—and whatever the hell that thing was. *Speaking of which?*

"What is that thing, Dr. Meyer?"

"A very large predator," Hugh replied. "If we get out of here alive, then I'll happily explain everything to you. What you will want to know now, however, is that its skin is covered in thick scales. Bullets won't harm it. Trust me, I found out the hard way last night."

"Not gonna stop me from trying," Sammy said. She drew her Glock and watched the water. The patrol boat's bow was starting to dip. Jesse was on her feet now, digging through the rubble that was once the cockpit. She was going for the shotgun.

The water erupted between the two boats. The Serpent hissed, then swung its head toward the tugboat.

Ben watched its eyes center on him. There was no doubt in his mind it would have the power to punch right through that windshield and snatch him up. He pushed the throttle to the max.

"Get out of my way," he said.

The bow struck the beast's neck. With a pained screech, the Serpent fell backwards and disappeared under the water. Its body struck the draft of the tugboat as it passed over. As the Serpent reeled, its head crashed into a rock, putting it in a slight daze.

Sammy and Hugh turned and watched over the transom, looking for any sign of it.

"Is it dead?" she asked.

"Believe me, we could only *wish* it could be that easy," Hugh replied.

The patrol boat's stern elevated as the water filled the forward compartments. Jesse climbed to the transom, shotgun in hand. Eight shells were loaded, with one chambered. Now, if only that damn Serpent would appear.

Ben brought the tugboat alongside her. Hugh and Sammy leaned over the side and reached for her. Jesse propped her feet on the guardrail and leapt across, landing on her knees.

"Go! Go!" Sammy signaled. The propellers jetted huge fountains of water, pushing the vessel toward the mainland.

"What's going on?" Jesse said. Sammy helped her to her feet.

"I have no idea," she replied. She glanced back at the doctor. "But we'll find out."

They watched the water, seeing nothing but ripples.

"Is it gone?" Jesse said, slowly catching her breath.

Hugh shook his head. "No."

Its previous kills had made it overconfident. Now, the beast was frustrated. Twice now, the humans had outwitted it. The Serpent fluttered its long tail, then rose for the smaller boat. It crashed hard against it, then dug its teeth into the side to drag it down further into the water.

There was no human aboard! The creature turned its head and spotted the larger vessel. It was fleeing—with its prey! Three times now!

It splashed down and swam, rippling its entire body as one enormous fin. Gradually, it was closing the distance.

Clearly, its prey had taken notice of this, as it felt the sting of the loud weapons skidding over its back.

Her ears rang from the repeated gunshots.

Sammy took a breath, squinted, and centered the creature's body in her iron sights. Its upper body moved against the surface, generating huge swells with each movement. She squeezed off a fifth and sixth shot. She was definitely hitting the thing, but it showed no signs of stopping. The doctor was telling the truth.

Jesse aimed the shotgun and fired. No result. The thing was getting closer. An empty shell bounced at her feet as she pumped the weapon. Jesse could see its head. She fired again.

"Jesus, what the hell is this thing?! I know I hit it!"

"Armor scales," Hugh said.

"Well, I'll have to hope for a lucky shot!" Jesse pumped the shotgun and sent another blast into the creature's face. Its eyelids locked tight, protecting the soft flesh underneath. The barrage of pellets did nothing other than make a few scratches along its snout—and spur it to move faster.

Ben looked over his shoulder. The thing had closed within a dozen meters. He was already at maximum speed! If he pushed the engine any more, he'd explode it. Both officers continued blasting away at it. An empty mag hit the deck, the click of its replacement slamming into place drowned out by Jesse's eighth, and final shotgun blast.

The Serpent's head rose. Its eyes opened, the evil black pupils fixed on its targets. Hugh's stomach tightened, his abdomen threatening to contract everything inside.

"Move!" he shouted. "It's gonna strike!" Both officers stepped back, then sprinted to the forward deck. The doctor's prediction was accurate.

The Serpent rose its ugly head and launched itself like a rocket, its jaws angling down and snapping shut where the humans had stood. The stern dunked under the sudden weight, the transom splintering and folding outward.

"Son of a bitch!" Ben grunted, cutting the wheel back and forth to wiggle out of the creature's grasp.

The passengers moved up along the side deck. Jesse flung her empty shotgun at the beast like a tomahawk. It bounced off its snout and into the water, leaving the creature completely unfazed. They were both down to pistols now.

A volley of nine-millimeter rounds struck its snout and forehead, forcing the eyes to clamp shut again. The boat teetered back again. Its jaws had clamped down on part of the decking, allowing it to hold onto the boat. Its body bunched behind its neck, ready to spring it on board the watercraft and finally seize its prey.

Sammy ejected another empty magazine, leaving one last one.

"It's climbing aboard!"

Ben veered sharply to the right, taking the boat into a tight circle. The creature held tight, the maneuvering delaying its attempt to slither aboard the boat. Its whiskers slashed the deck like whips. It was obvious it wasn't letting go, and the boat was not going to sustain its weight. On top of that, the gunfire was doing nothing to deter that. No amount of boat maneuvers was going to shake it loose.

He had a minute at best before they were all in the water.

"Hey, Sammy! Take the wheel!"

Sammy holstered her Glock and reached high. Their hands clasped, and he lifted her up onto the cockpit, keeping her from going around back to use the ladder.

"Keep doing sharp turns. If he's gonna come on board, he's gonna have to work for it," he said.

"What are you gonna do?"

"Improvise," he replied. He leaped off the back, landed on the main deck, then immediately ducked as one of the whiskers lashed his way. On his hands and knees, he found the cargo hatch then dove in face first.

In the small dark compartment, he didn't bother to turn on a light, as he knew the layout by heart.

Right in front of him was his welding torch. To the left was his buzz saw. Both of those would require him to get a little closer than he was comfortable with. He heard the clanging of air cannisters behind him. An idea came to mind. A crazy one, but it might just work.

He pushed aside his diving gear and grabbed one of the cannisters, then began climbing up out of the hatch. Right as he emerged, the boat shirted back. Jesse screamed and the doctor cursed as he fell against the deck. The creature was pulling itself up.

Ben popped out of the hatch and saw its body coiling around the transom, its head rising a few feet high, poised to strike the cockpit. The boat was leaning back, the transom just about level with the water. Another few inches, and the ocean would come spilling in.

Hugh and Jesse were clinging to the railing up on the forward deck, while Sammy held onto the helm. The beast had its eyes fixed on her. Had Ben arrived a few moments later, it would have.

The Serpent saw the human pop out of the small hole. It tilted its head and opened its jaws.

"Nibble on *this!*" He launched the cannister as the Serpent leaned in to snap. Feeling the sudden mass in its mouth, the jaws instinctively clamped down. Teeth breached the metal. Pressurized air blasted from the breach, launching the tank into the back of its throat like a torpedo.

The tight feeling of something lodging in its esophagus triggered a firing of nerves. It followed another instinct that usually served well whenever a moving thing was in its mouth; swallow! All of a sudden, the object was bouncing around in its stomach, causing all kinds of agony that the Serpent had never experienced before. Screeching loudly, it reeled backwards and plunged, its body twisting and turning in a turbulent display. The boat leveled out, its bow generating a splash equal to that of the creature.

Sammy wasted no time gunning the throttle. Luckily, the propellers seemed to be undamaged. The tugboat gained distance from the creature's splashes. The passengers watched in a mix of shock and awe as the beast struggled to get rid of the small, whipping mass that was crashing along its insides.

The Serpent managed to settle its movements. The cannister had finally run out of air, but the consequence of its movements had caused much discomfort. The Serpent regurgitated, expelling the cannister along with partially digested bits of its previous victims.

For the first time in its life, it hesitated before resuming an attack. It hovered a few feet below the surface, pumping water through its gills. After several seconds, the pain began to subside, and its instinct to feed took over once again.

It lifted its head like a vengeful demon, only to find that the boat had gained some distance. It thrashed its tail, initiating another chase.

Ben watched the huge swells caused by its rippling body. The damn thing was not giving up!

"It's still chasing us," Sammy said. She turned her eyes forward. With all the twisting and turning, she actually wasn't sure which way they were going...until she saw the yacht up ahead. It was Derrick and his crew, and most of them were gathered on the aft deck, watching the strange events unfold. Sammy cursed under her breath. She had accidentally led the beast right to them!

"Holy shit! Derrick! You see that?!" Josh said, pointing out.

"Everyone saw it, genius," the TV star replied. He watched the tugboat as it approached, relieved when he saw the familiar blond hair of the Officer he had spent the night with. His heart had nearly stopped when her police boat suddenly went down. What had followed was a series of gunshots and strange boat maneuvers, until the crew finally realized the police and the maintenance contractor were on the run from some gigantic sea animal.

And now it was coming for them!

"Keep those cameras rolling, boys! Melvin! Take the helm!" Derrick shouted. Melvin wasted no time running for the cockpit, with a cameraman at his back, of course. Though the production had a crewman specifically to drive the boat, nobody matched Melvin's feel for the controls. He knew how to push the engine and maneuver the large craft in strange situations, though they all paled compared to this.

Derrick tapped Josh and a few other crew on the shoulders.

"Come on," he said, leading them down into storage. At a juncture in the passageways, he pointed at the cargo hold. "Get as much bait as you can. Grab the heaviest weight you can, and meet me at the jet ski compartment. Josh, you're with me!"

The group parted ways, all moving with haste.

Behind the ship, the creature was maintaining its chase. Derrick watched the tugboat through a window. The Police Chief was at the helm, and it appeared that she was steering away to get it away from the yacht. Well intended, but doomed to fail. He'd been around wild animals his whole life, especially ones in the sea. What he learned about the predators was that usually a diversion was needed if you couldn't outrun them.

He and Josh entered the jet ski compartment. Josh opened the bay doors, letting in a rush of mist. Water splashed inside, the jet ski trembling from the movements. Derrick undid some of the restraints, then pulled a two-way radio from his waist.

"Hey! Jesse? Chief? You guys reading me?"

Somehow, the sound of Derrick's voice sent a ping of hope through Jesse's mind. The beast was moving closer, and she was unsure how they'd fend it off a second time. With bullets having no effect, it seemed like certain death was gaining on them.

She grabbed her radio. "Derrick! There's something in the water! Get your people to shore, now!"

"We saw it! Stay calm and listen carefully! Bring your boat back toward us! Right now! We need to distract it if we are gonna get out of here alive."

Hugh could sense both officers questioning the decision to put civilians in harm's way.

"He's right!" he said, interrupting their thoughts. "Go back, Chief! It's our only chance!"

Sammy tensed, then turned the wheel to starboard. The yacht had swung around and slowed to a stop, with its bow now pointed a few degrees to her right. A mechanical door yawned open along the starboard quarter. She could see two men loading a jet ski into the water.

The distraction.

"Derrick, you sure this'll work?" she asked. "I'm not sure if it'll abandon a larger meal in favor of that."

"It will if it smells blood!"

Sammy recited a brief prayer, then continued on.

"Bring it past us, then swing around our stern, and we'll direct it the opposite way. Then we'll all haul ass to the harbor."

Derrick stuck his head out of the door and watched the tugboat approach. It was three-hundred meters off and closing fast. The crew flooded the room, carrying the supplies he instructed them to bring. One had a huge piece of tuna slung over his shoulder.

"On the seat," he said. "That fish is going for the ride of its life." He took some wire from another crewmember and helped fasten the fish to the seat, while also securing a fishing weight to trick the electronic sensor into believing a rider was on board. He then tied a rope into a loop to wrap around the throttle. With the tug of the end, it would tighten like a noose.

He glanced at the entryway to make sure the camera crew had followed them in.

"Got ourselves a sea beast," he said. "Now, it's up to Derrick Crevello and his crew to save the day!"

He took a pocketknife and slit the fish's belly, then spilled some chum over the seat.

"You think this'll work?" Josh asked.

"It's got to work," Derrick replied, his tone a confident one. The tugboat was just about to pass by them. Just a few yards behind it was the big, moving creature. For a moment, he had fallen out of character. "Holy God!" He snapped back into focus, then leaned over the jet ski's controls. "Alright, somebody hold on to me, because this thing's gonna take off like a mother--, and I don't want it taking me with it."

Josh and another crewmember grabbed him by the shirt and shoulders, then braced for the sudden yank. He started the engine, then watched for the boat.

The Chief sped the boat within a few yards. Right behind it, the creature's head was starting to rise. His moment was now!

He tightened the knot around the throttle, launching the jet ski like an attack dog. Spraying water, it raced aimlessly into the open ocean...and bounced right over the creature's snout.

The Serpent dipped from the unexpected impact, then turned its attention on the culprit. It was fleeing rapidly. Its nostrils picked up a trail of blood. Whatever was aboard the man-made craft, it was bleeding! Hunger stirred in the Serpent's empty stomach, and it propelled itself after the new target.

"Yes!" Derrick exclaimed. The crew quickly closed the bay doors and rushed to the deck, with the TV star quickly getting on his radio. "Alright! Now's our chance! Let's make a break for shore. ASAP!"

In the pilothouse, Derrick pushed the yacht into full throttle, while keeping a watchful eye on the horrible beast behind them. Derrick's plan had worked, and it was now chasing the jet ski in the opposite direction. *His* jet ski!

"I better get a little credit for this escape!" he said into the camera. "And some compensation!"

He followed the tugboat to the west. After a mile, they could see the shoreline, looking like a little tan line at first. Dry land never looked so welcoming.

Derrick and Josh joined him in the pilothouse. The excitement of the adventure was now starting to dwindle, leaving them all in a strange state of shock. Derrick glanced at the helmsman.

"I think we figured out what ate your marlin."

CHAPTER 23

"Thank you very much," Sergeant Robert Shier said to the cashier after receiving his dollar-twenty in change. He stepped from the food stand and took a mouthful of his hotdog while watching the activity on the beaches. People splashed in the water, some going further out than others, but nothing too concerning. One particular event that made him chuckle were two kids battling each other on inflatables. One rode a great white shark, the other on a big black orca, and they were bumping each other, trying to knock the other off their raft. Finally, with a shriek, the one on the shark took a hit he couldn't recover from, and flopped into the water. His opponent raised his hands in victory, only to be pushed off from underneath.

Shier allowed himself a laugh, then kept patrolling. The boat patrollers had completed their checks on the shark nets, ensuring they were all in place. So far, no problems. Certainly beat working in Detroit, where he couldn't go two minutes without having to respond to an issue of some kind.

Waves of sand kicked up in front of him as a group of six-year-olds rushed by. Two were guarding one, and all three were glancing up to the air. Shier saw the football coming down, launched pretty impressively by another kid of the same age.

The ball landed a few inches from one of the 'linebackers' and bounced right for Shier. He lunged and swooped it up, then cocked it back over his shoulder, then pointed back at the thrower with his hot dog-wielding hand.

"Go long!" He gave the kids a few minutes to rush in that direction, then sent the ball soaring high. This time, the receiver snatched it right out of the air then gave a thumbs up at the Sergeant. Shier smiled and returned the gesture, then proceeded to walk the beach.

"Unit One to all units. We have an emergency! I need you to evacuate the beaches immediately. Call everyone in!"

It wasn't often that frantic radio calls made Shier's heart rush. He had heard them every day in Detroit. But he wasn't used to hearing the Chief like this. He glanced out at the water and saw the yacht coming toward the shore at twenty-knots, with the maintenance man's tugboat traveling ahead of it. No sign of the patrol boat used by Jesse Roper. Sammy wasn't the type to play pranks, and even if she was, she wouldn't go this far. Whatever was happening, it was serious.

"This is Shier. I read you, Chief. What sections need evacuating?"

"All of them!"

Shier glanced again at the water. There were thousands of people in the water. Evacuating it was not going to be an easy task, but there was no mistaking the urgency in Sammy's voice.

"All officers, report to the beach areas immediately. Bring everyone out of the water now. Boat patrols, turn on your flashers and use your loudspeakers."

"Boats as well," Sammy added. "Get a message out on the radios. Direct them to the harbor. I'll explain later."

"That'll be a hell of a debrief," Shier muttered to himself. He tossed his half-eaten lunch aside and rushed to the nearest lifeguard tower, immediately getting the attention of the man on post. "Get everyone out. Right now."

The puzzled lifeguard tossed aside his magazine and fumbled for his radio and bullhorn. First, he relayed the information to the other lifeguards across the beach, then raised the bullhorn to his lips.

"Everybody please, get out of the water!"

Whistles and bullhorns echoed across Spiral Bay. Despite the best efforts of the first responders, panic swept across the beaches. Cries of 'shark' filled the air, spurring people to run from the beach as fast as they could, while some skeptics complained that the shark nets were in place, so what was the danger?

Shier moved along the shoreline, aiding the beach staff in guiding the exodus of people safely from the water. A few shoving matches broke out, which he had to get in the middle of. In one case, he had to lock the arm behind the back of an agitated swimmer whose testosterone and attitude overshadowed any judgement. After threat of arrest, the man relented and moved on with the rest of the crowd.

The Sergeant looked out to the water, seeing the many boats moving in the distance. Some were heading into shore, but others were still adrift. Either their radios were off, or the people on board were just ignoring them.

He got on the radio. "We need eyes in the sky. Officer Murphy, I need you on the chopper. Officer Hayes, report to the hangar. You're driving. Those of you on boat patrol, tell any boater out there to come in. If they refuse, arrest them."

In ten minutes, he heard the whirl of the chopper passing overhead. All four remaining patrol boats had taken to the water, making a total of six in operation. All of them had their flashers on, their crew yelling through loudspeakers to get the boats in.

The Chief's voice came in through the radio. *"I'm docking now. Sergeant, what's your twenty?"*

"Section Forty-three," Shier replied.

"I'm on my way. Hold tight."

"Will do." He lowered the radio and let out a long, exasperated sigh. "Can't wait to hear this one."

CHAPTER 24

Sammy never appreciated the sensation of stepping on solid ground as much as she did in this moment. She walked toward Ben's shop, getting her breathing under control, while her mind replayed the seemingly impossible events that occurred in the last half-hour. Jesse and the doctor stepped off the tugboat, while Ben took a moment to assess the damage. Both officers had to turn their radio volume down from the non-stop chatter from the evacuation. The Fire Department was now getting involved. With such a large evacuation, there were sure to be a few injuries...and a visit from her father.

So much trouble in such a short amount of time. At least two vessels attacked—that she knew of, untold number of missing persons. Then there was the economic impact that this would cause if not dealt with quickly. Sammy was starting to sweat. There were so many factors to this, and they were all hitting her at once. She needed a course of action now. First, she needed answers.

She turned around and crossed her arms.

"Dr. Meyer, was it?"

"Correct. You can call me Hugh," he said.

"Alright, Hugh," she said. Her voice, while not accusatory, was not particularly friendly either. It was no coincidence that this guy and the Serpent showed up here at the same time. "Clearly, you know about this thing. What the hell is it, and why is it here?"

"And how the hell do we kill it?!" Ben added, dragging a few tools from his cargo hold.

Hugh rubbed his forehead, delaying his answer, but only to think of the best way to explain it. Would these people believe the truth of this creature's existence? Well, they did see it with their own eyes, and one didn't have to be a marine expert to know it wasn't part of the natural order.

"I work for a company called Timestone. Ever heard of them?"

"Yeah," Sammy said. "They're a medical research corporation. What does medical research have to do with a freaking sea dragon?"

"In the journey of trying to cure untold number of diseases, we decided we could look at the past. We started thinking that, if we could recover some of the flora and fauna that lived eons ago, in conditions that made Africa today look like a spa, we could discover all kinds of vaccines that could help people today."

"You're speaking about extinct species, Doctor. Are you a paleontologist?" Sammy asked.

"No. I'm a bio-geneticist. Or genetic engineer, if you prefer."

"Engineer? Wait..." Ben chuckled from disbelief. "You *made* that thing?"

"Yes," Hugh answered.

"What for? Medical purposes?" Jesse asked.

"The creatures had incredibly good adaptive capabilities," Hugh explained. "Our research has found that it has a highly resilient immune system. We created it to study its anatomy; to see if we could find a cure for modern day diseases or even cancer."

"We're getting a little ahead of ourselves here," Ben said. He stepped off his boat onto the dock. "We've skipped over the 'resurrection' part. What *is* that thing? Or specifically, what *was* it?"

Hugh hesitated again. The answer was fantastical, but then again, he was already spilling the beans.

"An extinct species of eel that lived during the Early Triassic Period. We've found that they've migrated across what is now the eastern coast of North America, and even went as far north as the polar regions."

"Let me guess the next part," Ben said. "You found one buried in ice!"

"Close. We found remains buried in ice. Preserved enough for us to uncover the DNA sequence, and resurrect a near perfect clone, with a few small components added from modern day eels. But all in all, that thing is all *Serpentem Vectem Cel*— Serpent Eel."

Ben's natural inclination would normally be to laugh in the doctor's face, but he'd seen the damn thing for himself. It wasn't a normal beast. As unbelievable as Hugh's story was, it had to be true.

"So, what are you doing out here?" Jesse asked. "Out to catch it? Probably sent out here by the company. I'm sure they'd like to have it back."

"Actually, no," Hugh said. "I'm here to *kill* it. That's what I tried to do, but its scales have hardened so much that it can withstand bullets, as you all discovered for yourselves today. The creature shows promise in developing medical breakthroughs, but we quickly learned that it's HIGHLY aggressive."

"No shit," Ben said, jerking his head toward the busted transom on his boat.

"We were transporting it by plane. It broke out of its confinement, killed the crew, crashed the plane, then found a nice shallow region to feed. That lighthouse back there."

"Did you know it was going to be that big?" Sammy asked.

"No. It shouldn't have gotten bigger than fifteen feet. But other doctors, working for the head of Timestone, were administrating accelerated growth hormones to the creature without my knowledge. They did it early on, and it's been growing ever since. I suspect it was given an extra dosage before the flight, because it was only twenty feet long the last time I saw it."

"Why would they do that?" Sammy asked.

"To save time. Time is money, and they didn't want to wait years for this thing to reach mature size."

"But I don't understand why they wouldn't want somebody to catch it," Sammy said. "I imagine it cost a fortune to grow the creature, let alone harvest the DNA of an extinct species."

"It did, but there's two other factors," Hugh said. "One is that Timestone has the technology and the knowledge to create a replacement. Two—and this is the more prominent reason, is that they don't want *any* knowledge of this creature out in the public. Hence the isolated facility we were shipping it to. Especially now, with people dead because of it, the loss from stock, lawsuits, lost product, shareholders backing out, all of that would be far worse than losing a specimen they could simply recreate. They figured, if it was discovered, it'd be chalked up as a newly discovered species that invaded the coast. Nobody would think there was a connection between a medical research firm and an oversized eel."

Sammy took a breath, then glanced at her companions. This was a lot to take in.

"So, what about you?" she asked. "If you work for them, and they don't care if it's lurking out here, then why are you out hunting it?"

"Because I created the beast to *save* lives, not to have them butchered," Hugh said. "Everyone that the Serpent kills is blood on my hands. That includes my colleague, Dr. Ryan Burg, who tried to help me last night. Him and the owner of that boat you saw half-submerged out there, all dead because of my creation. At the time, we thought it would be a simple enough matter to draw it to the surface and put a few slugs in its head. Unfortunately, that did not turn out to be the case."

Sammy nodded. There didn't appear to be anything sinister about the Doctor. After all, he was telling her several things that he had probably signed a non-disclosure agreement for. Just by talking to her, he was probably getting himself into hot water. He was probably risking having his name tarnished, his financials torn apart, wages withdrawn, as well as heavy lawsuits. On top of that, Timestone probably had someone penning a cover story right now, distancing themselves from the incidents, and doing so in a way that would put all the blame on Hugh Meyer.

"We can't have it swimming around out there. The waters between here and Lebbon Rock are in the jurisdiction of the Spiral Bay Police Department. We'll have to find a way to kill it," she said. "Doctor, will you be willing to help us as a consult?"

"Absolutely," Hugh replied.

"I'm not sure Shier and the others are gonna believe what we're about to tell them," Jesse said.

"That's where the bodycams come in handy," Sammy said. Her phone buzzed. She looked at the screen and saw the ID reading *Dad.* She swiped the green button and answered. "This is the Chief."

"Hey! I'm at the beaches right now. You're pulling everyone from the water? Boats included?! What the hell is going on?!"

"I'll tell you in person," she said. "We're on our way to the beaches right now. First, you need to make an announcement. Keep everyone out of the water, ESPECIALLY by Lebbon Rock!"

CHAPTER 25

"You've got to be shitting me."

Robert Shier shook his head as he and several other officers watched the bodycam footage of the huge beast laying waste to Jesse's boat. The room was darkened, the footage displayed through a projector, as though they were having a movie night.

Sammy stood at the front of the briefing room alongside Dr. Hugh Meyer and Richard. Jesse was seated at the front row of the group. Sammy kept an eye on her, hoping reliving the day's events wasn't too traumatic. So far, she seemed to be taking it fairly well.

"Holy shit," Officer Murphy said, watching the beast throw itself onto Ben's tugboat. After a few minutes, Sammy cut the footage.

"Lights please." Someone in the back hit the switch and lit the room. "Alright, everyone. That's what we're up against. We know that it has killed a number of persons, most of which we might not be able to identify yet. All we know are a Ms. Brianne Vase and a Sean Douglas. The families have already been notified. The other victims, we won't know until we kill the thing and can safely investigate that area. It's our responsibility that there won't be any more. Agreed?"

"Aye-aye," some of the officers said.

"In the meantime, we have officers patrolling the beaches to keep everyone away," Shier said. "We'll keep a guard on post all night long every few sections. Hopefully, tonight will be the only night we'll have to do that. There is a notice to mariners in effect. If we see anyone out on the water, we are to arrest them."

"Because of this, I'm gonna have to ask you to act quickly," Richard said. "I can only keep the media off of this for so long. If news breaks out, we'll have two problems, and interestingly, they're the opposite of each other. One is that there'll be a mass panic, which'll lead to an economic crisis, as tourists vacate our town. The other problem is that the event will actually attract attention from seafarers, scientists, and other people who want to get a look at the thing. We'll have boats coming down from Virginia, and up from Florida. It's more than I'm sure you'll be able to handle."

"That's why we need to do this quickly," the Chief said.

"Clearly this thing can withstand bullets. Even our high-powered rifles might have trouble penetrating," Shier said. "So, what can we do to get around this obstacle?"

Sammy pointed to the Doctor. "This is Dr. Hugh Meyer. Let's just say he's an expert on this species, and he'll be assisting us in bringing it down."

Hugh took a step forward. He hated that it had gone this far. The last thing he intended was to put more people in harm's way. Yet, it seemed like more and more people kept finding themselves in the middle of this situation. Unfortunately, there was no other course of action that he could think of.

"Because of its thick scales, we're gonna have to find a way to kill the beast from the inside."

"The inside? Why don't we inject a tuna with some poison and make the thing eat it?" Shier said.

"Not a bad idea, but it might not work," Hugh replied. "The creature is highly resilient to most toxins. Its immune system was one of the reasons we were studying it in the first place. No, we need a different method. Something that can be disguised as bait."

"I say we plant some dynamite in the bastard and make him chomp on that!" All eyes turned to Officer Raymond Lock, who sat in the back with his feet on the desk. His arms were covered in military tattoos, his features grizzled from his three tours in Iraq.

"That's actually not terrible thinking," Hugh said. "However, that method poses all sorts of problems. It could cause risk to whatever boat is in the water with this thing."

"Why don't we use the chopper?" Lock said. "I know those scales are thick, but can they really withstand a Remington 700?"

"Probably," Hugh said. "But I do like the idea of eyes in the sky. If anything goes wrong, the chopper unit could help to lead the creature away, while keeping out of reach of its jaws."

"This still doesn't resolve the issue of 'how do we kill it?'" Shier said. "Toxins might not work. We can't bomb the waters. Bullets can't penetrate it. I'm a little lost on any other available methods. Don't forget, we're talking about an animal as big as a humpback whale."

"What about electricity?" Sammy suggested. She looked at Hugh, whose eyes had lit up.

"Electricity might work, though I'm not sure how we can get a charge through its mouth...." He thought for a moment. "We know for a fact it'll go after bait. Last night, when my associates and I tried to lure it, it went after our bait first. And today, we diverted it with the jet ski. It can be tricked, so we can probably disguise an electric rod or something as food. If we can get the creature to bite it and hold on, then we might be able to shock it to death."

"Ha, no immune system can hold up against a good buzz," Sergeant Shier said. "Speaking of buzzes, once we kill this thing, drinks are on me." Murmurs of approval passed through the briefing room.

"We still need to figure out how we'll pull this off," Officer Lock said.

"I'm not sure yet," Hugh said. "I'm a geneticist, not an engineer, at least not in the common sense. I'm not sure how we can deliver a charge to the Serpent."

"I don't think that'll be a problem," Sammy said. "I know a guy who can take a pocketknife and socket wrench and build you a shopping mall. I think he can build us a lure."

CHAPTER 26

Ben sat behind his desk, absorbing the plans laid out to him by Sammy and Dr. Hugh. Sergeant Shier and Jesse stood inside with them, along with Mayor Richard Russell. Each of them was eager to hear his take on the issue.

"So, you want me to build a lure big enough to snag a creature with teeth over four inches long, so powerful that it can rip a boat in two, and has a temper that would fit right in on *Twitter*. Am I missing anything?"

Sammy cleared her throat. "Oh, and we need it to deliver an electric charge."

"Oh, that sounds fun," Ben said. "For a second, I thought you wanted me to reel it in. Or, maybe have Jesse do it, since she's the fishing queen."

Jesse smiled. Even despite of everything that had happened that day, the memory of catching that fish, and interacting with Derrick still made her feel giddy. If anything, she hoped that everything would go as planned and allow her to take advantage of the rest of his time here at Spiral Bay.

"Will it be a problem?" Sammy asked.

"Man, Sammy, we get back together, and already you're making up a honey-do list for me," he said. His smiled confirmed his use of sarcasm. "Yeah, I've got everything we need. How big do we need this lure to be?"

"Big enough to get the bastard's attention," Hugh said. "Probably about five feet at least. Once it's built, we'll cover it in fish guts or something to entice the Serpent."

"Best way for me to do this would be to build something from scratch, then," Ben said. He pulled out a piece of paper and started sketching a design. He drew an oval shape across the sheet, then added small lines along the body, and some arrows on the top and bottom. "These will all be hooks. Three or four inches would be enough to snag him well enough."

"I think that'll work perfectly," Hugh said.

"I'll get my welder out and get right on it," Ben said.

"Any idea how long it'll take?" Richard asked.

"Probably the rest of the day," Ben said. "I'm pretty sure I'll have it ready for use in the morning."

"Okay." Richard nodded, grateful for the young man's help. He would rather be celebrating the rekindling of Ben's relationship with Sammy, something he felt never should've ended. Unfortunately, that would have to wait for a better opportunity.

"However, there's still the issue of the electric charge," Ben said.

"Do we need a cable?" Sammy asked.

"No, I have a cable perfect for what we're looking for. As long as the Serpent bites the lure and not the cable itself, it should do just fine. No, the problem is the source of the electricity itself. We're either going to need a high-voltage generator, or plain and simply, a bigger boat. Specifically, a bigger engine."

"What about your tugboat?" Shier asked.

"Come take a look for yourself," Ben said. He led the group through the back door and onto the dock.

"Oh!" the Sergeant exclaimed, looking at the battered stern of the vessel. The bodycam footage didn't do it justice. The back side of the vessel had nearly been caved in by the beast. The boat was in no condition to go on a luxury fishing trip, let alone a monster hunt. "Yeah, I see what you mean."

"Any chance we can rent a boat?" Jesse said. "Maybe pay one of the fishermen for their trawlers?"

"You think any of them would let go of their precious boats?" Shier said. "Fishing is their livelihood. Even with promise of reimbursement, I don't see any of them letting us use their boats. Besides, boats like that require knowledge on how to operate them. It's not the same as steering a little patrol boat. I'm not sure if any of them would be crazy enough to go out there with us."

Jesse sighed. "There's one who might."

Richard cleared his throat. "Chief, would you walk with me please?"

They walked back into the shop, away from the others. Once the doors shut, his voice lit up.

"No. No! Bad idea."

"I know, Dad. I'm not keen on involving civilians in this either. But we might not have a choice."

"Those guys have cameras. We're lucky they haven't plastered this all over the internet yet! You know how bad it'll be if any of them got hurt or killed during this operation?"

"Worse than me?"

"Wha—" His expression soured. "Sammy, that's cold. You know that's on the forefront of my mind right now." Sammy regretted her response. If anything, she should've been grateful that her father actually treated her as a Chief and not as a little girl when in uniform. The lack of interference indicated a confidence in her ability to handle it, despite his concerns as a father.

"I'm sorry. I didn't mean—I'm sorry."

He nodded. "On that note, you sure you want to go out there? Perhaps you could be on the chopper?" The dad side was coming out, now that nobody was around. He knew how she would answer.

"This is my job. I'm not putting any more officers in jeopardy than I need to."

He smiled. "That's what makes you a good Chief."

"Dad, we're gonna need Derrick's help. I can make it so only a handful of people are on the yacht. But we need an engine that can deliver a charge, and that yacht can do it. Plus, it's the only thing available that might be able to withstand the tugging from the creature's thrashing about."

Richard hated to admit it, but she was probably right.

"Are you confident in this plan?" he asked.

"I've seen how this creature attacks. It'll go after the easiest prey first, thus, it'll go for the bait before even thinking of attacking the boats. I believe Ben can make a lure strong enough to snag it and keep it from escaping. Once it's on, we've won. We'll shock the hell out of it until its heart stops."

There was something about her confidence that made Richard feel better. Still, it was scary. Part of his reason for hiring her as Chief was to keep her off the frontlines. But, it was part of her job, and he refused to stand in the way...unless absolutely necessary.

"Alright, then. You think he'll even agree to do it?"

****

"Hell yes!" Derrick threw a fist in the air. His was the only voice of enthusiasm. On the pier behind him, several crew members shook their heads, their facial expressions shrunken. Even the swimsuit models, who seemed to have permanent smiles on their faces, looked forlorn.

Sammy bit her tongue. Already, she was second-guessing the decision to ask these outsiders for their help.

"Yeah, I don't know," Marty said. His eyebrows were raised high.

"Oh, quit being a bunch of babies!" Derrick said. "Think of this! We can film it. We'll make this a two-part, maybe even three-part special. And I'm sure the Chief here won't take issue with the idea of us getting a little camera use out of this ordeal." He leaned toward Sammy. "Right?"

"That's fine, as long as everything goes well," Sammy said.

"Wait! You mean there's a chance it won't?" one of the models asked.

"We're not gonna need a full crew aboard," Sammy said. "We just need enough people to operate the yacht, assist with communication and spotting, and maybe a person on standby to attach the cable to the engine." Already, there were numerous sighs of relief.

"Well, you can count me in," Derrick said. "What about you, Josh?"

"Well, uh, sure!" Josh said.

"This isn't like fishing for tuna," Melvin said.

"Of course it isn't!" Derrick said. "Why do you think I want to do this so bad?"

"Ratings," Melvin said.

"Yeah. It pays the bills and keeps you employed," Derrick retorted. "And besides, how often are we going to be presented with a challenge like this? We're gonna go out and kill a forty-foot eel thing! Imagine telling that story on your deathbed."

"Yeah, the problem is, I don't want to be there tomorrow," Melvin said.

"Fine," Derrick said. "For everything you want done, we'll probably need three people. Two in the bridge, one for the engine room. That's the bare minimum. I'm obviously on board. But, I'm not sure if…"

"Oh, fuck it, I'll go. I'm not gonna let you hog all the publicity," Melvin said.

"I'm in," Josh said. He struggled to put a smile on his face. Derrick snapped his fingers to the crowd. A moment later, a couple of cameramen approached, their equipment on tripods. They aimed the lenses at the TV star.

"Ladies and gentlemen, we have the opportunity of a lifetime. I, Derrick Crevello, will be going out with local law enforcement to catch and kill the large predator lurking near Lebbon Rock! This beast is a threat to the local population! It has already sunk one police boat, and the Police Chief barely made it out with her life! Now, she's braving the waters again, and she's asking ME for help. And you all know me; would I turn down the opportunity to fish for a giant monster?"

"Depends if there's money and fame involved," Marty replied. Derrick's expression soured.

"Cut. We'll edit that out. Thanks for ruining my monologue, dick."

"No problem! I was gonna have the writers come up with a better one, anyway."

"Uh…" Ben raised his hand to get the star's attention. "May we get a look at the inside, particularly the engine room?"

"Certainly. Follow me," Derrick said. He pointed at the cameramen and mouthed, "You too."

Ben, Sammy, and Jesse followed Derrick onto the yacht and into the passageway, with cameramen following them to capture each moment of planning. They proceeded down a small stairway, which led to a tight passageway which led to the engine room.

"Here it is," Derrick said. "MTU Two by eighteen-hundred horsepower." Ben stepped over to inspect it.

"This should work," he said. "The plan is to get the creature to snag itself on the bait. Once it's caught, the person on standby will then attach the end of the cable to the terminal."

"It'll be like jumpstarting a car battery, only we're stopping a heart," Hugh said.

"Right. We'll have the cable secured on the aft deck to keep it from getting yanked free. Derrick, I hope you don't mind a few screws and clamps in your deck."

"For this? Hell no. Do what you have to do," Derrick said. He clapped his hands together, the slap echoing in the small enclosure. "Alright! Looks like we're set to go. What time do we plan on kicking this off?"

"I want to do this in daylight," Sammy said. "Ben will be working on the cables for the rest of today, so I'm thinking ten a.m. tomorrow will work."

"Sounds good to me," Derrick said.

"Great! I'll have time to get one last meal in before I get turned into seafood," Melvin said.

The group returned to the dock then broke apart.

"Ten o'clock sharp," Derrick said. "Don't be late!"

"Never," Jesse said.

"Speaking of which…" Derrick took her hand and led her away from the others. "Uh, we still on for tonight?"

"Of course!" Jesse said. Derrick looked relieved.

"Thank goodness. I thought that maybe you'd get forced to work a double-shift or something because of the extra patrols on the beaches."

"No. The Chief wants me sharp for tomorrow's expedition. I'm off at three." Jesse looked at her watch. "Which is in twenty minutes!"

"That works out perfectly!" Derrick exclaimed. "I'm off...now!"

"Good. I guess that means I'll see you soon," Jesse said. She glanced back and saw the rest of her group getting impatient. She looked at Derrick, already backing toward them. "You want me to pick you up?"

"That's not how this works," Derrick said. "I'll pick *you* up."

Jesse laughed. "I'm all for the traditional way of doing things too. But you don't know your way around."

"Hmm, I suppose you have a point."

"Give me time to get changed. Four o'clock okay?"

"Nothing fancy. You know me," Derrick said.

"Makes me like you more," Jesse retorted. She spun on her heel and trotted back to the others.

"You're pretty cheery for someone who nearly got devoured," Ben said. "Especially considering that we're going back out tomorrow."

"I guess I'm just feeling optimistic," Jesse replied. She cleared her throat, then looked at Hugh. "You DO think this plan's gonna work, right?"

"As long as that bastard has no more tricks up his sleeve," Hugh said. "I think we have a good plan."

"I'm off to work now," Ben said. "Mind dropping me off, Chief?"

"You didn't have to ask," she replied. "Doctor? Do you have a place to stay?"

"Are there any hotels available?" Hugh asked.

"I think the Green Valley Inn has some. I'll call and check for you," Sammy answered.

They stopped at her Interceptor and contemplated tomorrow's expedition.

"Alright. Hopefully in..." Sammy checked her watch, "twenty hours, this will be nothing but a very interesting memory."

"Not to mention a *Catch my Drift* special," Ben said.

"You'll have to tell me about this show," Hugh said. It was the first genuine smile he had in days. It felt so good, that he hoped to be doing it more at ten-thirty tomorrow, after seeing his creation dead in the water.

"We'll tell you about it on the ride to the hotel," Sammy said.

CHAPTER 27

It gave Sammy chills to see the beaches so vacant, even in the late evening hours. The sun was starting its descent, and for the first time, she could count the unmoving shadows from benches, trash cans, lifeguard posts, and other static items along the beaches. By now, the crowds would start heading in, with a few hundred swimmers taking advantage of the quieter evening hours.

The Chief drove her Interceptor south along the beach for the thirtieth time. The only people she saw were the right ones: police officers. She had sent Sergeant Shier home, despite his dedication to remain on site and keep people away, but she needed him sharp for tomorrow's mission. The shark nets were in place, though Sammy knew they would do no good in keeping out that Serpent. She even refused to allow boat patrols out at night. Under cover of darkness, they'd be easy pickings for that damn creature.

Fourteen hours now. As it pressed closer, the butterflies in her stomach got worse. She wondered if Jesse felt the same way. Yeah, that girl always had a smile on her face, and always managed to put a good spin on things, but this had to be different.

She is scared too, right?

Sammy had entered the realm of overthinking her predicament, and she knew it. Unfortunately, anxiety was not usually quelled by a self-affirming statement that everything would be okay. She wanted to talk to somebody, and felt guilty about it. She was the Chief of Police, and had to maintain a relaxed demeanor of somebody in control. She couldn't let her officers even catch a hint that she was nervous, as that could create a downward spiral effect.

However, she needed to talk to somebody. Looking at the water was killing her right now. She had done her job for today. The beaches were clear, the second shift Sergeant was doing a good job of managing the shift. Her dad was keeping things under control from a media perspective. The story right now was that there was a shark spotted and that an operation would take place tomorrow to drive them away. Of course, it didn't explain why people couldn't be on the sand at least, but luckily, not too many questions were asked about it.

With a little luck, things would go smoothly tomorrow, and in twenty-four hours, she would have a nice restful sleep. She'd be hard pressed to get one tonight, thanks to that anxiety.

She finished her pass on the beach, then continued south to Beggar's Cove.

Ben Stacie was sweating as he pressed the flame to the cylinder piece of metal. He was outside, behind his building, with a sledgehammer and variety of other tools to the side.

With his focus on the task in front of him, he never heard the backdoor open. Only when it slammed shut did he look over his shoulder.

"Hey!" Sammy said to him. "Sorry. Hope I didn't almost cause you to burn yourself."

Ben grinned and shook his head. "No. I'm just wrapping this up." He turned the torch off and stepped aside to let her see the Turbo V6 Buick aluminum cylinder block. Sticking out from all sides were four-inch long barbs welded into the block. "Once that bastard bites down on this, it's game over. Aluminum is a good conductor of electricity. Made the barbs out of copper, which is even better."

"Wow," she said. "What about the cable?"

"I have some galvanized wire rope made with zinc electro plating. They use it on cranes and other heavy lifting machinery. It should hold the beast long enough to get the charge through. We can't skimp on the cable. Anything too weak will be torn in half."

"How much cable do you have?"

"Fifty-feet. We'll hook it to the boat, then attach a wire to the end to set the charge."

"Will the yacht be protected?"

"From the charge? Yeah, the hull has fiberglass covering."

Sammy nodded. "I guess we really did think of everything. All we need to do is cover this lure in bait, and we'll be good to go."

"Damn straight." Ben took his goggles off. He noticed she was still in her police uniform. "Have you been working this whole time?"

"I'm still the Chief. Gotta keep the town safe."

"It's safe," he said. "It's gonna be safer tomorrow. Why don't you call it a night?"

"I want to, believe me," she said.

"And you're not. Because?"

"I just don't want to sit at home alone dwelling on everything that's happening," Sammy said. Ben wiped his face with a handkerchief.

"Good thing you're here with me then," he said. She smiled, but only for a moment.

"You don't have to go out there tomorrow," she said.

"The hell with that! If anything mechanical goes wrong out there, you're gonna need my help," he said.

"It could go bad," she said.

"Babe, even the doctor thinks this'll work. We'll be in a hundred-and-twenty-foot yacht. The thing doesn't know what it's in store for."

"I guess I'm just nervous," Sammy said. She found a chair and helped herself to it. "So much has happened in the last twenty-four hours. It's a little hard to take in."

"I'll agree with you there." Ben sat down beside her. "But it'll be done. Then you can quit worrying. Don't forget, you'll get to be a TV star after it's all said and done."

That got her to chuckle.

"Maybe they'll want us to consult for the film adaptation," she said.

"Better. Have us star in it," Ben replied. He leaned over and kissed her. It lasted a few moments before she pulled away.

"Babe, I wanna continue and all, but you are covered in grease," she said.

"Well, I guess I'll have to remedy that with a shower. Wanna help?" He stood up and reached for her hand. She smiled again and took his hand, then followed him to his truck.

CHAPTER 28

Derrick Crevello was glad he made the reservation at Jason's Lobster Corral, or else he and Jesse would've been forced to wait hours. With the beaches closed, all the tourists took their activities inland, which included crowding the restaurants. Derrick was wise enough to get them a table in a somewhat secluded area of the restaurant to spare them the agony of listening to people complain about the situation.

Jesse was out in style tonight, wearing a dress that showed off her right shoulder, with a skirt that peeled back just enough to showcase her legs. Derrick went with a simple dress shirt and slacks. Fairly modest, but Jesse liked it.

They tried their best to avoid discussion of the Serpent, though it was evident that it was in the back of their minds. Instead, they tried to learn more about each other. To Jesse's surprise, Derrick seemed more fascinated to learn about her, when he could've easily won her over with the fascinating stories of his travels. Instead, they found common interests in sports and athletics.

"I ran track in high school. Had a mile run time of four minutes, thirty-three seconds," she said. "I was always a runner. I continued playing sports in college. Did a few years of Taekwondo."

"Judo for me," Derrick said.

"I can never seem to find any Judo schools," Jesse said. "I've always wanted to do it."

"Yeah, it seems they're a little harder to come by, nowadays," Derrick said. "Jiu-Jitsu has taken over the martial arts world. I did a few months of it. Not a bad sport, but it's all about preference, and I prefer the stand-up stuff."

Jesse took a sip of her wine. "Have you ever taken Karate or Taekwondo?"

"I started karate when I was thirteen, but we moved out of Ohio to California. That's when I found a Judo school, and fell in love with that. Then fishing came into play, and, I'm sure you know how that went."

Jesse took another sip of wine. She knew what she wanted to ask, but was afraid of where it'd lead. She certainly didn't want to spoil the evening, but her impulses got the better of her.

"So, what's the next place after you're done here?" she asked. "More coastal fishing? Hawaii? Or somewhere inland?"

"There's a big lake in Maine with some huge smallmouth bass," Derrick said. "I like to dial it up, then back. We have episodes like what we filmed with you where we catch thousand pound fish, as well as episodes where we dive in the kelp forests of California and spearfish underwater. Then, I like to bring it back to something more relatable, and just cast a line in a simple lake."

"I used to fish on a lake," Jesse said. "It was Evergreen Lake in Ohio. Sometime in the early 2000s it got completely covered in moss, and nearly all the fish died. Broke my heart. I heard it got replenished by now, but I'm not entirely sure."

"There's something calming about a lake," Derrick said. "Don't get me wrong, I love the ocean. Can't get enough of it. But there's something about a lake that I find more relaxing. If I had to choose between having a beach house, or a lakefront property, oh, it'd be a tough choice. But I think I'd go with the lakefront."

"Oh, me too!" Jesse said. She worried about how she sounded just then. She was genuinely agreeing with him, but it may have come off as 'Oh, I like lakes too. Take me with you! We'll live happily ever after, together.'

"There's actually a little lake in Michigan I really like," Derrick said. "Twin Lake. Nothing fancy. People would think I'm insane for wanting to settle down there. In fairness, I'd probably have that as my summer home...not the biggest fan of snow, though I do like ice fishing."

"I think I know where that's at," Jesse said. "Lupton, Michigan?"

"Yes," Derrick said, excitedly. "I didn't know you were from that area."

"A nostalgic memory," Jesse said. "I lived in south Michigan until I was twelve. Every year we'd go up north and rent a cabin on various lakes. We went there a few times, and I loved it."

"That's crazy. I can't believe you know what I'm talking about."

"You should do a show there...and check out properties. I'm sure you'd find something," Jesse said.

"I've thought of it. Right now, anything we do might be a step down if it follows the episode from tomorrow's footage. Like the stuff we're shooting in Maine. Be hard for the audience to go from fishing for marlins, to literal sea monsters, then down to smallmouths. Maybe I can convince the studio heads to air it prior to the Spiral Bay episodes. Now that I'm thinking about it, this would be one hell of a season finale."

"Too bad there's no red carpet premier," Jesse said.

"Nah, we're not that big of a show," he said. "Though that might change after tomorrow. Hell, it might change for you too. I can see you getting a hell of a promotion."

"I'd say thanks to a pay raise." Jesse smiled. "Too bad I can't take the sick day I promised."

"It'll be better," Derrick said. "We'll be hunting monsters together. How many people get to tell that story?"

"You nervous at all?" Jesse asked.

"The right kind of nervous, like what you feel when you're gazing up at a roller coaster before getting on. I think we have a good plan in place tomorrow. We'll kill the thing. The Mayor can open the beaches. Then, maybe you can get off work early and we'll spend the rest of the day together."

"We saw what it did to that other yacht," Jesse said.

"Yeah, but mine's bigger. And it'll go for the bait before it even gets the idea to go for us. That's what it did when it took Melvin's marlin. It went for the jet ski. It thinks it's badass, but has no problem going for easier prey. No, I think tomorrow's gonna go smooth."

Jesse smiled. "Sorry. I know we were trying hard to avoid the topic of tomorrow. It kind of crept in."

"Sweetheart, you could talk to me about digging up dirt, and I would still love it," Derrick said. Jesse leaned forward.

"After this weekend is done, you can always feel free to come back to Spiral Bay and talk to me about...well, I hope we can find a better topic than dirt." To her slight surprise, he didn't turn his nose up about returning and seeing her again. Might've been good at hiding it, but somehow, she didn't think he was.

"Maybe I will. Maybe I'll make it a weekend thing," he said. Jesse's heart was thumping hard. Her relief was displayed in a radiant smile. They leaned over the table and kissed.

CHAPTER 29

The beast was on a killing spree.

The waters belonged to it. In darkness or in daylight, there was no rock or crevice where prey could hide. The Serpent had fed repeatedly since its encounter with the humans, yet, it was still hungry. Even in comparison with its hyper-accelerated digestive rate, it was devouring prey at a rapid rate. Only when its body was developing, did it feel the need for excessive feeding. In captivity, right before a growth spurt, its handlers could not deliver enough food into its tank. In its dark enclosure, despite sedation, its hunger was so overwhelmingly powerful, due to the approaching growth spurt that would double its size, it had to break free and devour the humans nearby.

Now, it could feel the winds of change swirling in its body. Something was happening. The Serpent was not sure what, nor did it care. All it knew was that it needed to accommodate the needs of its biology.

It had traveled two miles south of the island it had claimed. Already, it had wiped out much of the existing ecosystem there, leaving only small crabs and fish that were not worth the effort of chasing. It had eaten a few sharks, but nothing large enough to sustain it. So, it had to branch out.

The Serpent stayed near the bottom, using its ability to blend in with its surroundings to mask its appearance. A lemon shark was its first victim out this way. The Serpent tore the fish in half with one single thrash of its head, then quickly mashed them into pulp. The blood helped to gain attention of other sharks. Blue sharks and makos approached, only to turn tail after seeing the leviathan that awaited. Mako sharks were among the fastest creatures in the ocean. Unfortunately, the only thing faster than them was the forty-foot Serpent that chased them.

It caught one by the tail and ripped the caudal fin away. The Mako spiraled deep, still swinging its tail in hopes of pushing itself away, but the bloody stump was useless. As it sank, the Serpent continued past it to catch up with another shark. The target ascended, hoping that a breach would somehow help it gain further distance. It broke the water with a tremendous splash. Before it reached the arch of its jump, another splash consumed the surface, making way for an air bound Serpent. It caught the mako shark by the head, then arched its body down, plunging headfirst into the ocean. The jaws squeezed tight, squelching the mako's head, before proceeding to ravage the rest of its body. It turned back to find the mako it had injured moments prior. It was squirming on the seabed, unaware that its caudal fin had been severed.

The injured mako tried to turn around after it felt the water distortions created by its pursuer. But there was nowhere to run. The Serpent snatched the mako off the seabed and shook it in its jaws. Teeth sliced through its body, dicing its organs and cartilage, until the mako was nothing but a series of ribbon-like flesh slurping into its killer's throat.

The Serpent wasn't done. Instinct dictated that it must continue killing. It followed the vibrations of the other sharks, leading it east into the open sea. After a half-mile of travel, it came across a group of hammerheads, which immediately scattered after sensing its presence.

A feeding frenzy pursued. The Serpent zipped into the middle of the school like an arrow, plucking one of the sharks out of the group like a bird snatches an insect. It mashed the shark in its jaws, swallowed, then came back for more. In a swooping motion, it snatched another shark with ease, torturing it briefly with the impalement of teeth, before ripping it apart.

The ocean became a bloodbath, which usually brought the attention of other predators. Yet, as though news of the evil creature had spread across the ocean, none came. Those that did draw near were quick to realize that there was something much larger and more violent than themselves doing the killing, and that there was no choice but to turn back, or contribute to the cloud of blood with their own innards.

Only the young and inexperienced were foolish enough to draw near.

The young sperm whale was thirty-six feet long, and had finally broken away from its mother three weeks prior. It had just returned from a deep dive, where it fed on squid, but not enough to satisfy its still-growing body. It had surfaced to breathe, and maybe satisfy itself with some bottom dwelling sharks.

It detected the anomaly with a two-hundred-and-fifteen decimal ping, which was louder than the sound of a jet engine taking off. Initially, it expected a call back, as it believed the lifeform ahead of it to be another whale. But there was no return click. Only movement. The young sperm whale ventured closer. It had never encountered large predators in its short life. Its pod had protected it from orcas and great whites, all of which were smaller than its current size. With growth came confidence, and with inexperience came poor judgement.

At a thousand feet, it realized there was no whale ahead of it. Whatever it was, it was coming in fast, a speed used either by fleeing creatures, or attacking predators. Despite having the largest brain in the world, the sperm whale lacked knowledge. It had never felt the plunge of razor-sharp teeth in its flesh. It hardly even encountered a squid that could mark its skin with its hooks. The youth was a stranger to pain, and because of this, it believed itself to be invincible. Further impairing its judgement were the memories of fights won against other young bulls. This strange creature was only slightly bigger than itself, and it seemed smaller in overall mass. A good blow to the head would probably kill it, or at least stun it enough to drive it away.

The youth led the assault with determination, fluttering its fluke with rapid speed. It closed the distance rapidly, ready to cave in the skull of the challenger.

The Serpent slowed, gauging the enemy's speed and trajectory. It was coming in fast, probably too fast for its own good. A few more moments passed. The whale had come within a hundred feet, which would be reduced to zero within the next second.

The predator dove at lightning speed. The youth kept on going, surprised at the lack of impact. It slowed, then spun back. The Serpent had evaded its attack. It could see the thing coiled on the surface. The youth had not realized the strange flexibility until now. The creature was like one of the arms of the squid it fed on, but alive, with a mouth armed with dozens of razor-sharp teeth.

Only now did the youth second guess its decision. But it was committed now. It couldn't run from a fight, especially after making the first move. It was still certain that a dead-on blow to the creature's face would be enough to ensure victory. It aimed itself downward at a forty-five degree angle then charged.

In the timespan of three rapid heartbeats, it closed the distance. This time, there was impact, not against the creature, but the sediment behind it. The Serpent had evaded again, but this time, it had planned its counterattack.

The whale felt the scaly body of the enemy constricting its own. Next came a piercing pain that it had never felt before. The Serpent bit deep into the whale's fluke, shredding the left lobe. The sperm whale twisted and writhed, unable to shake the enemy off of it. The Serpent bit again, this time tearing the lobe off entirely. Blood billowed all around the titans, and continued to grow with each bite.

The Serpent bit relentlessly, tearing chunks of flesh and blubber from the whale's underside, before working its way over to the right flipper. A dozen ear-piercing pings rang out from the youth's forehead, a cry of pain as the flipper was torn from its body. The Serpent had no aversion to the sound, nor did it have sympathy for the agony it was inflicting. It was answering a call from the highest authority it knew; its instinct. And that instinct demanded it finish the fight.

The Serpent slashed its jaw over the whale's head like a knife, lacerating the flesh with its teeth. It bit repeatedly, focusing its attention on the right eye. After a few strikes, there was nothing left in that socket except a bloody hole. It bit at the flesh on top, shredding the maxillonasailis muscle, then rupturing the distal sac. Fatty junk spilled into the water, along with the jelly filled compartments that separated it.

There would be no more pings, no more calls for help. The whale's head was ripped open now. It continued to struggle, but the loss of blood and use of senses were overpowering. It thrashed one final time, them spasmed after the Serpent bit along its airhole, ripping away a huge chunk that included the flaps. Water surged into its body. Had the whale survived a few seconds longer, it would've experienced the terror of drowning. That was the one bit of luck it did have this day.

The Serpent sank with the dead whale, then proceeded to devour mouthfuls of its body. It fed seemingly nonstop, until some of the skeleton was exposed.

Then, its body signaled that it was time for rest. There was change about to happen. Already, it could feel the pain in its throat. Its new evolution was ready to begin. It would be a painful process, but that was the cost of survival.

The Serpent lifted itself away from the corpse of its enemy then swam south to rest in its rocky environment.

CHAPTER 30

Sammy stepped out of her Police Interceptor and looked to the bright sky, seeing the chopper flying overhead. Officer Lock was leaning out the open fuselage, sniper rifle in hand. He waved to the Chief as the pilot, Ensign Hayes, circled around.

By ten o'clock, everyone had arrived at the docks. Derrick, Melvin, and Josh were waiting at the aft deck, helping Ben in securing the cable. Welding sparks flew high, nearly grazing the television star's left knee. Just a few feet to Derrick's left was Jesse, who stood with an M4 Carbine strapped over her shoulder. She was looking up at the chopper with her aviator shades on.

"I really like the whole badass look you have going there," Derrick whispered. Jesse grinned, still watching the chopper.

Two cameramen climbed aboard. Derrick threw his hands out as though about to hug them. "Hey, guys! Thanks for having the balls to come out with us." He slapped both men on the shoulders, then looked at the rest of the team. "This is Lewis," he shook the man on the right.

"Hi," Lewis said, waving a hand. He was a short man with a buzzcut. Judging from the sunburn on his face, Sammy assumed he was new to the production company.

Derrick shook the other, "And this is Ward. Don't mind them. They'll just be catching this on camera. If anyone is caught doing something embarrassing, don't worry, we'll remove it in post. Maybe."

"Good morning," Ward said. Ben looked over his shoulder to glance at the cameramen, then strained to tilt his head high enough to see Ward's face. He was freakishly tall. He should've been in a basketball league, rather than moving electronic equipment around. He was at least six-foot-seven, and was even dressed in shorts and a jersey.

"Hire him for wide shots?" Ben joked.

"Cheaper than a crane," Ward retorted.

"Speaking of that, why don't you take position on the fly deck, and Lewis, you take the main aft deck," Derrick said. With the director refusing to come aboard, the TV star was taking over directing duties—which he often tended to do anyway.

Ben drilled a few clamps into the deck, then made a few more welding patches. "Alright, I think this is as secure as it will ever be."

"I'll see to it that the town reimburses you for the repairs," Sammy reminded Derrick.

"Oh, nonsense. I'll probably get it covered as a tax write-off anyway," he said. "Come aboard, Chief! Don't miss out on all the fun!"

Sammy gave a thumbs-up, then went to the back of the Interceptor. She opened the trunk and grabbed two M4 Carbines.

"Ben, I'm sure you remember how to use one of these," she said. Ben glanced down at her, saw her with the weapons, then climbed down to help.

"Aye-aye, Chief," he said. His Army smile crossed his face. It had been a few years since he touched anything other than a handgun, but after two tours in Afghanistan, it was like meeting an old friend. He took the rifle, slung it over his shoulder, then took the case full of spare magazines. "You sure you don't want more officers on board?"

"Very sure. I'm not serving up a smorgasbord," Sammy said. She followed him up the ladder onto the deck. "Hopefully, if things go wrong, we can land a lucky hit with these. Maybe get him in the eye. But you saw the effect our weapons had yesterday. No, I don't want anyone aboard that we don't absolutely need."

Ben leaned in close. "What about the cameramen?"

Sammy glanced up at the fly deck, and could see Ward setting up his camera positions.

"Unfortunately, I don't have much choice in that matter. It's Derrick's boat, and while I'm grateful he's helping us, make no mistake, he's doing it for the show. I'm not a hundred percent convinced he'd do this if I demanded he couldn't bring camera crews aboard...on his own boat, no less." She sighed and rubbed her forehead. "Maybe I should've waited until we could've gotten the Coast Guard or had Dad purchase our own appropriate vessel for this."

"No, you're right, this is a time-sensitive matter that must be taken care of quickly. Sooner or later, someone'll be out on the water."

"That's right." Sammy and Ben turned to the left and saw Dr. Hugh Meyer approaching from the portside walkway. He was looking pale and sweaty. It was clear he had no appetite, and had possibly been vomiting due to the anxiety. "Listen, I'm sorry it ever got this far. My hopes were to kill this thing myself before anyone else even knew it existed. I hate to put anyone else at risk."

"No, Doc. You're doing the right thing," Sammy said. "Maybe after we're done, we'll work on exposing Timestone for their efforts in covering this up."

Hugh nodded, then began to inspect the cable. Most of it was coiled in a tight loop, with the huge lure dangling over the side of the deck, ready to be dragged into the water. On the forward side was a connecting clamp which was attached to a high voltage wire that led down to the engine room.

"So, all that needs to be done is attach the end of that to the engine terminal?"

"Correct. Once that clamp is on, you don't want to be anywhere near that lure," Ben said. "Too bad your pet won't realize it until it's too late."

Hugh looked at the welding patches. The cable was secure, but he was still wary. He had seen the creature's strength, and how easily it could tear steel hulls apart.

"I hope he doesn't yank it free before we can deliver the charge."

"Maybe with unlimited effort, but there's no way he'll get it off before we shock him to death."

Hugh nodded, feeling a bit relieved from the news. Melvin and Derrick stepped out on the deck, the latter looking increasingly animated.

"We have the bait set up and ready to go," he said. "It's your call, Chief. We're ready to go when you are."

Sammy took her radio speaker from her shoulder strap and pressed the transmitter. Before she spoke, she saw Lewis pan his camera towards her, then give a thumbs-up as though saying 'Action!'

"Unit One to all boats. We are leaving the harbor now. I want four vessels patrolling along the beaches. I want foot units on standby to make sure the area is vacant. Shier, I want your vessel and one other to go two-point-five miles out. If things go wrong, we might need a quick rescue."

"Whoa!" Derrick raced to the pilothouse with Melvin and started the engine. Right away, the cameramen got to work shooting B-roll footage. The yacht moved away from the dock and turned east toward Lebbon Rock. The least excited member, aside from Sammy, appeared to be Josh. He was staring at the wire nervously, then at the lure.

"You alright there?" Ben asked.

"Yeah. Just ready for this to be over," he said.

"Your job is easy, I promise," Ben assured him. "Literally, just wait for my signal and hook up the wire. Not much you can do wrong." Josh nodded and forced a smile.

"Yes sir," he said. "Just, uh, nervous, I guess."

"It'll be fine!" Derrick's voice swept over the deck. He waved to the camera, then leaned on the deck. "You are taking part in the most epic fishing adventure in history. Herman Melville has nothing on this! Only, I don't think anyone will come out of this with a peg leg! Right, Jesse!" He patted her on the shoulder, then directed Lewis to pan down to the lure. On the starboard corner of the deck was a large blue tub full of chum, and another with dead fish. He opened the latter and pulled out a ten pound tuna, recently caught from local fishermen. "We'll cover this bad boy with bait." He demonstrated by impaling the fish on a couple of the barbs. "When the Serpent comes around, he'll think this is a tight group of fish, and he'll think 'hey, why not try and take these all at once!' and then he'll bite down and lodge himself on these barbs, handmade by the great Ben Stacie over there!"

He ran his finger along one of the barbs, which protruded well over an inch from the tip.

"The Serpent will snag himself on several of these. There's no chance of escape. And before he even tries, ZAP! He'll think he swallowed a bolt of lightning. It's a big job, but honestly, a simple task."

Hugh's stomach was starting to turn again. He stepped away, letting the cool breeze calm his nerves. He continued walking along the side deck, not wanting to be caught on film like this.

"I certainly hope so," he muttered.

CHAPTER 31

The water was calm, the beaches smooth and golden-white. The only footprints were from those of the officers that walked along, turning away people who wanted to chance the swim.

"There's shark nets," many pointed out.

"Big shark. They're out there luring it away right now," the officers replied. Some spoke convincingly, others nervously, which led to the rumors to spread that there was something going on that the local government didn't want getting out.

Officer Clarence York was one of the more nervous officers. At twenty-three years old, he was more of a timid type who didn't like confrontation. He would not have even become a cop had his mother, father, and grandfather not pushed it on him. They were all cops, as were two of his uncles, his brother, and three of his cousins. They were competitive types, while Clarence was not. Unfortunately, he was short and not very muscular, and even with the badge and gun, he didn't have the most intimidating demeanor.

He walked alone on the beach and glanced up at a fellow officer who stood high in the lifeguard tower. It was Officer Peter Jay, keeping watch with a high-powered rifle. Though a bit gruffer, and a decade ahead of him in age, Peter took a small sympathy for the kid. Part of it was from guilt from chastising him during his rookie year, before finding out that Clarence wasn't even really suited for this job, but was guilted into it. It was a miracle that he found himself here in Spiral Bay, a relatively relaxed area compared to some of the places Clarence had worked in the past.

Peter watched the water with his binoculars. Every so often, he'd see one of the patrol boats pass by. The 'line of defense', as he called it, was about a quarter mile out, keeping an eye for any vessels coming in from the north or south sides. Warnings had been announced, but people often didn't listen. So far, there was only two instances where vessels had to be turned around.

Unlike here at the beaches, where someone was radioing in every few minutes to Dispatch for them to add to the log that they turned somebody away.

He heard the sound of an engine. Irritated, he closed his eyes. *Please let that be one of the mobile units coming in from town.* Of course, it wasn't. In fact, when he saw the *CBS* logo on the van, he realized he should've wished it was a simple resident. The Mayor had asked for the media to stay clear of the beaches, but that's like asking a four-year-old to keep his hands out of the cookie jar.

The big white van came to a stop, and right away, the big side door opened up. A female reporter hopped out with a cameraman behind her. Even from up in the lifeguard tower, Peter recognized the short black hair, and the white shirt with the top three buttons undone which was always sported by Tiffany Decker. She was an assertive woman who did not take no for an answer very well.

He could see her approaching Clarence.

Shit. She was going to eat him alive. Peter made sure his rifle was safely hidden behind the walls of the booth, then quickly made his way down the ladder to help his fellow officer in turning this reporter away.

Peter was halfway down the ladder when another vehicle pulled up. It was a blue SUV, with no markings indicative of any news organization. There was a glare on the windshield preventing him from seeing the man inside.

"Ma'am, you were already told. No press!" Clarence was trying so hard to be assertive, but Tiffany Decker was not the type to back down easily. If she smelled a story, she would stick her head in a hornet's nest to get to expose it if she had to.

"Officer, there are conflicting reports and rumors about the reasons this beach has been closed. There are increasing questions coming from the neighboring communities. People don't believe the danger is a killer shark. There have been shark sightings in the past. Even shark attacks in the past. Yet, such drastic actions have never taken place until now."

"Hey!" Peter's thunderous voice was enough to make Tiffany jolt, even though barely noticeable. "You heard the officer. No press. There'll be a press conference later in the day headed up by our Chief and the Mayor. You'll get your answers there."

"Oh, right. Give you guys more time to cook up a story to cover up what's really happening," Tiffany said. The reporter hadn't even been on this beach a full sixty seconds and Peter could already feel his blood pressure reach a boiling point.

"Does this look like a government conspiracy? You see FBI agents walking around? No. There's just a dangerous situation, and we're in the process of handling it. As long as people like you don't interfere, everything should be back to normal by this afternoon."

"There's something that's not adding up," Tiffany continued. "Drone footage reveals significant damage to the Lebbon Rock lighthouse, as well as wrecked fishing ships around the island. Then there were reports of the damaged luxury yacht, where a woman named Brianne Vast was reportedly killed."

"Again, you'll get your answers. But first…"

The SUV door opened up, and a man in his mid-forties stepped out. His hair was a mess. There were bags around his eyes, as if he hadn't slept in days. His button shirt added to that appearance. The top three buttons were undone, the white undershirt wet with sweat.

Oh shit… Peter recognized the man as the one whom he had to notify of Brianne Vase's passing. Jared Vase. Informing such bad news to a loved one was never easy, despite the varying results. At least half broke down in tears, as any decent person would expect. He'd seen people indifferent, some even happy and not afraid to show it. Jared's reaction was a mixed bag. At first, it was shock, then what appeared to be indifference, then he commented that 'the bitch deserved it.' Peter had to endure a monologue of how she was unfaithful and was in the process of leaving with some out-of-town jerk, which was where the glee started to show through. Then Peter watched that glee plunge into despair. 'You know the last thing I said to her?! It was that I hoped she got eaten by sharks!' Just the way he spoke was enough for Peter to know the guy intended to fight for his marriage in the long run. Sadly, he would not get his chance.

Clearly, Jared had met with Tiffany, which explained her heightened eagerness to expose the reality of the situation. Of course, she did it under the guise that she was serving the public. Obviously, not for money and attention. No, not her…

"I want to know what killed my wife," Jared demanded.

"Mr. Vase, I'm sorry. I really am. But you are interfering with a police matter. As are you, Ms. Decker."

"I'm not leaving until I find out," Jared continued. His face was welling up. "I need to know. Was it that prick she was with? Is there even a shark? Was that guy some serial killer? You said you never found any trace of him. Maybe he's on that island…"

"No. Just go home and grieve. You'll drive yourself crazy," Clarence said.

If Peter's eyes could burn, then Tiffany Decker's face would be a smoldering cinder. It was evident she sought Mr. Vase out and exploited his grief so she could get a good story out of the deal.

The radio crackled. It was the Chief, updating the units on the operation.

"Alright, we're approaching the island now. Backup units, be on standby."

Tiffany smirked. "All this for a shark, huh?"

"Alright, I'm gonna give you thirty seconds to leave," Peter said. "We have orders to arrest anyone who refuses to vacate this beach. That includes you, Ms. Decker. And you as well, Mr. Vase. I'm sorry about your wife, believe me, but you can't be here right now. You will get your answers later."

"What about me?" the cameraman quipped. Peter's tolerance was quickly running out.

"Get in the damn van," he said, pointing with one hand, while reaching for his cuffs with the other. Clarence did the same.

Tiffany scoffed, then proceeded to walk to her van, microphone held to her own mouth as she spoke into the camera.

"Is Spiral Bay as safe as we were always led to believe? What do the police know that we don't? Find out with us, as we dig further. This is Tiffany Decker, Spiral Bay, CBS News." They got in the van, while Jared slowly backed to his SUV, his eyes never leaving the officers.

"I just want whatever killed my wife to die. I'll do it myself if I have to," he said.

"You won't have to. We've got it covered," Peter said. Normally, he'd reply with 'you come back again, I'll arrest your sorry ass,' but such a verbal tactic would not faze a grieving mind like Jared's.

The widower nodded, then got back in his van. He followed Tiffany back into town.

Peter sighed, both in relief and frustration.

"Thanks for handling that," Clarence said. Peter looked out to the ocean, then back at the town. He looked nervous. Clarence watched him pull out his smartphone and start browsing the internet, searching for news regarding Spiral Bay. "What are you doing?"

"That woman's looking to stir the pot. I don't trust her. She'll use any means to get a good story, even if she has to instigate something. She did it thirty miles south of here at a place called Bayview," Peter said.

"Oh, shit. That was *her*?!" Clarence said. He was in the academy at the time, where a shooting had taken place at the Bayview Beach in southeast Georgia. Two boats met roughly two miles out, got into a spat, which led to one pulling a gun on the other. The twist was that the 'shooting' didn't involve any firearm discharges.

Tiffany Decker was already down there at the time, reporting on some mundane story, and decided to prance on the opportunity to turn it into a huge firearms debate issue. The event led to rumors of drug smuggling taking place in that area, and even issues of race relations, even though all parties involved were Caucasian. Tiffany got the clicks and the taxpayers got the bill. Useless investigations found what was already clear from the get-go. It was just a clash over one person getting too close to the other while speedboating, and things got riled. Not a favorable situation, but not nearly as bad as Tiffany and her fellow reporters made it out to be.

And that worried Peter. If she could make a mountain out of a molehill with an unknown situation such as the non-shooting in Bayview, he'd hate to see what she would do with something like the current situation.

He snatched his speaker mic. "All units, be aware, I've got CBS asking questions. Specifically, Tiffany Decker. She's gone now, but I don't trust that she's up to anything good."

****

"For the love of God!" Sammy exclaimed. She paced across the aft deck, holding a hand to her forehead as though nursing a headache. "Just what I need; that bitch sticking her nose into the situation."

"Perhaps you could detain her?" Lewis the cameraman suggested.

"Not for asking questions," Sammy said. "I've got nothing to go on. Our best hope is to kill this thing before she starts to rile up the town."

"You think things will go that wrong?" Ben asked.

"Generally, no," Sammy said. "But we've never had to shut down the entire beach before. We've got people here who've already paid big money for their hotels and luxuries. Chartering appointments are being missed. Plus, these people are out-oftowners. My Dad's already up to his neck in complaints. Now we've got this reporter, who's not even from around here, who hates cops, exaggerates or simply puts out false information…"

"Sounds like you're talking about the media in general," Hugh said.

"Maybe," Sammy said. She glanced to the northeast at Lebbon Rock. "Well, we're here now. Let's just find this thing and be done with it. The sooner we do this, the better for everyone."

"Fine by me!" Derrick said. He pranced out onto the deck and went straight to the tub of chum. "Alright, guys, you ready for this?!" A couple of people nodded, the rest stared nervously at the water. Derrick snatched a portable radio from his belt. "Josh. You all set in the engine room?"

"A-Okay, Derrick."

"Great!" Derrick snapped his fingers at Lewis, who turned to face him with the camera. Ben, Sammy, and Jesse stood at the port end, while Hugh stepped out of sight, not interested in being filmed. He remained on the portside walkway, where he could still see the lure going out. It was hanging off the transom, completely covered in dead fish, their bodies stuffed with chum, then sewn tight, allowing it to trickle out like a bleeding animal.

"Alright, my friends and admirers! This is Derrick Crevello, coming to you once again from Spiral Bay, Georgia! Yesterday, we discovered the beast that lurked in these waters, and narrowly escaped its wrath. Today, we take the fight to it! Until yesterday, this creature had never been seen before by human eyes. It is forty feet long. Its teeth can tear a killer whale in two. Its scales are so strong, it can deflect bullets! Only Derrick Crevello can stop it, with the help of Chief Samantha Russell and the lovely Officer Jesse Roper, and master handyman Ben Stacie.

"Yeah, don't forget Melvin and Josh, Dummy," Melvin said from the pilothouse. Derrick cocked his head and saw that some of the windows were open.

"Yeah, keep driving the boat. Speaking of which, go northeast. I'm about to start chumming." He turned to the camera again. "What we have here is a yummy mix of tuna and oil. How this works is that the oil and fat substance carries the mixture out with the current. This is how scientists typically attract sharks so they can observe them from diving cages. You might see a bunch of other critters come nipping at it, like blue sharks, barracudas, and yellowfins. Hopefully, the extra attention will help attract the big baddie."

Derrick took a plastic scoop and thrust it into the mixture, then launched it out into the water.

"Mr. Stacie, would you like to do the honors?"

"Certainly, Mr. Crevello." Ben went to the center transom and dropped the lure into the water. It floated at the top with the help of orange floats and the fatty contents of the tuna speared against it. Looking like a steel porcupine, it drifted thirty feet back.

"Thank you, sir! Now, we wait." He chuckled as he tossed a few more scoopfuls of chum into the water. "You know, typically I'd ask if anyone here would rather have this serpent grilled, but unfortunately they won't have the option, because when it bites that lure, that bad boy's gonna be fried! And if he tries to dive and get away, he'll be 'deep-fried!'"

Sammy and Ben shared a glance. Both started to chuckle, only because the joke was that bad. The laugh spread to Jesse and Lewis, and even Ward could be heard from the fly deck. The only one who didn't laugh was Hugh. The fact that they hadn't seen the creature yet made him nervous.

He remembered the last time someone wandered into its territory. It had hidden itself in the ravine, unseen by the submersible. It only hid for two purposes, for ambush, and when it was evolving. Neither possibility was favorable.

"Just show yourself, you bastard."

CHAPTER 32

Ben Stacie slumped on one of the fishing chairs. His eyes were glued on the lure, which wavered along the water behind the boat. Melvin kept a quarter-mile distance from Lebbon Rock and spent the last three hours going in a circle. The group's anxieties had turned into boredom and frustration. Sammy was leaning on the transom, staring at the water with a sense of distain, as if it was deliberately hiding the creature from them. Even Derrick seemed to have lost all sense of energy and charisma from the surprisingly long wait.

Sammy watched the chopper perform another pass in the distance, looking like a dragonfly buzzing over a pond. She leaned her chin to her speaker mic.

"Hayes? Lock? You guys see anything up there?"

"Nothing. Zip. No seals. Hell, even the birds have vacated," Lock answered.

"Chief, we're gonna have to stop back and refuel," the pilot, Hayes, added.

"Ten-four. Return to the station and refuel, then get back out here pronto."

"On it. Be back shortly."

Sammy watched the chopper fly to the west, then glanced back at the lure. The tuna had turned a pinkish white, the chum trail around it thinning. Derrick scooped up the last of the tub, then clipped the lid back on. There was only one other tub left. After chumming for three hours, the water around Lebbon Rock had practically turned a murky brown. There was no sense in continuing. If the creature didn't smell this bait, then it either wasn't here, or it wasn't interested. He wiped his hands with a sanitary cloth, then stepped to a cooler near the back cabin entrance.

"Good thing I packed lunch," he joked. He opened the cooler with his boot and pulled out a wrapped sandwich. There was no laughter, not even a smirk. Even Jesse looked like a braindead zombie.

"Maybe it's not here," she said. Everyone turned to look at Hugh, who was standing near the port railing. He shook his head.

"I doubt it. This area has served it well in providing prey so far. It would have to endure a few days of malnourishment before it gave up and moved further out."

"That's probably what happened," Ben said. "Doc, I don't know if you've noticed, but I haven't seen anything larger than a sardine come take a bite out of our chum trail. I think your fish has driven everything out of the area."

"Maybe it's scared of the boat," Jesse suggested. "It's only forty-feet long. The boat's a hundred-twenty? It probably thinks we're a big whale or something."

Hugh shook his head. "Not that thing. Even if it thought that, that wouldn't stop it from attacking. It knows no fear."

"Does it know boredom?" Lewis said. He had set his camera down and pulled a folding chair from the storage compartment. "I think it's moved on. There's no reason it wouldn't take our bait."

"Maybe it prefers live prey?" Sammy suggested.

"No," Hugh said, shaking his head. "It doesn't discriminate between the dead and the living. It must keep feeding because of its metabolic rate."

"Well, I think that goes back to the argument that it's no longer here," Jesse said. "Like Ben said, we haven't seen a single fish, let alone a forty-foot creature."

"That's what worries me," Hugh said. "I think, when we see it, it might be bigger than forty-feet. I think it's undergoing an evolution after feeding a considerable amount."

"An evolution?" Sammy said. "You didn't mention that before."

"I mentioned it grew remarkably fast, Chief," Hugh said. "I thought we had plenty of time before. But now, I'm starting to wonder…"

"So, wait a second, you said this thing is evolving?" Derrick said.

"Possibly," Hugh said.

"And how big will it get?"

"*IF* it's growing, it may be as large as sixty feet," Hugh answered. There were a few groans across the deck, accompanied by accusatory stares. "Hey, listen, I'm surprised it hasn't shown up just as much as you are. I was sure we'd be heading in by now." Nobody responded. The only one who didn't have a bitter expression on his face was Derrick. To add to Hugh's stress, Lewis had the camera pointed. Hugh initially wanted to verbally assault him with a barrage of f-bombs, but knew it would accomplish nothing but add to the tension.

"Listen," he continued, "if, and I do mean *if*, it's grown…it won't change a thing. It'll go after the bait. We'll hit it with the electricity. Stop the bastard's heart. End of story. And Derrick will have an even bigger trophy, and the show will get more hits. Right?"

Derrick's smile returned. A sixty-foot creature did make bigger headlines than forty.

"You know how the game works, Doc. I like it," he replied.

"He might, but it doesn't change the fact that we're empty handed." Melvin marched out on the deck, glazy eyed from lack of stimulation. "I've been turning that wheel for hours. I thought we'd be reeling in a Serpent by now."

"Just a little longer," Sammy said.

"It's not the time, it's the progress," Melvin said. He pointed his thumb at Jesse. "I'm with the officer here; I don't think the thing is out here. I think we should branch further out."

Sammy turned to Hugh. "Is there any other reason it would leave its territory?"

Hugh shrugged. "Only if hunting's scarce, it might branch further out, then return. Only if food was scarce for several miles out in any direction would it vacate permanently." He shrugged again, making it clear he wasn't confident that was the case.

"Well, shit, then," Melvin said. "I say we try and take it further east."

Sammy nodded. "I think it's worth a shot. If we turn up empty handed, we'll come back here and see if the thing's returned. Agreed?"

"Aye!" Melvin immediately answered with a raised hand.

"I'm good with it," Jesse said.

"I think it's worth a shot," Ben said.

"What do you think, Dr. Meyer?" Sammy asked.

"I suppose it's worth a shot," Hugh said. It was evident in his voice that he wasn't convinced, but he couldn't deny the fact that they were empty handed so far.

"Alright. Let's head east," she said.

"Yes, Captain," Melvin quipped, then scuttled back to the pilothouse.

CHAPTER 33

For Sergeant Shier, the one good thing about being on boat patrol all day was that he was out of the public eye, and thus, he could smoke a cigar on the job. With the water vacant, there was nobody to complain about the use of tobacco, and he knew that the Chief wouldn't mind in this particular instance. He was on his second one now, and was glad he planned for a long day, because it was turning out to be one. And judging by the Chief's recent transmission about going further east, it was looking to be an even longer day.

Officer Barber was at the helm. On the trash bin beside him were two empty water bottles and a can of coke, with an open one in the cupholder. He was swaying back and forth uncomfortably, sparking a chuckle from the Sergeant.

"What's going on there, Barber? Gonna go in your pants?"

"Very funny, Sergeant. We've been out here for over three hours. Coming up on four," Barber said.

Shier's eyes widened. "Don't tell me it's a number-two issue..."

"No, thank God. Just really need to take a leak," Barber said. Shier relaxed, then laughed again.

"Then what are you waiting for?"

Barber glanced back at him. "What are you talking about? There's no bathrooms on this little boat."

"There's a bathroom all around us," Shier replied, pointing at the water.

"Yeah...isn't there something in the manual about indecent exposure?" Barber said.

"Okay...under normal circumstances, yes. But there's NOBODY here," Shier said. "Just point it between the bars and let loose. It's not like anyone's watching. Just make sure your bodycam's not pointed at it."

"Yeah, they'll think we've found the Serpent," Barber retorted. He went for the railing and unzipped. The stream hit the water. Allowing himself a few seconds of amusement, the officer whipped the stream side-to-side. "Here, fishy, fishy, fishy!"

"It's a Serpent. Or an eel. And be careful, he might smell it and come after you," Shier said.

"Yeah, sure," Barber said. Despite sounding unfazed, he remembered reading how some sea creatures smell blood and urine to track down prey. If the Chief hadn't found the Serpent, then maybe it had moved. What if it was lurking nearby?

Hurry up, you damn full bladder.

"Are you giving the water a blood transfusion? What's taking so long over there?" Shier said.

"Almost done," Barber said. The stream dwindled into the final few dribbles.

An earsplitting roar made him jump, pants still unzipped. He yelped and tried to secure his manhood, while spinning toward the bow. In a heartbeat, Shier went from sitting quietly to uncontrollable laughter. He wasn't alone. Barber heard more laughs behind him.

It was Murphy's boat. On the deck behind him was a fellow cop in his thirties named Pollock, who was laughing hysterically.

Shier was restraining tears at this point. He opened his mouth to speak, but couldn't get any words out. Just laughter.

Barber scrunched his face. "You motherfuckers."

The laughter doubled in intensity. Pollock was leaning over the sides, his face now beet red.

"You oughta work at a ladies club the way you whip that thing around!" he shouted.

Shier wiped his hands over his face. "Oh, gosh, my eyes are tearing up. That was so good. Glad you guys didn't blow the horn on him five seconds sooner. The amount of piss he had in there, he'd have sprayed the whole deck!"

"Given ya some Mello Yellow, huh?" Murphy said.

Now, Barber was smiling.

"You pricks. Damn it!" *Yeah-yeah, have your fun. I'll get back at you eventually.* He noticed Murphy going for the speaker mic. "What are you doing?"

"Oh, nothing. Just, providing an 'update' for the others."

Barber pointed a finger. "Don't you even think about it."

Murphy steered his boat to the side and lifted the mic to his lips. He watched Barber's expression as he spoke. "Boat Four to beach units, no sighting of the creature yet, but there is something to update you all on. If any of you come across Officer Barber, make sure to honor him by blowing your horn whenever you see him." He depressed the transmitter and smiled in anticipation for the barrage of responses. Surprisingly, there were none. "Testing. Testing. Anyone read me?"

"Sergeant Shier. This is Officer Jay. We're getting a bunch of people over here demanding to use the beach."

"We've had five people show up over on Section Ninety in the last ten minutes. Make that six—got one coming in right now, actually," another officer said.

"We're arguing with a few right now," another added.

Shier stood up, his smile immediately fading.

"How long has this been going on?"

"There's been a few here or there all morning, but now it's getting worse," Peter Jay said. *"That moron Tiffany Decker put out some sort of story, and now everyone's wanting to know the real reason they can't use the beaches."*

"Oh, that bitch," Shier said.

"What do we do, Sergeant?" Murphy asked.

"Maybe we should go back and offer assistance," Pollock suggested.

"No. We have to stay out here," Shier replied. "Be on the lookout for boats, because you can be sure people are going to say 'fuck-it' and try to go out on the water." He snatched his radio again. "All patrol boats, remain on the water. Don't head in. I repeat, *don't* head in. Branch out and be on the lookout for any civilian vessels. Arrest anyone who attempts to go on the water. Beach units, same for you. Anyone refuses to leave, detain them. I'll call the station and order a wagon."

****

"Please do," Officer Peter Jay said. Already, another car was pulling up to the beach. To the north and south, there were flashing lights of Interceptors responding to other people arriving in other areas of the beach. Right now, they were trickling in one-by-one. At this rate, they'd be dealing with an invading army before shift change.

Clarence raised a hand and approached the vehicle. "Excuse me, sir, but you have to vacate the beach immediately!"

The tourist rolled his window down and shot him a vile glare. "I made this reservation a year ago. I didn't come here to be locked in my hotel room."

"I understand, sir, but I still need you to vacate the beach."

"I just want to be on the sand! You're worried about sharks, right? Sharks don't come up on the sand, dufus!"

Peter Jay started approaching to assist, only to turn his attention on another truck that was parked by the road. Without a care in the world, the family of three inside stepped out and began unpacking their beach towels and cooler. They had seen the officers, but clearly didn't care.

The Officer braced for the inevitable argument. He looked to the east. Somewhere on that horizon line, Chief Russell was out there hunting the thing. "Jesus. Hurry up, you guys. Please."

CHAPTER 34

The deck had gone quiet. In two hours, they had completed several passes over the course of a mile, laying chum the entire way. Out here, there were greater hints of sea life. A few blue sharks came by, as well as some other fish. But no Serpent.

Ward was smoking on the fly deck, complaining about getting no signal on his phone. On the aft deck, Lewis had set his camera down and had drifted into a snooze. He had started this trip borderline nerve-wrecked; and now, he'd kill for anything to show up. Sammy and Ben had a little small talk between each other, while the Chief checked in with the beach units via radio.

Only Hugh appeared to have unwavering focus, though the seeds of quitting were quietly starting to form in his mind. He was now considering the possibility that the thing had moved on. He wished Ryan Burg was here to consult with.

Ryan Burg…Timestone probably had people in mind to replace his position already. Hell, they were probably looking to fill Hugh's spot right now. The company would move on with their projects and leave any collateral damage buried in the sand. The L-100-30 Hercules crash had already been reported to the public as engine failure, with details of its cargo stated to be nothing more than mere medical supplies and equipment. The Captain of the *William Travis* had confiscated the recorded footage from the submersible, which was the only proof Hugh would've had to present to the public regarding Timestone's connection to the creature.

"Anyone want coffee?" Josh called out. Most of the people on deck shook their heads.

"I'll take one, please. Black," Hugh said.

"On second thought, I'll take one too," Ben said, after initially shaking his head.

"Yeah, me too," Jesse said.

"Now that I'm thinking of it, I'll take one. And get *him* one too," Derrick said, pointing at Lewis.

"Well, gosh! You guys are more indecisive than that monster out there. Want something—then you don't want it—then you do…" He continued the cycle as he disappeared into the passageway. Some of the group chuckled, then resumed watching the sea. It wasn't long before all sense of energy was once again depleted from the deck.

Even Derrick was bored out of his mind at this point. He wished he'd packed his guitar to entertain himself. He sat in the fishing chair and watched the horizon.

"What was the first fish you ever caught?" Jesse asked him. She dragged her folding chair over by him. He glanced over at her. Clearly, she was desperate for any conversation to pass the time.

"Largemouth in my uncle's private pond in Ohio," he said. "Fourteen inches. I was four years old."

"Really?"

"Well…my dad might've set the hook for me. And he may have helped hold on to the pole as I reeled it in. But who cares when you're that age?"

"I was six," Ben chimed in. "Atlantic salmon off my dad's yacht."

"I was ten," Sammy added. "I grew up inland, fishing in the rivers of Louisiana. Caught a trout this big when I was eleven." She held her hands about eighteen-inches apart.

"Seems like our kid-selves would've been better suited for this," Ben joked.

"True. At least they caught what they were looking for," Jesse said. The group shared a small laugh. Even Hugh smiled.

Lewis was snoring now. The crackling sound of air passage was worse than the dead silence that had preceded it.

A shadow appeared on the deck, and they realized it was Ward peering down on them.

"For the love of God. I can hear him from *up here*. Somebody better do something before I drop this camera on him."

"No, don't do that," Derrick said. "Waste of good equipment." He stood up, started to approach Lewis to wake him up, then stopped. A smile came over his face. He looked at Jesse. "Play along."

He crept behind Lewis' folding chair, knelt low, then grabbed the legs. He glanced at the others to see their expressions, then shook the chair.

"Holy crap! It's got the bait. It's pulling the boat along with it! Holy Jesus!"

Lewis shot out of his chair, eyes wide, immediately seeing Jesse and Ben pointing out to stern as if they were witnessing something horrific.

"Holy shit! Where is it? Where—" He tripped over his camera, and stumbled forward. He threw his hands out to catch himself, with one plunging down right into the chum mixture. Oil and guts splashed his neck and shoulder.

The group descended into laughter. Lewis yanked his arm out, watched the ocean, then realized what just happened.

"That's what you get for falling asleep on the job!" Derrick said. He was leaning forward, hands on his knees, face beet red.

"He's all chummed up. We should hook him up to the lure!" Ben said. Sammy slapped his shoulder.

"Oh, very funny guys," Lewis said. He held up two middle fingers to the group, then high up at Ward, who was filming the event from up top.

"Don't worry, we have extra shirts," Derrick said.

"Yeah, I hope so, because I'm freaking drenched in—" Lewis jumped as the water erupted behind him. All crew members launched to their feet, thinking the creature had surfaced. Lewis stumbled again, then turned around.

The dorsal fin emerged, with a caudal fin waving eight feet behind it. It was a tiger shark. It went for the lure and started biting at the dead tuna.

"Son of a bitch knew how to make an entrance," Derrick said. The group felt a mix of relief and disappointment all at once. The shark tore away a chunk of meat, scratching its nose on the barb without impaling itself. Derrick pointed a finger at it. "Hey! Get your own!"

Right after he spoke, another shark swam by and approached the lure.

Ben shook his head. "Fabulous. We're drawing in everything except the damn eel."

"This is just great," Sammy said. "Now, we're gonna lose all of our bait from all these critters coming around."

"I think it's safe to say our plan's not working," Lewis said.

"I'm starting to think that thing might've moved on," Ben said. "Have there been any reports of strange incidents up or down the coast?"

"Not that we've received," Sammy said. She could hear the muffled transmissions on the radio from the beach units. She twisted the knob then spoke into it. "Unit One to Shier. No luck so far. Can you give me a status on the beach situation?"

"That reporter really put us in a bind," Shier replied. *"She put out a broadcast about the beaches, and now everyone is thinking it's safe to come over. The guys on shore have more people than we can handle. Chief, if you haven't found the objective, then I suggest we do a press conference, because there's so much confusion already."*

"We did a flyby, and yeah, it's a mess, Chief," Officer Lock said.

"Damn it," Sammy groaned. She closed her eyes, decided on a plan, then lifted the speaker. "Alright, we're coming in. All boats, remain on patrol. I'll have a word with the Mayor on what to do about the beach situation."

"Chief, we can't give up," Hugh said.

"Doctor, you heard the conversation. We've got people flooding the beach area."

"And you being over there isn't going to change that," Hugh said.

"We'll figure something out, believe me," she said. "Right now, my cops need my help."

Hugh raised his hands over his chest, defeated, then leaned over the side to watch the water. Derrick patted his waist in search of his two-way radio, which had fallen off and ended up in his chair.

"Hey, Melvin?"

"Yeah?"

"Return to the harbor. We're going home with an empty dish today." He secured the radio and sighed as he felt the yacht rotate. "So much for my special."

CHAPTER 35

Sergeant Shier raised the microphone to his lips as Officer Barber ignited the flashers. Up ahead were two jet boats spraying waters as they performed tight circles a few hundred feet ahead.

"This is the Spiral Bay Police Department. Please vacate the water immediately!"

One of the boats turned west and slowed. For a moment, it appeared that they were about to do as instructed. As the officers came in closer, they realized the people on board were flipping them the bird.

"Can't arrest us for being on public water!" one shouted. The other boat continued zipping about as if the cops weren't there.

"This is for your own safety," Shier replied.

"Since when did cops care about safety," another young buck shouted. The Sergeant felt his blood boil. There were too many people out here. More boats were coming in from the harbor. He had stationed three officers out there, but they must've been overpowered by the mob. Not to mention all the private docks lining the nearby coast.

Officer Murphy had moved a mile northward to engage with vessels coming from that direction.

Back at the beach, the police placed barriers to prevent people from coming in. Most didn't risk climbing over, but many of them remained to protest the lack of access.

In the middle of it all was Tiffany Decker as well as a half dozen other reporters. Her cameraman stood with his back to their van, filming Tiffany and the crowds behind her.

"Behind me, you can see that the police have sectioned off the beaches. The official explanation is a shark attack. But is that really the case? Do they really need to close off the sand areas for a shark? What is the *real* purpose behind this? Why would the Mayor approve of such a tactic that is bound to hurt the local economy? As I speak, police are intercepting vessels in the water. Boats. I don't know about you, but I've never heard of a case of sharks sinking yachts and speedboats. Forgive the pun, but it all seems a bit 'fishy' to me. My word to the local government: Don't rely on lies. Tell everyone what's really going on. And open the beaches. People are paying big money to be here, and they didn't come with the intent of spending all of their vacation in cafes."

****

"That stupid, self-centered bitch," Sammy grunted. As soon as she was able to get a signal on her phone, she got on the internet to look for any current reports regarding Spiral Bay. What she got was a live report from Tiffany Decker, who undoubtedly was stirring the town up, which would lead to inevitable conflict with the police, which in turn, would create more coverage.

"We need to tell them what's really going on. If that thing comes to shore…" Jesse said.

Sammy nodded. There was no choice. Yesterday, it seemed like a simple enough matter to warn people from the beach, kill the beast, and prevent a mass panic. But she didn't account for Tiffany Decker lurking in the area like the snake she was.

They passed Lebbon Rock and started southwest for the harbor. Josh had stepped out to embrace the sunshine, after being stuck in the engine room for several hours.

"What a waste," he said, mirroring Derrick's disappointment.

"Eh, maybe we'll try again tomorrow," Derrick replied.

"What if it doesn't show then?"

"Then we won't have a show, I guess. All of this effort would be wasted," Derrick answered. Sammy snickered, then looked away. Derrick turned toward her. "Problem there, Chiefy?"

"No, nothing, Mr. Crevello," Sammy replied.

"Free speech is allowed on this vessel. No consequences," he said.

"No, it's nothing. Really."

"Spoken like every girlfriend I ever had," he said. Sammy sighed.

"It's really not my place. You're doing us a great service. You've allowed us use of your boat, which can't be understated…"

"Yet, you've got a problem with something…"

Sammy hesitated to answer. He didn't seem angry, but he didn't have that particular happy-go-lucky persona that she had grown used to either.

"This thing has killed people. We're trying to keep it from killing more. The failure of this expedition means it may kill more. Yet, you're more concerned with how it'll affect the ratings of your show. Doesn't it seem like a little bit of bad taste?"

"I don't know. Aren't documentaries about man-eating crocs in bad taste?" Derrick replied. "Or shows featuring sharks tearing people in two? What about all the movies that are released every year?"

"What you're referring to are either make-believe or strictly educational," Sammy answered. "This isn't. We're trying to stop a real creature responsible for the deaths of eight people—"

"More than that," Hugh added.

"I just don't see it as a laughing matter," Sammy concluded.

Derrick shrugged his shoulders. "I'm in the business of making money, Chief. I mean, aren't we all? Look at him," he pointed at Hugh, "Not saying you're a bad guy, doc, but don't tell me you made this creature just for the smiles."

Hugh didn't reply. He wished he hadn't chimed in at all. Who was he to judge anyway? This creature wouldn't exist if not for him, and all those people would still be alive. If anything, he should've been grateful Derrick had the good character to not stack all the blame on him.

"Doesn't matter anyway," Lewis said. He was wearing a black t-shirt, his Hawaiian one discarded after the chum incident. "Creature didn't show up. Not sure the studio wants footage of us cruising about for five hours. So, we're not making money off of this incident."

For the next minute, nobody spoke a word. Everyone on deck had the self-awareness to realize that the frustrations were finally starting to take their toll, and that they were moments away from pointing their fingers at each other.

Sammy glanced at her phone again and saw more reports from other agencies. *No wonder I'm pissed. And I'm taking it out on the guy who's helping me.* She stood up and walked around to the forward deck. Way in the distance, she could see flashing strobes from officers trying to intercept various vessels.

Back on the aft deck, Derrick leaned on the transom next to Jesse and stared out at the ocean.

"You feel the same way?" he asked her.

"Hmm?" She pretended not to know what he was talking about.

"Oh, come on. You were standing right here."

Jesse shook her head. "I don't know. The issue crossed my mind, but I guess it didn't bother me too much because, for one, the end result would be the same. Creature would be dead...considering it'd show up in the first place. Two...it's kind of exciting."

Derrick smiled. "Yeah? Really?"

"Let's face it. How many people get to say they're hunting a giant sea monster? I feel your state of mind," Jesse said.

"Girl, you're getting sexier all the time," Derrick said. "You're a daredevil at heart."

"I guess I am."

They shared a laugh, then leaned in to kiss, then jumped as something splashed near the lure.

Jesse caught her breath when she saw the dorsal fin. "That damn tiger shark again!"

The brown, striped fish went for the bait and bit one of the tunas, only to suddenly jerk away after getting probed by the barb. Derrick chuckled as it circled back again, not ready to give up the chase.

The others grouped at the transom and shared a unifying laugh as they watched it close in again.

"We should film it and say that's our deadly shark," Jesse said. Sammy, who stood at the starboard corner, nodded and smiled.

The fish fluttered its tail, opened its mouth, and lunged to bite. Water sprayed all around it, and suddenly the shark was lifted ten feet out of the water. Its head and tail fluttered, sticking out from the jaws of the huge Serpent that ambushed it.

"Ah, SHIT!" Derrick exclaimed, leaping back with the others. Lewis fell as he reached for his camera, while the rest of the crew stumbled clumsily, their guard having been let down.

The Serpent pressed its jaws down like a guillotine, severing the shark's head and tail, then swallowing the midsection. It dove down into the bloody water, sending large swells crashing into the back of the boat.

"My god, it's here," Sammy said.

"Time to party," Derrick said. "Josh, get your ass back in the engine room." Without saying a word, the TV sidekick raced below deck. Derrick watched the water. The thing's shape could be seen moving about. It was studying the lure with interest. "Alright, this is our moment of truth!"

"Should Josh hook up the cable now?" Jesse asked.

"No!" Ben said. "If the creature is shocked too soon, it might pull away before he can secure himself on the barbs."

"That's gonna happen any moment now," Derrick said. "He's watching it. He's like a bass following a jitterbug. Hey, Doc? You said he might have evolved? He looks to be the same size to me."

"I concur," Hugh said. He sounded bewildered at the assessment. "He must've wandered out of the area during our initial pass."

"Well, he'll be out again shortly...in the deli market!" Derrick said.

Sammy, Jesse, and Ben readied their rifles. Cocking levers clicked into place and muzzles were aimed at the water.

"Russell to Shier, we've located the target. I repeat, we've located the target. Do whatever you have to do to get people out of the water."

"I'm doing the best I can, Chief. There're too many people out here, and they're not listening. You HAVE to kill that thing!"

"We're on it," she said. *Please, God, let this work.*

The beast was shallowing. Its snout couldn't have been more than inches from the water.

"Come on," Ben muttered.

"You know you want it," Derrick said. Lewis the cameraman held back with the camera over his shoulder, while Wade filmed from up high. All hands tensed as they waited for the inevitable snap.

That tension released with simultaneous jolts as the beast lunged for the lure. It snapped its jaws tight, then reared back in pain.

"It's caught! It's caught!" Derrick shouted. The cable lashed in the water, then extended to the max as the creature started to run. Derrick snatched his radio from his belt. "Josh! Hook it up now! Do it! Do it!"

The creature pulled again, rocking the yacht backward.

The engine room suddenly turned on a slant, sending Josh tumbling from the terminal. The boat was being rocked by a creature a third of its size...all the more reason he didn't want it slithering aboard.

"Don't know what you're waiting for, Josh!"

"I'm trying!" Josh said, not into the radio but to himself. He climbed the 'slope' and found the terminal. "Let's spice up your meal, you oversized worm." He connected the clamp, then grabbed his radio to alert the others. "Cable attached!"

Electricity streamed from the roaring engine and traveled at lightspeed to the lure.

The beast was hit by a powerful force it had never experienced. Intense heat surged through the soft flesh in its mouth. With that heat came a loss of bodily control. Its tail spasmed and coiled. The beast had lost all will. Its heart fluttered, on the verge of bursting.

"Yeah!" Derrick shouted.

"Yes! It's working!" Sammy exclaimed.

"Another minute should do the trick," Hugh said. He held his hands in front of his chest, as though silently praying.

Derrick high-fived Jesse, then turned to the camera. "Ladies and gentlemen, what you're seeing here is the world's deadliest beast, on the verge of losing a very brief battle to the great Derrick Crevello...and the Spiral Bay Police Department." He held a hand toward Sammy, whom Lewis panned toward. Relieved that the plan was working, she decided to play along and smile for the camera.

"Town's gonna be thanking you when they see this," Derrick continued.

"They better. They—" Sammy watched the creature, noticing a huge plume of smoke billowing from its jaws. "Wow! Are we hitting it with *that* much electricity?"

The smoke started trailing their way.

Ben winced after sniffing it. "That doesn't smell like burning flesh. That smells more like...chemical fumes."

With a loud *ping*, the lure snapped, the cable slashing the air as it whipped to the side. The creature spat the lure and dove deep, its body jittery and in pain from the strange assault.

Ben watched the lure crash down a few feet away from the boat. Lewis rushed to his side to film it. He zoomed in. The barbs were gone, the lure itself shriveled and breaking apart. Smoke billowed while it bobbed in the water.

"Bastard did a number on this," he said.

Ben looked over at Hugh, who looked equally as dumbfounded.

"Doc? Is it just me, or is that acid corrosion?"

Lewis lifted his head from the eyepiece. "Acid?"

A thunderous impact struck the boat from underneath, rocking it to port. Lewis leaned against the transom, fumbling to keep hold of his camera. Water splashed his face, blinding him to the huge serpentine head that rose from the water.

"Oh shit!" Ben said. He aimed his rifle at the beast and fired. Hugh and Derrick backed to the starboard side, while Jesse and Sammy joined the fray. Bullets stung its face and neck. The beast opened its jaw, dripping blood from the roof. It bobbed its head, seeing the three people with the loud objects, and a fourth with a similarly colored piece of equipment.

Ben saw the smoke rising from the back of its mouth.

Acid...this thing spits acid!

"Clear the deck!" He took a step to pull Lewis out of the way, but immediately realized there was no time, and instead lunged for the side-deck to avoid the incoming nightmare.

The beast extended its jaws and bobbed forward as though to vomit. A hot yellow-green liquid sprayed the cameraman. The equipment dropped, not because he let go—as his hands were still clutching it. He raised his stubby forearms and turned around, screaming in agony. The acid had already consumed his facial features, and turned his flesh into mush. His forehead peeled away, revealing the smoldering skull underneath.

Panic swept the deck...which was also heavily corroding from the acid spray. It only took a few seconds for the portside corner to fold inward. The creature hammered its jaw down on the weakened second, smashing it to smoking fragments, and squelching what remained of Lewis.

Ben gritted his teeth and grabbed the rail to prevent himself from rolling overboard. The deck behind him had been pulverized, and now water was flooding the ship. Up above, he heard Melvin arrive on the fly deck.

"What the hell happened?"

"Get back inside. EVERYONE inside!" Ben shouted. He found an entrance and opened it, then heard the thrashing of water behind him. He glanced back just enough to see it in his peripheral vision, then slammed the door shut behind him.

Acid breath sprayed the side of the ship. Hot steam billowed from the bulkheads. Ben covered his mouth and coughed. The door was already peeling off its hinges, the frames corroding before his very eyes.

He heard screams from outside, then lost his balance as the yacht pitched to port. Next came the crackling of the side-passage-deck, overhead, and the corroding walls. The beast was slithering aboard the ship. Ben heard the screams again. They were Wade's.

Even while screaming, the cameraman kept his camera propped over his shoulder. It was not a dedication to the show or a loyalty to Derrick Crevello that kept him on the fly deck: he was frozen by fear. The beast rose, its snout bloody and reeking of breath and charred flesh. Now it wasn't just fear keeping Wade frozen, but the fictional belief that if he remained perfectly still, somehow he'd go unnoticed.

Only the pull of gravity snapped Wade out of his panic-coma. The boat leaned further to port, pulling him right for its jaws. Finally, he turned to rush for the wheelhouse.

The Serpent lashed out like a rattlesnake but bit like a crocodile. It took Wade in its jaws, pierced his trunk with its teeth, then worked his pulped corpse into its gullet.

The beast heard movement from inside the ship. The fly deck splintered as the creature slithered over it. There was no movement on any of the decks. The humans had all retreated inside.

Bobbing its head back, the creature summoned its new evolution. Its weapon, used by its ancient ancestors to combat larger reptiles of the land and sea, would now be used to draw its prey out of their hiding place. The beast filled the newly developed sacks within its throat with acid, then ejected the fluid over the top of the ship.

"Holy God! We're gonna die!" Melvin croaked. As he ran downstairs from the pilothouse, the overhead had collapsed from the creature's weight. He could smell the acid breaking over the top. He found himself in the main cabin with the rest of the group.

"Where's Wade?" Derrick asked.

"He never came in. That thing's breaking us apart," Melvin answered. Another pitch sent all six people stumbling to starboard. The creature was now smashing the upper decks, which were now weakened by its acid. The pilothouse was flying apart like feathers.

The smell intensified. Next came smoke. All eyes went up. Drops of acid trickled from the overhead.

"Oh, we're screwed," Josh said.

"Shut up," Sammy snapped. She reloaded her rifle and clutched her speaker mic. "Unit One to Aerial. Where are you, Lock?"

"We see you! We're coming in right now. I'll get the bastard off of you!"

Josh rushed to the broken window and looked up. The helicopter swept in like a hummingbird and turned to the side, allowing the sniper to take aim at the creature.

Another voice shouted over the frequency. *"Chief? What the hell's going on over there?!"*

"Sergeant," Sammy had to keep from shouting and adding to the panic, "You *HAVE* to get everyone out of the water. The plan failed and we're under attack. It'll go after everybody! It—
"

The creature slithered to the portside, rocking the ship again, and knocking Sammy headfirst into a wall. She fell to her knees, half-conscious. Ben and Hugh rushed to her side and pulled her up.

"Sammy!" Ben said.

The crack of a gunshot drew their gazes to the window. The chopper was hovering fifty yards over the port quarter.

"He's too close," Ben said. He snatched Sammy's mic off her uniform and shouted into it. "Chopper unit. You're too close. The thing sprays acid! Back off! I repeat! Back off!"

Lock landed another round between the creature's eyes.

"Come on, you bastard," he growled. He chambered the next round and aimed the crosshairs for its eyes. The beast constantly moved, making the shot improbable. Instead, he went for a wider target: the open mouth.

The creature was balancing on its lower half, which was coiled on the upper decks, or rather, what remained of them. The center-top of the yacht looked like a partially crushed soda can, with the sides buckling downward.

Lock steadied his aim and fired, seeing a small cloud of blood erupt from the thing's mouth.

"Ha! I knew I could hurt ya!" He watched the thing coil its neck backward. Its jaw clenched, its throat expanding. "Choking on it, are ya?!"

The beast tilted its head high and lunged. Lock's smile instantly disappeared, and simultaneously, he and Officer Hayes screamed in horror as a boiling hot liquid sprayed the hull.

Hayes banked the chopper to starboard. The windshield and portside window were covered in smoking green acid. In the fuselage behind him, he heard horrid screams, and frantic movements. He peered back through the passageway.

"Lock? You alri—" His jaw dropped as he saw the faceless head of the sniper looking back at him. The eye sockets were exposed, completely barren except for liquified flesh that dangled from the edges. The fingers were coiled, also burnt to the bone. Then in the blink of an eye, Lock dropped dead.

Alarms rang throughout the cockpit. *Rotor failure. Engine damage. Fuel pump failure.*

Hayes sucked in a breath, accidentally taking in the toxic fumes, which led to uncontrollable gagging. He felt the chopper descending. He pulled up on the joystick. *Climb!* It did for a moment, until the rotors grinded and broke apart. He was now freefalling.

Water rushed in through the melted windshield, knocking Hayes into the back of his seat.

The beast hissed as it watched the flying object go down. Eager to finish the fight, it plunged into the water and swam the few hundred feet of distance. It immediately found the skeletal body of the human in the fuselage, and snatched him up to digest whatever nutrients it could get from him. It arched its head to the cockpit, where a second human struggled to escape.

It wasted no time lashing at the weakened hull, peeling the top off like the lid of a can of spam. The human raised his arms over his eyes and screamed one final time. The Serpent impaled him in its jaws, shook him side-to-side, mashed his flesh and bones, then gulped.

It took a moment to rest and inspect the chopper for any other victims. Movement to the west caught its eye. In the distance were several vessels, most of which were much smaller than the one behind it. Though not likely to carry as much prey, they were likely much more accessible.

And there were dozens! It was looking at a buffet. And after the strenuous demands of its recent evolution, the Serpent desperately needed sustenance.

It didn't bother to look back at the yacht behind it. Had easier prey not been available, it would've returned instantly to finish the job. And should it still be there after it had finished, then it would seek out the humans inside once and for all. But for now, its interest lay in the vast activity levels on the horizon.

It dipped under the water and raced into attack formation.

"Where's it going?" Derrick asked.

"Is it coming back?" Melvin asked.

"Get out of the way, please," Jesse said. She held her breath to avoid breathing in the fumes and raised her binoculars to her eyes. "Oh, God. It's moving for shore."

As if hit with an adrenaline shot, Sammy went from half-conscious to bursting with energy. She fumbled for her radio, still dazed, only to realize Ben was still holding it. She took it back and held it in front of her face. This time, there was no calm to her voice.

"All units! Vacate the beaches! Clear the water! It's coming right for you!"

CHAPTER 36

"Come on, damn it! Move the boat!" Shier shouted, cupping his hand over his mic as he argued with a boat owner.

"There's nothing out here!" the defiant fisherman said. The boat owner shrugged from the fly deck.

"Gotta make a living, Sarge!"

Shier knew the man; Simon Brecht. Normally a nice guy, unless it got in the way of turning a profit.

"Won't make much after the fine!" Shier replied.

"You've worked here how long? And still don't know how much these people pay? Bring on the fine!" Simon said.

Shier kicked the transom. There were boats EVERYWHERE now. Nobody was listening, and even if he could somehow arrest them all, where would he put them? Adding to the overwhelming chaos was the non-stop traffic on the radio, and the uncertainty of what was happening with the operation. Half of Chief Russell's traffic was muffled with static, but it was clear that something had gone horribly wrong.

He heard screams to the east, followed by explosive booms of heavy impact.

"Christ!" Barber shouted, pointing at a speedboat that had been flipped over, bow over stern. It had twisted in midair and smashed into another vessel. The fuel tanks of both boats ruptured, sparked, and erupted into a gargantuan ball of flame.

The screams continued, and all at once, several of the defiant boaters turned to shore. Raising its head behind them was the Serpent. In its jaws was a human, bleeding profusely as he was mashed into jelly.

It hadn't even swallowed yet before it pushed through the flaming wreckage. It closed in on another vessel, tucked its head under the waterline, then flipped the boat over. The two people on board screamed as they were flung into the water. The Serpent swallowed its current prize then went for the next. It grabbed the first of the two by the legs, then yanked its head back, tearing the man in two. For a brief moment, his arms paddled the water before his brain shut down. Consciousness faded just in time, sparing him from the horror of being swallowed whole.

His companion paddled blindly, unsure of what direction she was going. She felt the swell of something large drawing near. She screamed, thinking it was the beast, then saw the sun's reflection off the bow of a retreating vessel. The man on the helm shrieked and tried cutting the wheel once he saw her, but it was too late. Her brains splattered over the underside of the boat, doubling the speedboater's panic and dismay.

"Oh my god! Oh my god!" He spun back, unsure of where he was going. At this point, he didn't care. He just needed to get away from the scene. He completed his circle and throttled to shore, only to see the dragon-like jaws a hundred feet ahead of him. He screamed and veered to starboard, hardly noticing the stream of yellow-green fluid raining down on him. Not until he felt it burn through his flesh.

He could see his knuckles poking through his skin. His shirt and pants started peeling away, revealing the mushy flesh and blood underneath. Right before passing out, he saw another boat ahead of him. It was a yacht carrying ten people. He never felt the impact.

The speedboat struck the yacht and exploded, pulverizing the starboard side and flipping the sixty-foot vessel over. All hands plummeted into the water, the swells pushing them far and apart.

The swells doubled in size, pushed along by the Serpent. It slithered toward the easy prey, snatching one of them out of the water. It clamped its jaws over the trunk, severing all four limbs at once. It crushed the body and gulped, then snatched another out of the water. Legs and blood rained down, while the upper half of the body was consumed.

A smack of its tail launched another victim into the overturned yacht, splattering his body against the hull. Red mist and body parts rained into the water, further panicking the remaining college-age people racing for safety.

Suddenly, Simon Brecht was no longer arguing. He cut the wheel and throttled to the harbor.

All vessels in the vicinity converged on the harbor like a flock of geese. As they closed in, they began crowding each other.

There was nothing Sergeant Shier could do but hope that they made it to safety. He yanked the M4 from the cargo hold, loaded a thirty-round mag, then took position by the starboard ledge, while Barber steered the vessel toward the beast. It was raising its head high, the person in its jaws squelching. Boat Seven and Six were already approaching from the north, their officers on deck armed with rifles.

Next came the cracks from rapid three-round bursts. Rifle rounds crashed into the creature's neck, only to spark like firecrackers against the hard scales. The beast dropped the dead victim and turned its eyes on the challengers.

It returned fire on the nearest one. The helmsman on Boat Seven let out a scream as he, and the cockpit, were burned away by the corrosive regurgitation. The hull withered away like a dying plant, its operator quickly void of all recognition, leaving the gunman behind him a terrified wreck. He emptied his magazine into the beast, making a defiant last stand before it lashed its tail like a whip.

The tip caught him across the waist. The two halves plopped in the water roughly twenty feet back, the torso landing a few meters away from the hips and legs.

Boat Six veered to port and throttled east, the gunner unleashing a volley at the Serpent's face. It jolted from the stings, the eyes closing shut to protect the vulnerable flesh.

It reared its head, then hyperextended its jaws. Only a few drops of acid sprinkled from its throat. The acid sacks had been drained, forcing the beast to resort to its teeth and tail to combat the aggressors.

It ducked into the water and slithered. The gunner depressed the trigger, launching the tiny rockets into the shape traveling under the water. It was like shooting a brick wall…a brick wall with teeth.

Those teeth were the first thing he saw emerge from the immense splash. Next, he felt their needle tips pierce his skin, and like a child with an action figure, it lifted his bleeding body off the deck. The helmsman looked over his shoulder, caught a glimpse of the horrific sight, as well as the tail that slashed from his left. It took his head off like a golf ball off its tee. Blood burst from the neck stub like flame on a match. The headless body staggered, twisted, then fell over the side, leaving the unmanned boat continuing to race east.

Shier shouldered his rifle. "Get us closer." Barber turned around, his thoughts evident as the glare on his face: *Are you insane?* "Do it!"

"Fuck! Sarge, I'm not going anywhere near that thing!" he stated. Shier opened his mouth to argue, but held back. The

Officer was right; they couldn't hurt it with bullets. Engaging with it would only spell certain death.

He grabbed his radio. "Chief! We're gonna need the National Guard. The Coast Guard! Hell, give the damn Space Force its first mission! This thing's gone berserk!" He waited. "Chief?"

"Sergeant, do the best you can," Sammy replied. Shier could tell by the urgency in her voice as well as the background chatter, that she was in distress.

"Chief? What's going on? Where are you?"

"We're still on the yacht. It's sinking. We're gonna have to abandon ship," she said.

"You have a way off?"

"There's two life rafts here on the boat. We're prepping them now. Just focus on getting everyone to safety."

"Chief, you'll be easy pickings coming in from out there. Where's the chopper?"

"Gone."

"What?!" Shier ran his fingers over his face. *It brought down a damn helicopter?!* His body tensed so hard, Barber almost thought he was having a seizure. He closed his eyes, breathed, then overcame the tension. "We're coming out to you. Just stand by."

"Sarge?!"

Shier looked ahead and saw the beast turning around. It was heading directly for shore.

"Oh crap!"

"What do we do?" Barber asked. "Sarge. SARGE?!"

Shier screamed into his radio. "All units! Clear the beach! It's coming ashore!"

Officer Peter Jay helped a fallen civilian to her feet and pushed her along until she was able to run inland. Clarence York was at the shoreline, helping a few people who had narrowly dodged an incoming boat.

Vessels were racing to shore like landing crafts on Normandy Beach, their owners abandoning the crafts and sprinting to town.

Shier's transmission was lost in the deafening screams of fleeing civilians. Several of them passed a white van, where Tiffany Decker observed the chaos.

"As you can see, it's pure mayhem! Whatever the police were hiding has come to light. There is carnage everywhere.

Boats have crashed. People are being mutilated. It's like a warzone. First responders are doing their best to control the chaos, but there's so much going on over a wide area, it's impossible to—"

The cameraman panned away from her and aimed at the increasingly large swells. Tiffany turned to look, then gasped when she saw the snake-like monstrosity glide ashore. It raised its head and lunged at a fishing vessel that had just struck the sandbank a moment prior. It shattered the wheelhouse with a devastating headbutt, then snapped its jaws at the man inside. The severed waist splattered blood, the upper half still thrashing in the mouth of the beast.

Clarence York shrieked, then fumbled for his firearm. He tugged twice, failing to undo the strap in the intensity of the moment. The creature turned and looked in his direction. The rookie stumbled backward, failing a third time to free the weapon. Finally, he turned around and ran for his life.

The beast glided over the sand, reared its head back, opened its jaws, ready to snap. Bullets struck its snout. The beast turned its attention on Peter, who continued firing his Glock. It shuddered a couple of times from each strike, then slithered his way.

"Fuck this," Peter Jay said, then ran with the rookie toward town. The creature hissed and pursued the humans, who ran past a large white vehicle, where two other humans foolishly stood. One, carrying a large black object over his shoulder, finally had the good sense to move, while the other stood frozen in fear.

Tiffany Decker babbled her last few words into her microphone. She had not expected to see such a horrific creature, let alone see it come on land. The slamming of the van door and the starting of its engine shocked her into reality.

Her cameraman was abandoning her!

"Hey, wait for me, you stupid—"

The creature clamped its jaws around her and bashed her into the sand, pulverizing any trace of her identity. It lashed its tail at the fleeing van, sending it fishtailing to the left. The driver spun the wheel, screaming for God's mercy, which ended in hellfire consuming him as the vehicle skidded around the back of a shop and into a propane tank.

A ball of flame erupted, flipping the van and two nearby trucks over, their fuel tanks simultaneously combusting like fireworks.

The beast backed away, repelled by the sudden heat, and slithered back into the water.

Peter and Clarence stopped to catch their breath, each shaking as another secondary explosion popped off. The experienced officer holstered his weapon then found his radio.

"Sarge…it's returning to the water. It's going back." He let the speaker mic drop, then watched the smoldering news van.

Shier held his binoculars to his eyes. He could see the smoke, as well as the movement of several people, including his officers. There were swells heading eastward, pushed along by the creature's mass.

Hearing the sound of an approaching boat engine, he lowered the glasses. It was Murphy and Pollock, both physically and emotionally drained from the horrific events they just witnessed.

"Switch off your flashers. Let's not draw its attention," the Sergeant ordered. Murphy quickly complied. They watched for another moment to make sure it wasn't coming their way. So far, it was continuing east.

"Oh, shit. The Chief's still out there," Murphy said.

"I know," Shier said. He kept an eye on the swells, which were roughly a thousand feet to the north. "It's going back to Lebbon Rock."

"It'll come across the Chief. They'll have no chance," Barber said.

"Nor will we if we head out," Pollock added.

"If you want, you can swim back to shore," Shier said. "I'm not leaving the Chief and the others to get torn apart by the thing. Barber, take us out. Full throttle."

"What can we do, though, Sarge? You saw what it did to the other vessels," Murphy said.

Shier thought for a moment. Murphy's logic was sound. He was on board with saving the Chief, but what good would their efforts be if it only resulted in the beast sinking their vessels and killing them as well?

The drone of chopper blades caught his attention. He gazed up, seeing at least three news choppers flying overhead.

"Flag 'em. Flag them down," he spoke urgently. "What frequency are they on?"

CHAPTER 37

The stern was completely submerged, the bow now pointed up at a forty-five degree angle. The waterline had crept past the port and starboard quarters and was gradually going past the middeck.

The six survivors gathered on the small foredeck. Derrick and Melvin inflated two red life rafts. Each came with a small motor that had to be attached manually, which would be enough to return to land. The downside was that they weren't strong motors, and would have no chance outrunning the beast should it appear again.

"Is Shier coming?" Josh asked. It was the third time in ten minutes he asked that question.

"He said he's on his way," Sammy said. She clutched her rifle and looked to the west. "Is that smoke?"

"It went to shore," Hugh said. "It's unstoppable."

"No shit. It spits acid?" Melvin said. Hugh could feel the barrage of accusations cocking back, ready to spring his way.

"We had discovered sacks in the throats of the species we uncovered in the North Pole," he said. "It was unclear at the time what they were for. Our marine biologist suspected they were for spitting venom, like a cobra."

"Well, I'd say close but no cigar," Ben said.

Hugh rubbed his brow. How long had the thing been developing acid? Is that how it managed to escape the steel container before it doubled in size?

Perhaps it started developing acid, but hadn't evolved enough to control it. Perhaps that's why we didn't find it until now. It was fully developing its throat sacs to contain the fluid, and waited on the ocean bottom until its evolution was complete.

He gripped the rail as the bow raised further. The group converged at the tip. They heard a crashing sound from within the *Liddy*; something in the passageways was collapsing. Now, the boat was sinking with increased speed.

"Alright, everyone in the rafts," Sammy instructed.

"We're dead meat," Josh said.

"Dude, shut up and get in," Derrick said. He dropped one of the rafts into the water, then skidded down the deck, and hopped inside. Jesse followed, her legs splashing down over the edge. Derrick pulled her in completely, then raised his hands to help Melvin and Josh get aboard. Meanwhile, Sammy, Ben, and Hugh boarded the other. The yacht slipped further, until the stern struck the bottom with a muffled *crunch!* The bow swung to the right then slipped beneath the waves. The rafts bobbed in the swells.

"Should we go for the mainland or to Lebbon Rock?" Ben asked.

"If we trap ourselves in Lebbon Rock, we may as well offer ourselves up to the thing. That lighthouse won't provide any protection at this point," Hugh explained.

"So, I guess we'll chance going to the mainland," Sammy said. Ben and Derrick yanked the ripcords to their motors, sparking propeller rotation. Slowly, the vessels went east.

Jesse held her rifle in her lap as she watched the water bounce from the rubber hull.

"We'll be fine," Derrick said. It was odd to hear him speak without the intense enthusiasm he was known for. There was a level of shock in his eyes. She wondered whether it was from the loss of his ship, or the death of the cameramen, or the show. Maybe all of the above.

"I know," she said.

The TV star watched the horizon, then leaned forward.

"What's that?" He pointed to the right. They saw flashing lights on a police boat speeding to the east.

"That's one of ours," Sammy said. "Patrol unit! Turn fifteen degrees starboard." There was no response. She checked her radio to make sure it wasn't wet or damaged. "This is the Chief…"

Ben and Derrick steered the rafts closer to the vessel. There was nobody aboard.

"What the hell?" Melvin said.

"Good God," Josh said in despair. "They came for us, and it got them first! We're totally dead." Melvin grabbed him by the collar, his face red.

"Dude, you knock that shit off, or I swear to God, I'll—"

"Knock that shit off, you two! Jesus," Jesse snapped.

"Chief, you think you can intercept it in time and get aboard?" Derrick called. The thought had already crossed her mind. Sammy and Ben exchanged spots, the latter positioning himself to grab hold of the side ladder. Sammy steered to the right, then angled back to the left, ready to pass within inches of the incoming police boat. It was coming in rather fast, forcing her to carefully measure the distance between them.

Ben balanced on one knee, held his hands at his chest, then threw himself at the diving ladder. The raft skidded against the hull, which quickly carried him off. Ben fastened a better grip on the bars, pulled himself up over the side, then collapsed onto the deck. He felt the wetness of human blood against his back, which made him spring to his feet. The deck and portside gunwale were covered in red. The throttle was left in forward position. He hurried to the helm, slowed the vessel down, then began circling back toward the others.

"Whoa!" Derrick called out. He knew they weren't out of danger yet, but still, he'd rather be on that police boat than these measly life rafts. He steered toward it. Melvin and Josh were already propping themselves on their knees, ready to climb aboard.

"At full throttle, we'll be back to the harbor in twenty minutes," Melvin told himself. *Twenty minutes. Just survive the next twenty minutes.*

"We'll make it, guys," Jesse said. She tapped Josh and Melvin on the shoulder. "I promise, all right."

"You guys don't happen to have an atom bomb in your armory, do ya?" Melvin asked. "Because it seems that's what it would take to kill that thing."

"Tried to include it in our budget, but you know how cheap Sammy can be," Jesse said. A few chuckles escaped their throats. Sammy pulled her life raft up to the police boat.

"Go up," she said to Hugh.

"No, you first, Chief. I'll be right behind you," he replied. Sammy grabbed the bar and hoisted herself onto the side of the ship. Once she was out of the raft, she allowed herself to embrace the humor in Jesse's remark.

The levity only lasted a moment.

Tidal waves rolled a few hundred feet to the east. All smiles quickly vanished as the whip-like whiskers soared high in the air. Those slit pupils followed, with a razor-lined jaw yawning open.

Ben grabbed Sammy and yanked her into the boat.

"Can't we get a goddamn break?" he muttered.

****

"Come on! Hurry up," Shier said, waving the choppers down. Two of them set down on the beaches, one for *Spiral News Network,* and another for *The Georgia Post.*

As soon as the fuselage door opened, the Sergeant rushed the aircraft, shocking the reporter stepping out.

"Officer, what's happening?"

"I'm commandeering your chopper and your pilot," Shier said. The cameraman remained in his seat with a dumbfounded expression on his face.

"You can't do that!" the reporter replied.

"Watch me," Shier replied. He yanked the cameraman out of his seat, threw him onto the sand, then pointed at Murphy, who stood a few feet back with Barber and Pollock. "Take the other and follow me. You two, help evacuate the wounded."

"You got it, Sarge," Barber said. Murphy gave a thumbs up and raced for the *Georgia Post* chopper.

Shier slammed the fuselage door shut. He leaned over to the pilot. "Take us out toward Lebbon Rock."

"Officer, you've pretty much ensured you've ended your career," the pilot remarked.

"Damn it, you asshole, there's people over there who'll be killed if we don't lift them up!"

The pilot removed his aviators, looked back at Shier, realized he was dead serious, then started liftoff.

"All you had to do was ask."

Both choppers lifted off and raced to the east.

****

The calm that had embraced the group had quickly erupted into panic. Josh was hyperventilating, while Melvin's fear manifested itself as anger.

"You did this, Derrick! I wouldn't be in this shit if not for you."

The TV star ignored the verbal assault while he steered the boat closer to the police vessel. He glanced back at the creature, then realized it was not closing in on them, but on the boat, leaving him no choice but to steer right and take them south.

Jesse cupped her hands to her mouth and screamed.

"Sammy! Look out!"

The Chief saw it. She positioned her rifle at her shoulder and launched a few rounds at the beast.

"Stop!" Hugh shouted.

"Doctor, get aboard!" she replied.

"Stop shooting it!" Hugh said. Sammy looked down at him. The doctor was knelt over the raft's motor, yanking the ripcord.

A hundred thoughts raced in his mind. The natural instinct to survive screamed at him to climb aboard that boat, only to be countered by deductive reasoning. There was no escaping his fate now. Getting on that boat would only change the location of where he would be torn apart. The Serpent would topple the vessel as though it were a paper plane.

His mission to kill the beast had failed. At this point, he'd settle for saving others.

He pushed the motor to its top speed and raced to the north. He snatched Ben's rifle, checked the magazine and safety lever, then pointed it at the creature. He wasn't used to the kick of a three-round burst, which almost knocked him on his back. He repositioned, sucked in a breath, then tried again. He absorbed the kickback, watching the creature jolt as he jabbed it with bullets.

"Doctor! What are you doing?" Sammy called after him. Ben grabbed her by the shoulders and pulled her back. It was obvious Hugh was drawing it off. There was no saving him now. All they could do was wait for the creature to turn before throttling north.

After taking several rounds to the jaw and neck, the creature went after its creator.

Ben throttled the boat, quickly pulling up alongside the other raft. Josh quickly climbed aboard, followed by his three companions. They gave one last look at Hugh. To their amazement, he managed to lure it almost a thousand feet away before it reached him.

Hugh fired the last round, then threw the empty gun like a tomahawk. It bounced off the creature's nose and splashed into the water. The creature coiled its head back, baring teeth lined with stringy fabric from clothing, and gazed at its creator.

In his last moments, he wondered if it recognized his face, and only hesitated to savor the experience of a creation destroying its creator.

No. It's just an evil monster that should never have been resurrected...

The beast proved his point, snatching him and the raft in one single swoop. The raft exploded, as did Hugh's midsection. It thrashed his body about, its teeth breaking his body into sections like deli meat, then swallowed. It nestled the ribbons of rubber floating about, concluded they weren't edible, then turned its attention on the fleeing police boat.

"Shit, it's coming back!" Josh said.

"So much for twenty minutes," Melvin said to himself. The creature began to glide through the water. In just a few moments, it started narrowing the distance between them.

Jesse pushed herself between them and fired her rifle at the beast. After fifteen shots, her weapon ran dry, leaving her with her sidearm.

"Chief! Chief! You there?!" Shier barked through the radio.

"Sergeant. Don't come out here. Your boats won't stand a chance," Sammy replied.

"Not in a boat."

The drone of helicopter rotors turned her attention to the sky. Two choppers were descending from the east, flying right toward them.

"Oh YES!" Melvin said, his anger shifting to optimism.

"Come to papa!" Josh said.

Shier gazed down at the group that crowded the deck of the police vessel. The creature was three hundred feet behind it and quickly approaching. He checked his rifle, made sure he had a spare magazine on standby, then tapped the pilot on the shoulder.

"Bring us low, if you can. Let's draw it off."

"You got it," the pilot said. Shier opened the fuselage door and aimed his rifle down at the beast. As the chopper descended to fifty meters, he began popping off rounds.

The creature shifted to the left, then raised its head high. The pilot descended another ten meters, then guided the chopper north, while Shier hit it with another dozen rounds. The creature bobbed its head, summoning any acid it was able to produce in the last fifteen minutes.

"Pull up!" Shier said. The chopper ascended. In the split-second that followed, a stream of steaming hot fluid passed underneath the landing skates.

"What the hell is that?" the pilot asked.

"I'll explain on the way back," Shier replied. He fired off another few rounds at the Serpent. Finally, screeching frustratedly, it sped toward them.

Murphy's chopper took advantage of the diversion and immediately descended near the police boat. Not being a rescue aircraft, there was no choice but to use a lifeline from the police vessel. Sammy tossed it to Murphy, who caught it and tied it to the base of a passenger seat.

"Go!" Sammy said to the civilians. Josh and Melvin went first. Derrick waited behind, taking Jesse by the shoulder.

"You next."

"No. You go," Jesse replied, her sense of duty not wavering. Derrick, half begrudgingly, grabbed the knotted rope and climbed aboard.

The Serpent sprayed again, only for the chopper to bank right and avoid its attack. It slapped its tail against the water, frustrated. The target was too high, its rewards too meager...unlike the one it was pursuing previously.

Shier continued hitting it until his magazine ran dry. This time, the diversion was not working. It was making a straight line for the vessel.

"Chief, it's coming right for you."

"We're already taking too many," the chopper pilot said to Murphy. The officer could already feel the shift in weight. There were five people aboard now, which was one more than what it was intended to hold.

"Sarge, you're gonna have to take the others, or we'll never make it."

"Copy."

"What? No," Derrick said. He stepped to the fuselage and reached for Jesse. "We have to get them up." Murphy pushed him into a seat.

"We do that, then we're as good as dead," he said. He looked down at the Chief. "Hold on. Shier's coming for ya!"

"Just go!" Sammy replied. The pilot wasted no time ascending, while the other chopper passed over the creature, which was now within a hundred feet of the vessel.

Jesse popped off several rounds at it.

The Serpent dived, slithered along the seabed, then angled up under the boat.

The chopper descended. Sammy tossed the line to Shier, who quickly secured it.

Before anyone could grab the rope, the beast struck the hull, rolling the vessel over to port. Water swept into the deck, weighing it further and completing its roll. Ben grabbed Sammy by the waist and lunged for the rope, catching it by the bottom knot.

The pilot ascended a few meters, the two people dangling below unable to get a firm grasp to climb up, forcing Shier to hoist them up himself.

The boat cracked as the beast struck again. It coiled around the bow like a python, gripped tight, imploding the hull.

Sammy finally got a grip on the knots and began ascending the rope. Shier reached down, grabbed her by the shoulders, and hoisted her into the fuselage. She spun on her knees to look back down. She saw Jesse emerge from the water twenty feet from the stern.

"Go back down," she told the pilot. He hesitated, seeing the beast abandoning its grip on the vessel, and circling back toward its victim.

"I hate having a conscience," he muttered, then descended.

Jesse saw the beast dive under the wreckage, and felt the swells raising her up. She had seconds before it would seize her in its jaws.

"Come on!" she screamed, panicking. The rope touched down within arms' reach. She grabbed it with both hands. She heard the Chief shout to the pilot, "Go! Go! Go!"

It lifted her out of the water, sparking immediate relief.

Following that relief was terror and intense pain. The beast raised its head, jaws agape, and extended half of its body out of the water to reach its target as it flew out of reach. The jaws snapped shut over her right leg and pulled away.

Jesse felt a jolt and *snap* simultaneously, which was immediately followed by a feeling of weight loss. Then came lightheadedness. She looked down and saw the stream of blood pouring from her thigh. Her leg was gone.

Shier and Ben pulled the rope, barely getting her into the chopper before she lost her grip.

"Stay awake," Ben said. He removed his belt and tightened it around the stump to slow the bleeding.

"Haul ass," Shier said to the pilot.

Sammy grabbed Jesse's hands. "Just stay awake, hon. We'll get you home." Tears ran down her face as she spoke. Jesse was in a state of shock. Blood was pooling on the floor. It took everything to keep herself from erupting into sobs. "Oh, pilot, please hurry."

CHAPTER 38

The questions came in rapid fire. There was no sense of order during the press conference; just question after question with barely any time for Richard Russell to respond. It didn't help that he didn't have the answer to most of these questions, not to mention the fact that his mind was fixated on the fact that his daughter was nearly killed by the creature.

"Mr. Mayor, you never answered how long you were aware of a creature in the water."

"It was discovered yesterday morning. Immediately after, Chief Russell ordered the beaches evacuated," he said.

"It was reported to be a shark, which is now understood to be false information. Why was the public deliberately misled?" a female reporter in the back called out.

"I'll take responsibility for that. It was poor judgement on my part. Yesterday, after going over our plan, it seemed like it would be taken care of quickly. I didn't want to induce a panic."

"Mayor Russell, do you have a comment on the disappearances of several different people."

Richard shook his head, not to avoid the question, but to get rid of the headache that was squeezing his temples.

"I understand reports of missing individuals have been coming in lately. The Chief of Police had reported several wrecks near the lighthouse that we're confident the creature had attacked before we discovered it," he answered. "This creature is very large and violent, and it appears to be territorial. Nobody is allowed in the water right now, especially near Lebbon Rock."

"Hey, what about *us,* Mayor?"

Richard looked to the stands to his right. The reporters turned their cameras to a slightly overweight man stepping from the back of the room. He hadn't shaven in days, his hair was ragged, his eyes glassy. Yet, every inch of him radiated anger and hatred.

Oh, this can't be happening...

One of the aspects that made Mayor Russell so favorable—up to this point, at least-was that he was very good with faces and names. He'd interact with town residents, remember their names, their children's names, businesses, which made him a likeable figure. And Jared Vase's name was particularly easy to remember, since he was right there in the police briefing when his daughter announced that Brianne Vase was a confirmed casualty.

"Mr. Vase..." Richard stammered.

"That bastard out there has killed our loved ones! It has killed friends. Neighbors. My wife! I was planning to—" Jared's voice trailed off. He realized he didn't want to broadcast Brianne's infidelity to the world. Fact is, he still didn't want her to go, and in the night she had run off with that prick whose name he still didn't know, he decided he was going to win her back.

"Mr. Vase, our hearts go out to you. Really, I'm so sorry for your loss. But PLEASE, let the authorities handle this."

"The authorities handling this is what led to that massacre today!" Jared retorted. Cameras flashed as several fishermen rallied behind him.

"This bastard is destroying our livelihoods," Jared's first mate, Leon, said. Nobody dared to interrupt him. He was a towering man with a face that belonged in a *James Bond* feature. Even in the face of the local government, he wore his sleeveless denim vest, exposing his muscular physique gained from years on the sea. Typically, he was actually a nice man. But Jared was his Captain and his best friend, and if Jared wanted to avenge his wife's death, then Leon would go with him.

"Mr. Vase, Leon..." Richard tilted his head to see a third fisherman stepping behind the pair, then recognized his thin black beard and short hair. "Aaron. All of you, listen up. I'm getting in touch with the Coast Guard. They'll be sending a Cutter within the next four days..."

"Four days!"

"There's severe storm damage in the Bahamas and in the Gulf," Richard replied. Hurricane Aurora had kicked off the season early, and struck the Caribbean with a vengeance before making landfall in the Gulf of Mexico less than a week prior.

"Four days is not enough," Aaron said. "That thing is driving away all the fish in the area. Willis Tyson went out early yesterday morning. When he came back in after the radio call by the police, he said he found no fish in the usual hot zones. I spoke with a crew member on that show that's being filmed here. They had a marlin on a line. Then something bit everything off behind the head! No doubt it was that snake-thing out there!"

"In four more days, it'll drive everything out of our waters," Jared said.

"Not to mention the effect it's having on the water itself," a reporter in the crowd said. "It spits acid. Who knows what other chemicals it's releasing into the water."

"And how will the Coast Guard handle it? Blow it up? Kill all the other fish in the area?" Leon said.

"Gentlemen, I know what you're getting at. You're not going out on the water."

"Try and stop me, Mayor," Jared said. "I'm going out there right now and I'm gonna kill that bastard. Wanna stop me? Send your little girl out there to catch me. Yeah, I'm sure you'd like your precious Chief on the water right now."

Richard tightened his jaw. He stood, trying to think of something to say, while ignoring the camera flashes that assaulted his eyes in the dusk air. Jared and his crew gave him one last defiant look before marching off to their vehicle.

As if the day couldn't get any worse. He was already facing the end of his political career. Any additional incidents would be on his conscience at this point. Yet, Jared Vase and his friends were not wrong. Waiting for the Coast Guard would kill the local economy. He was already feeling the heat, as hotels and resorts were reporting hundreds of cancelled reservations. It would take years to bounce back, longer if that creature was left to swim around for days. If it was killing the fish population, it would mean the other half of the local economy would be choked to death. So much damage, and in such a short time.

Still, he shouldn't let the guy go out. He pulled his phone from his pocket and scrolled to Sammy's number. His thumb rested over the *send* button, but failed to make contact.

That stubborn girl. She wouldn't place any of her officers at risk. She'd go out herself to intercept these fishermen. The current shift had a couple of officers stationed at the docks, but only a few, and it was a large area to cover. To add to the misery, both staffing and morale were at an all-time low, considering the vast number of officers that were lost during the incident.

He would alert them all the same, but it wouldn't matter. Jared would go out on the water. The officers would radio Sammy. And she'd try to go stop them.

Right now, she was at the hospital…

"Mayor Russell, do you have a comment on—"

"No more questions. I'll do another conference tomorrow. I got to go." Richard turned around, walked off the stage, and hurried for his car.

CHAPTER 39

Sammy hadn't smoked since college, but damn, she needed a cigarette so bad she may as well have been an addict. She flaunted her Chief of Police badge to the hospital security staff after they approached her in the lot regarding her smoking in the parking lot. The entire hospital grounds were considered a smoke-free area, though it was more about promoting an image than anything else. What would they do? Tell the Chief of Police to vacate the grounds? And if she refused, then what? Call the police? She knew this, they knew this, and considering the day she'd had, they were at least smart enough to have a sense of proportion. People were dead, including several of her officers…and possibly her best friend, and they were going to harass her about the smoking policy? Outside, of all places?

Not today.

Ben Stacie passed the security guards on their way in. They too were coming to the close of a busy day. There was a rush of family members coming in to see loved ones who were injured in the attack. Overcrowding became an issue, to the point where even the police had to start forcing people to leave.

Every doctor was called in to the ER and OR. Ben had heard through the grapevine that two officers that were out of town on vacation had been ordered back immediately. They would have to travel four or five hours, and be prepared to work for twenty-four at the end of it.

It was getting late in the evening now. Ben found Sammy sitting on a curb. Her police shirt was unbuttoned and untucked, the t-shirt underneath getting wet with sweat. Streaks of blood had dried on her trousers and boots.

"Come on, let me take you home," he said.

"No," Sammy said, near tears again. She had cried in his arms twice, both for Jesse, and the men she had lost today. It was so unfair! *Why did that thing have to spit acid?* She ran her wrist over her left eye. "We were so close to killing it."

"I know. Nobody saw the turn of events coming. Even Hugh didn't know."

"And now he's dead too," Sammy said. "Just like Lock. Hayes. Miles Peterson. Ian. Dawn. Tony—"

"Stop it," Ben said. Sammy took another draw on her cigarette, burning it right to the butt, while finishing the list of names in her mind.

"And Jesse," she concluded out loud.

"She'll make it," Ben said.

"If she does, she'll never be the same," Sammy said.

"You're not wrong," Ben said, "but she'll live. That's the important thing. She can have a life still."

"Yeah? Doing what? She lost her leg. She won't be a cop anymore."

"Sammy, it'll be tough for her, but she'll pull through. I've seen it. She'll be jogging past us in no time."

Sammy lit another cigarette with the old one.

"The others won't. Several people won't. They don't even know how many are dead. And it was all on my watch."

"No, you're not gonna do that," Ben said sternly. "It was that bitch Tiffany Decker in her quest to make a name for herself at the expense of the rest of the world. Had she not riled everyone up to create a scene, those people would be alive today. Including your officers. I'll say it a hundred times if I have to: it wasn't your fault."

"Good luck explaining that to the families of my cops."

They sat silently together, staring into the line of trees at the end of the lot as the sky gradually darkened. Cars went in and out, with people hurrying into the building to check on loved ones, while others left. Some were in tears after receiving terrible news of their friend or loved ones' fate, while others expressed relief that their loved ones would pull through. Watching their expressions heightened Sammy's anxiety. Which reaction would she carry when she left this hospital tonight?

A car pulled in. In the darkness, as well as her general numbness to the world around her, Sammy didn't realize it was her father until he stepped out.

"Dad?"

"Hey, kiddo," Richard said. "How is she?"

"Don't know yet," Ben replied. "Still in surgery. They've been giving her blood. They've been working on her for hours."

"Jesus." He gave Sammy a hug. "She'll be fine, I promise."

"How's the town?" Ben asked.

Richard looked down and shook his head, resigned. "People are leaving left and right. Who can blame them, really?"

"They should know we did the best we could," Sammy said.

"The media will print whatever they want to print. It's what they do," Richard said.

"Are they demanding action?" Sammy said. Richard's expression hardened. It was as though he was *afraid* to answer. "Dad? What's going on?"

"There's people who are going out on the water," he replied.

"People? Who?!"

"Fishermen. They're gonna try and kill the thing themselves."

"And you're *letting* them?"

"It's not that I'm letting them. I have no way to stop them." Sammy stood up and started digging for her keys. Richard closed his eyes. He couldn't have predicted her reaction any better. "Sammy, no. As the Mayor, I'm grounding you. You're not going back on the water."

"What the hell are you talking about?"

"I mean what I say," he said. "You're not going out."

"Those people are as good as dead if I don't stop them!"

"You won't be able to, sweetie," he said.

"No, you just don't *want* me to," Sammy replied.

Richard sighed. "Is that such a bad thing?"

"It is when you keep me from doing my job."

Ben put his arms around Sammy's shoulders to calm her. "Who's going? How do they plan on killing it?"

"It's Jared Vase and his crew," Richard said.

Sammy cocked an eyebrow. "His crew? Does that include Aaron Tabbert?"

"Y—yes," Richard said.

Ben yanked his hands back as though afraid they'd be torn away. "Aaron Tabbert? What's wrong with that guy?"

"He used to run his own fishing ship before I confiscated his boat. He was using illegal depth charges. I guarantee, if he's going with Jared, he's planning to use dynamite to try and kill the thing."

Richard shrugged. "Is that such a bad thing this time?"

Sammy tensed nearly to the point of screaming. "It's *my* job! You need to trust me to do it!"

"I can't, sweetie. I'm sorry. Let these men take care of it. You wait here with Jesse, okay?" He looked over at Ben. "Take care of her, will ya?"

Ben nodded. He wanted to speak up, but didn't know what to say. He didn't agree with the Mayor in this decision, but then again, how could he blame the guy at this point? He appointed

Sammy to this location to help keep her out of harm's way, not to throw her into the lion's den.

Maybe those fishermen could pull it off. Perhaps explosives were all that was needed all along. Maybe by tonight, the nightmare would be over. Ben could only hope. Unfortunately, his hope and his predictions were at a crossroads.

Yet, if Sammy were to go after them, he, like her father, would also try to stop her. It was a plain and simple fact; the water belonged to the Serpent now. Anything that went on it was doomed to face its wrath.

"I'll stay with her," Ben said. Richard wanted to give Sammy a hug, but she had already stepped away, tossing her cigarette against the pavement. He returned to his car and drove away.

Ben hustled to catch up with her.

"Sammy, don't..."

"It's all falling apart," she said. "He doesn't trust me to do my job. Because I got several people killed. Including Jesse..."

"Stop it. God, Sammy! It's that damn company's fault! They created that thing and let it go loose, all so they could avoid some bad press." Sammy ran her wrist over her eyes again. This time, the tears were free-flowing. The dam had broken and the rivers were surging.

She fell into Ben's arms and sobbed.

CHAPTER 40

The hours were like decades. Sammy leaned back in the lobby chair, half-asleep, but determined to find out Jesse's condition. With her parents in Ohio, Sammy was the closest thing to family she had in this town. It allowed her to keep up on updates of Jesse's condition. As far as she was aware, she was still in critical condition.

The lobby had quieted down as evening fell into night. Many of the visitors had gone home or back to their hotels for the night. There were only a half dozen other people waiting, with permission given by the hospital staff.

Sammy had run out of tears to shed. Her face was pink from all the energy spent from her emotions. Now, she looked like a mental patient, staring at a wall. She leaned against Ben, who had an arm over her shoulders. He spent the last hour in and out of dozes, constantly shifting to consciousness whenever those double doors opened.

Sammy rested her head against his shoulder. His presence was calming. God, if he wasn't here with her right now... If not for Jesse pulling her little stunt, they wouldn't have reunited.

Even in the OR, she's looking out for me.

She smiled, thinking of Jesse in her glory as she brought that marlin to Derrick's yacht. Derrick....

She looked to the far left side of the room. There was a man pacing back and forth, a hand constantly scratching his chin, his face worn with guilt and distress. She thought it was odd to see Derrick mildly annoyed back on the yacht. That was nothing to see him scared straight. It was clear he felt partly responsible for Jesse's condition.

If only I made her go up the chopper first. Or if I didn't make such a game of the situation.

His body language was all too familiar. Like her, he was dealing with the baggage of lost co-workers.

Sammy quietly slipped out of Ben's arms and stood up. He stirred a moment, opened his eyes, gave her a quick smile, then dozed off again. She stroked his face gently, then walked over to where Derrick was pacing. There was a coffee table nearby. Up until now, caffeine seemed like the last thing she needed.

But human beings are inconsistent creatures, with fluctuating needs.

"If you need to spend energy, the lot around the hospital is three quarters of a mile around," she said to Derrick.

Derrick forced a smile. "I've thought about that, actually. I just keep worrying that if I go out to walk, that's when the doctors will come out. I don't want to be away."

Sammy turned to make herself a cup of coffee, mostly to hide her surprise. Honestly, while she didn't think Derrick was a scumbag or anything like that, she had assumed that Jesse was just another fling in a long line of girls. He was a celebrity after all. She had seen the way he acted when he was with her. Yeah, they got along well, but Sammy figured that was his act. But here he was, ten o'clock at night, waiting here at the hospital to find out whether she would make it.

Sammy stirred the bland, lactose free creamer into her coffee then turned back to face Derrick.

"Hey, uh, I owe you an apology for the shit I said on your boat," she said.

"Hmm?" Derrick thought for a moment, genuinely confused what she was referring to. So much had happened, her remarks of his crew filming the operation being in bad taste had almost vanished from memory. "Oh, that. Chief, there's nothing for you to worry about. Can't say it's been on my mind, really. But, that said, you probably weren't wrong."

Sammy took a sip of the coffee. *Oh, that creamer is horrible.*

"I know you two were seeing each other, I just didn't realize it was getting so serious."

"Well, it's only been a couple of days. I don't wanna get ahead of myself…"

"Sure you do," Sammy said. "Normally, I'd tell you to slow down. But I think this is one of those exceptions. I'm not saying run off and get married when she's out of here, and DEFINITELY don't go rushing to use the L-word. However, I am detecting a unique connection, and maybe it's worth pursuing. Unless I'm wrong…"

"You talk like you're certain she'll pull through," Derrick said. "Are you?"

Sammy didn't answer.

The sound of the double doors opening made her look back. Jesse's doctor stepped out, glanced about, then spotted her. Ben snapped into consciousness then stood up to listen in. Normally, the doctor would be worried about confidentiality, but he was so exhausted, and was familiar with most of the people here except Derrick, so he didn't care.

"Let's find out," she said. She approached the doctor. The smile on his face said a lot. Already, Sammy felt another wave of tears threatening to break through. "She'll be okay?"

"Yes, her condition's improving," the doctor said.

Sammy cupped her hands over her mouth. "Oh, thank God."

"We were able to seal the wound. We had to trim the bone a bit. Her leg is gone with only six-inches of thigh to work with. Just enough for us to fit her for a prosthetic when she's ready. We've had to fill her with three units of blood, but the bleeding has stopped and she's stabilized. She'll probably be here for a couple of weeks at least before she can leave, and needless to say, she'll have a lot of physical therapy in her future. But she'll live."

"Oh, thank you so much, Doc," Sammy said. She gave him a hug, then hugged Ben and Derrick.

The three of them shared a sigh of relief. At least, in this disastrous day full of bloodshed, there was one ray of light.

CHAPTER 41

"Here snaky-snaky-snaky," Aaron called into the night as he tossed another scoopful of chum into the water. Bits of dead fish swirled about in the water, trailing out around Lebbon Rock. "We know you're still hungry. We have a tasty treat for you."

In the pilothouse of his trawler *Napoleon*, Jared winced. "Aaron, mind not doing that, please?"

Aaron looked up at him, unable to see the Captain through the glint of the spotlight against the window. After a little bit of thought, he realized the talk of feeding the thing made him think of his wife's unfortunate demise. Personally, Aaron felt she had it coming, but the dumb idiot still thought he had a shot of saving his marriage. Dumb idiot or not, Jared was his friend.

"My bad, Cap," he replied.

"Just find that thing and blow it up," Jared replied.

"Don't worry, boss. We'll give that bastard what he's got coming," Leon said. He stood on the main deck with his harpoon gun, firmly bolted to the steel deck plates. He had stolen it off a Norwegian whaler back in 2010, and was always seeking an excuse to use it.

Jared steered the eighty-foot trawler north of Lebbon Rock.

"Where the hell is it?" he muttered, loudly enough to be heard.

"Maybe it left town," Leon said.

"I doubt it," Aaron replied. He panned the spotlight across the water. He glanced back behind him at his case of dynamite. "Bet those cops wish they had this shit earlier. Instead, they tried electrocuting it. Dumb idiots."

"I'll give them credit for ingenuity," Leon said.

"I only give credit to plans that work," Aaron said. He tossed another scoopful into the water. "Anything on the fish-finder, Cap?"

"Nothing," Jared replied. Unlike Aaron, he was patient. He would happily cruise all night, as long as it ended with the creature's death.

Leon manned a spotlight on the starboard side. He moved the light across the water, then further out.

"Jesus, look at that!"

The others came out and saw the wreckage. It was a fishing vessel, just a couple meters shorter than theirs, submerged in the water. The pilothouse and parts of the bow prodded through the surface. Everything else was lost beneath the black water.

"Must be the wreckage the police reported," Jared said.

"No…that one is closer to the island," Leon said. "This is different."

"Hang on a second…" Aaron leaned over the edge. Leon pointed the light to the starboard bow where the name of the vessel was printed. They only caught the first few letters. *Diamo—*

"*Diamond Rough*," Leon said. "Jesus, Mary, this is Frank Russo's boat! Where—where is he?" He panned the light across the water. His movements started growing frantic as he realized Frank's fate.

"Maybe he was out here during the attack," Aaron said.

"No, I saw him earlier this afternoon. *After* it all happened," Leon said.

"I guess he tried going after it," Jared said. Leon glanced at him, shocked by the coldness of Jared's voice. Frank was a good guy. Did he not care?

"Hey, we've got movement," Aaron said, pointing several hundred feet past the wreckage.

Leon pointed his light stream. There was something in the water, though he couldn't make out what it was. There was fog in the way, and the clouds were blotting out the moon above. Aaron grabbed a stick of dynamite and eagerly held his lighter to the fuse, ready to light a flame at the flick of his thumb.

Spotlights beamed back at them.

"Is that you, Jared Vase?" a man yelled out. Jared stepped out of the wheelhouse. He recognized that voice.

"Redford Harper? What the hell are you doing out here?"

The sixty-foot fishing vessel *Royal Blue* came closer, then came to a stop at the other side of the wreckage.

They saw the first mate, an average-sized man in blue overalls named Leonard shining his light away. Up above, a man in his fifties stepped out on to the fly deck. He wore a thin grey shirt with holes in the armpits and midsection.

"My god, it bested Frank Russo. He must've been eager to come out here if he beat the rest of us," Redford Harper said.

"What are you doing out here?" Jared repeated.

"Same thing Frank was! I'm out to kill myself a sea serpent," Redford replied.

"In that little boat? Why? For Brianne?" Jared knew Redford was no admirer of him or Brianne, so there was no way he was hunting the thing out of the goodness of his heart. He had his own motive.

"Good ol' fashioned money," Redford replied. He cackled after seeing the puzzled expressions on all three men's faces. "What? Didn't you hear?"

Jared shook his head.

"Money? Who's offering money? The Mayor?" Aaron asked.

"Nah, not him. Families of victims," Redford said. "Reports are coming in from across the country. A bunch of families of the people killed by that thing are offering rewards for its death." He followed the statement with a smile. Having been banned from fishing due to illegal trapping…as well as a charge for drug smuggling aboard his boat, Redford had been hard-pressed for cash. "Have you seen it?"

Jared scoffed. "What do you think?"

"Fair point."

"Who else is out looking for it?" Jared asked.

"Jay Beaver and his crew are searching further north," Redford said. "By tomorrow, everyone's gonna be fighting to get out here. It'll be a money race! You started one hell of a movement, Jared."

"I beg your pardon?"

"This was inspired by you standing up to the Mayor and stating you were going after that thing! It's all over the news. Obviously, some of the victims' families are agreeing with you, because that's when the offers started coming in online." He glanced at Leon and the harpoon gun. "Got your whaling gun all set up I see. You're a true-to-life *Captain Ahab*. Hell, you'd get revenge AND a bunch of money for killing the thing."

"I'm not interested," Jared said. "I just want the thing dead."

"No? Altogether, it makes quite a hefty sum. Might even go in the millions. They're all willing to pay. Check it out on the net. It's for real."

Aaron's eyes widened, then turned to his Captain. "You know, that's not a bad bonus."

"Don't care about that. I'm here to get that thing for what it did to Brianne," Jared replied. Aaron shrugged. *As long as the reward comes in. I'll take your cut if you don't want it.*

"Brianne?" Redford said.

"Yes—my *wife*."

"Oh, her. Gosh, dude. I almost forgot. If anything, I figured you'd be thanking the beast for eating her sorry ass. Not to mention the guy she was banging."

"Redford, that's enough," Leon warned. He watched his Captain's body language carefully. Already, they weren't supposed to be out here. If Jared did something stupid to Redford, all three of them would be screwed.

"Imagine it, those two on that love bed in his cabin. Sea serpent comes peering in. 'Yoo-hoo!' *Chomp!*"

Jared sensed the urge to cut the wheel to starboard and send Redford into the rock below. Instead, he cut the wheel the opposite direction. He steered east, going past the lighthouse into open ocean.

Bastards. To hell with all of them. Who are they to talk about him trying to win his wife back? How many failed marriages did they have between them? At least Jared would've fought for his. If that damn thing hadn't intervened…

He would stay out all night if he had to. No money-grubbing fisherman was going to rob him of his revenge.

****

Another hour passed, and still, no sign of the Serpent.

Jared steered a mile northeast, suspecting it had gone further out. All they found was drifting wreckage from the catastrophe, and soon, a dead fish. Then another.

After traveling another half mile, they had come across a world of dead fish floating along the surface. It was a graveyard on water. The air was full of a terrible stench. It was the smell of rot as well as something similar to something he remembered smelling in his high school chemistry lab.

Jared steered the boat westward, still bumping against dead Atlantic salmon and tuna. Some were barely clinging to life, flopping their tails against the water. Some swam in tight circles, stopped, bobbed their mouths, then tried again, not knowing that they were doomed to succumb to the very illness that had taken the others.

Even Aaron was disturbed. He panned a spotlight out to the water. The ocean was full of dead fish. He began to wonder, if there were this many floating up top, how many dead ones were lying along the bottom?

"Maybe we should head back," Leon suggested.

"No. We're staying until we find that thing," Jared replied.

"But Jared, don't you see this?" Aaron said.

"Dead fish. It might mean that thing's close by," Jared said. To appease the crew, he continued westward. At least being a couple miles closer to shore might calm their nerves. The entire route was covered in fish corpses. The white spotlights showed bodies that had been badly burned. Eyes were pale white and showing signs of infection.

Adding to the dreaded atmosphere was the increasingly dense fog that lingered over the water.

"I don't get it," Leon said.

"There's nothing to get," Jared replied. "It's out here. We're seeing signs of it."

"That's what scares me," Leon said. He was regretting his unconditional support for his friend. It seemed reasonable at the time to go out and hunt this thing. But now? The thoughts of mutiny were starting to swirl around in his mind. The decision to come out here was a knee-jerk reaction, and that was usually when the worst choices were made.

He climbed up into the pilothouse. Jared glanced over at him, his eyes expressing surprise and irritation.

"What are you doing in here? Man the spotlight or we'll never see the thing."

"Are you even looking at the water?" Leon said. "We can't see anything past that fog."

"It's out here," Jared said.

"Jared…" Leon rubbed a hand over his face. "This was a mistake. To come out here tonight, I mean. Let's wait a day, come up with a better plan…"

"What better plan?"

"I don't know. I just think we were too rash to come out here and—"

"I'm not waiting for some other prick to kill it. I want to be the one to kill it. If you or Aaron deal the killing blow, I'll settle for that, but I'm not letting some stranger kill it to fill his pockets. This is personal, Leon. We're not returning until that Serpent is dead. You don't like it? You can swim home!"

Leon couldn't even recognize the Captain he also thought of as his friend. This guy was a sneering, cold-blooded psychopath.

"Hey, man, I'm not working for you right now," Leon said. "I'm out here as your friend! I thought I was helping you. I'm mad about Brianne too, okay. I have my opinions on whether she deserves what you're doing, but it's what you wanted so I chose to support you. But, something's wrong here. Frank Russo's boat, the dead fish…"

"Losing your nerve?" Jared said.

Leon shrugged. "So what if I am?!"

"Shouldn't have come out here, then. This is my boat, Leon. I'm killing that thing."

"It won't bring her back. It won't undo what she did. You're dealing with two shocks at once, Jared. She cheated on you, and before your mind could even process that, she died."

"I told her I hoped she'd be eaten."

"By SHARKS…not that it matters, you didn't mean it. She wasn't swimming. The Serpent attacked her boat, which she shouldn't have been on in the first place. You didn't get her killed. Man, you're not thinking clearly."

"My mind's perfectly clear. You're the one who's confused, or else, you wouldn't be out here."

"Can't argue with that point," Leon replied. "But I've come to my senses now. We're heading back."

The door opened and Aaron stepped in.

"What's this talk of heading back?"

"Aaron, this was a mistake. We didn't think this through. We can maybe come back out with a better plan, during the day so we can see, and—"

"And share the water with a hundred other fishermen? I don't think so," Aaron said.

Apparently, being interrupted was the popular thing tonight. Leon took a breath and tried to settle his rapidly increasing heart rate.

"I'm just saying—"

"No way am I letting some other asshole get the payday," Aaron said. He glanced at Jared. "No offense, boss."

Jared shrugged it off. He didn't care that Aaron wanted the money. Let him have it. In his mind, it was a good reward for his loyalty.

Leon took a step back. He realized he had become an obstacle in the paths of two very determined men, one driven by revenge, the other by greed. Both of which were notorious for the downfall of a men's soul. And it had already started. He'd known these men all his life. Even Aaron, despite his flaws, was a decent human being at heart. But now, he looked as though he would throw Leon overboard in an instant in order to keep his payday. Same with Jared.

The tension only increased by the echoes of loud pops in the distance. All three men raced out onto the fly deck and gazed into the thick fog. More popping sounds echoed, followed by a squeal. Then a crash. It reminded Leon of an accident he witnessed on the highway five years back. A semi weaved too far to the left and struck a pillar beneath an overpass. Even through closed windows, the crunch sounded as though it was right next to him.

Same with what he just heard.

There were more screams, which ended swiftly with the onset of another crashing noise.

Jared hurried back to the helm, muttering, "It's there."

"No! You'll get us killed!" Leon said. He went after Jared, then felt Aaron's arm squeeze over his neck. He arched backward, gasping for breath, and felt Aaron's chin near his cheek.

"Sorry, bud." He squeezed tighter, not to kill, but to render him unconscious…as long as he didn't interfere any further.

Jared accelerated the boat. The horrible smell intensified, even to the point of making Aaron want to gag while he choked out his friend. Not only was the smell horrid, but the air was getting increasingly humid.

Leon pushed against Aaron's weakened grip, prying it away to make just enough space to get a breath. He kicked a foot back, striking one of Aaron's shins, then pushed against the floor to drive them backwards.

"Motherfucker!" Aaron said, as if Leon was the instigator in this fight. They both stumbled backwards out the door then fell on the deck. Leon rolled away, only for Aaron to grab him again. Grappling with each other, they came to their feet. Each threw a couple of punches at the other's midsection, until one from Leon struck low. His fist connected with Aaron's groin, doubling him over. The fisherman let out a yell, then clutched his manhood.

Leon backed away against the guardrail, thinking the fight was over. Then he saw the glare. Now, he wasn't looking at a man who was merely greedy; he was greedy *and* vengeful. The rage would have only lasted a moment, then simmered to a more controllable level, if Aaron had simply not given in to it. He sprang with the speed of a small insect and thrust both hands into Leon's chest. Leon was upside down for the briefest of moments. By the time he realized he was falling, he felt the *crunch* in his neck after landing face down on the main deck.

Aaron gazed down at his fellow crewmate. Leon's body flopped once, then was perfectly still. His sizzling blood settled, and a cold numbness crept over him. Several thoughts ran through his mind. *Did that just happen? He's just unconscious, right? It was a hard fall, but men have fallen from longer heights and survived.* Of course, he was intentionally neglecting the angle in which Leon had landed.

Slowly, the reality of the situation struck Aaron. He raced down to the main deck, still forcing himself to think Leon was merely unconscious. Hell, he'd settle for paralyzed at this point. As long as he wasn't dead!

The blank open eyes and crooked neck finally sealed the reality. Aaron groaned. He was a killer now. He had done many things in his life. He'd stolen, looted, fabricated lies, sabotaged other ships' nets, even gone as far as to threaten people during intense arguments. But he never actually meant what he said. Here he was, looking at the warm corpse that was Leon. His *friend*!

His mind raced, thinking of impossible tasks to whatever higher power there was. He asked for this to be a dream and to wake up from it. Or for Leon to just be sleeping with his eyes open. Not so. Further ideas raced across his mind, each more insane and impossible. *There must be a way to rewind time! Just sixty-seconds is all I need to redo!*

"What the hell did you do?!"

Aaron saw Jared staring down at him.

"It was an accident!" Aaron said.

Jared gripped the rail bar so tightly, Aaron thought it would snap. What he didn't realize was that the anger wasn't directed solely at him. Jared was pissed at himself.

"Oh my god," he muttered. Only now did he realize the point Leon was trying to make. His goals had corrupted his mind. Aaron's too. Too bad it had gone too far. He felt as though the sky was falling. His world was crumbling. Now, he was going to end up in prison. Like Aaron, his mind started to race. He was in enough hell as it was, but there was no way he'd be able to handle the confined space of prison, especially surrounded by actual murderers.

Yes, he was guilty. But the way he saw it, he would suffer enough by living with it. To hell with prison. Yeah, Aaron would get the harsher sentence—if he didn't find a way to pin it on Jared. Aaron wasn't evil at heart, but he had less qualms about weaseling his way out of trouble. And this was the worst trouble. Jared could already see the future play out. It would be an endless cycle of back and forth between the two men in court, each doing what they could to lessen their own sentence at the expense of the other.

"What do we do?" Aaron said. Jared was slightly relieved to hear the question. It meant that Aaron's mind hadn't undergone working out sinister plots. There was no good solution, so Jared decided on the easier one.

"We find the creature and kill it," Jared answered. "Then we'll say that it got Leon in the process. People will believe it, considering the mass casualties from its attack."

"Yeah...YEAH," Aaron said, nodding his head. Anything but prison.

Another crash echoed in the distance. In the madness of what just occurred, they actually almost forgot they were approaching the sound of gunshots.

"Oh, God Al'Mighty!" a man shouted.

Jared gripped the rail again; this time, out of fear.

The thrashing was maybe a hundred feet in front of him. The fog started to break, propelled by heavy movement behind it. They saw a fishing vessel—the two halves of it separated by several meters. Both were gradually sinking beneath the waves. Debris was scattered all around them, drifting alongside several dead fish.

In the center of it all was the Serpent, with Redford Harper clutched in its jaws. His arms were locked out, fingers curling as though being electrocuted. He wasn't being shocked, but crushed. As the jaws connected with each other, one of the arms fell into the water.

The Serpent swallowed his still-twitching corpse, then turned its attention to the oncoming *Star Blaze*.

After overcoming the initial fright of seeing its horrifying face, Aaron opened his case of dynamite and grabbed a few sticks. Jared took the helm and steered to port. The beast was already moving in for the kill.

"Don't waste time! Kill it!" Jared shouted through the window.

Aaron broke off the fuse, leaving only a half-inch's worth. He lit it with the flame and chucked the stick at the beast. It bounced off its neck, fell away for a few yards, then exploded. The Serpent reeled to its right, letting out a hiss before hitting the water.

"A-ha!" Aaron shouted. The force of the blast rang his ears, but he didn't care. He'd go deaf, as long as the creature was dead. With the millions he'd rein in, he'd get his ears fixed anyway...and possibly find a way to wipe away the memories of what just happened to Leon.

The water settled, the fog twisting into in thick tornados.

"Did we kill it?" Jared asked.

"I don't see it," Aaron replied. He panned a spotlight where the creature fell. Nothing. The water was still, the air quiet.

Until it wasn't.

They heard the splash on the starboard side. The creature rose like the arm of a mythical kraken. The only sign of injury from the blast were a few chipped scales. Acid dripped from its mouth like drool, singeing the guardrails.

Aaron panicked and pressed the lit flame to the broken wick of the next stick of dynamite. Sparks flickered in the sky as he tossed it over the creature's head. The intense *boom* knocked the creature back into the water, its head butting the bow.

The boat rocked back, causing Aaron to stumble. His hands were so shaky he could barely clutch the next stick of dynamite. The fog was swirling around the ship, as though they were in the eye of a hurricane. Ghostly shapes twisted along the walls, some even appearing to reach out at them.

Below, the water was swirling. That thing was still alive. Aaron was on the verge of vomiting. It had taken a near-direct hit by a dynamite explosion and was still alive! What the hell was this thing?!

Something was coming through the fog. He could see the large shape emerging through the greyish-white curtain. He wasn't going to give it time to attack. He grabbed a roll of dynamite, lit the fuse, then chucked it as hard as he could.

The sizzling explosive arched through the air and landed right on the silhouette.

Aaron heard it touch down. It was like a tennis ball hitting a kitchen floor. Then he noticed the glint of flashlights streaming.

It wasn't the creature. It was another fishing boat...and he just threw the dynamite stick right on their deck. He heard the crew panic when they realized what had just landed on their ship. By then, it was too late. The dynamite exploded, rupturing the hull and sending men flying into the water.

Jared came running back out onto the fly deck.

"Aaron! What the hell did you do?!"

It was the second time that question was asked in that tone. Now Aaron was in hysterics. Not only had he become a killer that night—he was a killer of multiple people. It was a domino effect that was knocking over more pieces the further it went along.

The screams intensified. A huge splash swept over the wall of fog, the wind gust unveiling the sight of the creature going after the easy meal. The front of the boat was gone; completely blown away by the explosion. The stern half was angled down into the water. Splattered over the cabin structure were human remains. Someone had been standing right over the dynamite when it blew.

There were three people in the water. Two…one was in the creature's jaws. It swung its head and ripped him in half, then went after the next one. The fisherman screamed, threw his hands over his eyes, which failed to protect him from the oncoming wrath. His screams continued down the creature's throat and into its stomach. It didn't bother to mash him in its teeth—it just swallowed him whole.

The final victim tried paddling toward the boat, only to be snatched up by the legs. He dangled upside down for a moment. The creature flung him up into the sky, pointed its open jaws straight up, and let its prey twirl back down into its mouth. Its mouth shut, crunching the man's pelvis into his face, snapping the spine and ribs, then swallowed.

"Kill it!" Jared shouted to Aaron.

The world seemed to be spinning. The Captain yelled at him three times before the words even registered in his brain. Fed up, Jared hurried to the main deck himself and grabbed several sticks of dynamite. He snatched the lighter from Aaron's hand and lit the fuses, then threw them one by one. Repeated explosions popped around the beast, with one striking directly around its midsection. Small chunks of shell popped from its body. It let out a squeal, then thrust its head at the *Star Blaze*. Boiling hot fluid spurted from its throat and splattered over the bow. Steam rose around the fishermen, and it wasn't fog. The deck was melting before their very eyes. The creature was only mildly injured, even after taking a direct hit. They had underestimated its defensive capabilities. Those scales had become so strong, they could possibly deflect an anti-tank round.

Finally, Jared came to his senses. "Let's get the hell out of here!" He started climbing back to the pilothouse. All sense of bloodlust was gone. Now, he was just a terrified man desperate to survive.

Until this day, he was a law-abiding, respectable, well-liked fisherman who rarely ever got into a dispute. Now, he was an associate to multiple murder, with no intention of turning himself in. He always feared the thought of living a bad life and being greeted by the devil at the end of it all. Never would he have guessed that the devil would meet him first.

Instead of hellfire, this devil rained acid. It was equally hot.

Jared was almost up to the fly deck when the acid struck. The Serpent had aimed high, deliberately aiming for the Captain. The fluid splattered over his back, neck, and shoulders. Instantly, it started breaking down his flesh. He reared his head back and screamed. There were many emotions he wanted to express in his last moments. One was anger for losing to the beast that killed his wife. Another was regret for the human being it made him become in his final moments. A religious man, he wanted to beg God for his forgiveness and to receive his passage to Heaven, and to avoid the eternal tortures of Hell. He never got that far.

The acid burned through his neckbone. Jared's head flopped backward. It dangled from a few pieces of meat, staring down at a terrified Aaron. He stepped back, trying to scream, but unable to get it out. The Captain's fingers remained clenched to the ladder bar for several more seconds before coming loose. His body splattered on the main deck, the midsection almost completely dissolved by the acid.

The Serpent emerged over the portside, its evil eyes now fixated on the last remaining human. Aaron staggered backward. His foot hit Leon's corpse. He fell, then scampered backward after seeing his friend whom he had killed. Both Leon and Jared were right next to each other, their dead faces pointed right at him. Hovering over them was the Serpent. Its upper body slithered over the railing, then coiled back.

Finally, that scream escaped Aaron's lungs.

A waterfall of acid poured over him. His melting body flailed, then broke away piece by piece.

After a few minutes, not even the bones were left

CHAPTER 42

Sammy Russell awoke from one of the deepest sleeps she'd ever had. At first, she thought the knocking on the door was in the lucid dream she was having. She was terrified of going to sleep the previous night, certain that she would have nightmares regarding the creature and dying victims, or even a replay of Jesse's injury. No, instead it was really peaceful, featuring her childhood days of sitting on the beach with her parents and watching the other kids play.

It was actually Ben's shuffling in her bed that made her awaken. She pulled her head off his chest, then squinted at the window. The sun was out. She checked the time. It was only a little after seven-thirty. She had called the station and told them she would be in late today, after being at the hospital for so long.

"Who the hell is it?" Ben groaned.

"I don't know," she replied. She threw on some clothes, straightened her hair as best she could, then went to the door.

Standing on her front porch was her father, along with Sergeant Shier, Derrick Crevello, and a few other officials.

"Hey, kiddo," Richard said. "Sorry to bust in on you. I tried the office, but the Sergeant said you'd be here."

"What's wrong, Dad?" Sammy said. The Mayor frowned, then looked away for a moment, his face displaying shame from his poor judgement.

"At least five fishing crews went out to try and kill the thing last night," he said.

"Five that we know of," Shier added.

Richard nodded. "Derrick had a long-range drone among his toys. He was kind enough to let us get a safe aerial view of Lebbon Rock and the surrounding waters. None of them survived."

"The Serpent's out of control, Chief," Derrick said.

"What about waiting for the Coast Guard?" Sammy said.

"We can't wait," Richard said. "There's talk of rewards being put out against the thing. Fishermen from all over the coast are reported to be moving in. Several of the victims' families are offering substantial money for this thing's death. All added up, might be over six figures."

"That kind of money, concern of personal safety goes right out the window," Derrick said. "Trust me, I've seen it. Maybe not to this extent, but the human nature is the same."

"We need to kill this thing *now*, or else more people will die in the next few days," Shier replied. "There's no way we'll be able to stop the influx."

"You're kidding me," Sammy said.

"It gets worse," one of the local officials said. Sammy recognized him. He was Dr. Luke Chen, a medical consultant. "We've been receiving reports of dead fish all around the coast. My staff and I have been testing the water. I can't specify what the substance is, but it's some kind of poison. The acid that creature spills from its mouth; I think it has acid sacks in its throat that constantly fill up. Every so often, it has to expel the excess fluid."

"It's poisoning the water," Shier said. "God only knows how much of the ocean will be poisoned if we let it run loose."

"I've contacted the Coast Guard again, but they've got to do their own investigations, their own evaluations…" Richard said.

"God only knows how long that'll take," Chen said.

"We need action now," Richard concluded. He took a long breath. "Baby, I need your help."

Sammy leaned against the doorframe. "I thought you were done putting me at risk—that you wanted someone else to handle it."

"I never like seeing you at risk, babe. But now? I think you're the only one that can pull this off," Richard said. A moment of silence passed between them. "Please help. Or more will die."

Sammy could hear the emotion in his voice. She reached out to hug him.

"Of course I'll help. It's my job."

"I'm in!" Ben said. He stepped to the door behind Sammy, fully dressed.

"Me too," Derrick replied. Sammy heard a couple of car doors slam shut. Back along the line of cars stood Josh and Melvin.

"We're game if you are," Melvin said.

Sammy looked at Derrick. "I don't see any cameras."

He shook his head. "*This* situation? Bad taste. I just want to see that thing taken down."

He held out a fist. She took the hint and bumped it with her own.

"We almost had it last time. We just need to get around that acid spit somehow," Josh said.

"That's true. What about explosives?" Sammy asked.

"There's strong evidence that Jared Vase and his crew used them last night," Derrick said.

"Wait...dynamite can't even kill it?!" Sammy said.

"Caught a glimpse of the creature with the drone. There're small signs of injury, but nothing to boast about. Those scales are just too damn strong."

"So, we can't penetrate it," Sammy said. "We'll have to try electricity again. Like Josh said, it almost worked last time. But how the hell do we keep it from burning the lure off?"

Ben put a hand on her shoulder. "I think I know a guy that can help."

****

Professor Jeb Bordain was already at Fleichman Community College when he received Ben Stacie's call.

Urgent matter. Need your expertise. Must meet immediately.

What could Bordain say to that? Bordain waited in the classroom for his former student to arrive. He didn't expect the Chief of Police, the celebrity from that fishing show, and the Mayor himself.

"Dr. Bordain, thanks for taking the time to meet with us," Sammy said.

"My pleasure, Chief," Bordain answered. "Mayor. Ben. Why do I have a feeling this has something to do with that big thing swimming out in the water?"

"It's out of control," Ben said. "It's up to us to stop it, or else things are going to get way worse."

"We're going with our original plan again," Sammy said. "We're going to build a lure to electrify the beast, but we need to find a way around its corrosive saliva."

"Wait, the reports are true? That thing actually does spit acid?" Bordain said.

"Correct," Ben said. "I've seen it. Highly corrosive. Unfortunately, we don't have a sample for you to analyze."

"And nobody's willing to get close enough to get one anyway," Derrick added.

Bordain shrugged. "Best I can do is compare it to corrosive acids we already know about. Carborane is considered to be the strongest solo acid. It's very corrosive and extremely toxic. It's not something we would allow undergraduate students to handle. Only trained experts."

"The stuff that this creature spits is probably even worse," Ben said.

"Burnt my camera operator down to the bone in seconds," Derrick added.

"Good god," Bordain said. "So, I presume you're looking for a material that'll withstand the acid burn?"

"Correct. We need something that can cover the lure so we can hook the creature again and electrocute it until its dead," Ben said. "Its scales are too solid. We can't shoot it or even blast it with explosives. Our options are limited. Our plan to electrify it almost worked. Had it not had that damn pocket ace…"

"The best option I can think of is to use Hastelloy," Bordain said.

"I'm assuming that's acid resistant?" Ben said.

"Probably the closest thing you're looking for," Bordain said. "It's a nickel-molybdenum-chromium superalloy." He realized, based on the looks on everyone's faces, they had no idea what he was talking about. "It's highly resilient to corrosion."

"How well does it conduct electricity?" Ben asked.

"It's not the best," Bordain answered. "It's a highly resilient metal, that's why. That's the challenge; to protect the conductor, while allowing it exposure to deliver the electrical shock."

Sammy could imagine the wheels turning in Ben's mind. His eyes went to the ceiling as he thought up his plan.

"Does it weld pretty good?" he asked Bordain.

"Very easily," the Professor said.

"What are you thinking, Ben?" Derrick asked.

"We weld the alloy over the conductor, including the hooks," he explained. "We'll even coat the barbs in the material as best we can. The tip will remain exposed, that way they can deliver the charge into the creature's flesh."

"If the tips are exposed, won't they melt away when the Serpent spits?" Richard asked.

"Not if they're already buried in the Serpent's flesh," Ben said. "The acid comes from sacs in the back of its throat. The roof of its own mouth will provide the protection we need."

Sammy smiled. "That might work."

Bordain nodded. "Sounds reasonable. Hope you like welding, because you'll be doing a lot of it."

Ben chuckled. "Good thing it's early. But there's other factors to consider—like where to launch the attack."

"Good point," Derrick said. "While I'm confident in your ability to create a new lure, I think I speak for everyone when I say NOBODY'S comfortable getting back on the water. Unless we're aboard a freaking battleship."

"I'll second that," Melvin said.

"Is there any way we can hit it from land?" Derrick said.

Ben and Sammy shared a glance, and simultaneously came up with the answer. "Beggars Cove."

"We can lure it toward the edge," Sammy said. "We'll use a high-voltage generator from the police station. Connect a cable to the lure. Get the bastard to bite it...and you know the rest."

"I like that plan because it'll allow us to have vehicles on standby," Derrick said. "If the thing comes on land, we'll be able to make a fast getaway."

"I'm on board with that," Sergeant Shier replied. "But that leaves one crucial element on the table: how are we going to draw the thing in?"

"Leave that to me," Derrick said. "If there's anything I'm good at, it's finding whatever sea critter I'm after."

"Derrick..." Sammy said, her voice full of concern. "What are you gonna do?" The TV star cleared his throat.

"I'll plead the fifth on that. Let's just say, you won't like it. But it'll work."

"I'll take your word on that," Ben said. "We don't have time to debate. We're gonna have to start prep *now* if we're gonna have this thing ready by tonight. God knows your police force will be fixated with keeping fishermen out of the water." He glanced back at the Professor. "You know where I can get a good supply of that superalloy?"

Bordain nodded. "I know a place."

"Tell them to bill it to me," the Mayor said.

"You got it," Ben said.

Sammy clapped her hands together. "Alright. Let's stop flapping our gums and get started."

CHAPTER 43

Sammy was relieved to hear that Jesse had been moved into a regular hospital room. When she arrived at the hospital to visit, she ran into Jesse's father, who'd arrived just a couple of hours earlier with his wife. They shared a hug and went together to Jesse's recovery room.

Jesse was awake, though visibly drained. As hard as it was to look at, it was an improvement over the previous day. Still, that depression in the blankets where her leg used to be could not go unnoticed.

"Hey, girl," Sammy said.

"Hey!" Jesse smiled. Sammy forced herself to return the gesture. Never good in these situations to display your sorrow. The general rule was to wait until you've left to cry, as long as it wasn't in front of the patient.

"I owe you one," Jesse said.

"You owe *me*?!"

"Uh, yeah! You and Ben, for saving my ass. I suppose I should add Shier to the list…"

"Jesus, I never thanked him," Sammy said. So much craziness in the past twenty-four hours that she almost forgot that she would certainly be dead if not for Shier's quick thinking.

"Ah, he won't take it personal," Jesse said.

"He's good like that," Sammy replied. "I'm glad you're doing okay."

"Not as glad as me," Jesse said.

"Jesse, I'm sorry everything went wrong," Sammy said.

"Ah, no! Don't even think about going there," Jesse said. "There was no way in hell you could've predicted what happened. Even the doctor didn't know. Yes, we lost people. But it wasn't your fault."

Gosh, if I had HALF the good character she has. Lost her leg, will never work in law enforcement again, has every right to be mad at the world, and instead, she's taking it like a champ.

Sammy repressed the urge to ask Jesse what she would do now that law enforcement was off the table. Now was not the time to ask, but the thought was prevalent in her mind. Maybe she could open up an indoor position for light duty... no, Jesse wouldn't like that. She didn't become a cop so she could sit on her ass all day under artificial light.

"I know what you're up to," Jesse said.

"What?"

"You're gonna try and kill that thing again."

Sammy hesitated. "Yes."

Jesse smiled. "You have a plan?" Sammy nodded. "Good. Get that bastard for me." She reached out with her hand and clutched Sammy's.

"I will," the Chief said. "Take care. I'll visit you again soon."

Sammy squeezed her hand one more time then stood up to leave, only to stop right before exiting the door.

"Oh!" Derrick exclaimed. He stood in the hall after backing up a step to keep from colliding with the Chief. "Hey, Chief."

"Hey," Sammy said. She noticed the flowers. Lilies; Jesse's favorite. She wondered if he knew or just took a good guess. "She's awake."

"Thanks, Chief. See you later on."

"You know you don't have to help," Sammy reminded him.

"Not going over this again," Derrick said. "Besides, that thing sunk my boat. Nobody or nothing sinks Derrick Crevello's boat and lives."

Sammy smiled. "Fair enough." She continued down the hall to go to the main lobby, glancing back just long enough to see him go into Jesse's hospital room.

She could hear Jesse's enthusiastic "Hey!" as he went inside, and the first few words of her introducing him to her parents.

Maybe there really is something there. Maybe, just maybe, he might be the answer to her problems.

Jesse was the type who wanted to travel a lot after all...

Let's not get too far ahead of ourselves. However, even with the consideration that a successful relationship would take time, Sammy had a good feeling it would work out between those two.

Sammy exited the lobby and stepped out into the parking lot. It was time to visit the cove to oversee the setup.

****

"Alright, set it there," Shier instructed the forklift driver. The long mechanical arm lifted the high-voltage generator out of the truck and set it down twenty-feet from the shoreline.

Beggar's Cove was a semi-circular stretch of shoreline, with a large hill overlooking the water on the north side. Spotters were already setting up positions. Spotlights were being set up.

There was a small café behind him. Its owner had been instructed to close off the lot entrance and vacate the building. Shier could see sparks flaring inside the parking lot.

Ben Stacie was hunched over on the pavement, pressing the welding torch to the lure. Shier knew better than to interrupt him, even to offer assistance. Ben was like an artist; he had a particular method he used to complete his craft. The lure itself was similarly built as the last one. Shier had caught a glimpse of it before going out on boat patrol. The barbs were individually sculpted with the torch and attached to the body of the lure. Now, Ben was in the process of applying the acid-resistant plating. It was a meticulous task, as every single piece had to be fitted individually to get around the barbs and spikes. To compensate for this, Ben had to use fewer hooks, or else it would take days to fit every little piece of Hastelloy sheet metal between the little protrusions. As he attached the plating to the hooks themselves, it gave them the appearance of limestone stalagmites that hung from the roof of a cave.

Ben was only a quarter of the way done now. At this rate, he'd be finished by early evening. They still had to get the electrical cable and some bait, but in comparison, those were the easy parts.

Shier saw a Police Interceptor park on the main road. The Chief was just now arriving. She stepped out and approached, stopping for a brief moment to say 'hi' to Ben Stacie. She glanced at the generator, then back out into the water, then at the shoreline.

"We'll place trucks here and here," she said, pointing at spots thirty feet apart. "When we have word that the thing's coming, we'll have all engines started and someone in the driver's seat. If that thing comes ashore, we jump in the back and hightail it."

"You got it, Chief," Shier replied.

"We'll need something to lure it back into the water if it does end up on shore," Sammy said.

"Derrick Crevello had an idea for that," the Sergeant said. "He's supplying us with some of his drones that he uses for aerial footage. He sent some of his crew to a supplier this morning to pick some other drones that he thinks will work to attract the creature's attention."

"I don't know," Sammy said. "Would drones even be big enough to get its attention?"

"The agricultural ones are. They're designed for spraying fertilizer over farmland. I got a look at them when the crew brought them in. I gotta say, they're the biggest civilian-owned drones I've seen. To the Serpent, they'll probably look like dragonflies ready to be snatched out of the air."

Suddenly, Sammy heard a dull buzzing, and felt a tiny, but concentrated gust of wind from above. She looked up and saw the drone passing overhead, then heard Josh cackling from the hillside.

The machine was almost six feet wide, with two large plastic containers connected with sprayers through hoses. It was black and red in color, and considering its size, it moved pretty fast.

Sammy put a hand over her eyes to protect them from the downdraft. "Thanks, Josh, I get the point." The television co-star snickered as he steered the drone away and landed it near his truck. Sammy fixed her hair and collar. "Okay, that might work. Who's gonna operate them?"

The Sergeant shrugged. "Handling those controls takes a little bit of getting used to. I gave it a try and almost lost the damn thing. Josh had to take the control back and keep me from dropping it into the ocean. None of our other officers are comfortable handling it. It's up to you, but Derrick, Melvin, and Josh are the ones most fit to handle the drones."

Sammy nodded. "They're insisting on helping anyway. If anyone can find an overgrown sea creature, it's those guys."

"I'll drink to that. With a little bit of luck..." Shier stopped. Last time they relied on luck, a third of their police force was killed or maimed. No, he'd rather depend on good judgement and determination. "You know what, Chief? I think this plan will work this time. Let's just bring that bad boy here and finish him off."

CHAPTER 44

By six-o'clock, Ben Stacie completed the last welding patch to the lure. With the dark-gray covering and silver tips, the lure had the appearance of a wrecking ball in some post-apocalyptic movie. The cable itself was covered in Hastelloy pipes to keep any acid from burning through it. The downside to this was that it weighed the lure down further and eliminated any flexibility the cable had.

Buoys were set up near the lure to help keep it afloat. As before, the spikes were baited with freshly killed tuna.

Ben soaked a towel in water and wiped it over his sweaty face. His hair was a mess from the hours of work he put in. His clothes were ragged and blackened. Sammy chuckled, took the towel from him, then helped to clean off the residue.

"You got the racoon eyes thing going there."

"It was the goggles," Ben said, holding still for Sammy to scrub his face. When she was done, she handed the towel back to him, then turned to face the crew. To minimize risk of casualties, there were four officers on site: herself, Shier, and Officers Peter Jay and Clarence York, who volunteered to be spotters. Both held high-powered rifles as they stood at the edge of the hill. Behind them was a Police Interceptor, pointed west, ready for them to make a quick escape if needed.

In addition to the officers, Derrick, Josh, and Melvin were on standby. There was a pickup truck designated for them. Like the others, it was prepped for a quick escape if need be. Josh was already seated in the bed.

Derrick was on the ground inspecting another tanker drone.

Sammy approached him after realizing he had one of the chum containers nearby.

"What are you doing?" she asked.

"Gotta get the bastard's attention. Simply flying the drone over the water won't do the trick. We need to give it a reason to chase it. I loaded the tank with a thin mixture of fish blood. Had to avoid the chunks to avoid clogging the sprinklers. Should be enough to tempt the Serpent, though." He stood straight. "Melvin there will operate our standard drone to give us a bird's eye view. Luckily, the weather's decent, so we should be able to see the Serpent coming up for the bait. Once he does, we'll lead him here."

"How long will those batteries last?" Shier asked.

"For this model? Roughly two-hours continuous flight. We have three of them, each fully charged, so that'll help. Same with the model Melvin will be operating."

"How long should each spray last?" Ben asked.

"We'll keep hitting it on and off to make it last," Derrick said. "All in all, we can prolong it for maybe an hour."

"Don't know about you guys, but I'm ready to get crackin'!" Melvin said.

Sammy glanced once again at the shoreline. Her eyes went out to the lure, which was now being hauled out to the buoy by a couple of volunteer crewmembers. They attached the cable, then steered their vessel back to shore. Once they vacated, the eight of them would be the only ones in the area.

"Alright. Let's get started," Sammy said.

Derrick and Melvin switched on their drones, stepped back, then ascended the devices to the air. Sammy and Ben approached the pickup truck where Josh sat. Two monitors were set up for them to see what they were doing, along with a GPS tracker for the operators to see what they were doing.

"On their way," Josh said.

The drones zipped far out to sea, quickly disappearing from sight. The Chief watched the ocean passing by on the bottom of the monitor.

After twelve minutes, she could see Lebbon Rock in the distance.

Derrick lowered his drone, while Melvin hovered his several meters above. Josh watched Derrick's drone on the monitor, gauging its distance from the swells.

"Slowly. Just another few inches. Whoa! Too much! Move back up, you're gonna get it wet. These things weren't meant to be dipped in saltwater."

"You said another few inches," Derrick complained. "That's all I did."

"Quit whining like a little girl and ascend," Josh said. Derrick glanced back, surprised to see the lax co-host talking back to him.

"Well, fine then!" Derrick said. "How's this?"

"Better. Keep it level. Alright, you're good to go."

Derrick initiated the sprays. The group watched the monitors as red mist covered the water's surface.

In the course of the next hour, Derrick coated the ocean with blood. Much to his frustration, the beast did not show. With the tank drained, there was no other choice but to fly the drone back and send out the next one.

Roughly twelve minutes later, he landed the drone near the truck, switched off the power, then activated the next one.

"Alright. Take two," he said. He waited for Melvin to be ready with the standard drone. At once, they flew the machines to the same location and resumed the process.

After another hour, the creature was still yet to reveal itself. With the third drone, Derrick decided to try another side of the island.

Frustration was beginning to take hold of the group.

"Maybe it moved out again," Sammy suggested.

"That, or it's evolving again," Ben said. Just the thought of it made Sammy want to kick something. She leaned on the pickup truck and watched the drones do their work. Her imagination was starting to play tricks on her. She kept thinking she saw a large shadow forming underneath the sprayer, only for it to be just a cloud passing over or even nothing at all.

She stepped toward Shier, who was on his phone.

"Yeah, thank you. Bye." He hung up, then turned to look at her. "That was Dispatch. Our guys stopped two fishing vessels at the harbor."

"It's the promise of money," Sammy replied. "They're gonna be flocking here."

"They already are," Shier said. "Dispatch informed me that the State Police called. They too, have turned away people hauling boats out here. The roadblocks should keep people coming from inland, but I'm worried that we're gonna have trouble with people flocking in from Florida and Virginia. All police departments on the coast have maritime patrols out to keep a watch, but it's easy for boaters to get around them."

"I know. It's fine, Robert," Sammy said. "We'll get this thing before they get here. We just need to be patient." She was reminding herself as well as him. She returned to the monitors. Once again, her mind played a trick on her. She saw a swell, caused by the breeze, which she hoped was the Serpent.

Just need to be patient.

CHAPTER 45

It was starting to get dark. Even Derrick was showing signs of frustration. He moved the joystick back and forth, trying to get the drone's rotors to make vibrations against the water's surface.

"Maybe they're just too small," Melvin said.

"That's possible," Derrick replied. "It's a big ocean full of sizable food. Maybe a little bite-sized snack that's not even touching the water just doesn't appeal to it."

Josh leaned back in the truck. "Maybe we should call it in?"

"No," Sammy said. "We're gonna keep going until we find it."

"Well, one way or another, we're gonna need a new method," Derrick said. "It's getting dark. In a half hour, we won't even be able to see the sprays, let alone anything coming up under the surface. We'll probably have to start again in the morning."

"By then there could be a hundred boats here," Sammy reminded him.

"Hmm…" It was true; he couldn't deny that.

"Too bad we don't have some trained dolphins," Ben said. "Something that could move fast under the water. Something that can draw the creature in but evade it as well."

"Hmmmmmm…." Derrick's eyebrows raised. Something about the new enthusiasm made Sammy nervous. "We don't need a dolphin. We have *me*!"

"Huh?" Sammy muttered. Derrick started flying his drone back.

"Melvin, keep yours in the air. Spot for me while I have some light."

"What are you doing, Derrick?" Sammy asked.

"Offering our beastie something a little more enticing."

"How?" Ben asked.

"By putting one of my jet skis to use," Derrick answered.

"Are you insane?" Sammy said. Derrick shrugged. He was smiling. The cocky adventurer side of him was in full display. He flew the drone back as fast as he could, ignoring the calls from his companions to rethink his plan.

"Well, I guess I really will get to become the show's new lead," Melvin said.

"You wish," Derrick said. He landed the drone on the shoreline then hurried to Sammy's truck. "Give me a lift?"

"Hell no," she said, despite doing it anyway.

She drove him a mile north to the harbor, reminding him of all the different ways he could die, then went for the jugular by mentioning Jesse.

"She wouldn't want you to do this."

It didn't faze Derrick. "Jesse's sound asleep right now."

"But Derrick, if something happens to you—"

"I get it, Chief," he said. "Just trust me. She would."

Ugh! She would, too. Sammy knew there'd be no talking him out of it. Derrick was out the door before she pulled to a stop at the harbor. He hurried to one of his jet skis that he had on standby, then started the engine.

"Remind Melvin to keep an eye on me," he said. He glanced up at the western horizon. There was maybe twenty minutes worth of sunlight left. Thirty at most. No time to talk. "Alright. See you soon. Be ready, because I'll be bringing a rowdy partygoer."

He pointed the jet ski east then shot out toward Lebbon Rock. Sammy watched him speed off. In less than a minute, he was just a dot in the horizon.

"You crazy asshole." She hopped back into the truck and returned to the cove.

"Boom! Oh yeah!" Derrick let his wild side fly free. He pushed the jet ski to its top speed of ninety miles an hour, slowing only when he saw the busted lighthouse straight ahead. He turned to his left and circled around until he spotted Melvin's drone hovering in the sky. He waved to the camera, then started zigzagging across the blood-clouded water, creating large jets and vibrations.

"Quit showing off," Melvin said through the receiver.

"You're just jealous," Derrick said, though his co-star wouldn't hear.

At the cove, all eyes were back on the monitor with renewed interest. Hearts were beating. Now, everyone was hyper aware of every tiny bit of movement in the water.

"That guy's a crazy son of a bitch," Shier said.

"Probably why he's worth millions," Ben replied.

"Well, he better come out of this alive…" Sammy said, thinking of Jesse.

"Yeah, because I won't have a job, otherwise," Josh said.

Melvin snickered. "What? You don't think the show would continue? What about me?"

Josh glanced at him, then back at the screen. "Eh? Maybe a season. Two at most. Then we'd be cancelled."

"And they say it's good to have friends," Melvin said.

"Hey, I hear informercials are always looking for actors. Maybe you could get a voiceover gig and…" His eyes widened. He snatched the radio and smashed the transmitter. "Derrick! It's coming! On your left! Move now!"

Derrick steered the jet ski to the right. He felt the spray of jetting water as the Serpent launched its head through the surface, its jaws narrowly missing him.

"Whoa!" he screamed, terrified and exhilarated at once. He pushed the jet ski for few hundred feet then looked over his shoulder. The Serpent had splashed down.

Up ahead, the drone had ascended another few meters, then passed over directly above him.

"It's coming," Josh said. Derrick waved to the camera to make sure he had the viewers' attention, then pointed west.

I'm bringing it to you.

He made a circle, enticing the beast further, then shot for the west. His prediction was accurate, for as soon as he finished the turn, the water exploded again. The creature's immense snout snapped shut over nothing but air. Derrick's second prediction was accurate as well. Instead of circling back, he continued for another few hundred feet. He heard the raining of acid spit peppering the water behind him.

The Serpent hissed, then glided along the water in pursuit of its prey.

"Yep, that's right. I've got a hundred-and-eighty-five pounds of protein just for you! Come and get it!"

"It's working. It's following him," Josh announced.

"Everyone get ready," Sammy said. "Ben, you be on standby at the generator. Shier, wait in the Escape. Be ready to haul him out if that thing comes ashore. Jay? York? You two all set up there?"

Both officers waved back to her, then gave a thumbs up. Afterwards, York started the truck and let it run. He had narrowly escaped the beast once and was not eager to experience any more close calls.

Ben started the generator. Like with the engine, all he needed to do was connect the cable to the terminal. At his feet was plenty of slack, which would provide him precious time to connect the cable should the creature try to run off with the lure.

Melvin hopped into the bed of the pickup, while Josh got in the driver's seat, ready to speed away in case things got rough.

At the shoreline was Sammy, watching the horizon through her binoculars. It was getting too dark for her to see very far with the naked eye.

"Jay, switch on your spotlight, will ya?" The white beam struck the ocean and panned back and forth. "Melvin, how far does he have to go?"

"Hard to keep up with him. Maybe another mile or so. At this rate, they'll be here in a few minutes."

Sammy started loading the water with chum, then used a pole to move the lure left and right to give it some impression of living prey.

Derrick veered left then slowed. Should he get too far ahead of the creature, it may give up the chase. Looking back, he saw the swells from its recent dive. Already, those swells were increasing in size. It was coming straight toward him.

"Holy..." he throttled forward, then arched to the left. Again, he predicted the Serpent's acid spray. One drop landed right behind his buttocks. He heard the sizzling of corrosion. He glanced back. "Damn! Too close!"

The harbor was just up ahead. He had to steer left in order to lure the Serpent to the cove. After a few hundred meters, he could see the spotlight on the hill.

The Serpent was right behind him, its evil eyes right above the swells, looking at him. Despite the lack of expression, Derrick felt frustration radiating off the creature. He had evaded its every attempt to nab him, and it wasn't used to prey escaping. It would chase him all the way to California at this point.

"Come get me! You know you want it!" He turned to line himself up with the cove, then made a straight shot for the lure. He passed through the spotlight, right for the shoreline, where Sammy was waiting near the cable.

The Chief rushed out of the way as the jet ski came roaring past the lure. Derrick slowed it to a stop, jumped off, and ran for the pickup truck.

Huge swells rolled toward shore like a rogue wave sent from a devastating earthquake.

"I see it!" Peter Jay shouted.

"Put the light on the lure," Sammy instructed. The white beam panned into the interior of the cove, then bounced off the silvery flesh of the dead fish.

The Serpent slowed, intrigued by the smell of blood. It raised its head and fixed its eyes on the offering.

Sam backed up next to Ben. Every muscle tensed as they watched the creature study the bait.

"Come on. Take it," she whispered.

The Serpent was as still as ice, watching the bait. Slowly, it nudged the lure with its snout. The tip of one of its spikes prodded its snout. It leaned back, then turned its eyes to the humans watching from the shoreline.

At that moment, Sammy realized the beast wasn't fooled.

"Abort the plan! Everyone pull out! Pull out now!" she ordered. She and Ben sprinted for Shier's truck and hopped in the bed. Huge waves invaded the shore as the beast slithered after them, passing the bait and the generator.

The other groups sped off in their pickup trucks, with the creature's attention fixed on Sammy's. It moved remarkably fast out of the water, enough that it was able to keep up with the vehicle. Sammy fired off several rounds from her Glock, which failed to deter the beast.

Derrick's voice blasted through the radio. "Chief! It's gonna spray ya!"

The Sergeant heard this and jerked the wheel to the right. As Derrick accurately predicted, a stream of hot fluid splattered the ground behind them. Hot steam billowed from the decaying earth.

Sammy leaned up, realizing some of that steam was coming from the truck itself. Ben noticed as well. He looked over the side and saw the acid eating through the rear left tire. Though they dodged the main stream, a few drops had made their mark.

The tire ruptured.

"Shit!" Shier felt the rear of the truck lagging. It fishtailed, putting him right on a collision course with a tree. He veered to the left, then saw the Serpent in the rear-view, about to strike. He jerked the wheel back to the right.

The Serpent's jaws snapped shut on dirt and gravel. Furious, it jerked its head to the left. Its tail, like a chain wielded by a biker gang member, swung wide to the right and caught the bed of the truck.

The vehicle flipped, launching the two occupants over the tailgate. Sammy hit the ground on her stomach, with Ben managing to land in a summersault. He rolled to his feet, turned toward the love of his life, and grabbed her by the shoulders. The world was spinning when Sammy was lifted to her feet. In her blurry vision, she saw 'three' enormous sea serpents slithering toward the truck.

The truck rolled twice before settling on its back. The windshield shattered, the roof half-caved-in, the doors crumpled. They couldn't see any movement inside, nor did they know if Shier was conscious or unconscious. The urge to save him would've gotten the better of Sammy had Ben not pulled her backward.

He didn't have to say anything. They couldn't save the Sergeant. The only option was to run.

The café was up ahead. Just thirty more paces and they would make it.

They sprinted as fast as they could, but the grinding sound of the beast's scaly body scraping up dirt only got louder. It seemed that for every step they gained, the beast tripled the distance. After a few fleeting seconds, it was right over them.

Ben closed his eyes, accepted his fate, then turned to shove Sammy out of the way so the creature would take him instead.

Before he could commit, the creature violently jerked its head to the side and hissed. Something fell at his feet. They looked down just long enough to see that it was Josh's drone, and to hear the co-star yell "Bullseye!" after flying the drone into the creature's eye.

Later would be the time for 'thanks'. The couple ran as fast as they could. Ben had seen the café owner lock the doors before leaving, so he didn't bother with the front entrance. Not slowing down, he leaned forward, snatched a rock from the side of the road, then chucked it at one of the side windows. The rock burst through the glass, shattering it.

"Go! Go! Go!" he shouted.

The creature was already coming again, having forgotten about the nuisance that stung its eye.

Ben knelt slightly by the window, clasped his fingers, and boosted Sammy through the window. Glass shards nicked her elbows as she climbed through. They then proceeded to cut Ben's fingers as he reached up and pulled himself through.

Sammy was on her feet. Ben was halfway through the window. Ten feet behind him were the creature's jaws. She screamed, grabbed him by the belt, then yanked back as hard as she could. Ben reeled forward and hit the floor.

The creature snapped its jaws, bashing the side of the building. It hissed, leaned forward just enough to see the two walking snacks through the broken window, then struck the wall again.

Ceiling tile rained down on them. Cracks spread across the walls as though they were made of glass. Support beams cracked loudly. Another window exploded into the small lobby.

Sammy and Ben ran to the door on the other side. They opened it, saw that the Serpent was coming around, then slammed it shut. A heavy impact blasted the door off its hinges. The creature plowed its snout through the small opening, splintering the frame, but still unable to fit itself inside.

"That determined fucker! We're trapped," Ben said. He led Sammy behind the cashier counter. They heard the sound of something wet splattering the wall. Now, the café was filling with steam. "Oh, come on!"

"He's gonna melt the side of the building off," Sammy said. The steam grew into a grey cloud that filled the room. Sammy and Ben hugged each other and closed their eyes. Going outside would only mean certain death...then again, so did staying inside.

All they could hope for now was that their predicament would provide an opportunity for their friends to escape.

Josh drove the pickup truck near the police truck. Derrick and Melvin hopped out and rushed to the overturned vehicle. Robert Shier was conscious. He was bleeding from his forehead and neck, but nothing deathly serious.

"Hang on," Derrick said. He pulled a pocketknife from his belt, sliced off the seatbelt straps, then with Melvin's help, he pulled Shier through the busted windshield.

"Alright there, Sarge?" Melvin asked. "Any broken bones? Able to stand?"

"I'm fine," Shier said. Their eyes went to the café. Street lights reflected off the creature's scales. It was on the opposite side, unleashing its fury on the building. Its tail lashed like a scorpion's, lacerating the roof. Steam billowed high into the air. "My God. Ben and the Chief are in there."

"Sarge, I don't see how we can draw it off without getting ourselves killed," Melvin said.

"Use the damn drones! Wasn't that the original plan?" Shier said.

"It's not interested in them," Derrick replied. "Unless we filled the tanks with something that could attract its—" he stopped. His eyes went down to the leaking gas tank. "Sarge, you were in the service, right?"

"Yes?"

"I'm sure they taught you about IEDs…" He hurried to his pickup, where one of the spare agricultural drones was resting…its tank empty. Shier realized what he was thinking.

"Bring it here. I have a hose handy to syphon the gas!"

The walls were buckling. Sammy was sweating. It almost felt as though the creature was trying to steam them to death before dining. Most of the west wall was gone. She heard the sound of crumbling, then screamed as the side of the roof collapsed.

It struck down at an angle, angering the beast outside, as its newly opened passageway was closed off yet again.

A strike against the crumpling slab made Sammy and Ben jump back. Instinctively, they backed away toward the kitchen. They shined an iPhone flashlight inside, immediately realizing there was no way out except…go figure, on the west side.

"We can't catch a break," Ben muttered.

Sammy noticed a metal glint on the left-hand side. A CO_2 fire extinguisher.

"Maybe we just did," she said. She grabbed the extinguisher off the rack, ran back out into the lobby, and hurried to the crumbling roof slab.

"What are you doing?" Ben said, coughing between words. Sammy held her breath and waited with the extinguisher, making sure no falling debris would knock it over.

The Serpent nudged the slab with its snout, then finally found a place to bite. It tore away a chunk of debris, then peered into the newly created opening. There, its victim stood, staring right back at it. It punched through the opening and widened its jaws.

Before it reached her, something metallic landed in its throat. Instinctively, its jaws slammed shut over it, releasing a white spray of freezing cold CO_2 mist.

"Eat *that*, you son of a bitch!" She turned around, grabbed Ben by the shoulder, then ran for the east entrance where they came in. Their feet hit the pavement and carried them back toward the shore.

Between them and the ocean was Derrick's pickup truck. Coming in from the right was Officers Jay and York's vehicle.

The Serpent shook its head, its jaws snapping at the bizarre mist that assaulted its mouth. It sprayed acid aimlessly at the white cloud around it. After ridding the icy sensation from its mouth, it resumed its attack on the building. The roof caved in completely, the walls buckling and folding outward. The creature slithered over the wreckage, only to see its targets racing back the way they came.

"Shier! You alright?!" Sammy asked. The Sergeant was syphoning gas from the truck. They noticed that the hose led right into the tank for the drone. "What are you doing?"

"A little improvising," Derrick said. "Not quite the kind we learn in show business."

Shier pulled the hose away. "Alright. We're out of time. Let's hope that's enough."

"It'll do," Derrick said. "Josh, take it up to the sky."

Josh pushed the joystick to its highest level. The rotors swirled, lifting the big drone high into the sky.

The other truck pulled up nearby. Peter Jay poked his head out of the window. "Hop in, Chief!"

Those words weren't necessary, as Sammy and Ben were already climbing in the bed of the truck before he was finished speaking. She looked back at the drone, which was flying right for the Serpent's head.

Josh steered it by its eye.

Remembering the pest that stung it moments ago, the Serpent struck at the drone and missed. Josh steered it close again. The beast watched, then lashed out again, and again it missed.

Finally, the angered beast gulped a couple of times, stirring up its acid sacks. Sensing his opportunity, Josh raced the drone right for its mouth. The acid struck the container, igniting the fuel inside. Burning gas splashed over the creature's face. It screeched and reeled backwards, its body flailing like an electrified worm.

"That's gotta hurt," Ben said.

"Alright, let's move!" Sammy ordered. "Separate. Get out of reach."

"You sure about that, Chief?" Clarence York asked. "It might go after one of us."

"Not if we get out of reach. It's gonna have to return to the water soon. It can't waste too much energy on land, or it'll suffocate."

Peter Jay nodded. "Then we might get a second shot. Alright, we'll go south!"

"Then we'll go north," Derrick said. He hopped into the driver's seat, with Shier taking the seat beside him. Melvin and Josh hopped back into the bed, then held on to whatever they could while the vehicle sped off to the north.

The Serpent's tail slashed the pavement, causing a large crack to travel down the length of the lot. It rolled over repeatedly, then lifted its head, which still billowed smoke. Its left eye was heavily scorched, its scales discolored from the fire.

It saw the two vehicles fleeing in separate directions. For a moment, it started to pursue the one on its right, only to sense a considerable lack of energy. It needed to return to the water and oxygenate its gills. In a gliding motion, it crossed the landscape, passed the generator, and dipped into the water.

"Alright, bring us back," Shier said, watching the beast in the mirror.

"So, we're actually gonna try again?" Josh said.

"It's not gonna go after the bait," Melvin replied.

"Oh, it will," Derrick said. "It's just lacking a special touch." Melvin swallowed.

"Dude, I sense the crazy in you! You already lucked out once by not getting eaten by that thing when luring it here!"

"What exactly *are* you planning?" Shier asked.

Derrick started racing back to the shore. "Do we have a rope handy? I need a long one."

Shier grabbed his radio. "Ben? You there? We need a rope if you've got one. Derrick's going to attempt something crazy."

The two groups met at the rallying point. Peter and Clarence dropped off Sammy and Ben, then returned to their original post by the spotlight.

"What's your idea, Derrick?" Ben asked.

"Our lure is lacking in flavor," Derrick replied. "Get me a lifebuoy and a thirty-foot rope, and standby in that truck." He glanced out into the water. The spotlight was beaming down on the swells caused by the Serpent. "God, part of me wishes I had cameras rolling."

Ben was muttering curse words as he shuffled through his equipment. The generator was still running, ready for the cable to attach and send its deadly current.

He found a rope, tied a makeshift harness around Derrick, shaking his head in the process.

"I know what you're up to...and it's INSANE!"

"Well, that's me," Derrick said, shrugging.

Sammy approached. "Derrick. What should I tell Jesse if—"

"Chief...have a little faith, will ya?!" Derrick said. He faced the water and got in a sprinting position, glancing back briefly over his shoulder to make sure Ben was getting in the truck. Without saying a word, he raced into the water, then swam for the lure. Each stroke hit the water loudly, intentionally drawing the attention of the beast.

The Serpent turned around, feeling the water distortion caused by struggling prey. Had the beast had a higher range of intelligence, it would've questioned why the human was being so foolish. But it was a creature driven by instinct—an instinct not only to feed, but to kill.

It circled back, passing through the white stream of light, which panned back over it as it went. It wasn't fazed by the bizarre anomaly, as its attention was on the struggling human.

"Oh, boy. What the hell was I thinking?" Derrick muttered to himself. He watched the swells in the bright spotlight. His breathing intensified. He clung to the dull end of the lure. He heard the truck engine rev.

"Wait," he called back, raising a hand.

The swells got bigger. The light bounced off that armor plating.

He heard the truck again. Ben's eagerness to accelerate was almost telekinetic. There was a slight tightening of the rope.

"Wait!" he said, more intensely.

The water broke. Derrick saw teeth…and the back of its throat.

"NOW! NOW! NOW!"

Ben floored the pedal, yanking Derrick out of reach.

The jaws slammed down, not on the intended target, but the lure. Sharp spikes pierced the roof of its mouth.

The beast reared back, the familiar pain causing it to turn away. It chomped on the lure, unable to free itself of the barbs. Already, hot steam billowed from its mouth as the remaining acid in its sacs prepared to erode the foreign object.

Sammy waited, cable in hand, until Derrick cleared the shore. He grunted as he bounced along the sand, then rolled over his right shoulder as the truck came to a stop.

The Chief connected the terminal.

The Serpent convulsed as an invisible force surged through its body. Its tail thrashed, its scales lighting up. Smoke mixed with the acidic mist.

Its acid sacs unloaded, coating the object with its defensive mechanism. Only this time, it didn't break away.

The group watched from shore while Peter Jay focused the spotlight on the beast. Its muscles tightened, crunching the lure.

"Yeah-yeah, you're not getting away this time," Ben said.

Its scales fanned open, pushed apart by the intense muscle constrictions. Blood sprayed from its damaged eye. The lure was turning red now.

It rolled over and sank under the water, its dying movements causing huge electrified swells to roll onto shore.

Finally, its heart ruptured. The water turned red.

Sammy detached the cable and breathed a sigh of relief. The Serpent was dead.

Derrick stepped beside the Chief, wet and exhausted, while also relieved. As he gradually caught his breath, he started to chuckle. His laughter was having a contagious effect on the others.

"What?" Sammy asked.

Derrick wiped a hand over his wet face, still grinning ear-to-ear.

"You know, Chief, you were talking about bad taste before. You should ask the Serpent *his* opinion of 'bad taste'."

The others glanced at each other. The joke was stupid, but somehow, it had the desired effect. They slapped hands, exchanged hugs, and laughed long into the night.

CHAPTER 46

Flowers soared high in the air as the pastor said the triumphant words, "You may kiss your bride."

Ben didn't even have a chance to lean in, as Samantha Stacie pulled him close and pressed their lips together. Thunderous applause swept through the church.

"Well done! Well done," Derrick said to them as they finally turned to face the crowd. The TV star was quite flattered when he was asked to be the best man. Then again, he supposed he did deserve a little credit. The episode featuring those two was a smash hit when it aired a few months back...partly because of the additional footage released to the public, which led to an investigation into Timestone.

Ben took his new wife and led her down the aisle, allowing the best man to meet with the maid of honor.

Jesse walked with grace, the mechanical leg not slowing her down in the slightest. She wrapped her arm around Derrick's and followed the bride and groom outside.

He had returned every weekend since his stay at Spiral Bay. He even managed to wrap up shooting early in several instances so he could fly back and spend time with Jesse.

The applause lasted until the wedding party was outside.

Sammy waved a hand at a tearful Richard Russell. "You'll have to find someone else to run this town for the next week!"

"I've got it under control," Robert Shier called out from the crowd, dressed in a suit and tie. Standing beside him were Officers Murphy, Barber, York, and Jay...the toughened latter struggling to suppress tears, much to the amusement of the rookie.

"God, this event's eating you alive," Clarence York said.

"Oh, shut up," Peter Jay replied.

As the bride and groom approached their limousine, Ben stepped back to face Derrick.

"Oh, hey, weren't you gonna do the thing?"

"I, uh, now?" Derrick said. "You sure? I don't want to steal your thunder."

"Oh, give me a break," Sammy said.

"What thing?" Jesse asked.

Derrick was sweating suddenly. "Well, it's the bride's day, and she wants this to happen. So…" He contemplated his decision, reached into his coat pocket, and got down on one knee. Jesse Roper cupped her hands to her mouth as the sun embraced the silver ring.

"Jesse Roper, would you…"

"YES!" She threw herself onto the TV star and nearly suffocated him with kisses.

Another round of applause erupted. The two embraced endlessly, barely managing to hear the whooping of Jesse's fellow officers and Derrick's co-stars.

Melvin clapped alongside Josh. "Make sure this lasts longer than the typical Hollywood romance."

Ben slid into the seat besides Sammy. "I'm sure they'll do just fine."

Derrick and Jesse separated just long enough to wave to the newlywed couple, then embraced again as they drove off to start their future together.

The End

Check out other great

Sea Monster Novels!

Matt James

SUB-ZERO

The only thing colder than the Antarctic air is the icy chill of death... Off the coast of McMurdo Station, in the frigid waters of the Southern Ocean, a new species of Antarctic octopus is unintentionally discovered. Specialists aboard a state-of-the-art DARPA research vessel aim to apply the animal's "sub-zero venom" to one of their projects: An experimental painkiller designed for soldiers on the front lines. All is going according to plan until the ship is caught in an intense storm. The retrofitted tanker is rocked, and the onboard laboratory is destroyed. Amid the chaos, the lead scientist is infected by a strange virus while conducting the specimen's dissection. The scientist didn't die in the accident. He changed.

Alister Hodge

THE CAVERN

When a sink hole opens up near the Australian outback town of Pintalba, it uncovers a pristine cave system. Sam joins an expedition to explore the subterranean passages as paramedic support, hoping to remain unneeded at base camp. But, when one of the cavers is injured, he must overcome paralysing claustrophobia to dive pitch-black waters and squeeze through the bowels of the earth. Soon he will find there are fates worse than being buried alive, for in the abandoned mines and caves beneath Pintalba, there are ravenous teeth in the dark. As a savage predator targets the group with hideous ferocity, Sam and his friends must fight for their lives if they are ever to see the sun again.

Made in the USA
Las Vegas, NV
25 July 2022